... stylish ... dramatic, emotionally ... tales that are deeply pigmented by reality's paintbrush. This Brooklyn native writes unapologetically bold, character-driven stories. Her novels feature diverse ensemble casts who are confident in their right to appear on the page. Contact: dot.cards/laquette

Donna Hill began her career in 1987 writing short stories for the confession magazines. Her first novel was released in 1990, and since that time, she has more than one hundred published titles to her credit and is considered one of the early pioneers of the African American romance genre. Three of her novels have been adapted ... television. She has been featured in *Essence*, the *New York Daily News*, *USA TODAY*, *Today's Black Woman* and *Black Enterprise*, among many others. Donna is a graduate of Goddard College with an MFA in creative writing and is currently in pursuit of her doctor of arts in English pedagogy and technology. She is an Assistant Professor of Professional Writing at Medgar Evers College and lives in Brooklyn, New York, with her family.

Also by LaQuette

A Very Intimate Takeover
Backstage Benefits
One Night Expectations

Also by Donna Hill

Strictly Confidential

Discover more at millsandboon.co.uk

DESIGNS ON A RANCHER

LAQUETTE

AFTER THE LIGHTS GO DOWN

DONNA HILL

MILLS & BOON

First Published in Great Britain 2023
by Mills & Boon, an imprint of HarperCollins*Publishers* Ltd
1 London Bridge Street, London, SE1 9GF

www.harpercollins.co.uk

HarperCollins*Publishers*
Macken House, 39/40 Mayor Street Upper,
Dublin 1, D01 C9W8, Ireland

Designs on a Rancher © 2023 Harlequin Enterprises ULC
After the Lights Go Down © 2023 Donna Hill

Special thanks and acknowledgement are given to LaQuette for her contribution
to the *Texas Cattleman's Club: The Wedding* series.

ISBN: 978-0-263-31753-4

0223

This book is produced from independently certified FSC™ paper
to ensure responsible forest management.

For more information visit: www.harpercollins.co.uk/green

Printed and Bound in Spain using 100% Renewable electricity at
CPI Black Print, Barcelona

DESIGNS ON A RANCHER

LAQUETTE

To all my ladies who are bosses.
This is a reminder that you can and
deserve to have it all.

One

"Finally."

Keely Tucker fell backward onto the plush king-size bed in the middle of her lavish hotel room. After spending the last couple of hours at the Texas Cattleman's Club schmoozing local vendors during a mixer, all she wanted was the peace and quiet of an empty and blessedly silent room.

She lay there, soaking up the silence, wishing she could spend the next few days doing nothing but loafing while watching Netflix. Sadly, she knew there wasn't a chance in hell she'd actually get to do that.

"With everything you've got to do over the next three weeks, it's cute you think you'll have time for television, Keely."

At thirty-one, Keely was stylist to a handful of solid B-list celebrities, a career she'd proudly carved out for herself over the last decade. After tireless work, and the good fortune of ending up on Ariana Ramos's radar, she was strategically positioned to transition from simply styling celebrities to creating original clothing designs for A-listers.

"You've come a long way from making dresses for your big sister's Cabbage Patch Kids Cornsilk dolls."

Keely laughed at the thought of her older sister Kyrie's most treasured childhood toy. It was a ridiculously ugly thing, but so popular, kids from the late '80s to the early '90s had to have one.

At that time, the doll was expensive for their parents, who were blue-collar workers living in a low-income housing project, scraping by to make ends meet for their small family. They'd splurged to give her sister that doll and she'd treasured it like it was gold. Unfortunately, after spending twenty-five dollars on one doll, there wasn't a great deal of money left over for all the accessories that Coleco peddled to children.

Necessity being the mother of invention, Keely's young self started drawing dresses she imagined her sister's doll wearing. Their mother, recognizing her little girl's talent, pulled out her sewing machine and showed Keely how to turn those pencil drawings into real-life clothes.

That doll was the best-dressed toy in all of Marcy Projects and Keely's very first client. A crucial step that led her to Ariana's door. Thanks to the actress's fame, and all the hard work Keely had put in over the years, her small design house, Low-Kee Designs, was about to hit the big time with respect to the fashion industry.

As excited as she was about her dream coming true, it also meant her work life was about to become more demanding, as if it wasn't high-pressured enough already.

Success wasn't for the faint of heart or the weary. It mostly boiled down to hard work, dedication and sacrifice. This week she'd sacrificed more sleep and energy than she had to spare as she traveled from one client to the next.

She'd started out in her hometown of Brooklyn, New York, before she'd flown to the West Coast to meet with Ariana. After spending a few days in LA to finalize details on the sketches for Ariana's wedding dress, Keely was taking off from LAX and landing in the small town of Royal, Texas.

Keely sighed, trying to quell the restlessness she felt creeping in from the edges of her mind. City-hopping alone wasn't as glamorous as one might think. Perpetual exhaustion wasn't the only result of putting her job first while she stuck to such a rigorous schedule. Loneliness ran a close second as an occupational hazard.

Traveling in multiple time zones in such a short amount of time meant there was no room in her life for the three Fs: fun, flirting and fornication. Case in point was the lost opportunity to accept a dinner invitation from the handsome man one of her friends had worked so hard to set her up with.

Though loneliness was a constant companion, she had to admit things weren't all bad. As tired as she was from all that travel, a smile bloomed on her lips as she thought of her job. At thirty-one, most people couldn't say they were living their best work life and poised to reach their professional zenith. She was grateful for that, so she wouldn't dare let her exhaustion or her desire to connect with another human being on a personal level keep her from living the absolute dream as a stylist-turned-clothing-designer to the stars.

"If you're gonna make this dream work, you can't

lie about all night, Keely." She felt around for the phone she'd had in her hand when she dropped like a spent ton of bricks onto the mattress. Just as her fingers curled around it, the device vibrated in her hand.

"Ariana," Keely greeted her client. "You're gonna live a long time. I was just thinking about you."

"I should hope so since you traveled all the way to Royal to finish my wedding gown." Ariana's reply made the grin on Keely's face spread wider. Although the woman was a bona fide Hollywood star, she was still so down-to-earth she could relate to regular folks like Keely. That quality alone made Keely want to create the dress of Ariana's dreams.

"I literally just walked into my hotel room. I plan to hit the ground running first thing in the morning."

"Did Jay drop you off?" Ariana's question made Keely draw a blank.

"Who's Jay?"

"Jacob Chatman," Ariana replied. "Tripp and Ex's friend. Tripp said he asked him to take you back to your hotel."

Recollection smacked Keely in the middle of her forehead.

"Oh, I told Tripp not to bother. I'm sure his friend is cool and all, but as a city girl, I'm not all that comfortable jumping into a car with someone I don't know."

"How did you get back to the hotel, then? I know you came with Milan in her car and she left well after you."

"I ordered a Lyft," Keely replied.

"Keely." Ariana's voice had a slight note of chastisement in it that made Keely chuckle. "How is jumping into a Lyft any better than accepting a ride from Tripp's friend?"

Keely let out a small sigh before answering. "Because at least with the Lyft, there's some documentable record of whose car I'm in. It's a Brooklyn thing. We don't trust anyone."

Ariana's full and throaty laughter traveled through the line, making Keely's shoulders shake with amusement too.

"Keely." Ariana's voice dropped a note, making Keely sit up and take notice. "I truly want to thank you for coming all the way out here three months before the wedding. It means a lot to me that you're working so hard to make my dress perfect."

Warmth bloomed inside Keely's chest as Ariana put her kind, everyday girl on display. Even a brash city girl like Keely could appreciate the subtle way Ariana made everyone around her feel like a longtime friend.

"Girl, don't even worry about it. As much money as you're paying me, I would've come down here as soon as you got the ring if you'd wanted me to."

Keely joined Ariana in a full laugh that nearly brought tears to Keely's eyes. Once she caught her breath, she continued. "For real, though. I'm really appreciative of this opportunity you're giving me, Ariana. You could've chosen Vera Wang, Alexander McQueen or Oscar de la Renta to make this gown."

"True," Ariana replied. "But there was something about your designs that just called to me. Those designers are great. But everyone wears them. Me? I like being different. And your designs are the best kind of different on the market, Keely."

"You're damn skippy they are." While Keely was grateful for the opportunity, she knew her work was stellar and no one could give Ariana the dress she'd created for the woman. All she needed now was to find the perfect final touches for it, and Ariana would be the best-dressed bride of the year.

"If you don't mind, while I have you on the phone, I'd like to go over a few final—"

Keely's sentence was interrupted by her hotel room falling into darkness.

"Keely, you were saying?" When Keely didn't respond, Ariana tried to get her attention again. "Keely, you still there?"

"Yeah, but I've got a problem. The power just went out in my hotel room."

Two

"What exactly do you mean I have to exit the hotel?"

Keely stood in front of the hotel's front desk watching the attendant exude the practiced calm that was probably part of his employee training.

"Ma'am, this blackout has created unsafe conditions and we have to evacuate our guests."

Keely's jaw dropped as she processed what the attendant said. "For how long?"

"Indefinitely, I'm afraid. According to the city, they are trying to pinpoint the problem. It could take days to fix."

"Did you just say *days*?" The gentleman nodded, giving her a small smile filled with a lot of regret.

She could feel panic rising, so she pushed it down, trying her best and barely managing to keep a level head.

"All right. Can you at least refer me to another hotel

that has suites available? I need a large space for my work."

Keely could see the unwanted answer in his apologetic blue eyes. "I'm sorry, ma'am. But this is a citywide problem. Half the town is without power, and the few hotels that haven't been affected are booked solid."

Keely gave a stoic nod and turned away from the front desk. Panic was climbing up her spine. Determined to get a grip on the situation, she took a breath and pulled her phone out of her back pocket.

With the press of her finger, Keely was dialing Ariana's phone.

"Keely?"

"Hey, Ariana. Apparently, the blackout isn't specific to the hotel."

"We've heard. Are you okay?"

"Physically, yeah. But I'm gonna have to leave the hotel. There aren't any more rooms available nearby with the space I need to work. I may just have to cancel this trip and try to get back down here next month."

Keely was already trying to rearrange appointments in her head to see where she could possibly make time for a return to Royal. Even though she didn't have her beloved planner with her, she knew there weren't any openings in her schedule.

"Before you leave, let me see what I can do." Ariana's voice held a cautious note of optimism that Keely was afraid to hold on to.

"Get your stuff together and be ready to move when I call you back. I promise, we're gonna figure this thing out."

Jacob Chatman slumped down into his favorite recliner, too tired to do anything more than breathe. After helping his staff with mucking stalls, replenishing water and grain, the daily health check of the boarded horses and getting the two newly acquired American quarter horses checked in and settled, Jacob had little energy for anything other than showering before plopping down in his favorite chair.

Tonight he had even less energy to spare than usual after stopping by the TCC mixer to show his face in support of Ariana and Xavier's upcoming wedding.

Closing his eyes, he'd just leaned into the cushions and was about to press the recline button to put his feet up when he heard the familiar, "Jay, where you at?" from his good friend Tripp Nobel.

The stupidest thing I ever did was give that man an access card to my front gate.

He sighed deeply before calling out to his uninvited visitor. "In here." Tripp had been to the house enough that he knew exactly where "here" was. The sound of the man's heavy boots plodding through the foyer and around the corner until he reached the great room was proof of Tripp's acquaintance with both the house and Jacob himself.

"You look beat. Rough day?"

"No rougher than most." Jacob's answer was filled with exhaustion laced with a little bit of annoyance that his friend was interrupting his peace. Tripp knew the only thing Jacob coveted more than his ranch was his peace, quiet and solitude after a hard day's work. "You need something?"

Tripp's lopsided grin wasn't unexpected. That was both the blessing and curse of friendship. What most people found abrasive, a good friend understood all that growling was just you. Since Jacob didn't have too many good friends to spare, he partially lifted one corner of his mouth into a pseudo smile for Tripp.

"Damn, man." Tripp's feigned offense filled the room, lifting Jacob's mood. Even though he was tired and wanted to be alone, Tripp always managed to make him feel glad to be in the man's presence. "You could at least offer me a beer. I know your mama taught you better than that."

She had. Both Tripp and Jacob had been raised by women who insisted on a clean house, good manners and thoughtfulness from their sons. If you violated any of those expectations, you risked a wooden spoon upside your head. All these years later, those values were still ingrained in them. But Jacob had to admit, after a hard day's work on the ranch, those last two requirements weren't as instinctive as the first.

He prepared to sit up when Tripp held his hand up. "Like I said, you look beat. I know where to find them."

Jacob nodded, and when his friend was around the corner and out of sight, he yelled, "And make sure you wash your nasty hands before you go in my refrigerator."

Tripp's resulting laugh erupting through the halls and filling the air brought on his own laughter. Both their mothers had spoken those exact words to them as boys running into the house looking for snacks after playing outside all day.

Tripp didn't disappoint, coming back with the expected "Yes, ma'am" they both would've rendered to either of their mothers. The sound of the half bath's exhaust fan followed by the splash of running water further amused Jacob. Leave it to Tripp to bring him a good time even when he didn't want one.

Jacob had expected that fact to change since Tripp

fell hard for Dionna Reed. Women needed attention, and as happy as his friend was, Jacob wouldn't blame him one bit for focusing all his energy toward Dionna. Yet the gratitude that filled him as he soaked up Tripp's presence in his house threatened to overwhelm him.

Ranch life could be lonely, especially when you're the owner and overseeing everything is your number one responsibility. Jacob had done well for himself, turning his family's once farm into the premier horse ranch in all of Royal. But the cost was giving up any chance he had at finding the kind of happiness Tripp seemed to have with Dee.

Tripp returned with one longneck in each hand, giving one to Jacob before sliding onto the nearby sofa.

"So, what is it?" Jacob's question lingered in the air as they both took sips of their beer.

"What's what?" Tripp's reply yielded a lifted brow and pursed lips from Jacob.

"You offering to bring me a beer because I'm tired screams you want something. So, what's the ask?"

"I guess I can't get anything past you."

"Never could," Jacob replied. "Now, out with it."

"I know this is a huge favor."

"No," Jacob interrupted, "attending that mixer at your insistence immediately after spending all day doing ranch work was a huge favor. Both you and Ex are lucky I love you."

Tripp conceded to Jacob's statement with a nod.

"Unfortunately," Tripp continued, "I'm out of options and you're the only one who can help."

Jacob shifted in his recliner before leaning over with his forearms braced on his knees as he waited for his friend to drop whatever bomb he was holding.

"You might not know it yet since you left the mixer

early, but a blackout is affecting nearly half of Royal. I remembered you installing that fancy emergency generator a few years back, so I figured you'd still have power."

Jacob nodded. "True, but the generator hasn't kicked in yet. There hasn't been any power disruption here."

When Tripp tilted his head slightly, Jacob answered his silent question.

"My ranch runs on a separate transformer than the rest of the town. As long as nothing happens to that transformer, I get power. It's too remote out here for me to rely on the town's equipment. Having my own means I control the maintenance and I'm not reliant on the municipality as much."

"Even better," Tripp replied, his response waving in the air like a giant red flag.

Jacob took a long swig from his beer before he looked at his good friend with suspicion.

"I know you didn't come all the way out here to check on the status of my power. A phone call would've sufficed for that. What you want, Tripp?"

Tripp's shoulders shook as a loud huff of laughter escaped his lips.

"Same old Jay." Tripp's comment triggered an acknowledging smile.

"Cutting through the bullshit keeps me sane. Now out with it. What do you want?"

Tripp drank from his longneck, before placing it on a nearby end table.

"You know the entire town is getting ready for Xavier and Ariana's wedding, right?"

"I'm aware," Jacob replied. His ranch may be remote, but even he caught wind of the scuttlebutt surrounding this local-turned-celebrity event. "Even a hermit like me can't avoid all the noise about it."

"Ex never could do anything small." Tripp laughed. "Including his wedding. Some of the vendors at the TCC mixer you dropped in on are already doing prep for the big event. As best man and bridesmaid, it's fallen to me and Dee to try to sort out arrangements for them."

Jacob noticed the sparkle in Tripp's eye as he spoke of his lady, Dionna Reed. Jacob's acquaintance with the woman was extremely short, but even he could tell just how smitten his friend was with her.

"No," Jacob answered before Tripp could even get the question out. "I've got too much work to put some stranger up on my land."

"Jay," Tripp pleaded, using Jacob's nickname to lay on the extra helping of guilt. "The woman who's designing Ariana's wedding dress is stranded. She needs a lot of room to work…"

Jacob shook his head but Tripp ignored him and kept going. "…and since you have a whole cabin you're not using…"

"Doesn't matter if I'm using it or not. She can't come here. I don't have time to babysit some fancy dressmaker from Hollywood."

"Technically, she's from Brooklyn, New York." Tripp's clarification did nothing to quiet the alarm bells going off in Jacob's head.

"I wouldn't care if she was from Timbuktu, she can't stay here."

Tripp hung his head and for just a moment, Jacob worried that his response might've been too strong. Fortunately, the sight of amusement in Tripp's eyes put him at ease.

"Man, do you know how much you sound like our

parents with that 'I wouldn't care if she was from Timbuktu' line? You gotta stop, brotha. We ain't that old."

Jacob groaned before he stood, carrying his beer bottle over to the fireplace where pictures of his parents greeted him. Bixby and Geraldine Chatman were the epitome of getting to reap the benefits of your hard labor. They'd endured the hard and rigid life of farming to keep him fed, clothed and happy.

When they retired a handful of years ago, turning the then farm over to him completely, he'd started working on his dream of converting the farm into a horse ranch. He'd had no idea then how successful and gratifying his accomplishment would be. He also hadn't contemplated on how lonely his success would be either.

Looking down at his parents, he realized they had each other to weather the storm with. Jacob had to make do on his own.

"Tripp, she can't stay here. I don't need strangers on my land." He spoke those words while still staring at the happy picture of his parents, slightly envious of the joy their union seemed to bring them, something he knew he could never have of his own.

He turned around, planning to restate his position when he saw the familiar hangdog face Tripp was making. Something the man had perfected over the years to tug at Jacob's heartstrings more and more.

"Technically she's not a stranger. She's the woman I tried to get you to give a ride to when you were leaving the mixer."

If Tripp thought mentioning that made things better, he was mistaken.

"The one who disappeared without telling you? Oh, she definitely can't stay here."

"Please, man." Tripp had gone into full-blown begging mode at this point. "You're the only one with enough space for all her dressmaking stuff. Help a brotha out."

Jacob tried his best to scowl at his friend, but watching Tripp mock-beg was too amusing to be mad at.

"How many times has your 'help a brotha out' line gotten me into a world of trouble?"

"Too many times to count," Tripp easily admitted. "What harm could having a beautiful and talented woman stay on your ranch do? She needs a big space to work without anyone bothering her, and since you've sworn off women, I know you won't pay her one bit of attention."

Tripp was right. He didn't have the time nor inclination to pay this woman or any woman the time of day.

"Fine, she can stay on one condition."

Tripp's eyes widened with excitement. Jacob could tell the man would agree to just about anything to get Jacob to do this favor for him. And that was exactly what Jacob was counting on.

"If I agree to this, you gotta agree to let me off the hook for all future mixers. I don't wanna hear nothing about me attending another one. Understood?"

Tripp hesitated for just a minute, then reluctantly nodded in agreement.

"Agreed," Tripp replied quickly. "I promise, man, you won't even know she's here."

"I'd better not," Jacob responded. "'Cause if I do, I'm taking it out on your hide."

Three

"You're certain this dude isn't some sort of axe murderer living up in these dark-ass woods."

Ariana's laughter came through the speakers of Keely's rental loud and clear. "While I'm pretty sure that Jacob owns an axe living out there on a ranch, Ex hasn't mentioned anything about him being homicidal."

Keely groaned, hoping she hadn't made an already untenable situation worse by agreeing to stay with this perfect stranger.

"Okay, so he's not a killer." Keely's relief bled through her body. Even with Ariana and her fiancé vouching for him, the suspicious New Yorker in Keely didn't easily trust anything or anyone.

Not that she thought everyone was out to get her. She'd gratefully not reached that level of paranoia. She was, however, always on the lookout for a scam. If it didn't smell right, Keely's intuition would know before her nose did.

"And you're sure me staying there isn't going to be an issue?"

Keely glanced at the GPS screen, preparing to take the next turn to lead her to her new digs.

"Ariana, your silence isn't making me feel great."

"According to Xavier, Jacob is a stand-up guy, just used to his solitude. So, as long as you stay out of his way in the cabin, he'll be fine."

Keely tapped her fingers on the steering wheel, trying to quell the uneasy feeling she had about this. Although she'd just jokingly asked about any homicidal tendencies, Keely was confident Ariana wouldn't knowingly endanger her.

With only three months remaining before her big day, there was no way in hell Ariana would be able to get a luxury designer to pick up where Keely left off.

Besides, the woman was a good human being. Keely was pretty sure Ariana wouldn't risk her safety because of how kind she was. Ariana's kindness notwithstanding, there was still some anxiety there that Keely couldn't seem to shake.

Chalking it up to the unexpected upheaval of getting caught in this blackout, she blew out a breath and attempted to calm herself.

Keely was great under pressure. She had to be when dealing with celebrities and their clothing. For instance, she was attending an award ceremony when she went to the bathroom and found Coco Jones nearly in tears because the zipper on her designer dress broke. Without even thinking, Keely pulled out the spool of invisible thread and the emergency sewing kit she always kept on her person and literally stitched the woman into the dress.

Relieved, the young actress and singer had taken Keely's name and number just in case she needed her again. She hadn't, but Keely's sure and confident demeanor had stuck with Coco, and when she was in need of a stylist and designer for the next award season, she called on Keely.

Regardless of the nerves in her belly, she had to keep her eyes focused on the goal. There was too much at risk to let nerves keep her from her prize now.

"All right, girl. My GPS says I'm pulling up in a couple of hundred feet. I'll text you if there's a problem."

Ariana signed off, and Keely ended the call just before pulling up to a large wrought iron gate. Pressing the intercom button before the slight rumble of apprehension in her chest made her execute a quick K-turn to get the hell out of Dodge seemed more difficult than hailing a cab at rush hour during bad weather in Manhattan.

The only thing stopping her from giving up was her pride, and the fact that there was literally no place else to go with this blackout affecting most of the town.

A crisp and notably cool "Hello" came through the speaker, reminding her of what Ariana had just said about her host.

Jacob is a good friend of Xavier's cousin Tripp. According to Xavier, Jacob is a stand-up guy, just used to his solitude. So, as long as you stay out of his way in the cabin, he'll be fine.

"He had better be, Ariana," Keely mumbled under her breath, hoping the speaker wasn't sensitive enough to pick up her muffled words.

"I'm Keely Tucker. Tripp Nobel and Ariana Ramos sent me here. I'm looking for a Jacob Chatman."

There was a pause before the speaker crackled to life again.

"Take the road past the main house until you come to the cabin on the other side of the pool."

The voice was abrupt, instantly making her worry. Dealing with assholes on this trip wasn't the number one thing on her to-do list. She hoped it was just the speaker making him sound cold and robotic and not an actual personality trait.

Keely followed his instructions until she drove past a beautiful two-story home with stucco siding and a terra-cotta rooftop bathed in the soft lighting along the trail of the road. She drove past a large swimming pool and spotted the cabin. After idling in the car for a few moments, she grabbed her Prada bag and groaned as she reached for the door handle.

"Big-girl pants, Keely. Big-girl pants. Gotta put them on and notch that belt tight to keep 'em in place."

The reminder was enough to straighten her shoulders and allow her usual confidence to slide through her veins like a loud reminder that she could and would do this because she was awesome at her job. And nothing, not even a real-life growly cowboy, would make her renege on her promise to deliver Ariana's dream wedding dress.

"Tripp, this woman better be as quiet as a church mouse. I can't deal with any distractions. I've got a six-month-old foal coming in and a mountain of intake work to go along with it. I can't have some citified diva getting in my way or getting on my nerves."

"Jacob, you gotta calm down some." His friend's normally easy demeanor was poking at Jacob's annoyance receptors like a petulant child seeking attention.

"I'll be calm when Ariana's fancy dressmaker leaves my property."

Tripp snickered, cranking up Jacob's annoyance factor even more. "Listen, Jay, the city will probably have this fixed soon. Once the lights come back on, she'll be outta your hair and back into a big hotel suite in downtown Royal. Until then, she'll stay in your cabin and you won't even know she's there."

Jacob watched from the window of the cabin as a set of lights from what looked like a pearl-colored SUV in the darkness slowly cut through the night.

He shook his head. A light-colored car on a dusty ranch was a rookie mistake in these parts, making the car and its owner stand out even in the pitch that shrouded the ranch in the evening.

"Jacob," Tripp interrupted him, pulling his eyes away from the window for a brief moment. "Ariana's already talked to her and she's promised me Keely won't be an issue for you. No distractions, no problems. You have nothing to worry about."

For a moment, the silent hope that his friend was right calmed the disquiet rolling around in his head since he agreed to host this stranger. Jacob had learned long ago that nothing and no one was worth the success of his ranch.

He'd sacrificed the good times of most of his twenties to make the Slick Six Stables something his mother and father would be proud of. Something that would continue to keep them in comfort for the rest of their retirement. He wanted his ranch to keep every generation of Chatmans who followed in wealth and comfort.

He'd already accomplished the first two, but the third and most important goal was to have such a prominent brand name that everyone in the equestrian business would be clamoring after a Slick Six Stables–bred-or-trained horse.

That goal was just within reach, with the possible sale of one of his Thoroughbreds to a renowned Kentucky Derby trainer. This could be the career opportunity he needed to go from local praise to global horse-breeding notoriety. With his dream in reach, this was the worst time for any sort of distractions on his ranch.

"We'll see. She just pulled up." The fact that his voice sounded like crunchy gravel under tires didn't escape Jacob's notice. Still, he couldn't find enough give-a-damn to attempt to smooth out his voice and his mood for his friend.

"Good," Tripp responded. "Just remember what your mama used to tell us, Jay. If you can't be nice, be quiet. Don't mess this up for Ariana. If you do, I will never hear the end of it from Ex."

Jacob groaned. If Ex got at Tripp over this, Tripp would in turn grouse until Jacob was willing to do just about anything to shut him up.

"Fine," Jacob spat, hoping his friend understood just how much of a sacrifice he was making for this favor. "I promise to be on my best behavior while the diva is here. But if she steps outta line or gets in the way, all bets are off, Tripp."

"Thanks, man." Jacob could hear the stupid smile on Tripp's face coming through loud and clear on the phone. "Talk soon. Bye."

Jacob slid his phone in his back pocket and took a breath before heading out to the front porch of the cabin.

He opened the door and stepped one foot over the threshold when the door to the luxury SUV currently parked on his property opened, and a long, thick and

curvy leg covered in the sexiest pair of thigh-high stiletto leather boots he'd ever seen appeared.

The boot held his rapt attention until its mate joined
it and the door closed loudly. The sound made him draw
his eyes up beyond the top of the boots to more curves
than any woman had the right to possess.

She was a thick woman. And since Jacob liked them
thick, he was having a hard time focusing on anything
but the luscious curves she had on display. His eyes
had just reached her full bosom that her fitted V-neck
T-shirt accentuated when she spoke.

"Hi, I'm Keely Tucker. I'm looking for Jacob Chatman."

Jacob's eyes instinctively closed at the sound of her
voice. It was a rich contralto, smooth and earthy like
a fine cognac, and the sound of it wrapped around his
name stirred urges he hadn't much paid attention to
while trying to dominate the global horse-breeding
market.

"Are you him?"

He opened his eyes and instantly regretted it when
wide, whiskey-brown eyes met his. Her body was damn
near perfect with curves on top of thick curves. But her
eyes, they drew him in like some sort of conjure woman
stirring her cauldron, blending magic that would break
down even the strongest man to do her bidding.

He shook his head. He didn't know what the hell that
was that had gotten hold of him. But he'd be damned
if he acknowledged it, or had him forget that women
and work don't mix.

"Yeah, I'm him."

He knew his words were curt, but her slight flinch
made him check his inner-asshole and find the home
training his mama had instilled in him.

"I hope I'm not putting you out."

He stepped out onto the porch and down the few steps until he was standing in front of her. That was a big mistake. She was gorgeous from afar. This close up, she was absolutely delectable, making him search his memory for the last time he'd held a woman close under an entirely different set of circumstances.

She looked like heaven wrapped up in the most decadent dessert you could think of, and she smelled like a cross between lemon and mint, and everything in him wanted to lean in closer to get his fill. Especially after working around animals all day. Whatever perfume she was wearing was a welcome refresher.

"Glad to see you made it here safe. These roads can be a little difficult for visitors to navigate."

She smiled then, the gleam of perfectly straight white slicing through the country darkness, warming him in places he had no business being warm right now.

"This terrain is definitely trickier than anything I've ever driven on in New York."

"I'll take rough terrain over rush-hour traffic any day of the week."

"Touché."

When her smile widened and the dimple in her cheek deepened, he locked down the smile that was slowly curving the side of his mouth. Too bad the warmth radiating from him, spreading out from the center of his chest to his limbs, wasn't as easy to control. This was a favor. It shouldn't involve him smiling like a goofy teenager in the front yard.

"Why don't you come inside and let me give you a quick tour." When she looked back over her shoulder, pointing to the cargo area of the SUV, he waved his hand.

"Don't worry about it. I'll have a few of my hands bring your things in. I'm sure today has been hectic enough without you trying to lug heavy suitcases out of your truck."

She nodded, and he turned, extending a hand to help her up the stairs onto the porch. He wasn't prepared for the sharp zing of electricity that the simple feel of her fingers against his palm caused. And when she crossed the threshold, he shook his head and remembered Tripp telling him the dressmaker wouldn't be any trouble.

As he watched Keely walk in front of him, the fitted material of black leggings hugging what looked like a helluvan ass, he wanted to hog-tie Tripp's lying lips together. Because the way his dick wanted to plump up at the sight of her backside in those leggings and boots, Ms. Keely Tucker was most definitely going to be a problem.

Four

"Wow, this is not what I was expecting when Ariana told me I'd be staying at a cabin."

"And just what *were* you expecting?" Jacob's mellow voice was fire on ice, burning away her frozen layers one scorching degree at a time.

Certainly not you.

There was no way she could've anticipated this stranger with his bulky muscles straining his flannel shirt and faded jeans. She definitely couldn't have fore-seen how the rumble of his deep voice would vibrate through the night air into her chest and rattle around inside her. And she knew damn well there was no way she could've prepared herself for how absolutely fine this man was.

His skin was a beautiful shade of brown that lay somewhere between tan and sun-kissed sand. Smooth with its golden undertones, she would give up her next cup of coffee to touch it—considering the way she loved coffee, that was saying something.

"I thought Ariana was talking about a little log cabin without heating or indoor plumbing. She had me imagining I'd be living on the frontier."

He didn't laugh. Stoic and serious as he had been when he'd opened the door, he just stared at her with those dark brown eyes that were so mesmerizing, she had to focus on the cabin just to keep her cool.

She looked around, not just because she was in awe of the design. It boasted a large open space where an eat-in counter separated the kitchen from the living and dining areas.

The walls were wood panels, stained to the perfect color of tanned oak, making the room both warm and bright. There was a stone fireplace with a flat-screen TV she'd swear was at least eighty-six inches, and the soft gray sofa, armchair and love seat made the room seem cozy and lived-in while still elegant.

She could see the stairs leading to a loft, and just beside them were the front windows that had a perfect view of the stone patio area and the pool that sat between the cabin and what she assumed was the main house.

"This is much nicer than a log cabin in the woods."

"Glad it meets your approval." The sarcasm dripping off his response grated on her nerves.

"It's nice, but far. How do you live in such a remote area? I don't know if being this far away from civilization will pose a problem with the dress design and production."

"Beggars can't be choosers."

She turned her head slightly, narrowing her gaze as she pored over his words. Just who in the hell did he think he was talking to? She might be an indie designer on the come-up, but she didn't take shit from anyone. Not even this fine-ass rich cowboy in his wooded palace.

He locked gazes with her, as if they were in a battle of one-upmanship. He was about to say something, something she was sure would only piss her off and escalate the problem. Even though everything in her Brooklyn soul was telling her to cuss his ass out, she couldn't allow anything to ruin the opportunity she'd worked so hard for.

Resigned to extricating herself from the situation without ruffling any feathers, she took a breath, closed her eyes, counted to five and then opened her eyes again. Feeling more in control, she nodded and gave him as kind of a smile as she could muster.

"I know me staying here has to be a great imposition for you and I'm grateful you'd go out of your way to help me out. But the fact that you've growled at me more than once since I arrived tells me you're a lot more bothered by my staying here than Ariana let on. If it's really that much of an issue, I'll find other accommodations."

"I'd like to see you try."

His wry smile kept her eyes firm on his full lips even when his smart-ass comment made her want to pop him in the mouth.

"You know what? You're an asshole and this obviously isn't going to work."

He raised a sharp eyebrow as if he couldn't believe she'd spoken to him that way. Keely was a lot of things, but a pushover wasn't one of them. She gave as good as she got.

"Gee, don't hold back on my account."

"Trust me, this *is* me holding back. You don't want to see the real Keely let loose."

There was a flash of something bright and hot in his eyes that confused her. It wasn't anger, even though she was certain she was getting on his last nerve. A fact she was proud of considering he'd stomped all over hers.

"Lady, don't blame this all on me. You don't seem exactly thrilled to be here either."

He pulled off his hat, and for the first time, his jet-black wavy hair was free, adding to his sexy factor. For the record, that was just another thing about him that pissed her off. He had no right being as sexy as he was when he was this much of a pain in the ass.

Get it together, Keely. As much as he gets on your nerves, you need him right now.

"My work is really important to me. Making sure this dress is perfect for Ariana is my priority. If I seem ungrateful, it's only because I'm worried. I'm sorry if what I said about the cabin made you think I was somehow being critical of your home."

She watched his shoulders relax just a little, the small change letting her know he was stepping back behind the arbitrary line.

"I get it. I'm in the process of trying to close a deal on a few horses that will take my ranch to the next level of success. Distractions and inconveniences have a greater impact when you're working at this tier of entrepreneurship."

She nodded silently, glad to have found some common ground with the grumpy cowboy and too afraid of him rubbing her nerves raw to speak. He must've felt the same because he nodded in return before putting his Stetson back on and grabbing the doorknob.

"The kitchen is fully stocked if you're hungry and

the master bath upstairs has towels and toiletries. Go ahead and make yourself at home while me and the boys bring in your supplies. I'll make sure we set everything down in the living room."

He looked back over his shoulder, confirming that his stated plan was agreeable. When she nodded, he opened the door and was gone, leaving her alone with her thoughts and her desire. Because even though he annoyed her like a pebble in her shoe, there was no denying that Jacob Chatman was one fine-ass man. Yes, she'd said that before, but it was a fact that bore repeating.

Five

Keely sipped from her steaming cup of coffee, then looked down at the list of vendors on the screen of her iPad mini. She was trying to figure out how to organize her day, except there was one pesky little thing that kept distracting her.

Jacob Chatman.

He came back with help to unload her car as promised, giving her a front-row view of those big arms and tree-trunk legs of his on display. Those images had stayed with her well beyond the few minutes it took Jacob and his crew to bring her things in the cabin. And even though he'd come and gone like the efficient workman he appeared to be, all night long she replayed the ongoing reel of him lifting and setting down trunks' worth of design supplies.

To try to get her mind on work, she'd set up her mannequin and took Ariana's dress from the garment bag she'd laid across her back seat with the utmost care. Now it hung carefully over her mannequin, which was perfectly designed to mirror Ariana's specific measurements, in the center of this luxurious open-floor cabin.

That was a task that should have taken her little time, but because she was so distracted, she caught hell getting that damn mannequin reassembled.

Keely looked at the rest of the unpacked boxes, promising herself she'd get to them by the end of the day. Right now, she had to make a stop at the Rancher's Daughter, Royal's high-end clothing boutique, to find the perfect bridesmaids' dresses to complement Ariana's.

A tap on the door caught her attention, so she closed the case on her device and walked to the other side of the large room to open the door.

Right there in the flesh was the object of her distraction, Jacob Chatman. Today he wore a plain white T-shirt that stretched across the solid wall of his chest like it was painted on. She closed her eyes, instantly reminding herself that this was so unprofessional.

She was a clothing designer and stylist. It wasn't like she hadn't seen well-built men as a matter of course in her workday. Hell, she'd even had cause to glance at a naked form or two all in the name of her job and she hadn't so much as batted an eyelash.

But standing here with this gorgeous man filling her doorway, and keeping her eyes up and focused on his face, was proving to be harder than it should have.

"Morning, Jacob." She cleared her throat and forced herself to lock eyes with him. "Did you need something?"

He tipped his hat, bringing a much-needed novelty to the moment that distracted her.

Dammit, he was beautiful, slightly bullheaded if their little spat the night before was any indication, but in the dawn of a new day, that didn't seem to matter.

"I just wanted to check on you, see if you need anything before I go back out to the training arena in the back."

"Back out?" She tossed that phrase around before she lifted a questioning brow. "As in you've been out working already?" She looked at the Apple Watch on her wrist and saw it was just after seven.

"Darlin', this is a ranch. We get up before the cock crows 'round these parts."

Did he have to say cock? She was doing so well at pretending he wasn't affecting her. Before her lecherous mind could make her do something stupid like try to steal a glance at his crotch to see what she could see, she stepped aside, letting him in, and headed for the kitchen.

"Would you like a cup of coffee? I just brewed it."

"No," he said quickly. "I've got to get back. I just realized in trying to get you settled last night, I never gave you my number so you can call if you need something. It's a pretty big ranch and as you pointed out last night, we're far enough away from the town proper that it can make going back and forth difficult."

There was something off about him. The hard edges were still there, but there was some genuine warmth there that she hadn't seen last night.

"Is it dangerous out here?"

Keely was a city girl through and through. Even with all her travels for work, the closest she'd come to seeing the woods was when she visited her parents in Washingtonville once they moved out of the city when they retired.

"No. Not during the day anyway." She spread her

hands on the nearby counter as she listened to him. "The horse pastures are much farther out, so if you wanna go exploring about, you'll be fine. At night, though, I wouldn't advise you to go off on your own. It's really easy to get lost out there in the thicket of those woods if you aren't familiar with the terrain."

She nodded, then reached over to grab her iPad mini. She tapped the screen until her messaging app opened and handed it over to him.

"Text yourself and I'll lock your number into my contacts."

He looked at the small device in its folio keyboard case, then brought his gaze back to hers with a tilt of his head.

"You actually type on this thing?"

Keely crossed her arms, prepping for whatever nonsense he was about to sling her way. It was too early to fight with this man. But if he threw the first metaphorical punch, she'd be sure to have a blow of her own waiting.

"Yeah. Why?"

He studied her for a moment, as if he was trying to find the words to express himself. "It's just that everything I've seen about you since you arrived last night seems so bold and noticeable. You're at least five-nine. Even though the truck outside is a rental, something tells me your personal vehicle isn't much smaller. You stepped outta that car with stilettos on, and even though you tried to keep your cool last night, you weren't above getting into it with me five minutes after our hellos. A woman like that...this tiny little device that's barely bigger than some phones, just doesn't seem like you at all."

There was something about the way he said "bold and noticeable" that made a spark of fire blaze in her belly, swelling until she could feel the heat moving quickly through her body. They'd spent a handful of minutes together and he could already read her so well.

Who was this man?

She'd worked all her life putting up a hard shell to keep people from really seeing her. Brooklyn was a beautiful place, but it was also cutthroat. You had to be as big, bad and bold as the next person to garner respect. That rule didn't just apply to the streets either.

Even in her family, she'd had to erect that wall to keep their slick words about her chosen profession from getting to her. Her family wasn't terrible. They loved her. They just wanted something practical and reliable for her.

They wanted her to be financially secure, and to them that meant getting a job with a steady paycheck. They weren't elitist. They didn't think that being a designer was somehow beneath their status as medical professionals. No, they would've been just as thrilled if she'd found a civil service job with steady pay and benefits. Knowing what it felt like to struggle to make ends meet, they simply wanted their girls to be secure.

"Astute observation." She turned away from him, hoping he wouldn't observe the flush she felt burning under her skin. "I'm from Brooklyn, where everything is big and bold by nature. You got a problem with big and bold?"

She'd figured by going on the offensive, she'd get better control of herself, finally find a way to not react to whatever it was that set her on fire when she was in a room with him. As soon as she turned around to face him, she'd realized she was wrong. So very wrong.

"I like big and bold."

There was a smile in his eyes and an indecipherable

expression on his face that made it hard to tell if he was joking or… Was he flirting with her?

"I live on a ranch in Texas. Everything is big and bold out here."

It certainly was from where she was standing. Jacob was a hulk of a man. He'd clocked her at five-nine, but she was actually an inch taller. Standing in front of him in her sock-covered feet, she had to look up at him. That wasn't usual for a girl who was almost always the tallest person in the room.

"Is that so?"

She was playing with fire and she knew it. But somehow, even knowing it didn't make her pull away. Keely knew damn well she shouldn't engage in any type of flirting with this man that she hardly knew. Less than twenty-four hours ago he'd been a prickly son of a bitch she'd wanted to throw one of her stiletto boots at. Considering they were $2,000 Dolce & Gabbana boots, he'd worked her nerves pretty good to make her want to risk scuffing one of them.

"It is."

They stood there watching each other, locked in a silent battle attempting to see who had the stronger will.

"If you hadn't noticed, I'm a big girl."

By the way his eyes dropped, scaling the length of her body, letting his gaze caress each one of her curves, yeah, he'd definitely noticed she was a thick sistah. And by the barely there hitch in the corner of his mouth, he liked the fact that she had some meat on her bones.

Okay, Jacob, you like 'em thick.

Just as the thought slid across her brain, her common sense snatched her by her proverbial collar and set her straight.

You are not out here to flirt with this man, no matter

*how mouthwatering he is standing in the kitchen look-
ing like he wants to make a meal out of you. You're here
for work. That's it and that's all.*

God, she hated her work ethic. It was always spoiling her fun by making her be responsible when all she
wanted to do was press her nose into that man's corded
neck and see if he smelled like grass and earth, and any
other scents one might find on a ranch.

"Well." She could see the moment her response broke
the spell and they were back to just being strangers
sharing land. "Even big girls like to feel delicate every
now and again." When he quirked his eyebrow in disbelief, she smiled. "I'm constantly on the go. This is
lightweight, and fits in almost every handbag I own.
It's practical and helps me get the job done."

Sensing the change in her playful mood, he nodded,
then quickly handled the exchange of numbers, handing her back her device.

"Well, you seem like you've got your day planned
out. I'll leave you to it." He walked to the door, grabbing the knob as he turned toward her. "Before I go, it's
Friday. There's always a big meal at the house to celebrate the hard work the hands put in all week. You're
welcome to drop by and get a plate you didn't have to
cook. Grub's on the table at six."

Before she could respond, he was out the door and
she was left in her kitchen wondering how the cowboy
she'd met last night was getting under her skin with so
little effort.

Determined not to get lost in thoughts of Jacob Chatman, she looked down at her iPad mini and opened her
agenda again. She started humming the tune of Rihan-
na's "Work." *That's what you're here for, Keely. Nothing less, and certainly nothing more.*

Six

Keely found the Rancher's Daughter Boutique in the middle of a quaint street. She'd parked closer to the corner, noticing the street sign that marked Main Street in bold letters.

"Wow, so small towns really do have streets called 'Main Street.' I thought that only happened in Hallmark and Lifetime movies."

Amused, she followed the numbers until she was standing in front of the address she was looking for.

A quick press of the bronzed door lever and a pleasant door chime announced her entry. A gorgeous and visibly pregnant redhead with pale green eyes came from the back, greeting Keely with a wide grin.

"Welcome to the Rancher's Daughter. I'm Morgan. How may I help you?"

A genuine smile bloomed on Keely's lips. Although the young woman was elegantly dressed in a sharp pantsuit in a vibrant green, her welcome was warm and friendly, something Keely didn't always find present in the rag industry.

"Hi, I'm Keely Tucker. We spoke on the phone about material and color swatches for the Noble/Ramos wedding."

Morgan's face lit up and she opened her arms, surprising Keely by embracing her as if they were old friends.

"I'm so happy to meet you in person. My best friend and I have been working for the last two days to get the swatches perfect for you. Come to the back and we can get started."

Keely followed Morgan through a heavy velvet curtain into a large room with smaller dressing rooms lining the back, and a round dressing stool in the middle of the room with a mirrored wall in front of it and a sofa and love seat behind it.

Keely saw movement near the sofa that drew her gaze in that direction. There was a woman sitting there whose frame and posture looked familiar as she was hunched over a book on her lap. Familiar eyes and mahogany-brown skin greeted her when the woman looked up. Before Keely's brain could make her speak, the young woman stood, staring at Keely in disbelief.

"Keely, it *is* you!"

Keely chuckled as she laid eyes on a face she hadn't seen since she was a sophomore in high school.

"Zanai James? What on earth are you doing in Royal, Texas?"

Zanai walked over to Keely, wrapping her arms around her. "I've lived here since my father and I left Brooklyn."

Zanai turned to Morgan, whose entire body jiggled

with laughter as she watched the two women reunite. "Morgan, Keely used to live in the same building as my aunt Deja. Since I spent every spare minute at Deja's house, Keely and I were inseparable. When you mentioned her name, I wasn't sure if your Keely and my Keely were one and the same. It appears they are."

"Again, it's a pleasure to meet you, Morgan. I'm so glad you were able to still open considering the blackout."

Morgan shrugged. "I grew up on a ranch. This isn't the first time I've lost power. I have a portable generator for the essentials. Thank goodness for credit card readers you can attach to your phone or tablet. Otherwise, business would really be impacted."

"I'm glad you weren't too terribly affected. I've been dying to see what you came up with ever since we spoke."

"And I am excited to show you," Morgan replied. "Sit down and make yourself at home while I go get the swatches. I'm sure you and Zanai can find something to chat about in the few minutes I'll be gone."

As soon as Morgan turned on her Louboutin heels, Keely and Zanai squealed like the little schoolgirls they used to be.

"I hope you don't mind me showing up at your meeting without warning, but when I realized Morgan's Keely might be *my* Keely, I couldn't stay away."

"Are you kidding me?" Keely's reply seemed to widen Zanai's grin. "I'd be so through with you if I found out you were in the same town as me and you didn't stop by. It's been too long."

They finally made it to the sofa, sitting with both their hands linked as if they were afraid they'd somehow slip away and lose each other again if they let go.

"You always said you were gonna design clothes for celebrities. Look at you living your dream, Keely."

Pride swelled in Keely. Zanai had been there from the very beginning when Keely was sketching in her faithful composition notebook. Watching her friend's eyes light up with sincere joy made her buzz with glee.

"So, what are you up to in a town like Royal, Zanai?" The last time she'd seen Zanai had been at Zanai's aunt Deja's funeral. There'd been no time to catch up then with both their hearts so heavy with sadness. Deja may have been Zanai's biological aunt, but she was loved by so many in Marcy, there was standing room only in the chapel.

"I run a developmental psychology clinic for neurodivergent kids."

Keely couldn't help the smile that bloomed on her face. For someone as compassionate as she'd always known Zanai to be, Keely could see how this was the perfect job for Zanai.

"That sounds like a perfect job for someone as smart and kind as you are."

"It is the perfect job for me. I love my clients, and providing them with quality care is truly fulfilling." Zanai waved a dismissive hand in the air. "Enough about me. Where are you staying in town? If you're still at a place with no power, Jayden and I have plenty of space at our place."

Keely leaned forward a bit. "Jayden? Who's that?"

The contented sigh that slipped from Zanai's mouth made Keely chuckle. Even without Zanai confirming it, Keely had a pretty good idea who this Jayden was or, at least, who he was to Zanai.

"He's the most wonderful man to walk the face of the earth, if you ask me." Zanai shrugged and shared a playful wink with Keely. "But I'm deeply biased, so you can't really go by what I have to say."

From what Keely could tell, Zanai's bias told her all she needed to know about her friend's beau. Zanai had always been a reserved, quiet girl. Seeing her sit here aglow in what had to be love, or at the very least, very strong like, Keely was pretty certain it would take an awesome person to bring that out of Zanai.

"Sorry, but that goofy grin on your face says you and Jayden probably don't need me underfoot. Besides, I'm staying at the guest cabin at the Slick Six Stables."

"The Chatman place?"

By Zanai's question, Keely surmised that whole small-town bit about everyone knowing each other had to be true.

"Yeah, you know the owner? His name is…"

"Jacob Chatman," Zanai offered. "He's a friend of Jayden's. I don't know him very well yet. But he's always been kind, very serious, but kind. If he and Jayden are friends, I'm sure he'll take good care of you while you're staying on his ranch."

At that moment, Morgan reentered the room with what looked like two giant old-school photo albums. She set them down carefully on the coffee table in front of Keely.

"Here are the fabric and color samples." Morgan's voice was brimming with excitement. "Even if we don't have the material or color in stock, I can get it here in a handful of days."

Zanai stood up, grabbing her clutch purse before returning her gaze to Keely.

"I'll get out of your hair and let you two get to work."

Keely shook her head, patting Zanai's vacated seat cushion. "No, you won't. Unless you've got a patient waiting, you are going to sit right here so we can catch up while I sort through all these samples. That way I can work and get all the juicy details about how you and Jayden got together."

Zanai folded her arms, lifting a sculpted brow into the air. "Those terms are agreeable. But only if you tell me about all the celebrity men in Hollywood who are begging for your time."

Keely nodded in reply. Those terms were agreeable because there were no Hollywood stars chasing her. There never had been. Keely had been too focused on work every time she'd traveled to Hollywood. There was never any opening in her schedule where she could cut loose and have a little fun and companionship.

No, all there was, all there ever was, was work. A fact she'd been happy about because it meant she was giving 110 percent to growing her brand. But sitting here in Zanai's obvious glow, Keely wondered for the first time if she were missing out on something more important.

Seven

Jacob wiped the same spot on his kitchen counter for the fifth time. To say he was a bit preoccupied would be an understatement.

All throughout supper, even while his ranch hands were being their usually boisterous selves as they sat down to dinner, there was only one thought running through his mind.

Where's Keely?

He was well aware that it shouldn't even matter to him where she was or if she ate or not. But it did. So much so, he kept glancing toward the door looking for her.

That didn't sit right with him. He tried to tell himself it was just the home training his mama instilled in him to be concerned for his guest's comfort. But even he knew that was a lie.

He'd gone to the cabin this morning with the intention of just telling her about dinner and giving her his cell number. His plan was to stand on the porch, deliver his intended message and get back to work. Unfortunately, when Keely came to the door dressed in a simple T-shirt that put her ample bosom on display and a pair of skinny jeans that wouldn't quit, when she'd opened the door and silently invited him in, all he could do was follow.

He didn't like that.

Not one bit.

Jacob wasn't a man who was easily enticed by anything or anyone. The only thing that soaked up all of his attention was work.

Chatman Farms had been reasonably successful when he was coming up. His parents worked hard every day and instilled a fierce work ethic in him. If he wasn't working, he was thinking about work, and that single-mindedness had been the thing to spark his innovation and inspiration for turning the moderately successful Chatman Farms into the popular, and therefore lucrative, Slick Six Stables.

According to his exes, Slick Six was all he cared about. The truth was, he couldn't actually dispute those accusations either. He'd dated. He'd tried his best to treat the women he was seeing well. Inevitably, it never worked out that way. He always became the absent-minded boyfriend, forgetting scheduled dates because he was caring for a sick horse or trying to break a new arrival in. Whichever the case, he'd end up alienating his girlfriends because it was obvious to them that his ranch and his work came before anything else.

That was why he was single. That was why he would probably always be single. He could never put a woman first.

But here he was, the perpetual bachelor, standing in his kitchen while scrubbing an already clean countertop, fixated on a woman who was a perfect stranger.

His ability to focus and effectively close everything out that wasn't work-related was the most important reason for his success. But since the moment he watched Keely step one long, thick, gorgeous leg out of her SUV, his focus had been practically nonexistent.

Realizing he would soon clean the paint off the counter, he tossed his sponge aside, braced both his hands on the counter and dropped his head into a helpless lull. This was his contemplative stance. It usually meant he was about to do something stupid that would get him in a world of trouble.

Breathing deeply, one slow breath after the other, he tried to settle the uneasiness that quivered in his stomach. Just once he hoped that tempting voice in the back of his head that whispered *Do it*, over and over again, would get lost in the soothing sounds of air filling and then leaving his lungs.

He shook his head when the voice became louder than his breathing, knowing full well today wasn't going to be the day that sanity won out over his uncharacteristic impulsivity. Resigned to his fate, he walked over to the sink, washed his hands, then opened the refrigerator door. As soon as his gaze landed on the plate he'd fixed for Keely when he was putting away the leftovers, he groaned.

I'm just being polite. It's only my mama's home training, nothing more.

As he reached for the plate, he could hear the little devil on his shoulder produce a huge, raucous laugh that came deep from its imaginary belly.

You keep telling yourself that, it taunted as it slapped

its knee and gave in to another round of laughter. It seemed even his conscience wouldn't let him hold on to his delusions to placate his discomfort.

"Screw it," he whispered before grabbing the plate and marching his way across the expanse of the patio and finding himself standing on the cabin's porch.

Yes, he found himself there. He would never admit to himself or anyone else that he'd willingly go to Keely of his own accord. It was a small fiction that was currently the only thing helping him hold on to his sanity. Because to admit to himself that he was here simply because he wanted to see her again was too dangerous a thought for him to give in to.

Keely stood at the fridge kicking herself for not stopping for something to eat while she was in town. She'd spent most of the day with Zanai and Morgan going through material samples and color swatches, comparing them against sketches of the finalized dress while she and Zanai entertained Morgan with their stories of running around in Brooklyn as kids.

By the time she'd packed up her sketchbooks and a handful of swatches to send to Ariana, she'd completely forgotten about food and headed straight for the Slick Six Stables.

The loud grumbling in her stomach was an obvious protest to that unwise decision. Looking in the fridge and its freezer compartment, she groaned. Everything required prep, and between travel, the mixer and getting herself situated during this blackout, she still hadn't recovered.

She scoured the cabinets until she found unopened jars of peanut butter and jelly and a box of saltine crackers.

"You've had worse in a pinch, Keely. This'll definitely do."

She set her fixings on the kitchen counter when a tap at her front door caught her attention. Even from the kitchen, she could tell who was on the other side of the door by the quick set of taps against the wood and the large yet distinct shadow blocking out the porch lights.

She pushed the curtain aside to glimpse the one and only Jacob Chatman at her door. She might be in a small town where everyone knew each other, but her inner Brooklynite had a healthy dose of suspicion no matter where she traveled to.

He gave a quick nod that made her bite down on the inside of her lip to keep the aching groan building in the back of her throat from leaping out of her mouth. How a nod could be categorized as sexy, she didn't know. Yet everything about it was steady and sure, two things her wayward mind imagined Jacob had in spades when it came to matters of intimacy.

"Sorry to bug you. Just wanted to drop off a dinner plate to you."

He held what looked like a mountain of food beneath aluminum foil.

"Thanks, I really appreciate this."

She stepped aside and he walked into the cabin, following her as she turned around and headed for the kitchen.

She'd hoped the few seconds it took to get from the door to the kitchen counter would be enough to compose herself. Color her surprised when it didn't. In fact, the brief loss of eye contact seemed to make his powerful gaze that much more intense.

"Fixing a snack?"

She shook her head, lifting her gaze slowly from her

makeshift dinner on the counter to the sultry half grin sitting on his smug face.

"No, more like working too hard and forgetting the dinner invitation your generous host offered you this morning."

She expected to see him gloating. She certainly deserved it after flaking on his invite. But there, in the depths of his eyes, arrogance was absent. Something akin to…familiarity stared back at her, warming her through and through.

"I thought I was the only person who works so hard, he forgets to eat."

"I've missed so many meals getting caught up in work that if being plus-size was solely about eating too much as society believes, I'd be thinner than this saltine cracker right here."

He didn't say anything. Instead, he silently took her in, all of her. She could feel his hungry gaze slide slowly, oh so slowly, down every bit of her five feet ten inches. Its steadiness made small sparks of desire flutter in the bottom of her empty belly, making her feel just the tiniest bit woozy. Either that, or she was hungrier than she realized.

"Society usually doesn't know what it's talking about." He stretched one of his hands flat against the counter and leaned in. "Plus-size is what we call healthy 'round these parts. Frankly, I don't trust anyone who can willingly walk away from a good rack of ribs, a juicy burger or my mama's banana pudding."

She snatched up another cracker and crunched loudly on it. "I'd kill for ribs right now. And when you say banana pudding, are you talking about like a bread pudding or that banana-flavored Jell-O mess?"

"Alternating layers of sliced bananas and Nilla wafers covered in a milk, egg and sugar mixture and baked to perfection."

"Please stop," she moaned. "Unless your mama is on her way in here with a slice for me, don't torture me like this."

The deep rich tones of his chuckle washed over her, making goose bumps pebble up on her arms. How his laugh managed to be as sexy as the rest of him, she didn't know. But it damn sure was. Even her work-obsessed self wasn't immune to it.

"If she wasn't cruising around the Caribbean with my dad, I'm sure that could be arranged. But I've got the next best thing."

He lifted the foil cover from the plate he'd placed on the counter.

"So, you can just magically tell when people are hungry and then bring them plates?" Yes, she was teasing the man, who up until this moment hadn't seemed like he had an amusing bone in his body.

Teasing him was far better than giving in to the uninvited want that seemed to move into her body and mind, squatting and getting comfortable, without consulting her first.

"I have many talents."

Keely was certain he did. Everything about Jacob Chatman, from his easy gait and powerful stance, to his broad shoulders and tight waist, reinforced the idea that this man knew how to handle himself at all times.

"I'm sure you do." She pointed to the plate sitting on her counter. "Apparently answering telepathic calls for food delivery is one of them."

He silently went about setting the foil aside, revealing what looked like the best-tasting baby back ribs, baked macaroni and cheese, and steamed cabbage she would ever taste.

"You ordered takeout?"

He scoffed, glaring at her as if she'd kicked his favorite pair of cowboy boots.

"Don't insult me like that. I made everything on this plate."

She pursed her lips, trying to hide how impressed she was. Yes, men cooked all the time. But the lovely aromas wafting up from that plate indicated that man could burn, and a man who could burn in the kitchen was a rare treasure to find.

"It looks decent."

She was lying through her teeth. It looked like it came straight from somebody's grandma's table. She wasn't about to tell him that, though. The look of defiance settling over the strong angles of his face was too delicious for Keely to come clean.

"I see I'mma have to show you better than I can tell you." Within seconds, he'd somehow made it around to her side of the island. He was standing so close, too close in fact, that his clean and spicy scent pushed away the appetizing fragrance of the food, filling her senses, triggering that heady feeling of floating. "You go'n and sit down."

There was something about the way his voice commanded her, something so visceral it connected with something deep and unfamiliar inside her. Keely wasn't a person who took well to orders. She wasn't a joiner or follower, didn't feel the need to follow the rules of the group just to get along. But the deep rumble of the hint of bass in his voice triggered something inside her that wanted to just relent without question.

For the briefest moment, her inner Brooklynite

fought the idea of being told what to do. But the commanding sound of his voice, paired with the stern look that graced his face, soothed something inside her she couldn't explain.

She nodded, doing as she was told, taking the bar stool on the opposite side of the island counter as she watched him wash his hands, put the plate in the microwave, then set about retrieving cutlery and a napkin to place in front of her.

Keely sat quietly, almost mesmerized by his seamless movement in the kitchen. Yes, this was his cabin. Yet he moved around it with such ease, as if he spent most of his time here and not at the big house where he lived.

She was about to say as much when he returned with her plate and tipped his chin in her direction, signaling her to eat without speaking so much as a word. And she complied, willingly picking up the cutlery and loading up a healthy forkful. Any notion she had of resisting died when she saw the satisfaction her compliance gave him gleaming in his eyes.

She didn't know why it mattered that her acquiescence pleased him. The small lift of his full lips into a barely noticeable smile was like high praise poured over her. It unnerved her, yes. But she was much more intrigued than put off and that in and of itself should've had her running for shelter. Yet she couldn't find the slightest bit of desire to run, so she did what she instinctively knew they both wanted: she ate.

She hummed as the savory and sweet tastes collided on her tongue. Just for a second, the flavor explosion was enough to shake her free of whatever hold this man had on her as she loaded up another forkful while chewing her current mouthful.

"Damn, I take back every slick thing I was thinking

about your cooking abilities." She managed to speak around her packed jaw. "This is amazing."

"I know it is." He stood in front of her with his arms crossed and his eyes locked on her. "I told you my culinary skills were unmatched."

She was enjoying the food too much to worry about taking him down a peg or five. He was arrogant, but as good as the food was, he damn sure had a reason to be.

"Did you go to culinary school or something?"

With an arched brow, he cocked his head to the side as he continued to watch her eat. "Yeah. Bixby and Geraldine Chatman's soul food culinary arts program."

Keely picked up a juicy rib covered in a sweet and tangy sauce that was going to leave a mess all over her mouth as soon as she bit into it.

"I'm sure there's a joke somewhere in there meant for me to find." She took a generous bite out of the smoky-flavored meat before continuing. "But this food is too good for me to check for your sarcasm right now."

Her response brought an easy chuckle that she found almost as tempting as the delicious food he'd prepared—almost.

"My parents were big on cooking when I was growing up. Since I'm their only child, they doted on me by teaching me. Anything that could be baked or roasted in an oven, my mama taught me how to cook, and if it could be deep-fried or grilled, or covered in a sauce, my daddy had a recipe for it."

"God bless them." She licked some of the sauce from her fingers, not caring how uncouth she appeared. "I really mean that. They deserve to be nominated for sainthood if they taught you to burn like this."

"I'll make sure to tell them you said so when they get back from their cruise."

"Again," she managed between bites, "I'm sure there's some sarcasm in there, but the food is too good for me to care."

He laughed, stepping away from the counter and grabbing a bottle of water out of the fridge and sliding it over to her. He stood in silence for the remainder of her meal, which should've been weird. She should've questioned why it wasn't. But instead of overanalyzing this scenario like she did everything else, she simply went with it, finding his silent company a comfort she hadn't even known she'd wanted.

When she was finished, he cleared her plate and washed up the dishes. "You cook and you wash dishes. Your woman is a very lucky girl."

"If she existed, she'd probably disagree with you as much as any of my exes on that account."

Even though Keely was in a near food coma, she was lucid enough to catch that fleeting wisp of something in his voice that made her think he might not be joking.

"You can't possibly be trying to tell me you don't have women hanging off you."

"I don't have a problem getting women. Keeping them, however…is another matter altogether."

Stunned momentarily silent, she shook her head, preparing to delve deeper into his meaning. But before she could get her brain to work properly, he nodded, said good-night and closed the door quietly behind him, leaving her watching the door as she murmured, "What the hell just happened?"

Eight

"Everything all right, boss?"

Jacob shoveled the last bit of straw into the stall before turning to his foreman, Matt Santiago, standing just outside the now clean stall.

His muscles ached, and his body was covered in sweat, proof that he had done more than laze about thinking about the beautiful woman squatting in his guest cabin.

"Yeah," he muttered. "I'm good. You need something, Matt?"

Matt stood with a mischievous grin on his face, like he knew something Jacob didn't. He'd been Jacob's first hire when he took over the farm from his parents and began converting it to a horse ranch. His tanned brown skin and ink black hair spoke of his Mexican ancestry, and the gleam in his dark eyes revealed his good-natured playfulness that made him a good working match for Jacob. He was a hard worker, but he had a knack for reminding Jacob not to take himself too seriously when he became too consumed with the ranch.

"You've been breaking your back since sunup. I'm used to seeing you work hard, but even this is a bit much for you. You wanna talk about it?"

Jacob walked out of the stall, putting his shovel away and pulling his work gloves off, shoving them in the back pocket of his denims.

"Nothing to talk about. I just wanted to make sure everything that needed to get done today was taken care of."

"Or—" Matt raised a finger, ignoring Jacob's excuse for working himself to the bone with little more than a few water breaks throughout the day "—your guest in the cabin has you so rattled you can't think straight."

Jacob shook his head. "You know I don't get wrapped up in women, Matt. Keely is a guest and nothing more."

Matt's grin spread wider. Somehow the sight of it seemed to worsen Jacob's mood. That didn't seem to stop his friend and employee, though.

"Keely is it, now?" The playful note in Matt's voice somehow made Jacob feel more seen, generating the weird sensation to duck and cover. "A couple of nights ago, she was Ms. Tucker when you came to get me and the rest of the hands to help unload her truck. Today she's Keely. Seems like you've gotten cozy with her."

"Matt." Jacob purposely used a deeper tone to try to ward his foreman off. But he could tell by the good-natured gleam in Matt's eyes, the man didn't care a whip about Jacob's attempt at being stern. "Speak your piece so I can go shower, eat and go to bed. It's been a long day."

"All I'm saying is, you've been a bit outta sorts today

and I think it has to do with the pretty lady in your cabin. Maybe that's a sign you should be taking the time to have a little bit of fun. Lord knows if anyone deserves a good time, it's you."

Jacob huffed. "I appreciate you trying to look out for me, Matt. But I don't have anything to offer a high-maintenance woman like Keely. She's glitz and glam, and I'm dirt and sweat. She would require a whole lot of time and attention I don't have to give."

Jacob turned, making his way outside of the stables, hoping Matt would take the hint and leave the conversation alone. He didn't need anyone reminding him of what his brain had him thinking of all last night.

The few minutes he'd spent watching Keely thoroughly enjoy the food he'd prepared had been a singular joy he hadn't expected to experience. As someone who worked in the fashion world, he'd expected her to be too prissy to eat in front of him, let alone dig into the plate with the reverence and joy that she had.

The look of serene pleasure on her face and the soulful sounds coming from her took his mind from food to the physical in less time than it took to blink an eye. Instantly, he'd gone from enjoying watching her indulge to wondering if she made those same sounds when she was receiving another kind of pleasure. One he was certain he would give anything to be the one giving it to her.

But when Keely mentioned a fictional lucky woman in his life, it was like the harsh spray of a fire hose slapping him in the face, melting away the fantasy building in his mind.

Sure, there had been women in Jacob's life. None of them were lucky, though, not as far as they were concerned. Each one of them had wanted the one thing he couldn't give. Devoted attention.

"Jay." The pointed tone in Matt's voice meant he had every intention of ignoring Jacob's need to be done with their chosen topic. "You need to blow off some steam, my friend. And if the visitor in the guesthouse piques your interest, maybe you should do something about it."

"I'm busy."

"Yeah," Matt continued. "So is she. That might mean she's game for a little fun too. You'll never know if you don't ask her."

Jacob cut his eyes at Matt, making the man raise his hands up and walk slowly back toward the stables.

"Just think about what I said, Jacob. There's no harm in asking."

Jacob stalked away from Matt, heading back toward the main house. He was in need of a shower, a beer, solitude and peace. If he could make those things happen, maybe they would get him out of this funky mood that had dogged him all day long.

He realized those things might be harder to acquire than he imagined when he rounded the corner of the main house and found none other than Keely Tucker sitting on his front porch waiting for him.

He'd laugh if he found the universe's sense of humor the least bit funny. He'd worked himself to exhaustion today trying to erase their short time together last night. He was just tired enough that he thought he might be able to successfully clear his mind when the object of his apparent obsession was sitting on his porch like the big beautiful distraction she was from the very first moment he'd laid eyes on her.

"Whatever it is, it's gonna have to wait until I've had a shower."

She said nothing, simply nodded, then stood. He walked past her, opening the front door, then moved to the side to let her walk in ahead of him. One look at the large swath of honey-brown skin on display in a pair of denim shorts and he was convinced he'd made the worst decision of his life. There was absolutely no good that could come of this woman being in his house… with him…alone.

Nine

The apology she had for him was on the tip of her tongue when he walked up to the porch. She'd intended to come and talk to him, tell him how sorry she was for making things weird by making jokes about the women in his life. She honestly hadn't meant any harm, but that brain-to-mouth connection of hers didn't always work properly. Keely said what was on her mind. Not to be hurtful, but because lying took too much energy. She wasn't built for things like small talk and diplomacy. Shooting straight from the hip was how she operated.

Except for last night.

Last night, she'd done anything but be honest. If she had, she wouldn't have allowed the hyperawareness she seemed to suffer in his presence to make her try to fill the silence with something cute and sarcastic.

It had worked for a bit. But somehow without realizing it, she'd crossed a line. And since finding a place to stay that had both power and the space to accommodate her work wasn't easy, pissing off her host was the last thing she needed to be doing.

Seeking to prevent more damage, when Jacob told her he needed to shower before he spoke to her, she'd nodded and followed him to the front door. Now, instead of being back at the cabin working on Ariana's dress, she was trapped in this man's living room with the knowledge that he was naked and wet in another room.

And there she went again, thinking about things she shouldn't. Keely paced back and forth in front of the fireplace, trying her best not to imagine Jacob's light brown skin covered in sheets of water as he stood underneath the shower spray. Every time her mind would go there, she'd sketch on the iPad mini with her Apple Pencil, and when the thoughts persisted, she'd walk in front of the fireplace again.

"If you keep that up, you're gonna wear a hole in my rug."

She turned toward the sound of his deep voice to find him standing in the doorway clad in a pair of beltless jeans that hung low on his hips with a crisp T-shirt that stretched against every muscle of his torso, putting every sinew of his solid upper body on display.

"Sorry. Pacing helps me think. I do it a lot when I'm working on a design that I'm trying to get just right."

"Ariana's dress giving you grief?"

"No," she replied quickly. "I'm just trying to figure out the final touches to take the dress from being a wedding dress to Ariana's wedding dress. I'll know it when I see it. Until then, I'll just keep doodling until I figure it out."

He leaned against the doorway, watching her carefully as if he was trying to figure out the answer to a question he hadn't asked.

"As fascinating as all that sounds, I'm sure you didn't come all the way over here to find me and talk about Ariana's dress design. Did you need something?"

She scratched her head before she began, remembering her mother telling her that was always her sign of contrition. Whatever Keely said after that was usually a heartfelt admission of whatever it was she'd done wrong.

As grown as she was now, she somehow hadn't kicked the habit. Something her mother still thought was cute, while Keely despised the habit because she thought it made her look weak. And weakness couldn't be tolerated when you were trying to build your own empire.

"I don't want to take up too much of your time. I just wanted to stop by and say I'm sorry."

He stood to his full height then, his brows pulling into a pointed V. "And what exactly are you sorry for?"

"I was out of line last night joking about the women you date. I truly didn't mean anything by it. But by the way you shut down the conversation, obviously I said something that bothered you."

She waited for him to say something, say anything. The silence seemed louder if possible.

You said your piece, Keely. Time to leave the man to his brooding alone.

She went to walk past him, but stopped dead in her tracks the moment his long fingers came in contact with her forearm.

He looked down, his brown eyes searing into hers, burrowing through to her very core.

"Don't go." When she didn't respond, he squeezed

her forearm with those deft fingers of his, ensuring she couldn't move from that spot if she wanted to. "If we're gonna have this conversation, I'm gonna need a beer. Don't let me drink alone."

He probably hadn't meant those words to sound so loaded, so needy. Their intensity rang inside her head, making it hard for her to think straight. If her brain were working right, she would've carried her happy hips through his front door and back to the cabin. But the neediness in his voice, it called to her like sugar to ants, and she was right on his tail, following him to his kitchen.

He pointed to the bar stools aligned against one side of the counter while he stepped toward his chrome fridge.

"You eat yet?"

"No. You?"

"No. Too tired to cook, so I'm gonna make a sandwich from some of the leftover ribs. You're welcome to eat with me."

"I hope you don't think I came over here seeking food."

"I wouldn't mind it if you did. I hate for food to go to waste but I still haven't learned how to cook for one person."

He turned away, pulling plates and seasoning jars from the cabinets and setting them on the counter and then grabbing a sealed food container from the fridge. Once he grabbed the bread, he layered the fixings in an assembly-line fashion and slid a thick sandwich that required both hands for her to eat.

"Thanks for coming all the way over here to apologize. Wasn't necessary, though."

He chose that moment to bite into his sandwich. She

wasn't certain if his timing was based on hunger, or a need to silence himself. Either way, she knew there was more to his words than his easygoing lilt relayed.

"Then why did you leave so suddenly when it seemed we were having a friendly conversation?"

He pushed his plate aside and leaned forward. Even with the counter still between them, she could feel so much heat emanating from him, she was tempted to place a cool hand on his face to test his temperature for herself.

"Dating is a bit of a sore subject for me. I don't indulge in it much."

"I don't understand why not." She blurted out the words before she could catch herself. And since she'd already said as much as she had, she figured she might as well continue with her train of thought. "As fine as you are, I know damn well the women in this town must be trying to break through your gates to get to you."

Something bright flashed in his eyes that she couldn't quite identify. Figuring she'd better quit while she was ahead, she took a bite of her sandwich, letting her food stop her mouth, as her mama always said.

"Thank you for the vote of confidence. My fineness notwithstanding, meeting a woman who can put up with my nonexistent work-life balance isn't as easy as it might seem."

"Meaning?"

He raised his brow, silently asking if she was sure she wanted her question answered. When she nodded, he continued.

"I spend most of my day doing something to build this ranch. Relationships take time and attention I don't have to spare. So, if a woman wants more than a good time every now and again, then I'm not the man for her."

"And by a good time every now and again, you mean...?"

"Sex."

No hesitation at all, he just put it all out there. With her thumb on her chin and her pointer finger tapping at the corner of her mouth, she contemplated his response. To be fair, she did ask him, so she shouldn't have been surprised he gave her an answer.

She couldn't help the cheeky smile blooming on her lips. Finding a man who was blunt about what he wanted, doing away with the "hey, baby, hey" games a lot of men tried to play as a matter of course, Keely found his openness...refreshing, to say the least.

"I hope I didn't offend your delicate sensibilities by speaking out of turn."

Keely's shoulder shook from the hard bark of laughter bubbling up in her chest.

"Bruh, I'm from Brooklyn, Do or Die Bed Stuy to be exact. The worst thing a man can do is try to run game on me. I appreciate when people just tell me what they want instead of beating around the bush."

"I want people to know what to expect with me. Things can go sideways when all parties involved aren't clear on the expectations."

In that moment, more than anything she could remember in recent times, she wanted to know exactly what a woman could expect from that good time with the sexy cowboy standing in front of her. For a moment, she pondered whether or not it was rude to ask the burning question singeing the inside of her brain.

Something changed in his demeanor as she sat there watching him, pondering her next step. The exhaustion dogging him from the moment he'd rounded the corner to the house seemed to drip away. In its wake was an awareness she couldn't quite describe. Whatever he was noticing or looking for, he hadn't shared. But the intensity of his eyes sliding down her face made her skin burn hotter than the Texas sun during a heat wave, pushing her to ask the question lingering in the air.

"What exactly can a woman expect from you?"

He took another bite of his sandwich, taking his time chewing every morsel before grabbing the longneck he'd pulled out of the fridge and taking a long, slow swig from it that put the thick muscles of his neck on display.

"When a woman is in my presence, she can expect to have my total attention. I might not be boyfriend material, but when I do indulge, I make sure the woman I'm spending time with understands how much I appreciate her company. So, anything I can do to show my appreciation, I will."

Keely was always an imaginative, creative person. It was a trait that had served her well in her life. Tonight, however, it was going to land her in a world of trouble she didn't need.

Sitting here in front of Jacob, listening to him talk about showing his appreciation to a woman, her overactive imagination was banging against the mores of her barely there tact, desperately wanting to know what that appreciation looked like in real time.

"You could teach some of the men I've encountered a lesson."

He lifted his brown eyes, encouraging her to elaborate, and even though she knew she shouldn't, she took a swallow of her beer for courage and continued.

"I travel a lot for work. I'm never home more than a couple of weeks at a time. The men I meet that want to treat a woman well also want commitment. My career is just taking off. I can't focus on anything other than work."

"And the men that don't want to treat a woman well?"

She broke away from his dark gaze to peel an edge of the bottle's label away from its cool surface, trying to figure out how to answer him without seeming desperate or uncertain of her own mind.

Keely knew what she wanted. She just hadn't found anyone willing to give it to her yet. Or maybe she had? Jacob chose that moment to walk around to her side of the counter, leaning his hip against the marble and staring down at her with such desire she had to wonder if for once she'd met a kindred spirit that understood her boundaries where relationships were concerned.

"The men who wouldn't mind the friends-with-benefits thing only seem to focus on the benefits and not the friends part. Just because I don't want a ring doesn't mean I want to be treated like I'm disposable either."

He moved his hand slowly toward her face, giving her more than enough time to pull away if she chose. He needn't have worried about that. She wanted to know what Jacob's touch felt like, if only something as innocent as a fingertip caressing her cheek.

Fortunately, she didn't have to concern herself about innocent touches. When his finger and thumb clasped her chin, bringing her gaze up to his, there was no mistaking the fiery need burning in his heated stare.

"There is nothing disposable about a woman as gorgeous as you. Any man that doesn't recognize that is a fool who doesn't deserve a second of your time."

"For a man that just met me a few days ago, you seem mighty certain of your assessment of my value."

"You saying you disagree with me?"

"Not at all," she replied. "I know my worth. I'm just

questioning how you can be so certain of it after spending so little time with me."

He didn't drop his gaze, didn't retreat into some slick pickup line. Instead, he scrutinized her face as if he was committing every line, slope and angle to memory for his assessment.

"Only a fool could stand in your presence and mistake gold for rusty old tin. I would never make that mistake."

By the drop in the timbre of his voice, she knew he was going to kiss her even before he moved slowly but intentionally toward her. By the time his mouth hovered just above hers, she parted her lips in hungry anticipation.

She knew she was too eager, that her best bet would've been to play it cool and reserved as if she didn't care. But damn her need to present a put-together facade, she wanted his mouth on hers and she wanted it now.

Too desperate to know if he tasted as good as he looked, Keely lifted her hand, curling each finger into the cotton of his crisp white T-shirt, dragging him down and pressing her lips to his.

If he was put off by her forwardness, he didn't let on. Instead, it seemed to urge him on as he threaded eager fingers into her loose strands, tugging just tightly enough to keep her exactly where he wanted her.

When she moaned in appreciation, he pressed his lips harder against hers, moving them with a controlled urgency that both satisfied her while making her ache for more.

She spread her fingers wide across the hard plane of his chest. This wasn't sculpted muscle from being a gym rat. She was certain Jacob's solid physique didn't come from staring in a mirror all day while he curled hand weights. She'd bet his solid frame came from roping cows or whatever it was that cowboys did on a ranch all day. Whatever it was, she was grateful for what resulted in a gorgeous specimen of man that was waking up parts of her body she'd apparently neglected for far too long. Because the taste of this man's lips and the rugged smell of spice and soap that wafted up from his skin was an intoxicating mix that made her blood pulse and sex clench.

Girl, you did not come here for this.

True, but she couldn't say she was all that upset at the turn of events either. Not when every nerve in her body was vibrating with desire.

When he gentled the kiss, pulling back slowly, her senses were so overrun she could hardly distinguish light from dark.

She blinked several times, trying to get her vision to clear and her eyes to focus again. Still under the influence of Jacob's kiss, she closed her eyes, leaning into the hard wall of his chest.

"I think you kissed me blind."

She could feel his laughter move through him as he held her closer.

"I'd like to take credit for that." He whispered just loud enough for her to hear. "I haven't enjoyed kissing someone like that in a while. But I think your temporary loss of sight has more to do with a power loss than my kissing technique."

"Wait, what?"

He set her back from him, tracing the side of her jaw. "Seems like the Slick Six is experiencing a blackout too."

Ten

Jacob passed his flashlight beam once more over the backup generator, making certain everything was in working order.

He'd cringed at the exorbitant cost of the thing when he'd had it installed. That was then. Now, he was grateful he'd had the foresight to purchase it.

He looked over to his side to see Keely standing next to him with her arms crossed and worry pinching her brow into a sharp V. For him, being out in this kind of darkness was a usual, comforting thing. He imagined being from the city, where the lights were always bright and plentiful, this kind of night had to be unnerving if not outright alarming.

"Everything working okay?"

Her voice was steady, but he could see the concern in the rapid movement of her dark brown eyes. He reached out his hand, hesitating slightly before placing it carefully on her biceps.

Just before the blackout, he'd had his mouth plastered to hers in the most titillating kiss he'd ever experienced. But Keely's agreeing to kiss him in the confines of his kitchen didn't mean he had the right to touch her anyway he wanted, wherever he wanted, even when his only desire was to comfort her.

"Everything's working as it should. There's only one problem I can see."

"What's that?"

"We have enough propane to keep the lights on until my scheduled propane delivery next week—"

"That doesn't sound like a problem." He smiled, trying to keep from alarming her. Keely was bright, bold and loud, and as much as he hated those qualities on most people, they were downright attractive on her. So, seeing her with the slightest bit of concern dampening her natural boisterous persona didn't sit right with him.

"You didn't let me finish. We can keep the lights on until my delivery next week if we shut down power in the guest cabin. Running electricity in both residences is gonna consume a hell of a lot of gas in a short amount of time."

"Are you evicting me?"

"From the guesthouse? Yes. From the ranch? No. You'll just have to stay in the main house with me."

"Ugh," she groaned. "Why does the universe hate me?"

He chuckled a bit. Her dramatic display of frustration was entertaining if nothing else.

"I'm sorry the idea of staying in my guest room is so unappealing."

She shook her head. "It's not you." Her voice was soft

and resigned, as if she'd just decided fighting wasn't worth the energy. "I'm very grateful for your hospitality. The issue is space. Space and solitude."

She must've noted the confusion in his furrowed brow and narrowed gaze because she continued without being prompted.

"Ariana's dress is huge and white, and needs to be guarded like a national treasure. She's a celebrity. The tabloids would do anything to get a sneak peek at it before the big day. I can't let that happen. Moving to another location, especially a house where other people have access to it, will increase the chances of the dress getting leaked."

"Is that all?"

She looked a bit annoyed if the sharp glare she aimed at him was any indication. He held up his hands quickly to slow the fire he could see growing in her stare.

"My great room is large enough for you to work, and the double doors have a lock and I'm the only one with a key. You can keep the room locked up to keep the gown safe. I also have blackout blinds on the windows, so we can make sure no one can get a sneak peek of the gown before the wedding day. Does that work for you?"

She blinked at him, as if she were still attempting to process everything he was saying.

"Yeah, that works. Thank you."

"You sound surprised I'd try to help."

Her face was open and bright, and even without the beam of the flashlight, he was certain he'd still be able to make out every glorious angle of her beautiful face.

"To be frank," she began.

"Do you know any other way to be?" he asked, hoping she didn't find his sarcasm offensive.

When she chuckled softly, warmth spread through

him. "Actually, I don't. Being forthright is a personality quirk of mine."

The smile on her face lightened his mood even more and he had to wonder if he should be so concerned that a mere smile from this woman could make him feel light and free.

"I'm not surprised you'd try to help me. You seem to be someone who looks out for people. That first night I was here when you and your hands came to unload my truck, you were very kind and open with them. That kind of connection isn't always present between employees and bosses. I'm just surprised you didn't look for another option that would get me off your ranch and out of your hair."

She was right. He could've called around to see if he could find somewhere else for her to stay. But the truth was, the thought had never crossed his mind. He'd never once thought of her being anywhere else but with him.

He should be unnerved by that. But he wasn't, and he wasn't naive enough to ignore why. The kiss they'd shared, along with the conversation where she'd told him she didn't want to be treated as disposable, had flipped some kind of switch in him. Suddenly, he wanted her around if only to prove to her that he would never be the kind of man to treat her so poorly.

He wouldn't tell her that, though. He knew from experience that telling a woman something like that gave her ideas he couldn't possibly entertain because he wasn't boyfriend material. He wouldn't play games with Keely like that. Even though he'd only known her a short time, he had a great deal of respect for her. So instead of telling her the truth and risking her misunderstanding his meaning, he simply said, "I'm not that much of an asshole, Keely, that I'd turn you away in

your time of need. Especially when I'll be out of the
house most of the day so the only time our paths will
cross will probably be at dinner. I think I can put up
with that little intrusion on my solitude for however
long you're here. How about you?"

She smiled again, nodding her agreement. And as
they made their way back to the main house, he prayed
his assessment was right. Because Keely was temptation on legs, and he had too much to lose by giving in
to his baser desires.

"Is that the last box, Matt?"

"Yes, boss." His foreman came over to help Jacob
pack up all of Keely's things and get them settled into
the great room. "You need me for anything else?"

"No, Matt. Thanks for coming out this early and
helping me out."

"You know I always got your back, boss."

Matt may have called Jacob *boss*, but they both knew
the man was more than just an employee. He was a treasured friend, which was probably the only reason he got
away with half the things he said to Jacob.

"'Preciate, man. Since you came out here so early,
take the morning off." Before Matt could resist, Jacob
held his hand up. "I'll take care of your duties."

Matt tipped his head toward Jacob with a jubilant
smile plastered across his lips.

"Shoot, you don't have to tell me twice. I'll see you
this afternoon."

Matt clapped him on the shoulder just as Keely made
her way into the kitchen.

"Thanks for all your help, Matt." Jacob turned to
see the gracious smile on her face and the relaxed features that made Keely appear more comfortable in his

ranch home than one would think a city socialite like her would be.

"Welcome, Ms. Keely. I'm just glad you won't be alone in all that darkness. Holler if you need anything else. Jacob knows how to find me."

She nodded and waved as Matt made his exit, sharing the kind smile she'd just gifted Matt with Jacob.

"He's such a nice guy." Keely's comment brought a wry smile to Jacob's face.

"That's because you don't know him well enough. He's a great worker and a better friend, but a royal pain in my ass all the same."

"Good friends often are." She looked around the kitchen before bringing her gaze back to his. "I really appreciate all the trouble you've gone through to accommodate me."

"Wanna make it up to me?" Her pointed stare made him shake his head. "Don't worry. It's not that kind of proposition. Since we've gotten your things sorted in the great room, how about going on a ride with me?"

The suspicion on her face went from paranoid to cautious as she contemplated his request. He'd met a few New Yorkers in his travels and their suspicious nature of anything friendly was a great source of entertainment for him.

Keely wasn't off-putting. In fact, her open smile and boisterous nature drew you in like a carefully placed lasso on a calf, tugging at you until you couldn't help but surrender to her call. But even though everything about her pulled at you, you could tell by the cut of her eye and the intensity of her stare that she was always attempting to anticipate your next move.

"I'm taking over Matt's morning duties since he came over and helped me get your stuff moved over here. I need to check the perimeters of the land, make sure the posts are secured and safe so none of the horses we let roam free in some of the open areas get injured. I figured after all the work you put in setting up the great room, you might've wanted to take a break and take a nice horseback ride with me."

She folded her arms, tipping her head back and forth before she raised her gaze to his.

"That depends."

"On what?"

"On whether you've got a really even-tempered horse that won't throw me. I haven't ridden since I was a kid."

Horseback riding was usually something people in elite circles indulged in frequently. He was slightly taken aback to hear she hadn't ridden in so much time.

"I do." His reply seemed to calm something in her and he realized this wasn't a show. She really was concerned with the temperament of the horse. "Her name is Tildy and she's the sweetest horse you'll ever find. She loves people, and if you feed her a treat, she'll be loyal for life."

Besides his mother, Tildy was the most loyal female he knew. Because she was so sweet, Jacob was extremely protective of whom he paired her with. If a rider was too hard or vigorous, they didn't get to ride his sweet Tildy. But somehow, he knew that Keely would appreciate the old girl and be as kind to her as Jacob was.

Keely was a person who paid attention to detail. He was sure that skill had to be useful in her line of work. She noticed enough about him to understand that something was wrong and she cared enough to seek him out to smooth things over. He didn't know why, but her actions had meant something to him. Now, he wanted to spend a little more time in her presence.

He ignored the warning bells that were clanging loudly in his head, trying to remind him that he didn't have time for whatever it was he thought he was doing. Then he watched a smile bloom slowly on her face, the single gesture making warmth and contentment spread through his chest, and he knew right at that moment there wasn't an alarm bell loud enough to make him withdraw his invitation.

"Sure." Her easy response lured him even more into the depths of the fog he found himself in when he was near her. That fog was thick, surrounding him, blocking out anything else from his senses but her. "I'll ride with you. Let me just run upstairs and change into something appropriate."

Appropriate.

As she turned around, heading up the back stairs to the guest room, all he could think of was that the titillating thoughts running through his head as he watched her perfectly rounded ass climb the stairs were anything but appropriate.

Eleven

"Damn, this place is big."

Keely stepped inside the stables, turning in a circle as she took in the wide space. Not that she had much to compare it with. She'd only ever ridden when she'd gone on her high school's annual field trip to a small farm upstate. The rickety old building where the handful of horses on that farm resided wasn't even in the same category as this large horse palace that boasted of high ceilings, a loft that bordered the entire interior structure, and stalls lining a long wall.

"It's a'ight." His knowing smile belied his faux humility. He knew damn well this place was amazing.

"How many horses do you have here?"

"In here? Five." His response made her take another glance around the interior. This place was too big for five horses.

"We have three stables on the property. This one

houses ten. It's the smallest. My personal stock is kept here. The other two are for sales and boarders, respectively. They can house up to fifty horses each."

Keely's mouth dropped open. Again, she had no context for how many horses could or should be on a ranch. But she certainly didn't think having more than one hundred horses on your property was to be expected.

"Do you really have enough room for that many horses? I'm not talking about the stalls. I mean, I imagine they need space to run around or something."

He nodded casually as he led her down the hall. She took in each stall whether it was occupied or not. From growing up in Brooklyn, to all the traveling she did now as a stylist and designer, her travels had never taken her to a bona fide ranch. The rural landscape and lifestyle were more foreign to her than any country she'd set foot in beyond the borders of the United States.

"They do. A safe measure is ten horses per acre. At fifteen thousand acres, we can technically house fifteen hundred horses."

She turned to him, ready to interrupt, when she saw his mouth curl into an amused grin.

"No, we never take on that many horses at a time. We may have the acreage to support that many, but not the staff. I employ about sixty full-time hands. A third of them live on property and the rest commute in every day."

He walked ahead of her as they neared the middle of the stables, grabbing an apple from a nearby table.

"Tildy girl, I've brought you some company."

Keely watched a golden beige pointed head with a white snout peek out of the middle stall on their right.

"Tildy girl, you ready for a visit?"

Jacob got close enough to rub the animal's snout.

Apparently, she enjoyed Jacob's petting her because she pushed her head in his hand, encouraging him to stroke her again.

Lucky girl. Keely shook her head at her ridiculousness. *Gosh, Keely. You know things have been running slow in the man department if you're jealous of the attention he's paying a horse.*

Once she stopped lamenting the fact that the horse was getting more action than she was, Keely took notice of the gentle timbre of Jacob's voice as he greeted Tildy.

Here was this big man, standing well over six feet with a wide and muscular body to boot, and he was speaking in hushed tones to this great animal who was soaking up all his affection and sharing a bit of her own. She kept bobbing her neck and almost nuzzling the side of Jacob's face.

"That's my good girl. I'm happy to see you too." He waved Keely toward him, pulling her close to him, but standing between her and the stall. She realized he was trying to make her feel safe around Tildy.

That kindness made her want to settle against his side. But since she was trying to keep things platonic, she stayed where he'd positioned her.

"Do you want to get closer to Tildy so you can meet her proper?" When she nodded, he held out his hand and pulled her close enough that their shoulders touched. A brief sizzle of electricity sparked between them and Keely had to use all of her willpower to not jump away in surprise.

"Always approach a horse from an angle. You want to make sure they see you and know you're coming. Tildy weighs about a thousand pounds. You don't want something with that kind of heft surprised by your presence."

Again, she nodded, paying close attention to his impromptu lesson on getting comfortable with horses. She was certain going riding when she was younger was born out of the invincibility teenagers believe they possess. But as a grown woman who understood a healthy dose of fear could save your life, she was grateful for Jacob's care.

"Tildy is a Norwegian fjord horse. This breed is short, no more than thirteen or fourteen hands, but built stocky. It can carry a full-grown adult and then some. These horses are also bred for their calm temperament. They don't spook easy, making them good for first-time or novice riders who need to get used to being up close and personal with our big, four-legged friends like my girl here. When you're ready, give me your hand and I'll help you pet her."

He reached out to her, slowly curling his fingers around hers until her entire hand was swallowed in his. He gave her hand a gentle squeeze before laying it flat on the horse's shoulder.

"You wanna make sure you pet her in the direction of the grain of her hair. Doing otherwise can be uncomfortable for her. So, start at the top of her neck and brush down toward her shoulder. Make sure your strokes are slow and soft."

She listened to him; his deep voice was so soothing. She couldn't blame the horse from being lulled into ease. Keely's own nerves calmed to the relaxing tone of Jacob's voice.

He continued to talk her through more steps to getting acquainted with Tildy, including feeding her apple slices from a flat gloved hand and attaching a lead rope and pulling the golden-haired horse from her stall to the tack area at the back of the stable. By the time he'd put Tildy's tack on, Keely felt relatively comfortable, and the way the kind creature began to seek affection from Keely, budging her hand the same way she'd seen Tildy budge Jacob's, Keely felt she'd probably just made a new friend.

Jacob saddled up his horse, a large black beauty he'd called Midnight, and they walked them both outside in the fresh open space. After demonstrating how to mount a horse, and giving her pointers on how to make the ordeal less awkward for herself and Tildy, she was soon sitting astride Tildy. After instructing her on how to hold the reins and how to get Tildy to move, Jacob mounted Midnight.

"Since you're learning, we're not really gonna ride today. We'll just walk around at a gentle pace."

Her nerves started to flare and he must have somehow recognized her apprehension because he reached across to her, silently asking for her to place her hand in his. When they touched, and she felt his warmth and confidence flowing through her, their gazes met.

"I'm a man of my word, Keely. You can trust me when I say I won't let anything happen to you. You're safe with me and Tildy."

For no other reason than he'd said it, Keely believed him. If she were thinking clearly, she'd acknowledge how out of character for her that was. But Jacob's firm yet soft hold on her hand made her forget about all the reasons she shouldn't blindly trust this man. Namely, because anyone who said "trust me" generally couldn't be trusted farther than they could be thrown.

"So, is there anything in particular we came out here for, or did you just really want to give me an impromptu riding lesson?"

Jacob glanced at Keely from the side, finding himself fighting the smile her blunt words brought to his lips. He was beginning to notice this lightness in his chest whenever he was around her. It was persistent, scraping away at the loneliness that had settled there.

He'd always believed his penchant for solitude was a blessing. It kept him focused on his work, and focusing on his work had helped him build this ranch from nothing. The Slick Six had become everything to him. But listening to and watching the easy yet daring way she approached everything, it was hard for him not to acknowledge her presence offered him something good, something that had been missing in his life for so many years, he hadn't realized how vital it was until this moment: companionship.

"We're going to check on the transformer. The ranch isn't connected to the city's transformers."

She turned her head to him while looking upward as if the sky was gonna give her the question she was searching for. When her soft brown eyes connected with his, he realized she wasn't searching for the question. She knew exactly what she wanted to ask. She was trying to decide *how* to ask the question.

"Keely, you don't have to censor yourself. If you wanna ask something, ask it."

Her shoulders relaxed a bit, telling him his assumption had been correct.

"I get being a diligent landowner and checking in on your property. But don't you think checking on a transformer is something a professional should do?" She lifted a sleek brow, drawing his attention to it, causing him to fight the urge to stop and reach out to touch it.

He cleared his throat before speaking, trying his best to hide the impact her voice and forwardness had on him from her, but himself too.

"Yes and no."

She nodded, beckoning him to continue. Usually his one-or two-word answers would've been as far as he would've bothered going by way of an explanation. But again, this was Keely, and he was finding her harder and harder to resist.

"This is something a professional should handle, and if the problem is too complicated, I'll definitely have to wait for someone to come out here and check on it. But with the town's power still out, electricians are in high demand right now. This way, if it's something minor, I can get it fixed now."

"Ready to be rid of me already?"

He didn't answer immediately. He needed time to process the answer. If she'd asked him this when she'd arrived a few days ago, the answer would've been a resounding yes. But after knowing what her luscious mouth felt like pressed against his, having her around him wasn't such a difficult task.

"If I wanted you gone, Keely, you would be."

Her face was impassive, and he wished he knew her well enough to be fluent in her particular code.

Before he could explore that thought further, the outpost cottage came into view. She followed him, watching him dismount, and when he was standing next to her with his arms stretched out, she surprised him by repeating the same movements herself. Granted, she wasn't as graceful as him, but the fact that she'd been game to try any of this won her all the bonus points in his book.

"Are we visiting someone before we get to the transformer?"

"No," he replied. "This is one of a handful of cottages placed on some of the more remote locations of the ranch. The last thing you wanna do is get stuck out here with no means of communication or provisions. We keep these cottages stocked with nonperishable food and a landline just in case someone needs help, or when one of the hands has to work out here." She opened her mouth to ask another question and he lifted a pointed finger to stop her. "And to answer your next question, the transformer is behind the cottage."

He grabbed the saddlebags from both horses, resting them both on the verdant grass before he took their lead ropes, petting both of them as he spoke in the same hushed tone he had in the stables.

"Now, I'm depending on you two to behave while me and Ms. Keely go check on a few things. Can you do that for me?"

Midnight tapped one of his front hooves and Tildy bobbed her neck, pushing into his hand as he gave her a good rub.

"All right, now. Remember to come when I call." He removed their lead ropes before giving each of them another comforting pat. "Go play, y'all."

She watched the horses gallop away, then turned her bemused gaze back to him.

"Do they really understand what you're saying?"

"I've had them both since they were foals. Trained them myself. They understand the commands they're given. But more than that, they understand my body language. If I'm petting them and talking gently, they don't sense any fear or danger. Horses are very in tune to the emotions of humans."

They made their way inside the one-room cottage. Unlike the cabin behind the main house, Jacob had had these cottages built for utility instead of luxury.

There was a small sofa and two recliners in the center of the room, each flanked by end tables. A modest TV hung over the fireplace, completing the living area. The kitchen was a corner in the east side of the structure. It housed a small kitchenette table with four chairs, a small gas stove, a refrigerator and a chopping block that couldn't have been more than three feet long.

Behind the couch there was a double bed against the wall with a nightstand on each side of it. He tried really hard to ignore that particular piece of furniture. With Keely standing in this room, it was far too tempting. He was here to do a job, not engage in some sleazy seduction fantasy.

"Here's the place." He waved a hand around the entire expanse, stopping briefly to point to a door next to the bed. "That's the washroom, if you need it. Since the power is out, I wouldn't trust anything in the fridge. I've got a few provisions in the saddlebags if you get hungry, or I could pull out a can of something from the cupboard."

She crossed her arms, staring him straight in the eye with that unforgiving confidence of hers. It might've come off as arrogant and condescending on most women. But on her, it was like a shining light that drew you in from the darkness.

"Jacob, I didn't get my happy hips on a damn horse just to keep you company on the ride. I plan to be out there with you."

She leaned into one leg, jutting one of her aforementioned hips out, making his hand itch with the desire to touch it, rest up on it, hold on to it.

"Keely, other than the ones from Hasbro, do you know anything about transformers?"

She pursed her lips into a sexy pout that had Jacob

more than a little fixated on their shape and how soft and silky they were.

"I don't know anything about electrical transformers. But I can hand you tools, and if you manage to get yourself electrocuted, I can call for help."

"Fair enough," he relented as a soft chuckle escaped his lips. "Come on with me if it suits."

Amused by her chastisement, he headed toward the back door. As soon as he stepped outside, he knew exactly what the problem was. A few large tree branches from a nearby oak lay on top of and littered around the sides of the metal encasement that protected the transformer at ground level.

When he reached the encasement, he didn't see any physical damage severe enough to interrupt power.

"I don't think anything's broken. But the vibrations from those branches dropping from high up could definitely have loosened or disconnected one of the connectors."

"Can you fix that?" He could hear the slight apprehension in her voice, and everything in him wanted to hold her and soothe it away.

"Yes, I can fix that. Let's just hope that's the issue. Otherwise, we'll have to wait for an electrician to arrive."

They set about working, Keely standing by his side, helping him remove the branches she could and stepping out of his way when he grabbed those that were too heavy for her to lift. He was glad for her help. It had taken a good block of time to get the transformer case cleared of the debris and without her, he might have been out here past dark trying to get this thing up and running.

He finally opened the case, scanning the darkness of

the internal chamber with a flashlight. Relief flooded him when he saw two disconnected cables on the transformer.

"Is it worse than you thought?"

The sound of her voice made him look back over his shoulder. She was standing, but leaning hunched over at the waist with her hands on her knees, putting all the golden-brown skin of the top of her cleavage at his eye level.

There wasn't anything remotely erotic about her intentions. This was just her trying to help him get the lights back on at his ranch. But being this close to her was short-circuiting his brain. He was having a time forming words, but his traitorous cock seemed to be working just fine as it strained against his denims.

"It's a…it's…" He wet his lips, trying to get his brain to focus on the transformer and not her. Unfortunately, that was easier said than done because Keely was wearing the hell out of that V-neck T-shirt and he was a grown man who adored and appreciated a beautiful bosom. And from just this little peek, he could tell hers was better than most. Beginning to feel like a creep, he shook his head and focused his eyes on the transformer. "It's exactly what I thought it would be. I just need to tighten these cables and hopefully that'll restore the power."

"Good," she responded. "Because it's hot as hell and we've been out here all day. If I sweat any more, I'm gonna start smelling like who did it and ran. I need a shower in the worst way."

Great, exactly what he didn't need. Images of Keely naked, covered in suds and water. Was she trying to kill him?

"I'll work as fast as I can. But sunset is approaching soon. We ate up a lot of time on our ride and clearing the debris. Are you okay with staying out here with me, or do you want me to call one of the men and have them come take you back to the house?"

He turned, waiting patiently for her answer. He wasn't exactly propositioning her. But by the spark in her eyes, he could tell she was contemplating the unspoken invitation lining his offer.

The delay between him asking the question and her answering seemed to stretch out for hours, even though he knew in his mind it couldn't have been more than a few seconds. Still, he didn't push. He gave her all the power in this situation because ultimately, he wasn't about coercing women to be with him. They were either game or they weren't. He had no problems whatsoever accepting a no the first time around. Though he would certainly be lying if he said a no from her wouldn't disappoint him more than most.

"Do you have a place to shower in that one-room cottage of yours?"

He nodded slowly, like if he was approaching one of his horses.

"Yes," he replied. The bright smile on her face told him he needn't have worried about her being as skittish as a colt. The sparkle in her eye was bold, brilliant and confident. She was definitely game. However, he still waited to hear the words.

"Give me first dibs on the shower and you've got a deal."

He let his eyes slide down her bent form, his better judgment screaming at him that this was a mistake he couldn't afford to make. With ease, he tuned out the sound until it was all but gone. Because there was one thing he knew—however they spent their time tonight, whether it was talking or burning up the sheets, he was not going to miss out on the opportunity to spend the night with Keely Tucker.

"It's a deal."

Twelve

"God that was amazing."

Jacob looked up from the food fixings he'd kept surrounded by ice packets in his saddlebags and time stopped when his gaze landed on Keely. The outposts were stocked with food and clothing for any hands that might find themselves stuck out here unexpectedly.

They kept unisex clothing that could be worn by any gender, so anyone who found themselves out here could comfortably remain huddled down here if need be.

Their offerings mostly comprised sweats, denims, flannel shirts and tees. And because they were gender neutral, they didn't exactly hang in a flattering manner from most bodies.

But Keely Tucker wasn't most bodies. He'd known that from the first time he'd met her. She was full-figured, sexy as hell and currently the object of his fixation as she sauntered out of the bathroom dressed in a pair of sweatpants and a baggy white tee that hung from one of her shoulders as if it was made to do so.

How she made that shapeless piece of cotton look like the sexiest piece of lingerie he'd ever seen, he didn't know. All he did know was that he was grateful for the kitchen counter standing between them. If he had to stand directly in front of her without any barriers, he might be tempted to do something stupid like pull her close to him so he could know how she fit against him and if that fit was just as decadent as he hoped it would be.

"What's for dinner? It smells amazing."

"Leftover ham. It's not a grand meal, but a little seasoning will take it from an average sandwich to something memorable."

She sat down on the opposite side of the small counter, her gaze focused directly on him. He shouldn't have been surprised to find her watching him. Keely was a designer. Her observational skills were probably better than most. But her gaze made him feel exposed in a way he couldn't ever remember, as if there was nothing he could hide from her, no matter how much he desired to.

He was a twenty-nine-year-old man, and he'd never experienced that kind of connection with someone where all his pretenses and defenses wanted to naturally lie down. He couldn't understand for the life of him why his brain decided Keely should be the one he felt comfortable enough to do so with.

"Everything okay?"

"Yeah," he replied. "I'm just feeling a bit antsy after all that physical labor. I'm gonna shower while the food finishes heating up in the oven. If I'm not back when the timer goes off, would you take it out of the oven for me?"

She nodded, and he headed into the bathroom. His brain might have decided Keely was the one to let down his guard with, but his instinct wouldn't let him do it. If it had, he might just have told her she was the most beautiful woman he'd ever come across, and her personality made him want to spend as much time as possible in her presence.

Old habits died hard and Jacob's habit of keeping women out was just too ingrained in him to just stop without consideration. He checked the food one last time before heading across the room to the shower.

Once the door was closed behind him, he made quick work of stripping and showering. Part of his haste was because he had food in the oven and burned ham wasn't something anyone with a decent palate wanted. The other part was that he knew what he wanted to happen tonight, and if he stayed in here too long, applying that obligatory consideration he'd been so dead set on a few moments ago, he might just talk himself out of this unspoken thing that was happening between him and Keely.

"Stop with the back-and-forth, Jacob. Just go out there, share a meal with her and let things naturally evolve from there."

It had been so long since he'd done this dance with a woman, he felt awkward trying to execute the steps. Sex, he remembered. But this connecting with someone to get to the sex part didn't feel as simple as it used to.

His last girlfriend exited his life over a year ago. Since then, he'd indulged in a hookup or two, but Keely wasn't a woman who could be easily placed in the hookup category.

She wasn't forgettable. He'd certainly tried. But over the last few days she'd been here, she'd somehow managed to make her presence so noticeable, he was beginning to find it strange when she wasn't around.

"Stop frettin', Jacob."

Resigned to his new plan, he dressed quickly in much the same attire as Keely, except the garments didn't manage to look anywhere near as fashionable on him as they had her.

When he entered the room, she was standing at the counter, layering bread and the ham on plates.

"You didn't have to do that." She looked up at the sound of his voice, gifting that self-assured yet warm smile of hers.

"You've fed me for the last couple of nights and made sure I wasn't in the dark. The least I can do is make you a plate."

He sat down on a bar stool, feeling at a loss of what to do. At least when he was in the kitchen, he had the preparation of the food to keep him busy. But standing here as she moved gracefully around the small space, he had nothing else to do but look at her.

And looking at her was a problem, because every time he laid eyes on her, he wanted to break his own rules and learn more about her, making her more than just a random lay.

No matter how he wanted her, that was a risk he wasn't sure he could take. Not when he was so close to finalizing his dream of making the Slick Six the number one horse stable in the world.

When she was finished plating the sandwiches, she came around to his side of the counter and sat next to him. She wasn't touching him, but she was close enough that he could smell the store-brand vanilla shower gel in the bathroom wafting up from her skin. On him, it smelled like run-of-the-mill soap. On her, mixed with her particular body chemistry, it smelled like the most tantalizing thing he'd ever had the pleasure of experiencing.

"So, tell me how you got into the horse business. Is it like a family thing?"

He should've been relieved she was going for small talk. That was especially true since the topic was his business, the thing that had been his sole focus for the last eight years of his life.

"Yes and no. My parents were farmers. It provided a good living, but it was their passion so it never really seemed like work to them. That wasn't the case with me."

She took a bite of her sandwich and shared a sly smile with him. "Let me guess, you thought you were too cute for all that? You needed to do something cooler like raise horses?"

He couldn't help but be amused by her easy way of saying whatever was on her mind.

"Something like that. Horses just always got me. I was a later-in-life child, so there weren't any other kids to play with. Horses always seemed to get me better than people. So, while my parents were farming, I was spending all my time with the few horses we had on the farm."

She watched him intently as he spoke, as if she was taking in every detail and committing it to memory.

"So, because you liked playing with the horses, you decided you were gonna be some sort of cowboy as an adult?"

"Honestly, that's every little boy's dream at some point," he replied. "But it wasn't that obvious to me."

He cracked open the water bottle she'd placed in

front of him before she sat down and took a cool swig as he remembered that day.

"I just knew I liked horses as sort of a hobby. It never dawned on me that working with them could be a career. Then, when I was in college for business management, I went with a few friends to a horse show. A trainer was catching hell trying to get one of his more stubborn steeds to cooperate. I walked over and asked if I could try. I talked to the horse, showed him a little love, and he was literally eating out of the palm of my hand by the time it was all said and done.

"The trainer told me I should really think about going into horse training because I was a natural. That's when the idea of training and possibly breeding horses became solidified in my head. I told my parents and they supported me. They allowed me to take a bit of their land and start with a few local horses here and there. The business took off. I did so well, soon I was bringing in more money than their farming. They allowed me to expand over the years, and when they retired a few years back, they gave me the business and told me to run with my dreams. Hence, the Slick Six Stables was born."

When he looked up from his plate and turned to her, he expected to find her eyes glazed over with boredom. To his surprise, they were anything but. Her gaze was focused on him, as if she was fascinated by every word he spoke.

"That's pretty impressive." She cleared her throat, looking downward at her plate. "Both your tenacity and your parents' support of your dream."

Her voice was tinged with the slightest bit of melancholy that the average person probably wouldn't have picked up on. But he realized he paid so much attention to Keely, even the slightest change in her made him sit up and take notice.

"You sound as if that's…rare."

He hedged his words. They hadn't known each other long enough for him to be bulldozing his way into her past. But he wanted her to know that if she wanted to talk about it, whatever *it* was, he was interested in listening to her.

"It is. My parents were not supportive of my dream."

He couldn't help but raise both brows in surprise. People who were as bold and confident as Keely was often had a host of people behind them telling them they were the best at everything. It never would've occurred to him she didn't have the support of anyone who came into her orbit.

She paused for a bit before she returned her gaze to his and continued. "My parents were great parents. They loved my sister and I to pieces. It's just, we grew up really poor. We lived in the projects." She took a sip from her bottle of water as if she needed a moment to gather herself. "I'm not sure if you know what that is down here, but it's low-income housing. In New York, they're dark, dank apartment buildings that resemble prisons more than someone's domicile."

He was familiar. His family wasn't so far removed from their humble beginnings that he was completely ignorant of the topic. In Texas, the Housing Authority looked like cookie-cutter shacks rather than the high-rise brick-and-metal monstrosities Keely was speaking of.

"My parents struggled a lot until they were finally able to scrape enough together to put my mom through nursing school. Once she got a job, my dad went to school and became an X-ray tech. Once he finished school and started working, he went on to medical school and became a radiologist."

Jacob could see the pride she held in her parents as her eyes lit up with awe and her cheeks sat high on her face as her wide smile bloomed across her lips.

"The medical field literally took us from the projects to a four-bedroom house in Washingtonville just before I started high school. Their choices gave us security. So, listening to their teenage daughter talking about how she wanted to go to fashion school instead of doing something practical like going to school or getting a good civil job, it didn't really compute for them."

Context truly was everything. "So, they weren't being unsupportive, just cautious and concerned. They couldn't see beyond their limited experience."

Her brow pinched into a deep V as her eyes locked with his.

"You're the first person I've ever told that story to who understood their perspective. I love my parents and they love me. They were just deathly afraid I'd end up unable to support myself. They understood what that felt like and wanted more for me."

He could understand that, especially after learning how they'd used their education in a practical field to pull their family out of poverty.

"So how did you get around their restrictive thinking?"

"Before they would pay for me to go to FIT, that's Fashion Institute of Technology."

He raised a hand. "I'm not that country that I don't know what FIT stands for."

She gave a quick nod before continuing. "I had to complete a twelve-month LPN course—"

He held up his hand again. "Okay, I'm not so familiar with that acronym."

Her smile bloomed into full-on laughter. When she was able to get a hold of herself again, she picked up where her story had stopped.

"LPN stands for Licensed Practical Nurse. In addition to earning it, they demanded I get and hold a part-time job in a medical facility or doctor's office while I attended FIT. They wanted to make sure I had the education and work experience necessary to fall back on if my fashion dreams didn't pan out."

"That's some serious parenting right there." It might not have been the route his parents had chosen to go, but he definitely saw the value in the path Keely's parents had chosen.

"It really was. Although I didn't love being an LPN, the money I saved while working and going to school helped me create a nice little nest egg that became my start-up money for my stylist business. I can't say I was happy about their stipulations to begin with, but in the end, I couldn't really be mad."

"And do they accept your decision now?"

"They do. But I can tell they still worry that there's no stability in my chosen profession. I think that's the worst part of it. That thing in their eyes that says they're worried about me. It's why I've worked so hard. I need to make sure this works for me and for them. I don't want them to worry. That means I can't fail."

He felt that determination in his soul. He understood the drive to guarantee success no matter what. That need had dogged him since his parents gave him his first opportunity. He knew what a gift it was and he refused to squander it.

"There's nothing wrong with being determined, Keely. I'm sure your parents are very proud."

"They are." She turned slowly to him, scanning his face for something he couldn't exactly name. Maybe it was understanding and commiseration. Perhaps it was comfort. Whatever it was, it made him lean in closer than he should have.

"You're right, there's nothing wrong with being driven. It just doesn't leave room for much else in your life. It leaves you…"

"Lonely."

He could see the surprise in her eyes that he would understand. But every time he sat down to talk to her, he realized he understood her a whole lot more than most people around him.

"Don't be so surprised. The other night when you thought you'd offended me by talking about how lucky the women in my life must be, I wasn't offended. I was just reminded that no woman would ever have that luxury because my work always comes first."

She leaned in a little closer as if she was trying to soak up every word he spoke. Like maybe she'd been waiting for someone to speak words like this to her. He wouldn't find it so strange if she were. He certainly never thought he'd find a woman who understood why work had to be first.

"All the women I've dated since I've started this place say they understand my determination. But after a handful of cancellations because something work-related comes up, they're either complaining about my neglect or writing me off altogether. I just got tired of it and decided I should probably just stick to being alone."

"So, there's been…"

"Hookups," he answered. "There've been hookups.

But there hasn't been anyone I could sit around having a laugh with or someone I could talk to about how demanding my work is. There's been no one I could really look forward to getting to know because most women I encounter haven't dealt well with my absence in the relationship."

She gently placed her hand on his thigh, using it to steady herself as she leaned closer into his space. Their lips were close enough to touch save for the thin sliver of space just big enough for air to slip between them.

"And what if you found someone who was just as career-focused as you? Someone who couldn't afford the distraction of a relationship, but would really love the chance to get to spend some time with a man that respected her work ethic and didn't need her constant attention to feel validated. Would you be willing to indulge in a friends-with-benefits situation-ship if you found a woman like that?"

Her voice was sultry, its deep tones sending jolts of electricity up his skin that were so enticing, he could already feel his cock twitching in his very revealing, very loose sweatpants. He watched her brow rise in anticipation as she waited for his answer. And when she allowed the pink tip of her tongue to slide across those full lips of hers, there was only one answer he could utter.

"Hell yeah."

Thirteen

She'd only intended to press her lips lightly against his to seal the bargain they'd just agreed to. Somehow, the peck she'd intended morphed into something needy and hot once her flesh touched his.

The fire poured from his lips to hers, spilling inside her, spreading through her, consuming her until she thought she just might turn to ash right there. But then she felt his large hands move confidently up her thighs, moving on to her hips, curling his fingers into the fabric there, pulling her toward him.

She went willingly. There was no way in hell she was going to miss out on getting closer to him, of feeling the hard planes of his body that she was sure had been carved in the very fields they'd ridden through earlier.

He deepened the kiss, tightening his hold on her, splaying his tree-trunk thighs wide and pulling her between them, letting one of his hands dip to that sensitive spot in the small of her back. If she let this continue, if his fingertips made their way under her shirt, touching her there, she'd be lost.

She pulled away from him, moaning as the sweet ache of need coursed through her veins, begging her to reconnect her mouth with his.

"You are very good at that." She trembled in disbelief as the unrecognized huskiness in her voice rent the air.

"I am very good at a lot of things, sugah."

The cockiness in his hushed tone was as much of a turn-on as his searing mouth and blistering touch. Men who bragged of their sexuality never did it for her. But somehow, she knew that Jacob wasn't boasting. Everything from the certainty in his tight embrace to the sure way he pressed his lips against hers confirmed he was going to deliver on everything that hard, big body of his was promising her.

"I can see that. But are you sure you really wanna do this? I mean, someone who guards his freedom and privacy as much as you do, I don't know if you really understand what you're getting yourself into."

She allowed her hands to slide down the corded muscles of his arms until her fingers were covering his at the small of her back.

"Why don't you come a little closer, and I'm certain you'll understand just how interested I am in your proposition." He pulled his full bottom lip between his teeth, taunting her to give in. And she wanted to give in. But Keely was in Royal for a reason. No matter how tempted she was by her sexy host, she had to make certain they were both aware what they were agreeing to. She couldn't afford to lose sight of what her goal was.

"I'm serious, Jacob. I need to know you can agree to

this just being for fun. No catching feelings. Neither of us has time for that."

"Are you really worried I don't know what I want?"

She took in the sight of him, his mouth curled into a cocky grin, the muscles in his thighs flexing and his cock, long and thick against her as he kept her caged between his legs.

"I think it's pretty obvious you know what you want in this moment. But my concern is maybe your eyes are getting too big for your belly."

"Are you asking me if I can handle you?"

He placed his hands on her hips, tugging her toward him. His grip was firm enough to keep her right where he wanted her but loose enough that if she truly wanted to free herself from him, she could.

"No." She looked him directly in the eyes, making sure he knew she was serious about what she was preparing to say. "I'm trying to make sure you can really accept who I am and what my focus is. I've had men tell me before they can handle keeping it easy. But sooner or later, they catch feelings, and then get upset when work is my priority. I can't lose sight of what I'm here for. I can't get mixed up in anything that's going to get in the way of me taking over the fashion design world."

He stood up, backing her up against the counter and confining her between his thick arms.

"Keely." The sound of her name on his lips shook something loose in her, something that had her wanting to scale this mountain of a man like professional climbers on Everest. "I'm a grown-ass man and I know how to entertain myself. It's not my expectation that you coddle me and keep me entertained."

He moved closer, pressing her into the counter as he

leaned down, kissing along her jaw, until his lips were at the sensitive area of skin right underneath her ear.

"Now that we've got that outta the way, for the record, you also don't have to worry about me biting off more than I can chew. I'm a big boy and I like grown-man portions. I like my cut of meat tender." He punctuated the word with a kiss to her neck. "Browned to perfection." His lips traveled again until they were at the junction of her neck and shoulder, forcing a hard shiver of pleasure through her body. "And thick as all hell."

His lips touched just beneath her collarbone, making her body arch as if it were begging him to continue his journey downward. "If you're willing, I promise you, my appetite is more than hardy enough to appreciate exactly what you're offering."

He stepped back from her, letting his hungry gaze slide down the length of her, making her long for everything that heated stare promised her.

"So, are you ready to dine, or do you still need to check out the offerings?"

"I'm…ready."

His crooked smile returned right along with that brazen spark in his eye. He held out a meaty hand to her as he cocked his head to the side.

"Then come here, thickness."

The way that word rolled off his tongue made every cell in her body quiver with need and want, and desire so strong she could feel heat burning through her like molten lava through a Dixie cup. And without the slightest bit of hesitation, even though smart money said she should probably leave this sexy-ass man alone, Keely laced her fingers through his and eagerly followed him in the direction of the double bed against the far wall.

She made one stop on their way to the bed, pulling

up next to the couch and grabbing her mini backpack to quickly search for the condom she usually kept in her wallet. When his brow furrowed, she rummaged around in a zipped compartment of the bag, smiling when she found the wallet and pulled out the foil packet she'd been looking for.

"Now." She winked at him, biting her bottom lip as she took in the full image of him with a very generous dick print behind his loose sweats. "Now we're ready."

Considering the short amount of time she would be in town, he naturally assumed that if he ever got the opportunity to have her body wrapped around him, it would be a one-off and he would take his time to savor the delicacy that was Keely Tucker. Apparently, he lied to himself, an emerging pattern he was beginning to notice where Keely was concerned.

From the moment she placed her hand in his and allowed him to lead her to the double bed, it was like a match to gasoline-soaked kindling. When he pulled her into his arms, and her lush body fit so perfectly against his, any designs he had on taking his time were out the window.

A fact that was spurred on by the hungry, needy sounds spilling from Keely's lips every time he held her tighter, or touched her.

He could get drunk off this woman. Presented with this opportunity, that's exactly what he planned to do.

Their clothes came off in a flustered hurry as they tried to navigate how to remain touching while needing to separate to undress. It was frantic and clumsy, but soon, Keely Tucker was standing before him naked, pulling him atop her as she lay across the bed like an all-powerful deity waiting to be worshipped by the un-worthy commoner standing before her.

Would he ever be worthy of a woman like Keely? So self-assured, so in control of her own dreams that she was well on her way to building an empire. Probably not, but that didn't stop him from reaching for what he wanted either. And right now, more than shelter in bit-ter cold, more than cold water in a Texas heat wave, Jacob wanted Keely with his whole being, and he in-tended to have her.

The thought occurred to him that he should at least try to curb his craven appetite, take things a little slower and give Keely time to adjust to what was happening between them.

But when he attempted to pull away, she wrapped those gorgeous, endless legs around him, locking her ankles, keeping him right where she apparently wanted him.

"We can do slow later. Need you now."

How had he gotten so lucky to stumble across this treasure of a woman? She was his match in so many things. It was as if they were living parallel lives. But what were the odds that she'd be just as desperate as he was to press their flesh together until they blended into one.

She tossed the condom at him, spreading her legs wider as he sat back on his haunches to sheathe himself. But as he tried to open the foil packet, he was distracted by the sight of Keely's fingers disappearing inside her body and all of his motor functions seized up.

In an instant, his cock went from hard to steel in just a matter of strokes. He growled, half enjoying watch-ing her pleasure herself, but also jealous that it wasn't his fingers she was riding.

"Dammit, woman."

"I'd suggest you hurry up. I'm almost there."

With each roll of her hips and each dip of her fingers into her cavern, she was taunting him, daring him to join her or watch her bring herself to bliss. The message was clear. Either way she was going to get hers, and he'd be damned if that wasn't the sexiest thing he'd ever seen.

Determined not to miss out on much more, he found just enough focus to carefully remove the condom and quickly sheathe himself.

By the time she removed her fingers, now slick with her desire, and slid them between her folds, caressing her clit like he wanted to, he was ready to burst. He placed himself at her entrance, silently asking if she was still game for all of this. She reached down, wrapping him in the fingers she'd just used to pleasure herself, and that was all the confirmation he needed that she was still on board with the plan. And in his mind that plan was to get each other off as hard and fast as they could, hopefully without injury.

He pressed in until her warmth was completely surrounding him, taking a moment to get a handle on his senses that were screaming with excitement.

"Move, dammit." Her face was contorted in a strange mix of need and satisfaction, and he took her biting words as a compliment.

"God you're so pushy."

"Like you don't love it," she replied, and he couldn't deny it. He was loving every second of this experience so far.

Determined to give them both what they wanted, he set out a punishing pace that had her quivering around him. She was squeezing him so tight, he knew it was only a matter of time before she reached her peak.

He grabbed her hips, changing the angle of his stroke just so, and without hesitation, her body spasmed, tensing around him as she climaxed beneath him.

Watching her fight her way through such a powerful release made fire burn in his veins.

"That's it, darlin', give in, let me have what I want."

Yes, he was one of those men who got off on knowing he could get women off, and he didn't even have the decency to be the slightest bit ashamed of it. Watching her be consumed by the pleasure he gave her, it was the headiest aphrodisiac he'd ever felt and if he could, he'd keep her like this, coming on his cock, wild and brazen beneath him, forever.

His traitorous body vetoed that idea as he felt his own climax climbing up his spine. His rhythm faltered as he tightened his grip on Keely's hips, anchoring himself lest he lose complete control. And when she wrapped her legs around him again, keeping him pressed against her, he gave in to the temptation to let go.

His orgasm ripped through him, causing him to falter, losing his grip and collapsing against her. She wrapped her whole body around his, planting sweet kisses along his neck as she rubbed his back and spoke to him in soft words.

"Shh, I got you, Jacob."

And she certainly did. There wasn't a force on earth that could cause him to relinquish this precious space in her body that she'd so graciously gifted him with nor the comfort he found in her arms. There was only one problem that he could think of as the orgasmic fog began to clear his head.

Now that he knew what she felt like in the throes

of passion, what her flesh felt like pressed against his, Jacob wasn't certain he could let this go when the time came. And it would. He knew that with a certainty. It would come.

Fourteen

Keely sat at a table in the rear of the Royal diner, waiting for her guest to arrive. As she sipped on her coffee, the dark, sleeping screen of her iPad mini mocked her idleness. There was a time when every free moment she had would be spent on this device, sketching, arranging her business schedule or jotting down ideas for things future Keely should take care of. Not today, however. Today, she'd been sitting at this table for at least twenty minutes reliving every moment of her time in Jacob Chatman's bed.

She shook her head at the irony of her drilling Jacob about his acceptance of the no-distractions rule when she sat here unable to abide by said rule herself.

Keely girl, it was one night. It's not like you've never had sex before.

Yes, she'd certainly indulged before. But never to the point where she'd been so desperate for another taste that she'd had to fight herself to get out of bed and make it to her meeting on time.

If only it were just last night, though.

If it was only about their one shared night together, maybe she could eventually put that out of her mind and focus. But anticipation of their date tonight made her a little too eager to get back to the Slick Six Stables and Jacob Chatman in the bold, living flesh.

Not the time, Keely. Not the time.

She glanced up at that moment to see Rylee Meadows, Ariana's wedding planner, step into the diner, and she knew it was time to shake off this postcoital fog clouding her head. The two women had only spoken once on a brief video chat, but Keely couldn't risk seeming flighty and unreliable because her senses were still overwhelmed by Jacob's ability to please her.

She took a large swallow of coffee, hoping the caffeine would jump-start her brain, before waving to catch Rylee's attention.

"It's so nice to finally meet you in person, Keely."

Keely stood, extending her hand to the young woman when she finally stood at Keely's table.

"Same," Keely offered. "I can't wait to talk about some of the ideas you have. I'll be meeting with the florist and caterer later in the week to see how we can incorporate touches from the dress into the floral arrangements and the food."

Rylee sat down opposite Keely and pulled out her laptop. Setting it up quickly, she pulled up a list of ideas and sample pictures for Keely to peruse.

"Ariana talked about doing an Old Hollywood theme for the wedding decorations." Rylee pointed to the screen for Keely to follow along. "I was thinking we could use cream, gold and black to really amp up that elegance factor."

"That's gorgeous," Keely responded. "I like the idea about the Hollywood glam. In fact, Ariana's choice of dress design fits perfectly with that. The only problem is she's decided she wants to add a little bit of Texas into the dress design to represent Ex's home state."

Keely swiped her fingers across her tablet until she found the picture she was looking for.

"I had the idea that we could incorporate the blue-bonnet, the Texas state flower, into her dress. As you can see here, it's a bluish-purplish color. The gold and the cream might coordinate well with that. I'm just not sure the combo of gold, cream and black will work."

"Hmm." Rylee twisted her mouth to the side as she looked back and forth between her laptop screen and Keely's tablet. As a fellow creative, Keely recognized that look—it meant Rylee was running down all the configurations and combinations of the aforementioned colors to see if she could come up with a solution. "I see what you mean. How about if we toss the black as you suggest and use gold as the primary color, the bluish-purplish color as the secondary and the cream as the tertiary? I think those three would make a striking trio. Could you make that work with her dress?"

"Absolutely," Keely replied. "Her dress is made from an antique white satin. I'm toying with adding color to the piping for a subtle yet vivid accent. Hopefully the florist will be able to procure enough bluebonnets for the bouquets, boutonnieres and the venue decorations."

Keely looked up and saw a light spark in Rylee's eyes. It was the result of collaboration between creatives when their ideas came together into a beautiful explosion.

"This is going to be amazing." Rylee's excitement was contagious, and soon Keely was feeling like her normal, focused self. It was a relief to feel some of her usual dedication to detail and determination filter back into her system. This was what she was in Royal for, to make Ariana's dress the linchpin of the wedding of the century. And if the excited way Rylee was tapping away at her laptop keys was any indication, Keely was halfway to accomplishing her goal.

See what you're capable of when your mind is on the right things?

Yeah, she saw. But as a memory from the previous night in that outpost tried to claw its way back to the surface of her mind, she had to wonder if keeping her head screwed on right would be as easy as reminding herself of her purpose. Because right now, the only purpose her head wanted to acknowledge was how she would purposely enjoy stripping that man naked and running her tongue over every inch of his glorious skin.

Rylee chose that moment to look across the table at Keely with a concerned look in her eyes.

"Are you all right, Keely? You seem a bit flushed."

She was flushed all right. But since there was no way in hell Keely could tell Rylee the truth about what had her blood rushing through her vessels right now, she waved her hand in front of her face and said, "It's this Texas heat." She dropped back against her chair and grabbed the tepid glass of water the waitress had provided twenty minutes ago when Keely first arrived. "I guess it's turning out to be more than I bargained for."

"Well, good morning to you, sunshine."

Jacob walked into the stables with a travel cup of coffee in his hand. It was closer to afternoon than morning and he was just beginning his workday. He knew he was supposed to feel bad about that, but after spending all night buried deep inside Keely's warmth, there was no way he could give a good goddamn about the flogging his foreman was about to give him.

He and Keely had gotten precious few hours of sleep before they headed back from the outpost at the first rays of dawn. He was supposed to get dressed and head out to work, but watching her curled up in his bed as she found her way back to the land of nod had proved too tempting for him to resist. He'd lain down behind her, just to embrace her nearness for a few seconds— or at least that was the lie he told himself at the time. The next thing he knew he'd woken up to the sun high in the sky and a folded note explaining she'd gone into town where Keely's warm body had once been.

"I know, I know," he said with as much vigor as a man tired from having amazing sex all night long could muster. "I'm late. But I'm here now, so let's get on with our day."

"You rib me if I'm only fifteen seconds early to my post." Matt's raised brow and amused smile entertained more than annoyed Jacob. A result he could only attribute to his night with Keely putting him in such a good, relaxed mood. "You know I can't let the fact slide that you're more than a couple of hours late."

"You wouldn't be Matt if you did."

Matt nodded his agreement and turned to Jacob, smiling like he was in on a secret no one else knew.

"I couldn't help but notice your guest didn't come down until late this morning too. What exactly were you two doing at that outpost last night?"

"We played chess," Jacob offered with a straight face,

not caring one bit if his friend believed him. That was his story and he was sticking to it.

"Chess," Matt echoed. "That's what we're calling it now?"

"I know I pay you to do more than get on my nerves."

Matt nodded. "You do. But getting on your nerves is a job perk I plan to take full advantage of."

Jacob couldn't help but chuckle at that. Matt's antics had been Jacob's only source of entertainment for so long, he had to admit it would be strange if all the man did was do his job without giving Jacob crap every chance he got.

"Have the new arrivals been assigned to their trainers yet?"

Matt grabbed a nearby clipboard and handed it to Jacob.

"Yeah. The staff has been briefed and they've already met their new charges. Also, while you were taking your time getting here, I took a call this morning from Ezra Stanley, the owner of a world champion horse. Apparently, he isn't too happy with his current trainer and is interested in talking to you about bringing his horse down to the Slick Six for training for the next round of qualifying events."

Jacob's jaw dropped open as he took in what Matt was saying. This wouldn't be the first prize-winning horse the Slick Six had trained. But a medal winner? That was gold right there as far as word-of-mouth advertising. If Jacob and his staff could make this owner happy, he'd have the hype to his reputation he needed to pull bigger and definitely more lucrative contracts.

"Hot damn," Jacob yelped, the sharp sound drawing out a loud bark of laughter from Matt. Both men knew there wasn't too much that could get Jacob this excited.

He was solemn and serious on his best day, ornery and grumpy on his worst. This was damn near euphoria where Jacob was concerned.

"Hold on, big man. He wants to schedule a visit out here to take a look at our facilities and meet our training staff before he makes his decision. I told him you'd call him back with the schedule after you met with the staff."

Jacob nodded, so thrilled, all the fatigue he'd walked into the stables with was now replaced by a jolt of adrenaline.

"Tell the staff we're having an emergency meeting now. Wherever they are on the property, they need to be in the conference room at the main house ASAP. We've got a world champion to court."

He turned around, leaving the stables and heading straight for the house. This was just the chance he'd been waiting for and finally, after so many years of backbreaking labor, he was about to get the chance of a lifetime.

He made it to the house in what seemed no time. He made quick work of getting the conference room ready. Despite dropping everything he touched at least twice, he still managed to get the space set up before his staff arrived.

Too full of energy, he couldn't sit still, so he paced back and forth, hoping to burn off some of these excitement jitters he just couldn't seem to shake.

"Jacob… Jay… Are you home?"

Jacob stopped moving the second he heard Keely's voice traveling through his halls. The sound of her rich alto soothed his need to be in motion. Eager to see her, but pressed for time since he knew his staff would be converging on the house soon, Jacob didn't stop to wonder why the moment he heard her voice calling his name, everything inside him stilled in a way even a soothing cup of rum-spiked coffee couldn't have managed.

When he found her in the kitchen, he didn't stop to speak. He simply planted his hands on her waist, pulled her until she was pressed against him in the most delicious way and locked his mouth to hers.

The sweet mewling sounds she made while he nibbled at her bottom lip was pure addiction, a sound he wanted to hear over and over as many times as she'd allow him to hear it. But as much as he enjoyed the taste of her, unless he wanted to share all their business with his employees, he had to find some decorum and set her free.

"Well, that was a very lovely greeting. What did I do to deserve that?"

He pulled her hips toward him again, loving the feel of her pressed so tightly against him.

"I am celebrating some feel-good news. And since you spent all night making me feel good, I thought it was appropriate I share it with you first."

She lifted her eyes to the ceiling while her coy smile lit up a flame in his chest that was growing brighter and brighter each time he encountered her.

"I did put a lot of work into making you feel good last night, didn't I?"

"You certainly did," he agreed, taking the opportunity to steal another kiss while they were still alone. "Also, you left me alone in bed. Since I also put in a lot of work too, I think I deserve a sweet treat as well."

She nodded, easily agreeing with his recollection of events. "Hard work like ours deserves to be rewarded."

"True," he replied. "So, sit down and let me tell you my news so we can both be rewarded."

She stepped out of his embrace and hopped up on one of the stools at the counter in the center of the kitchen.

"Don't keep me guessing, man. What happened?"

"Today, we got an inquiry from the owner of a medal-winning horse. He's interested in bringing his horse here to start training for the next quals season. He wants to come down and tour the place, and check out my trainers to see if the Slick Six is as good as our reputation claims we are."

He watched her eyes grow wide and her jaw drop in surprise, and it was as if something inside him clicked for the first time that he couldn't understand.

"Jacob, I don't know a thing about horses," she spoke in a rushed, excited cadence. "But even I can see how huge an opportunity this is. Congratulations."

Her exuberance over his accomplishment made him want to yank her close to him again. No other woman he'd been romantically involved with could give a damn about hearing about his work. He understood it. He didn't have one of those sexy jobs like corporate CEOs and the like. His work was dirty, backbreaking and, most of all, time-consuming. There weren't too many women he'd come in contact with who wanted to know anything about what he did.

But seeing Keely celebrate with him, even though this opportunity didn't have a thing to do with her and there was no way for her to benefit from it, softened something in him, making him ache to keep her closer for a while longer. But just as soon as the thought crossed his mind, he realized the other half of the news he had to share with her. Suddenly, his good mood began to fade as he prepared for what had been the start of many arguments in the past.

"I'm about to hold a staff meeting to hammer down

the logistics of this visit so I can put in a call to the owner before close of business today. That pretty much means I'll be unavailable for most of the day and probably part of the night."

She watched him carefully, understanding dawning in her eyes. He could tell the moment she realized what he was getting at and he braced himself for the usual antics he'd experienced whenever he had to cancel plans with a woman before.

"Jacob, don't worry about us going out tonight. This is way more important than you showing me around Royal. We had a deal, remember?" She waved her hand back and forth between them. "This can never get in the way of work. This is a huge opportunity. You can't half-ass it because you're hanging out with me when you should be handling your business. I wouldn't let you do it even if you tried."

Damn, just when he thought he had things figured out, here comes this woman turning him and his world upside down.

He stood there staring at her because he wasn't quite sure what to say. So many times, a moment like this would blow up into a tense fight about how he was neglecting the woman he was seeing. It was such a frequent occurrence he honestly didn't know how to respond to how well Keely was taking the cancellation of their first proper date.

The sound of worn cowboy boots on wood steps shook him out of his stupor. He glanced at Keely again.

"How did I get so lucky to find a friend as wonderful as you?"

She shrugged. "Truly, I don't know because I am pretty great."

She was. Even with her not so humble brag, they both knew she was telling the truth.

He stepped closer, taking a peek out the window to make sure they didn't have any spectators before he pressed a quick kiss to her smiling lips.

"You really are," he agreed.

"Glad you know it," she countered. "And if you go take care of work like the dedicated horse trainer I know you are, I'll make sure to reward all your hard work when we're the only two people in the house tonight."

"Is that right?"

She nodded her reply, and not for the first time, Jacob wondered how different his dating life might've been if he'd had an understanding partner like Keely.

"It certainly is, Mr. Chatman. Now go'n and get that bag."

Jacob took in the special woman standing before him, tipping his imaginary Stetson as he gave her an enthusiastic "Yes, ma'am."

She was gorgeous, creative and smart as all hell. But the thing he was most enamored with at this moment was how much she was like him when it came to dedication to work. Keely was proving to be a woman of her word by pressing him to take care of his business. She was also making it abundantly clear that she was the total package, every man's dream. And if he wasn't careful, he might just find himself falling for her.

Fifteen

Keely stepped away from her travel sewing machine, stretching the kinks out of her back and moving her fingers to get the circulation flowing in them again. Once she'd left Jacob to take care of his staff meeting, she'd locked herself away in the great room working on Ariana's train. The starlet wanted a detachable train that she could remove at the reception so she could party like the movie star she was.

In response to Ariana's request, Keely had designed a grand cathedral train that would've made the former Hollywood actress the late Princess Grace of Monaco jealous.

It was made of two panels. The first created the outer silhouette with a scallop lined of appliqué that perfectly matched the bluish-purplish color of the bluebonnet. The second panel was inset with the matching lace and chiffon of the sheer arms of the dress, speckled with tiny, hand-sewn, satin replicas of the flower's petals in the bluebonnet color. Now that the panels were sewn together, there was six feet of glamorous detachable train Keely was certain Ariana was going to be ecstatic about.

Keely stood in the middle of the room with her hands on her waist in a mock superhero pose. Considering how sluggish and unfocused she was at the start of the day, she was proud of how she'd managed to turn things around and make the day productive. She'd even managed to schedule meetings with the florist and the caterer next week so she could finalize Ariana's dress design once she saw some of the bouquet samples the florist would bring and the signature dishes the caterer would provide to accent the color scheme of the wedding.

There were still a couple of hours before the sun would begin to set, so she decided a quick trip into Royal proper for some supplies would be the best use of her time.

She found her way easily back to Main Street, taking in the quaint setting of what was probably one of the busiest streets in Royal. It was definitely the "city" part of town, but unlike some metropolises such as New York or LA, there was still a mindfulness to the atmosphere that major streets in larger cities didn't possess.

Keely parked at one end of the shopping area, hoping to peruse the storefront windows to figure out exactly what she was looking for. The sidewalks weren't crowded like in New York and she had to wonder if that was just the way of life here in Royal or if the blackout was keeping most people off the street.

As she walked by, she only saw a handful of shops with "Closed" signs hanging in their windows. Again, she didn't know if they were already closed for the day, or if they were still dealing with issues from the blackout. After everything that had happened between her and Jacob, she couldn't deny this blackout had the power to turn lives upside down. That was certainly the truth when it came to hers.

The sight of a candle shop with the lights on drew her in and before she knew it, she was entering the shop, taking in its soothing decor and aroma.

A smiling young woman with jet-black curls and blue eyes greeted Keely from behind the counter.

"I'm Jen. Welcome to Flicker. How can I help you today?"

Keely continued to look around as she made her way to the counter where Jen was standing.

"I'm so glad you were open. I was worried most of the stores might still be affected by the blackout. As soon as I saw your lights on, I knew I had to come in."

She saw the young woman's face soften with gratitude, sprinkled in with compassion. "I think most of the businesses are fine. Some are just closed down because people are waiting at home to deal with whatever issues losing power caused them. And with the advent of PayPal, Venmo, Cash App and card swipers that can attach to your cell phone or your iPad, most vendors are able to make sales without needing to plug in an old-fashioned cash register."

Keely could certainly commiserate. As uneasy as she was about staying with Jacob in the beginning, she'd at least been lucky enough to have a roof over her head and power at her disposal. Not everyone in Royal fared so well.

That gratitude over her circumstances was part of the reason she was here. Jacob had done something kind for her by letting her stay in his home, and she wanted to return the favor by doing something nice for him after his long but productive day.

Keely took a long sniff of the mixtures of scents and knew she was in the right spot. "It looks and smells wonderful in here." She could pick out berries, vanilla and lavender among the varied aromas. "I don't know how I'm going to make a selection."

Jen chuckled as if she'd heard this very same thing from every customer who'd walked through the shop's doors.

"Well, that's what I'm here for. Tell me who and what the candle is for, and I'll try to recommend some scents based on that."

The image of Jacob's marble-like body surrounded by water and the soft glow of candles brought a smile to her face. Jen must have picked up on Keely's expression, because without the slightest bit of hesitancy or discomfort, the woman matched Keely's grin.

"So, we're looking to set a romantic mood, are we?" Keely nodded and Jen continued. "Does your intended have more masculine or feminine energy?"

Keely thought about Jacob and tried to place his energy. "He definitely taps into the masculine. He loves physical labor, dirt and animals. But he does have this softer, nurturing side too. You see it when he cooks for the people around him or when he's caring for animals. Do you have anything for someone like that?"

"Sure do," Jen replied. "I think something like a sandalwood with a splash of vanilla could work for someone like that. It's a great combination of both masculine and feminine energies. I just made a fresh batch about forty-eight hours ago. They should be perfect now."

Jen waved her over to the back display wall, grabbing a squat candle in an elegant glass jar. She opened the cap, and handed it to Keely. "Do you think this will work?"

Keely brought the jar to her nose and moaned at the warm and woody scent wafting into the air.

"Definitely." Keely's excited answer broadened Jen's friendly smile. "I'll take as many as you have."

"Sure, it will take about fifteen minutes to get them packaged. Are you okay with that time frame?"

Keely gave a nod and walked over to the counter to complete the transaction. "I'll just continue browsing your shop in the meantime."

"Well, since you're my largest-selling purchase today, I'll add a little something special to your package." Jen gestured for Keely to follow her to a shelf to the right of the candles where she saw a huge oil display. She handed Keely a bottle and encouraged her to smell it.

"This is my best-selling product. It's a light massage oil that makes the skin silky smooth. You can add essential oils to it to make the most delightful fragrances if you choose. Since you like the sandalwood and vanilla, I'm thinking I could mix some of that up in the massage oil for you as a freebie in the candle basket."

Keely clapped her hands together like an excited child. "Free-ninety-nine is my favorite price." She might be able to afford luxury items with the huge come-up in her earnings, but Keely loved a bargain as well as a small business owner who offered small touches like this to make a client feel special.

Jen rung up the sale, her generous smile making Keely feel right at home. "I hope you love everything. By the looks of it, this is for a special occasion."

Keely stopped for a moment, realizing Jen was right.

This was a special occasion. She intended to enjoy Jacob and all his wonderful touch had to offer, and considering the dry spell she'd had in both good company and good sex, *that*, along with celebrating Jacob's new opportunity, made tonight very special indeed.

But somehow, her plans ran so much deeper than the physical. She realized this wasn't just about the anticipated outcome, it was also about getting to share something with a man she was beginning to care for more than it was safe for her to admit.

When Jen informed her that her order was ready, she took her bags and headed out the store. As she stood on the sidewalk watching people mill by, it struck her as odd that the world around her was just running its normal course. She, on the other hand, was primed to have a partial existential crisis about what was happening between Jacob and her.

She took in a long, slow breath, allowing a calm smile to spread across her lips as she quieted her thoughts.

"Just keep it chill, Keely, and everything will be fine. Don't make it more than it has to be."

Jacob entered the back door to see all the lights turned out in the kitchen except the one over the stovetop. It left the room in a soft, warm glow that felt more inviting than usual.

Most nights when he came in late, he stayed in the kitchen long enough to grab something light to eat before he showered and headed to bed. But the adrenaline from all the plans he and his team had made today for the world champion's owner still had excitement buzzing through him.

In a week's time, Ezra Stanley would be visiting the Slick Six and, if everything went right, Jacob's plan to expand his business would finally get underway. He wanted to celebrate, and he wouldn't allow himself to feel the least bit bad that Keely was the only one he wanted to share this good time with.

Hoping she was still up, he took the back stairs two at a time and walked down the long quiet hallway until he reached the center, where the door to the master bedroom awaited.

He opened the door gently. He might be excited as hell, but he didn't want to startle Keely if she'd already fallen asleep. But when he stepped inside and swept his gaze from one side of the room to the next, the only thing he found were two candles, one on each nightstand, gently flickering.

"Keely?"

"In here," she called out, making him turn toward the en suite bath. The lights were turned down here as well, candles acting as the only source of light here too. His eyes swept across the vanity, to the large shower stall, and then finally to the huge Jacuzzi tub at the far end of the room.

There she was, leaning back against the porcelain, her head lolling against a bath pillow with her body submerged beneath water filled with suds and rose petals. One of her arms lay languidly against the edge of the tub, while the other was invisible underneath the suds.

He remembered when he'd had the master suite renovated, the interior designer and the contractor had practically twisted his arm to agree to installing that big thing. The truth was, in all the years he'd had it, he'd never actually used it. But the cost and the maintenance were all worth it just to glimpse this goddess looking like sin and temptation.

The golden-brown skin of her face, shoulders and neck

seemed more bronzed in the dim candlelight, making him want to touch her even more. But when a soft moan escaped her lips and he watched her pull her submerged hand from the water before letting it slide down her neck, then chest and then lower, while her gaze locked with his, he thought he was going to combust right there on sight.

"Do you need a formal invitation, or are you gonna get your tail in here and join me?"

The lustful spark in her eyes dared him to respond. And he would. Just not verbally. Words wouldn't do right now. Action was what they both needed and he didn't plan to hesitate one moment longer.

Without a word, he shucked his clothing, then stepped in the opposite direction of the tub toward the shower. He'd spent most of his day in the conference room, but he'd still gone to the stables. And while he didn't mind the familiar scent of horses, he didn't want to taint the atmosphere Keely had obviously gone through the trouble of creating for him, so he took a quick shower, keeping the water as cool as he could stand it, because his only purpose was to get clean under the spray so he could get as dirty as he wanted in those suds with Keely.

Refreshed, he stepped out of the shower and headed straight for the tub. Dripping from head to toe, he didn't bother with grabbing a towel. His only focus was getting to the woman who had him harder than he'd ever been, and he hadn't touched her yet.

She greeted him with a wicked gleam in her eye that promised so much satisfaction, he quickly stepped into the tub, sloshing water over the sides and not giving a damn about the mess he was surely going to have to clean up later.

"Come here, you."

He settled behind her, pulling her back against his

chest, sliding his hand down her lush sides and bringing them in front of her until his palms were cupping her heavy, luscious bosom.

"When you said you'd have a reward for me tonight, you weren't playing, huh?" He nuzzled her neck, placing a trail of soft kisses against her sizzling skin as she settled between his legs.

"I don't kid about my rewards, Mr. Cowboy. As hard as I work, I try to remember to play as hard too. Otherwise, I'll get burned out, and no one wants to deal with a burned-out Keely. She is decidedly not fun."

He kept one hand cupping her breast while the other traveled down her soft torso and abdomen until his fingers traced the top of her slick mound. She trembled in his arms and the vibrations brought a sly grin to his lips. This was only the beginning. By the end, he planned to have her breaking apart from his touch.

He slipped his fingers down to her folds, letting the edge of his fingertips tease the seam until she was canting her hips forward, proving just how much she wanted his touch.

"Mmm," she moaned deeply, gripping the sides of the bathtub for purchase when he grazed her sensitive button. "I'm supposed to be rewarding you." Her voice hitched as he pressed the pads of his fingers, stroking her clit in a painfully slow rhythm that she desperately wanted to chase.

"That's where you're wrong." He sped up his movements just slightly. "Feeling you pressed against me while my fingers commit every inch of your sex to memory." She tensed against him, rolling her hips underneath the water as he built up momentum. "That's the only reward I want right now."

He was telling the absolute truth. There was something about watching Keely come completely undone by his own hand that made him harder, hungrier for her than he could ever remember being.

Every twitch of her hips against him, his cock slid in between the crease of her bottom as if he was made to be there, and considering he was hard enough to cut glass at this moment, he was damn certain this was exactly where he belonged.

Keely spread her legs wider, giving him more room to work, planting her feet against the porcelain tub to give her more control in the water. He sped up his strokes, wrapping his open palm gently around the base of her neck, exposing the elegant line where her neck met her shoulder.

He licked a long, slow line from her shoulder, up her neck, until his mouth rested against her lobe. She trembled in his arms, her opening clasping at his fingers in desperation of the climax he gauged was just out of reach.

Jacob whispered cooing, soft sounds in her ear as her pleasure-filled moans filled the dim room. Increasing the speed of his strokes, he kissed her lobe and smiled against the shell of her ear as he flicked his thumb against her hard nub.

"Let go, baby. Let me see you break apart for me."

Her body tensed and she keened, the sound so guttural and explosive, he could feel his heavy cock twitch against his stomach, begging for a release of his own.

She held on to the sides of the tub, bracing herself, as she splintered into tiny pieces, sloshing water over the sides. The water could flood the entire room for all he cared. The only thing he wanted was to witness the beauty of this woman shattering beneath his touch as he brought her to completion.

It may sound chauvinistic in today's world, and he'd probably never admit this aloud. But he had never felt more like a man than when he had this woman in his arms, falling to pieces from his touch.

And as she settled against him, her body still wracked with tremors as she tried to come down from her powerful climax, he knew for certain nothing in his future would ever compare to this.

When she recovered, she turned around on her knees, taking him in one hand while reaching to the side of the tub for the condom she'd placed there earlier. Once she had him sheathed, she slowly, almost painfully so, lowered herself over him, taking him into her warmth. And when she was completely seated, she leaned over him, kissing him deeply, before she leaned back, locking her sultry gaze with his, luring him into her web.

She knew she had him. He knew she had him, and by their mutual needy smiles, he figured they both were fine with that realization.

"It's my turn now," she murmured while rolling her hips in a slow, teasing pace. "Please, let me return the favor."

He spread his arms against the width of the tub and leaned back before whispering, "Be my guest."

"How did you come up with the name 'the Slick Six'?"

Jacob looked down to make sure he'd heard the sleepy voice tugging at the end of his consciousness. He wrapped an arm around Keely's waist and pulled her closer in his embrace. After their lovemaking escapade in the bathroom, they'd dried off, lotioned up and crawled under the covers of his king-size bed, slowly drifting into sleep in each other's arms.

"Now, why would you wanna hear a boring story like that? I guess I didn't put in enough work in that bathtub to tire you out if you need me to tell you a bedtime story."

She peered up at him with a lazy smile pulling at

her full lips as she snuggled closer to him, entwining her legs with his.

"See that deflection tactic right there? That tells me that this is definitely a story I want to hear."

He leaned down, stealing a quick kiss before he spoke.

"Smart and sexy as hell. What have I even been doing with my life before you."

She smoothed her hand over his hip, gliding it along his skin, and then playfully pinching his backside.

"Yes, I am both those things. But you're still stalling. Get to talking, cowboy."

"Okay," he relented, realizing she wasn't going to drop the subject. "When I was a kid, my father introduced me to *Lone Ranger* reruns. And from that moment, everything in my life revolved around those characters. I didn't just love *The Lone Ranger*. I wanted to be the Lone Ranger."

He paused for a moment, remembering the joy he felt every time he sat down to watch his favorite show with his dad. That show was a seminal event in his young life, shaping his ideas of right and wrong.

"Well, when Halloween came along and my class was having a party, there was only one choice of a costume for me."

"I bet you were the cutest Lone Ranger too."

"My mama certainly thought so," he replied, laughing as he recounted how many pictures his mother had made him stand for before he could leave for school.

"When I got to the party, my classmates asked me if I was a sheriff or a regular cowboy. I told them neither, and proudly announced I was the Lone Ranger.

"Some of the kids didn't know who he was because they hadn't seen the show. But there was one boy there who was familiar and he yelled out, 'You can't be the Lone Ranger. You're Black and the Lone Ranger is white.'"

He could feel Keely flinch in his arms, as if she was trying to take the pain of that past blow for him. He smoothed a hand over her shoulder, calming her, letting her know he was all right.

"I don't think it bothered me so much when the kid said it because he was a kid. I figured there were people smarter than my fellow eight-year-olds. But what cut me was when my teacher, Mrs. Abernathy, agreed with him. Her saying it made it true. And when I made it home from school in tears, relaying what had happened, my parents were seething. But even though they were both hurt and angry for me, they set aside their feelings and set to figuring out a way to help me deal with what had happened."

She leaned up on her elbow, her gaze locked firmly on his as if she were completely invested in his tale. He didn't know why, but it was a source of comfort that she cared enough to listen.

"How'd they do that?"

"My dad, who absolutely hates the internet, got online and found a bunch of information about Black cowboys. Namely, that the Lone Ranger was actually based on a real-life Black cowboy named Bass Reeves, who was the first Black US Marshal. Learning that healed something in me that I hadn't realized the experience had tainted. It made me believe I could do, be anything, no matter what anyone else said.

"Bass Reeves, Bill Pickett, Isom Dart, Stagecoach Mary, Nat Love and Daniel W. Wallace, my dad looked at those six and said, 'Jacob—'" he thickened his Texas drawl to sound more like his father "'—these six cowfolk right here were slicker than a can of oil. They were innovative, and created the game. Everyone else is a pale imitation. Never let anyone's ignorance define who you are or who you want to be.'"

He couldn't help the warmth blooming through him as he remembered how great his father made him feel in that moment.

"I can see from your smile that what your dad did meant a lot to you."

"It really did," he replied. "It also didn't hurt when my mama went up to the school the next day and read my teacher the riot act and showed her how absolutely ignorant she was of actual history."

"So that's how you came up with the name, the Slick Six Stables?"

He nodded. "Yup. It's me paying homage to those the world has forgotten. Keeping their contributions to our history—" he moved a pointed finger back and forth between them "—American history, alive."

He wrapped a loose lock of her hair around his finger, loving how soft it felt against his skin. It was in that moment he realized it wasn't just her hair or any particular physical feature about her that was doing it for him. Well, not just that. It was also her presence. It was his ability to tell her something so personal, that only his parents knew that particular truth.

How this woman had found her way into the secret places of his mind, and if he were honest, his heart, he didn't know. What he was particularly aware of at this moment was that he liked it, and even though everything in him said he should fight this, all he wanted was to settle deeper into this feeling that Keely Tucker was stirring in him.

Sixteen

"What the hell, Matt?"

Jacob stalked toward his foreman just outside one of three training pens on the property. Matt visibly tensed at the barking sound of Jacob's voice while his eyes flickered back and forth rapidly as if he were trying to figure out what in the world Jacob was hollering his name for.

"Everything all right, boss?"

It was certainly a reasonable question in response to Jacob's displeased tone. As far as Jacob could remember, there weren't too many times in all the years Matt had worked with him that Jacob had found fault with the man. Especially nothing that warranted the kind of frustration currently running through him. But these weren't normal times. In two days, Ezra Stanley would be visiting Jacob's ranch to decide if he wanted to send his medal-winning horse to the Slick Six for preseason training.

As far as Jacob was concerned, that meant everyone on this ranch should be as jumpy and fixated on perfection as he was.

"Matt, I specifically asked you to take over lead trainer duties for the duration of Stanley's visit. You scheduled me instead. What's this all about?"

Matt loosened his shoulders a bit, relaxing his stance before sharing an amused grin with Jacob.

Since he found no humor in this situation at all, Jacob's annoyance ground harder against his nerves.

"I fail to see why you're laughing. You're the person I trust most on this ranch, Matt. If you're not in the pen when Stanley arrives, it could definitely impact whether he signs with us or not."

"Jacob." Matt said his name slowly, like he needed to make sure Jacob didn't miss a word of what he was about to say. "You didn't ask me to put myself down for training during the visit. You asked me to put your best trainer on the roster that day."

"Exactly," Jacob countered. "That's you."

Matt shook his head, confusing Jacob even further. "Jay, you are the best trainer the Slick Six has ever had. You know the ranch inside out because you built it from the ground up. You're a freakin' horse whisperer. No one can get these proud animals to respond like you do. Trust me, friend, you want Stanley to see you running things when he arrives, not me. You are the one who will sell the Slick Six. Not me."

Jacob stood back, taking in all his foreman, his friend, had said to him. It wasn't that Jacob didn't know he was good. He was damn good at his job. He'd broken his back to build this ranch into what it was. But now that he was on the cusp of getting everything he wanted, he suddenly had a case of the doubts.

"I'm sorry, Matt. I was out of line."

Matt chuckled, making Jacob's overreaction that much more prominent. "You were. But I won't hold it against you. You've been burning the candle at both ends since last week. It's got you rattled and tense. Maybe you should find a way to blow off some steam between now and then."

"No time."

Jacob shook his head, hoping to exaggerate the point. Matt was right about his not getting enough rest. He'd work his tail off all day and then spend his nights tangled up with Keely in his bed.

He wasn't complaining, not in the least. Having her around gave him an energy, a zeal he hadn't had since he'd first started the Slick Six. But his mood was definitely suffering from his lack of uninterrupted rest.

"I'm gonna finish up some admin work in the office. By the time I'm done, there will barely be enough time for a shower followed by dinner with Keely."

Jacob purposely left out the sex-with-Keely part. Matt didn't need to know all of his business.

"Dinner? Is that what we're calling it now? Because the way you two make eyes with each other whenever you're together, I'd figured there was a whole lot more than dinner going on at night."

"And just like that—" Jacob pointed a finger at his friend, fighting hard not to let truth permeate his expression "—you are once again the asshole in this situation."

"It's a gift, really." Matt placed a firm hand on Jacob's shoulder as his devious grin lit up his face. "You know what else is a gift?"

Jacob had no clue what Matt was going to say. There was no telling what would fly out of the man's mouth.

"No, but I'm sure you're gonna tell me."

Matt squeezed his shoulder, then pointed in the direction behind Jacob. "That beautiful woman walking this way with a smile as wide as the horizon over water. And as much as I wish it, I doubt she's in such a good mood over me."

Jacob turned around, nearly forgetting his friend was standing beside him. His brain only seemed to recognize the beautiful, golden-brown woman with that luscious body that tied him in knots and then some. She walked toward him with the enticing rhythm of her swaying hips pulling him further under her spell.

"Don't let *dinner* keep you up all night, my friend. The Slick Six needs you functioning on all cylinders to make this visit work."

Jacob knew Matt was speaking the truth. But somehow as Keely stepped closer to him, the only thing he seemed to be able to focus on was her.

He'd debate with himself later about how problematic his thoughts were. But right now, the only thing he wanted was to walk back to his house so he could spend as much time as he could revisiting all the wonderful things about Keely and her body that he just couldn't manage to get enough of.

Why does that man look this good in dusty jeans and a faded plaid shirt? There has to be a law.

If there wasn't, there sure as hell should be. No one, absolutely no one, had the right to be that sexy standing in dirt and grass and all other manner of nature that her city-girl self was usually so far removed from. Concrete was her happy place and greenery usually made her nervous. But everything about the Slick Six ranch made her feel like dirt and the smell of trees and hay were her new oasis. That was all for one reason only. Jacob Chatman.

Jacob Chatman was somehow changing her slowly but surely, and as much as she wanted to pretend it was nothing, it was definitely something.

And if she doubted that, one look at him standing on his ranch, looking like the poster boy for sexy and rugged cowboys everywhere, and she forgot how to focus on anything but him.

The fact that she was out here instead of being hunched over her iPad jotting down notes or stitching the million and one buttons onto Ariana's dress was proof that she only had Jacob on the brain.

"Howdy, Ms. Tucker."

Keely heard Matt's voice, but she didn't bother to take her eyes off Jacob. As fine as he was, she was certain Matt could forgive her this momentary lack in social graces.

"Hey, Matt." Her voice was bright, and her step had just a bit more pep in it as she stopped in front of Jacob. Matt chuckled, his voice getting more and more distant, signaling the fact that he was moving away from them.

"Well, I'll leave you to it, Ms. Tucker. I can see already that you're the cure for Jacob's sourpuss mood."

Matt's parting words barely registered through the haze being around Jacob caused. Without thinking about where they were or who was around them, she raised her arms and hooked them around Jacob's neck.

It took only a split second to realize how forward she was being. She and Jacob had never talked about public displays of affection before. He was at work, even if he owned the place. Maybe this wasn't such a good look.

He must've sensed her hesitation, because just as she was preparing to step back, Jacob wrapped his arm around her and pulled her closer to him.

"You don't ever have to question me wanting your hands on me."

"Thank you for that." She linked her arms around his neck again. "But I should've asked before I just assumed. Now—" she sought his gaze, needing to connect with him "—what was Matt saying about your mood?"

She could feel the muscles in his shoulders and neck tense. Instinctively, she began kneading the strong line of his neck with her fingers, hoping to relax him.

"Is everything okay?"

"Yes and no," he replied, huffing an exhausted breath into the air. "I'm just anxious about this visit. There's so much riding on it that it's got my back up. I'm not proud of the fact that I took it out on Matt."

Keely felt for him. She understood this kind of anxiety and the pressure owning a business put you under. When it was your company, everything began and ended with you.

"Anything I can do to help?"

"There is, but we should probably take it indoors."

She shook her head. Even under the pressure of anxiety, he still seemed to remember how well their bodies fit together when they were naked.

"It's cute how you really thought it would be that easy to get me into bed."

"Come on, Keely," he whispered in her ear. "Help a brotha out."

With his Texas twang, that phrase was slightly comical coming from him. Aside from how good the sex was, it was moments like these where they let themselves be the slightest bit silly with one another that was creating a bond between them. She'd been here for nearly two weeks, and she felt so comfortable in his presence that it should worry her.

It didn't.

It should. But being with him felt so good that she'd resigned herself to the ache she knew she would feel when she finally had to go back to her real life and leave Royal.

Keely wasn't a masochist. She didn't seek out pain. She was falling for Jacob Chatman and she liked it. Even though she knew that ultimately this thing that was building between them had an expiration date on it.

"We can have a good time tonight when we're both finished with work. But if there's anything else I can do to help between now and then, I'd be glad to lend a hand."

He lifted his brow, searching her gaze before he spoke again.

"Do you mean that?"

"Of course I do. What do you need?"

Jacob looked up to the open sky, taking it in as if he needed strength to continue. When his gaze met hers again, she could see his earlier anxiety returning.

"Me talking about the ranch and what we offer on the grounds is easy for me. My work is there to speak for me. But people like Ezra Stanley require schmoozing, and I'm not really the best at that. That's where I need you to come in."

"How so?"

"I have to take him to the Texas Cattleman's Club to wine and dine him after the tour. The idea of small talk and me saying something foolish is going to worry a hole in my gut. So, I was hoping you'd attend the dinner with me to keep me from shoving my foot in my mouth."

She stepped back, running her fingers through her hair with one hand as she pulled out her phone and scrolled through her calendar with the other. She didn't need to look at the schedule to already know she had a conflict. But when she looked up at him and saw the silent "pretty please" in his eyes, she knew she had to finagle some things to make this a possibility.

"I'm supposed to be meeting with the florist during that time."

She could tell by the sad, puppy dog eyes he was giving her that he was anticipating her no. That certainly should've been her answer considering how important this meeting was to both finishing Ariana's dress and coordinating its accents into the wedding and reception.

"It's all right, Keely. I would never ask you to compromise your work for mine."

She smiled at him then, genuinely relieved at his statement.

"Thank you for respecting my work as much as yours." She took a deep breath and did some mental maneuvering to see if there was any way she could move some things around.

"Let me call the vendor and see if she'll be agreeable to seeing me a bit earlier. I hate to make last-minute changes, but this is important, you're important."

It wasn't the yes he wanted but she could tell he was grateful for the maybe she was offering instead. And knowing she put that glowing spark of hope in his eyes made her happier than a trip to the fabric store.

Keely, girl. What is you doing?

Seventeen

"Welcome to Sheen. How may I help you?"

Keely's gaze followed the voice offering her the warm greeting until her eyes found a very tall man with straight ink-black hair and a light beard staring back at her. At five feet ten inches, Keely didn't often find men so much taller than her that she'd classify them as tall. This man, however, had to stand at least five to seven inches above her head.

"Hi, I'm Keely Tucker of Low-Kee Designs. I'm here to meet with Corryna Lawson."

Bright blue eyes flashed at her as he extended his hand.

"You're in luck, she's already here waiting for you."

Keely eagerly followed him to the back, stealing a quick glance around the dimly lit restaurant as she went.

"Ms. Tucker," the host began, "this is Ms. Lawson." He looked down at Corryna before speaking again.

"Ms. Lawson, this is Ms. Tucker of Low-Kee Designs."

With a nod from both women, the host made his exit. Keely shook Corryna's hand before sitting and quickly pulled out her trusty iPad mini to start taking notes. As soon as she pulled her Apple Pencil from its case, she noted the time. She didn't have a moment to lose if she was going to glam up to sit by Jacob's side tonight.

"Well, there is one thing I need from you to make our bride a happy camper." Corryna stared at Keely with wide green eyes, waiting in anticipation for her to drop the proverbial other shoe. "I'm gonna need a ridiculous amount of bluebonnet flowers. I'm talking enough for bouquets and boutonnieres, ceremony decorations and table centerpieces at the reception hall. Essentially, I need to know if you can you make it rain bluebonnets. Can you do that?"

A slow smile beamed on Corryna's face before she answered, "Hell yeah."

"Keely, we're gonna be late."

Jacob paced back and forth in the kitchen as nervous energy coursed through him as he watched each moment on the wall clock ticking by. He'd been up before the sun to make certain everything was perfect for Ezra Stanley's visit. Jacob had personally escorted the man every place his feet had touched on Chatman land.

Ezra was a squat man with blond hair and dark brown eyes who wore big shades and an even bigger hat. But whatever he lacked in height, he more than made up for in his knowledge of and love for horses. He'd pressed Jacob about his methods, his philosophies and outcomes when it came to horse training. He'd taken such careful inspection of the premises, Jacob was certain he was more thorough than any state inspector that had ever come through the Slick Six.

No matter how vigorous the interview process had been, Jacob had come away from the experience confident that he was more than halfway to securing what would be a very lucrative contract. All that remained was this dinner, and if Jacob understood, it wasn't about mingling, it was to look Jacob in his eye and see if he could be trusted with such a precious gift as his horse.

If he was handing Tildy over to a stranger, he'd want to know if the man could be trusted to take care of his dear companion too.

"Keely!" he hollered again, rubbing the back of his neck as he tried to calm himself down. Getting tense this close to his dinner meeting wouldn't do him any favors.

"Jacob, stop screaming the walls down. Creating this kind of perfection takes time."

He turned around with a sly barb on the tip of his tongue, but the smart-ass comment dried up when his gaze took her in.

Their dinner wasn't formal, but the Texas Cattleman's Club was upscale enough that even he dug a suit out of his closet and threw it on. Keely wore a white bodycon dress that made her look like sin and heaven all rolled up into one.

"I rest my case." He couldn't get upset at her remark, or the fact that she'd taken so long to get ready. Watching her strut past him with an extra sway in her hips as she glided on those impossibly high heels she was wearing, he realized two things. First, she knew she was the total package. Two, she also knew that he knew she was the total package.

He shook his head, trying to get his wayward mind

to focus. "Keely, the point of you attending this dinner is to calm me down, not raise my blood pressure."

She turned slowly, waiting for him to catch up to her. She cupped his cheek, giving him a playful wink as their eyes met.

"The point of me attending this dinner is to keep your anxiety-fueled bad mood in check while you try to schmooze Stanley. So, tell me, are you thinking about your anxiety right now?"

He sure as shit wasn't, not by a long shot.

When she knew she'd made her point, she turned toward the door again. "Come along, Jacob. I wouldn't want you to be late."

Late? He couldn't give a damn about late right now. All he wanted was to continue to watch her strut back and forth in his kitchen as if she were on a runway. To follow behind her until he was close enough to wrap his arms around her and pull her flush against him. But duty did call. So, he vowed he'd do his level best at this dinner to keep things running smoothly, because outside of this contract, there was nothing as important to him as peeling that dress off Keely the moment they stepped through his front door.

He watched her saunter out onto the front porch, the sway of her hips nearly lulling him into a trance. He lifted his eyes to the night sky and shook his head.

"If anyone is up there listening, help me keep my eyes off this woman long enough to get us there and back safely."

He opened the passenger door and saw her safely seated before he slipped inside of his driver's seat. When he did, he found her shifting items in the small clutch purse on her lap.

"You forget something?"

She looked up, her body relaxing as she closed the purse and settled into her seat. "No." She pulled the key to the great room out of the purse for him to get a quick glimpse of it before she tucked it away. "I changed so fast, I just needed to double-check that I had this key on me. I didn't have a chance to do my usual check when I'm moving things from one bag to the other."

He kept his eyes on the road, but lifted a sharp brow. "*Fast* is relative."

She squeezed his thigh playfully. "Whatever. I told you that this level of perfection takes time to achieve. I essentially performed a miracle in less than an hour."

"You're actually carrying that thing around. You could've left it in the bedroom."

She shook her head. "Not on your life," she replied. "This key never leaves my possession. As long as Ariana's dress is in there, no one can go in or out of that room except me."

"Is there really this much interest in what Ariana is wearing on her wedding day? I get that she's a celebrity, but most folks around here don't care about her or Xavier's notoriety. We treat 'em like normal folks."

"This town is built different, I guess. Ariana can barely eat without someone snapping photos of her." She looked out the window, watching the road pass by as if she needed time to contemplate what she was about to say next. "Not to mention, there's this celebrity wedding crasher that has Ariana and Ex's wedding on his radar. If he got hold of any information, he'd leak it all over his social media just for clicks. It would devastate Ariana and ruin my business. No celebrity would ever trust me to work on another design."

He could feel tension building in her through the hand she still had propped on his leg.

"I know to most people, what I do doesn't seem all that important. But this is my passion and I take it seriously."

There was something about the dip in her voice that conveyed how serious she was. As if she'd had to have this conversation one too many times in her past.

The idea that she'd been forced to justify herself, her choices, didn't sit well with him. His arms twitched with the need to scoop her out of her seat and pull her as close to him as she could get.

Since being confined in a car made that sort of impossible, he slid his right hand over hers, lacing his fingers through hers, pulling her hand to his lips and placing a comforting kiss there.

"There is nothing frivolous about what you do. If I gave you the impression that's how I felt, I don't. I see how damn hard you work. It's evident in the details of your creations."

He could see her shift in her seat from his periphery.

"You've seen my work?"

The surprise in her voice tickled him. It was an addictive sound, sparking something bright inside him that he wanted to stick around. Not because it felt good to him, but because he enjoyed knowing he could give her something no one else could.

"Of course I have. After watching how dedicated you are to creating the perfect dress for Ariana, there's no way I wouldn't want to see more of your work. I may have even purchased an item or two from your men's business collection."

She turned in her seat, with an amused but confused smile blooming on her lips.

"I'm trying to figure out where a cowboy who loves

denim like a mouse loves cheese is gonna wear one of my designs."

He shrugged. "On occasions like tonight where I'm forced to leave the land and play in society. Also, I figured it would make a good impression on you if I showed up in New York to take you out on a proper date."

When she didn't immediately respond, he wondered if he was presuming too much. Keely had never made mention of wanting to see him outside of her time in Royal. He fought the desire to squirm. Instead, he straightened his spine as best he could in his seat.

"That is…if you'd care to keep seeing me when you go back home."

Before she could answer, the Texas Cattleman's Club came into view and he could see Ezra getting out of his car ahead of them in the valet line. Now, instead of worrying about how this dinner was going to go with Ezra, it seemed he'd spend his time worrying about Keely's answer.

"I tell you, I've been to some of the finest restaurants in the world, and there is no one on this planet that knows how to cook a steak like Texans."

Keely watched Ezra stab the last piece of steak on his plate and couldn't fight the enjoyment that stirred in her while taking in his antics. She hadn't known exactly what to expect of him. While he was inspecting the ranch and interviewing Jacob and his team, Keely had been tweaking her sketches and sewing her behind off to make up for the time she knew she would miss while acting as Jacob's wingman. As tense as Jacob had been about this meeting, she'd expected an uptight asshole.

"No offense to your home state, Ms. Keely." He

popped the perfectly cooked piece of meat in his mouth and hummed in satisfaction. "But even New York steak-houses don't have a thing on this."

"I'm not offended." Keely picked up her fork to fin-ish off her own steak. "The truth is the truth. This is one helluva good piece of meat." She cut her eyes at Jacob, thoroughly entertained by his attempt to keep from choking on the broccoli he was currently chewing.

"Smart, beautiful, honest and eats more than twigs in front of people. Where on earth did you ever find someone like her, Jacob?" Before Jacob could answer, Ezra turned to Keely and gave her a genuine smile. In Keely's industry, she'd come across enough men who wore their sleaze like a bad cologne. This wasn't some lecherous old man. This was charm gained through ex-perience with a little flirting to boot. "Do you have a sister?"

"I do," Keely answered. "But she's taken too."

She'd picked up her wineglass and had it less than an inch from her mouth when she realized what she'd said. She chanced a glimpse at Jacob to see if he'd heard her slipup. The moment their gazes collided, she knew he heard exactly what she'd said.

If the sharp look in his eye didn't clue her in, then the way his jaw tightened certainly did. The only problem was she didn't know if his reaction was good or bad.

Tiny spikes of cold sliced through her as she waited for this awkward impasse they were having while sitting at a table in the fanciest place in Royal, Texas.

"I didn't find her. She found me." Jacob may have been answering Ezra's question, but the way he looked at her, with so much heat in his eyes, she could feel her skin being singed by the flames. "And every day since, I wake up asking what I did to get so lucky."

The world narrowed down to the two of them. The voices of their fellow diners became insignificant murmurs. The large dining room became a tight corner with only room for the two of them, and the air was so thin, she felt light-headed from the lack of oxygen.

Her fingers began to tingle and somehow, without her recognizing how, her glass went from sitting firmly in her hand to lying on its side on the table. The heavy thud of the crystal against the cloth-covered table snapped her out of whatever strange trance Jacob's voice had lulled her into.

And when he opened his mouth to speak, she interrupted.

"My goodness," she exclaimed. "Seems that all that time sewing yesterday has given me a case of butterfingers." She grabbed her napkin and dabbed up some of the excess liquid spreading on the thick table linen, getting her hands sticky with it. "Excuse me, gentlemen, I'm gonna find my way to the restroom and wash my hands."

She stood up and let her stilettos carry her as quickly as they could from Jacob's scrutiny. Because whatever that was that happened between them sure as hell wasn't the fun they'd both signed on for. This... This was as serious as serious could get.

Eighteen

"Who are you?"

Keely sat at one of the stools along the vanity that took up one wall of the anteroom in the TCC's ladies' room.

She was fortunate enough that room had been empty when she'd entered in a near state of panic. As relieved as she was to find a precious few moments alone, she knew at some point, someone would find their way inside her hiding space, and unless she wanted them to see her falling apart, she'd have to get herself together.

Keely didn't have to ask herself why she was so out of sorts. That answer was clear. Jacob Chatman had made her feel easy enough around him that she'd let some Freudian-type slipup reveal something she hadn't even admitted to herself. She wanted Jacob Chatman. All of him. Not just the great-sex part, or the "he's funny and makes me laugh" parts. She wanted every piece that made up the sexy cowboy. She didn't just want him, she wanted to tattoo "Property of Keely Tucker" across his forehead so everyone would know, including him, that he belonged to her.

She released a deep breath and let that admission settle into her bones, seeping down into the marrow of her being. She wanted Jacob Chatman. But more importantly, she wanted to belong to Jacob Chatman too, and that reality would bring so much chaos into her life, she knew it was something she should never have.

She was here for work. Yeah, she'd taken the meetings she'd needed to. But she hadn't put in half the stitchwork that she should have by now. She was supposed to leave next week. The gown's first iteration should've been done by then.

If she were home in her little studio, nothing could've taken her focus away. But languishing on his ranch and in his arms, Keely had pushed her work to the side, not because Jacob had asked her to, but because everything in her being wanted to focus on him and the pleasure she derived from being with him, rather than do her work.

She couldn't blame this on Jacob. He wasn't some chauvinist demanding she give him all her time and attention. He never acted as if her work wasn't as important as his. This was all Keely. That meant only she could take responsibility for it. She had to fix this somehow. She had to extricate herself from the pull Jacob had on her. Otherwise, when this was over, her career would be in tatters, and she'd have no one to blame but herself.

Committed to holding herself accountable, she opened her clutch, rooting around in it for her lipstick. Feeling more confident once she'd applied the rich color, she smiled at herself.

"You can do this, Keely. It's about your work. You've made a million sacrifices to get this far, this is just one more."

Satisfied with her pep talk, she dropped the lipstick back in her purse and rooted around to take a glimpse of the great room key. Concern nipped at the edges of the encouragement she'd just given herself when she couldn't find it.

On the verge of a panic attack, she dumped everything out of the small purse onto the vanity table, hoping to find the key underneath her compact. But she knew her luck wasn't that good. Somehow, between getting out of Jacob's car and entering the TCC, she'd lost the literal key to her success all because she'd put her focus on the wrong thing: Jacob.

"You are one lucky bastard."

Jacob pulled his eyes away from Keely's disappearing form to focus on Ezra. The task was more difficult than it should have been, because his head was so preoccupied with whatever had just happened between Keely and him before she bolted for the bathroom.

"Trust me, I know." Jacob saw no need to sugarcoat his response or pretend he didn't know what Ezra was talking about. He didn't want to pretend where Keely was concerned.

He picked up his glass at that realization, needing to wet his suddenly dry mouth. Keely was a beautiful woman and any man would be lucky to have her. The fact that she'd chosen to spend her precious time with him made him feel as if there was no man in the world that could compete with him, not when he held the interest of the best woman who was the best at everything.

He lightly shook his head as a small, amused smile

bent the corner of his mouth. This woman had gotten under his skin and that fact should make him anxious, scared; he should be planning a tactical retreat.
Instead, he wanted to run to Keely, to announce it to
everyone who would listen that he was the most fortunate man alive.

"I like that."

Jacob raised a questioning brow, trying to figure out
if he'd missed out on part of Ezra's conversation while
his mind was focused on Keely.

"Like what?"

"The fact that you're smitten with Ms. Tucker and
you don't have even the slightest inclination to hide it.
I like that you recognize you have a gem in that lovely
young woman who graced us with her presence tonight.
Everything about the way you are with her shows me
you have the kindness and the resilience to care for
my horse."

"You're basing your decision to give me your business on my choice in a woman?"

Jacob was hoping this wasn't a blatant display of
chauvinism. So far, everything the man had said about
Keely had been complimentary. Jacob wasn't certain if
that remained to be the case so he waited, leaving the
pause after his question to convey his need for Ezra to
expand on his statement.

"I'm not that foolish or sentimental. Your facility is
top-notch and your training techniques are some of the
most innovative I've ever seen. Not to mention, your
outcomes are nothing to dismiss either. You know what
the hell you're doing when it comes to horses. But I
could find a hundred horse trainers who could do the
same. There has to be something more."

Jacob tilted his head, still not completely understanding where Ezra was going with this conversation.

"And you think Keely is that something more?"

Ezra leaned forward, bracing his forearms on the table. "Your companion is a powerful woman who is entirely her own being. Some men would be foolish enough to try to smother the light that exudes from her. But you're wise enough to understand that controlling beauty and power is much less rewarding than giving it the room to grow and thrive. If you can understand that with a force like your Ms. Tucker, then you'll certainly do fine with my horse, who is equally as aware of her power as Ms. Tucker is. So, if you want my business, the contract is yours."

Ezra stood, extending his hand to Jacob, who gladly accepted the gesture.

"I'm gonna head on out. Please share my goodbyes with Ms. Tucker. I'll have my lawyers contact you tomorrow about the contract. I look forward to working with you."

Ezra gave Jacob's hand an excited squeeze before he headed toward the door, leaving Jacob to contemplate all the man had said.

Of all the things Jacob had expected to hear from Ezra, an endorsement of his connection to Keely hadn't been it. Not by a long shot. But as Jacob took in the man's words and settled into his seat, he knew Ezra wasn't wrong. Ezra's observation had one other purpose. It sparked this burning need to lock things down where Keely was concerned.

He wanted more than just fun in and out of bed. And as he looked in the direction Keely had walked, he knew it was high time he shared those desires with Keely. If he was as lucky as Ezra believed, then maybe she'd have him as something more than a friend with benefits. Because the more time he spent with Keely, the more he realized she wasn't just a friend. With her fun and flirty ways, her supportive nature and her singular focus on her own excellence, Keely was fast becoming the woman of his dreams. Now, he just had to convince her of that fact.

But when he turned his head in the direction of the restrooms to see Keely walking quickly toward the table with sharp lines drawn on her face, he pushed his ruminating thoughts aside to focus on what looked like panic settling across Keely's face.

He stood before she reached the table, placing a calm hand against her cheek as soon as he met her.

"What's wrong?"

"It's the key, Jacob. I've lost the key."

Fear gripped him, squeezing tightly around his rib cage as he processed what she'd just said and what it meant. Nodding, he grabbed her hand, and headed back to their table. He released her hand long enough to wave and catch their server's attention.

"Put all of this on my tab and give yourself a healthy tip."

Before the server could nod in agreement, Jacob grabbed Keely's hand, directing her to the exit.

With each step, his heart rate ticked up another anxious notch, mostly because he could feel her worry turning into tense panic as each moment passed. But there was also another reason, a wholly selfish reason, he easily admitted to himself. If they didn't find this damn key, his plans of talking to Keely about their situationship were as good as dead in the water.

Jacob pulled his car into the garage. He'd usually let it sit in the driveway, but he needed the light the structure could offer. He spared a quick glance to find Keely sitting ramrod straight, her body practically vibrating with tension.

He shut off the car, and when she reached for her door, he rested his hand on her thigh and gave it a gentle squeeze. The touch wasn't meant to be sensual. It was all about comfort, about unraveling the knot he'd watched her twist herself into the moment she told him she'd lost the key.

He'd done his best to look around in the car once they left the TCC. But with the pitch-black dark surrounding them, and few streetlights, even with the flashlights from their phones and the small flashlight he kept in his glove compartment, there was no way they could sweep through the car the way they needed to.

"We'll find it, Keely. The last place you had it was in the car. It probably slipped out of your purse when you rested it on your seat."

She shared a soft smile with him, one he assumed was for his benefit, not hers. However, he'd spent enough time staring into her eyes that he could see they were still fraught with worry.

"Go on up and change and we'll start looking when you get back."

She nodded, silently exiting the car. Jacob stepped out of the car, pulling off his jacket and heading straight for the tools lined up against the garage walls. He grabbed his father's old-school droplight, plugging it up quickly before kneeling down on the concrete floor to inspect the passenger seat.

He was sure his suit pants would be ruined by the time this was over. It was a small price to pay for Keely's peace of mind, as far as he was concerned.

He looked in every crevice in the passenger seat,

the floor, between the cushions, the well in the door. It wasn't until he opened the back door and looked behind Keely's seat that he saw something sparkle when the light touched it. It was wedged between the seat and the wall of the car. There was no way his big fingers were fitting in that space. He moved back to the wall to get a flathead screwdriver. Within seconds, he'd pushed the metal object to the floor of the back seat.

He huffed a sigh of relief when he picked it up, confirming it was the key. If they hadn't found it, he would've just changed the locks to give her secure access again. But that would've had to wait until he could get a new lock from the hardware store in the morning. The idea of her spending the entire night tied up in worry and fear was something he couldn't tolerate, so here he was, on his knees in one of the few pairs of good pants he had, fiddling with a droplight and a screwdriver.

Keely's return to the garage brought a smile to his face, and when he stood up, waving the key in the air for her to see, the relief spreading throughout her entire body was well worth the effort.

"Thank goodness! Where did you find it?"

"Wedged between your seat and the side panel. I told you it was just too dark for us to see properly at the club."

He stepped closer to her, placing the key in her hand and noting how tightly she clutched the piece of metal. Despite holding the key in her hand, her eyes were still serious, and her mouth was pulled taught into a flat line, making him wonder if this was just her way of processing her earlier fear, or if this was something else.

He placed a gentle kiss on her lips and felt no response to it. He pulled back, his gaze searching hers, but her stare was nearly blank.

"Hey, it's been a day and you've had a lot of excitement at the end of it. Why don't you let me draw you a bath or give you a massage to help you relax?"

She stepped back from him, putting what he could see was intentional distance between them.

"Thanks for the offer. As tempting as it is, I'm gonna have to ask for a rain check. I need to get in some stitch-work tonight."

"At this hour?"

"We're business owners. You know we don't punch a clock."

She turned to the door that connected the garage to the house. Just before stepping through, she looked over her shoulder at him.

"I know you need to get up early. Don't wait up. I'll be up as soon as I can."

She gave him a final nod as the definitive end to their conversation. As he stood there alone in the quiet garage, he couldn't help but feel that gesture foretold something ominous he wasn't going to like one bit.

Nineteen

Keely bent down to spread the train of the dress out as she prepped for her video chat with Ariana to show her the new elements she'd added to the dress.

Her neck and back cracked when she tried to stand upright, a clear indicator that sleeping on a couch for days at a time to avoid the man sleeping in a bed above her wasn't the smartest idea.

She rolled her neck, trying to distract herself from the conflicting thoughts bouncing around in her head. She was almost there, almost to a place where her professional mask could push down the big emotions threatening to swallow her whole, when a knock at the door broke through her concentration.

"Keely?"

She didn't need to open the door to see who was on the other side. She knew that deep voice that coiled around her like a thick python, squeezing out every bit of resistance she attempted to muster up.

It is his house, Keely. It's not like you can refuse him entry.

Yes, it was his home. But she also knew Jacob well enough that he would not tread where he wasn't welcome. Before she could continue that line of thinking, another knock landed hard on the door, making her reconsider her thoughts of the limits of Jacob's actions. The booming sound was loud enough, she figured if she made him wait any longer, he might do something drastic like take the door off the hinges to see why she wasn't responding.

"Be right there."

She opened the door, and there he stood in his usual work uniform, a plaid shirt that stretched across his torso in an almost obscene fashion. As he walked by her, settling into the great room, she realized his jeans were presenting an equally tempting picture of the lower half of his body.

Keep your head together, girl. Your work is all that matters.

Keely took a breath as she closed the door, repeating that mantra over and over again in hopes that it would give her the fortitude to do what she needed to do: keep her head and her heart focused on leveling up her business and ignoring anything else that didn't fall in line with that.

"Did you need something?"

His eyes contracted into tiny slits, his gaze sweeping over her like searchlights looking for the guilty.

"Look," he began cautiously. "I don't mean to upset you, but I feel like something's changed between us and not in a good way."

She walked over to the mannequin in the center of the room, fiddling with the stitching on a side panel. There was nothing wrong with it. It was perfect, nothing less than Keely's usual when she was in her zone. But that was the problem. She hadn't been in that zone since she'd met Jacob.

"I'm not sure I know what you're talking about."

She spared him long enough of a glance that she could see the muscle at the side of his jaw twitch in frustration.

"I'm talking about the fact that I haven't seen you in days. It's beginning to feel like you're avoiding me."

No one could ever accuse that man of being stupid. Without much difficulty, he'd figured out her ruse. But just because he'd figured her out didn't mean she had to admit that he was right. Denial was the name of this game, and she'd hold on to it for as long as she could.

"Listen." She tried her best to sound annoyed, trying to forget the way his smoldering gaze made her burn for him, trying to keep the need out of her voice. "I'm not sure what you think is going on, but I'm working. We both know that's what I came here for so I'm not exactly certain why you're trippin'."

His nares widened as he drew in a deep breath, placing his hands on his waist.

"Why I'm trippin'?" She could see the anger building in his stiff stance and tight features. But underneath the frustration, she also saw a glimpse of something like disappointment coloring his dark irises. "I know what you're doing, Keely. It doesn't have to be this way."

She turned away from him, locking her joints, forcing her posture to be ramrod straight. She knew if she saw the same need in his eyes that she was certain filled her own, she'd never be able to resist him.

"This cowardly bullshit is beneath you, Keely. I thought you had more heart than this."

So did she, but apparently her feelings for him had changed her on a chemical level. She was changed. And as she listened to him walk out of the great room, the quiet click of the closing door resonating like a loud gong, vibrating off the walls, she wondered if she would ever be the same again.

For fifteen minutes she stood in the room, praying Jacob would return while simultaneously hoping that he'd be strong enough for the both of them and keep his distance. Her chest felt heavy as if some kind of heft pressed down against it, restricting her breathing.

She wanted to curl up and bawl her eyes out, but duty called. Her meeting with Ariana was moments away, and she had to prepare herself.

She gripped the back of a nearby high-back chair, squeezing until her fingers ached and her palms blanched from the pressure.

She knew she didn't have to punish herself like this. But the pain of the carved wood biting into her skin was much more preferable than feeling that gaping chasm that was growing between them.

But as her mind lingered on his parting words, she realized she was punishing Jacob for a crime he hadn't committed. He hadn't done anything wrong, and her needing distance wasn't about him. It was about her needing to focus. Yet she couldn't bring herself to tell him those words. Not when there was so much riding on her ability to stay away from him.

She stayed downstairs stitching or sketching away until she was too exhausted to climb the stairs, settling for the couch, using his early sleep schedule as a means to put distance between them.

Trifling. Just trifling.

She would've agreed with herself except her Face-Time notification on her iPad mini broke through her thoughts, giving her a momentary reprieve from her mixed emotions.

"Hey, Ariana."

"Hey, girl," Ariana replied as her huge smile filled the screen. "How's my dress coming along?"

"I won't lie, even though I suggested them, it took me a bit to figure out how to get the bluebonnet accents into the dress. But I think I've got it now. You ready?"

Ariana squealed at the sight of her dress and it made all the discomfort Keely was experiencing before the call slowly abate.

"Keely, I know it's essentially just the frame without all the adornments and embroidery, but this is magnificent. I can't wait to try it on. You were right, the bluebonnet accents were the perfect addition."

Keely's neck began to ache again and she couldn't help rubbing it in front of the camera.

"You okay?"

It was a simple question, but Keely wasn't sure how to answer Ariana. Sure, save for the few kinks she'd developed from sleeping on the couch, she was physically fine. But how did she explain this hefty weight sitting on her chest that grew larger and more powerful every minute she kept herself away from Jacob?

"I'm fine. My neck's just a little out of whack from working too long without enough breaks."

"Well," Ariana said with a sparkle of something wicked in her eyes. "We absolutely can't have that.

When I hang up this phone, I'm gonna book you into a spa for a full day of pampering."

"You don't have to do that, Ariana. You're paying me a ridiculous amount of money for this dress. That's compensation enough."

Ariana shook her head like a displeased school-teacher. "I'll hear nothing of it."

Keely attempted to open her mouth in protest, but Ariana held up a silencing finger, relaying her position on the matter was final.

"All right, I'll accept your generous offer. Besides, afterward, maybe I can hook up with my girlfriend Zanai and her best friend, Morgan, so I can catch up with Zanai and discuss some final thoughts on the fabric selections for the bridesmaids' dresses with Morgan too."

"I have a better suggestion. Find out Zanai's and Morgan's availability and I'll send all three of you."

Before Keely could protest, Ariana waved her hand as she smiled. "Send me the deets and I'll set it up. Later."

And just like that, Ariana was gone.

"No wonder she's such a great producer and actress. She has no problems getting exactly what she wants."

Figuring it was easier to go along instead of argue at this point, Keely found her phone on a nearby end table and called Zanai. Maybe hanging out with her old friend would help her clear some of the fog in her head. Because one way or the other, Keely had to get her head right.

Keely moaned as the loose feeling permeating every muscle, tendon and bone she possessed moved through her body.

She managed to find just enough energy to turn her head to find her two companions in much the same condition. Zanai was stretched out on her back, and Morgan was on her side gently cradling her baby bump.

Keely lay on her stomach with her arms crossed underneath the plush pillow cradling her head.

"This is the life," Zanai half whispered in response to Keely's satisfied moan.

"You mean rich folks don't indulge in spa treatments like this every other day and twice on Sunday?"

Morgan lifted her sleep mask from her eyes and peeked over at Zanai, then they both turned their gazes to Keely and answered, "Hell no," simultaneously.

"We're too busy working ourselves to the bone." Morgan's comment brought an amused smile to Zanai's face. "Since I cut ties with my dad, I'm a broke health care worker. There's no way I could afford to splurge like this on the regular. Please send my thanks to Ariana."

Morgan threw a small hand towel at Zanai that landed on her leg.

"Yeah," Morgan countered, "but she's got a rich boyfriend who would love to pamper her like this if she'd allow it."

Keely turned onto her side to get a better look at Zanai. "Girl, what is wrong with you. You'd better let that man spoil you."

"Trust me." Morgan's voice pulled their attention. "I am wholeheartedly supporting Ryan's spoiling of me while I'm carrying his child."

"Lucky heifers," Keely groused, drawing the collective laughter of the two women.

"I can't believe a woman as gorgeous and successful as you doesn't have her pick of suitors. If you wanted someone, all you'd have to do is bat your beautiful lashes. Those Hollywood folks have to be blind."

If only Morgan's assumption was correct. Keely was in celebrity circles all the time. But it was work. And since she didn't play where she ate, all of these beautiful suitors Morgan was mentioning were nonexistent.

"First, I don't live in Hollywood. I'm in New York. But even if I were, I'm just too busy to focus on a relationship."

Zanai lifted her brow, silently noting Keely's BS the way only a longtime friend could.

"So, you're saying there's no one tickling your fancy?" Zanai countered.

The lie was on the tip of her tongue, but when Morgan's and Zanai's dual gazes locked on her, she realized she just didn't have the energy for pretense. She sat up on her table, preparing to bare her soul. Maybe talking it out would help her work through the conflict in her head.

"Whatever I tell you two has to stay between us." They both eagerly nodded, sitting up on their individual massage tables, giving her their rapt attention.

"Jacob Chatman and I have been indulging in a lighthearted fling for the last two weeks and everything about it has been wonderful."

Her shoulders dropped with the last syllable spoken and the two women with her leaned in with concern painted across their faces.

"You sound like that's a bad thing."

"It is, Morgan," Keely replied on an exhausted huff.

"But why?" Zanai's question was logical. Unfortunately, logic had nothing to do with how Jacob made Keely feel.

"He's a distraction from my work. A very sexy distraction, granted. But still, a distraction. Every time he touches me, every time he slides me that slick look of his, every time he winks and crooks his finger, and uses that deep Texas drawl of his to say 'Come here, thickness,' it's all too damn distracting."

Morgan pointed a single finger up. "Wait a minute. Did you just say you find him calling you 'thickness' sexy, as in you like it?"

Keely smiled. As a size 16 woman and after spending so much time working in the rag industry, she understood Morgan's dismay. American beauty standards told women you have to be a size zero to be considered attractive and if you weren't, you should be ashamed of your body. Fortunately for Keely, she'd never subscribed to that limiting belief.

"I think it's more of a cultural thing, and beyond that, an individual situation. But culturally, Black people celebrate having larger bodies. So, when we say thick or thicc, we are actually using the word as a compliment, not a pejorative."

Zanai nodded in agreement with Keely. "She's right. If Jayden doesn't grab a handful of my ass every morning before I leave for work, I'm insulted and questioning if he's got a problem."

Keely couldn't help but chuckle at that. She couldn't lie and say she didn't have an appreciation for a slap on the ass as a sign of appreciation between lovers. Some might find it crude, but to her, it tickled her fancy...a lot.

"I realize that people may have different experiences when it comes to body image and being called something like that can be triggering for them. But every time Jacob calls me 'thickness,' he's telling me how irresistibly sexy he finds me and how much he appreciates every roll and curve of my body. So yeah, it's kinda hot as hell and ultimately a distraction."

Morgan had a peculiar expression on her face and Keely wondered if she needed to clarify what she'd said any further.

"In that context, I can see how uplifting that is. But what I can't figure out is if you're enjoying him so much, why can't there be room for both work and Jacob in your life?"

"Because unlike you," Zanai began, "Keely doesn't understand how to balance being a business owner with having a life. It's the reason we haven't seen each other in so long."

Keely winced from the sting of Zanai's words. She could see by the concern and care in her friend's eyes that Zanai wasn't trying to be hurtful. But deep down, the truth of those words cut Keely deep.

Zanai gave Keely a compassionate smile, soothing over her singed feelings.

"I know it wasn't intentional, Keely. I'm so proud of what you've accomplished. But I'd be lying if I said I didn't want you to make room for me, and people like Jacob, who from the sound of it, wants to care for you too."

"I wouldn't be so sure of that."

Morgan and Zanai shared a confused look before returning their questioning stares to Keely.

"Jacob is just as dedicated to his work as I am. He's not looking for anything deep. So, even if I were willing to try and make space for him, I'm not exactly sure he would want to pursue anything. We promised that we'd never interfere with each other's work. I can't just change the rules now."

Morgan slid down off her massage table, waddling

carefully until she was standing next to Keely's table. "Sure, you can. Feelings change. And if the lovin' is as good as you seem to believe it is, isn't that worth the risk to everything else?"

"In a fantasy world, I'd say yes." Keely tapped her fingers on her table, the feedback helping her focus a bit on what was important. "But this is reality. And in my reality, if I'm distracted from work, I can't build the empire I'm striving for. I've put everything I have into this business. I can't just let it all go up in flames because Jacob Chatman is the sexiest thing walking."

Zanai cleared her throat to grab Keely's attention. "Let me put on my therapist's hat for a moment. Now granted, I don't practice general therapy, but I remember enough from my clinical rotations to give you a little bit of advice. Keely, I don't think your business is the problem at all. I think there's an even larger issue at play here."

Keely folded her arms like she used to when they were kids, bracing herself to hear something she knew she wasn't going to like.

"Okay, Dr. Z. Lay your rusty psychobabble on me."

Zanai laughed, keeping the levity in the room.

"I don't think Jacob being a distraction is the issue. The issue is, I think you've gone and fallen in love with Jacob Chatman and you're so determined to fight against it, you'll use any excuse to keep you from pursuing it."

Keely gripped the edge of her massage table to keep herself from falling over from that shot Zanai aimed at the center of her chest.

Panic grew inside her, but Keely had worked around too many celebrities not to have learned a trick or two about deflection. Because there was no way in hell she could explore this option, and all its complicated ramifications, while wrapped in a towel on a massage table with her friends.

"That's your theory, huh?" Keely quipped. "I'm afraid of being in love with Jacob? Well, if you're so smart, use your psychological superpowers to tell me why."

"That's something you've got to take the time and figure out on your own, Keely." Zanai left her table and walked over to Keely, placing a comforting hand on her shoulder. "And when you do, you need to talk to Jacob. There's no greater regret than the one of not trying at all."

Keely closed her eyes, pinching the bridge of her nose as she tried to keep it together. Zanai was right about one thing: Keely had some serious soul-searching to do. The question was, with less than a handful of days left in Royal, could she figure out what she wanted before it was too late?

Twenty

"I guess you're done avoiding me?"

The annoyance in Jacob's voice reached her long before she could see his sharp features as she walked into the stables.

"Jacob, I don't want to fight with you."

He stepped away from his horse to look at her, and the cold pouring off him made her shiver in the Texas heat.

"Seems of late you don't want to do much of anything with me, so I guess you're consistent at least."

"Jacob." She called his name again, hoping she could soothe his apparent irritation with her.

"What did I do?"

The sharp sound of his voice cut through the air. It was laced with anger, but she couldn't ignore the obvious pain mixed in it too.

"What do you mean?"

He placed both hands on his hips, staring her directly in the eye.

"Things were getting real good between you and me, Keely. I didn't imagine that. And then you just shut me out."

She shook her head, not because what he said wasn't true, but because it wasn't her intention to make him feel whatever he was feeling that had him so annoyed and angry with her.

"Don't deny it. You've been deliberately locking yourself away in that great room so you wouldn't have to be near me. And I need to know why. What did I do to screw things up so much that you don't even want to be in my presence? What were you punishing me for?"

The angry tick in his cheek compiled with the sadness clouding his eyes tugged at an invisible cord deep inside her. Unable to do anything to hold them back, she closed her eyes and let hot tears fall.

"You didn't do anything, Jacob. I wasn't trying to punish you." Her voice quavered and every bit of pride she had leaked out with her flowing tears. "I was trying to punish myself."

His world narrowed down to the wet streaks her falling tears left behind on her skin. Something possessive and raw clawed at him and the only thing his mind would let him entertain was pulling her into his arms and holding her until her quiet sobbing receded.

"I'm so sorry." Her face was pressed into his shoulder and her words were muffled, but he could still somehow make them out with perfect clarity. It was like everything else with Keely Tucker; he'd been hyperaware of her from the moment they met. That awareness had only become stronger, clearer as his feelings and desire for her had become less of a want and so much more than a need.

"I'm sorry too," he cooed while rubbing a flat palm against her back. "I shouldn't have attacked like that. I let my temper get the better of me and I should…"

She pulled away from him, seeking out his gaze and holding it firmly once her eyes found his.

"No, don't you dare apologize. You were right when you said this cowardly bullshit was beneath me. I should've come to you and talked to you. You deserve at least that much after the way I've treated you." She took another shaky breath, steadying herself by placing her palms flat against his chest.

He reveled in her closeness. The pressure of her body against his provided comfort the way nothing else had. But he knew he had to keep that to himself right now. Keely was as skittish as a new arrival on his ranch, and he'd bet money she would bolt if he didn't find a way to make her feel safe.

"Can we go back to the house and talk? Tildy and I are cool and all, but I don't need her up in my business right now."

The gentle-natured mare huffed, letting Keely know her comment wasn't appreciated. Tildy might be good-natured. But that didn't mean she still didn't have spunk.

Jacob cupped Keely's cheek, needing to hold their connection. Things just made more sense when he was this close to her.

"I've got a better idea. You up for a ride?" He could see the protest building on her lips. The house was closer, but there was something magical about riding on his land, and right now, with them both wound so tightly, they needed some recreational activity to clear their heads. "We'll nix all this weirdness that's been going on for the last few days between us and hopefully, you'll find the words you're looking for."

With a nod, she acquiesced, and he took her hand, leading her to Tildy's stall.

"Now, I'm not trying to tell you what to do." He pointed his finger toward Tildy's bobbing head, smiling down at Keely. "But iffin' I was, I'd suggest you apologize to old Tildy before you saddle up. Nothing like a sore rump from a bad ride with a horse that's got you in her crosshairs."

They took a leisurely and silent ride to the outpost they'd settled in when they'd fixed the transformer. The last time they were here, they'd both let down their walls enough to find something exceptional between them. There was no doubt in his mind that if they could just get there, shut out the rest of the world, that maybe they could wade through the confusion they'd found themselves in.

They dismounted, and Jacob removed their tack as he prepared to send the horses off to frolic. He stopped, waiting for her to join him at his side, when he heard Keely speaking in a hushed voice to Tildy.

She'd been cautious but open with the horse since the first day he'd introduced them. Although he could still see that cautiousness that came with new riders, he also saw her reaching for something more with each tentative stroke she gave Tildy's neck.

He couldn't make out what she was saying to the horse, but whatever it was, Tildy seemed to enjoy it because she lowered her head, a silent incentive given to encourage Keely to keep stroking her.

The sight of this picture tugged at him, making him ache with the idea that Keely would be leaving soon, and he'd quite possibly never have the opportunity to experience this kind of simple yet profound joy again.

Another few strokes, and Keely stepped back as the horses took off. She fell in step with Jacob and they made their way inside the cabin.

"You want me to make you a snack? I'm sure I can find something to put together quickly."

He took her hand, squeezing it to give her the support she needed in this moment.

"I'd rather we sit down and talk. With so little time before you leave, I just want us to clear the air."

He stroked his thumb across a tiny patch of skin on the back of her hand, continuing their physical connection as he led her to the sofa.

Even after they sat, he kept her hand enclosed in his because things just worked better when they touched.

"I was afraid."

He took note of the honesty shining in her eyes, but remained quiet. This was her moment, and he needed to step back and let her have it.

"Things were fun, and even though there were a few moments where I questioned the wisdom of us hooking up, it felt right. It felt like we were headed in the right direction."

He agreed. Things felt right when they connected.

"But your little slip of the tongue at the dinner with Ezra sent you careening into a dark place that has made it easier for you to hide yourself from me than talk things out."

Her eyes widened with surprise. "I notice everything about you, Keely."

She seemed to take his admission in stride. But he knew from the way she sat stiff next to him that she somehow struggled with this idea.

"Jacob, this thing between us… It started with this explosion of friendship and sexiness that I thought would keep things light and fun. I… I…"

She shook her head, looking up to the ceiling as she searched for more words, he assumed. The only time he'd ever seen her so flummoxed was at the end of their dinner with Ezra.

"Keely, you deal with highfalutin celebrities on a regular basis. I'm assuming some of them are demanding as hell and you still manage to get through it. Why is talking to me so hard?"

"Because this matters," she softly replied before bringing her eyes back to his. "Because you matter in a way no one else has ever mattered before, and that scares me."

She turned to him, squeezing his hand as if it was an anchor she was checking to make sure it was still there, holding her steady.

She needn't have worried. Nothing and no one could've dragged him away from her at this moment. Not when his heart was beating so fast in his chest he could hear its loud thumping in his ears.

"I have given everything to get where I am in my career, Jacob. My family still doesn't believe I have a real job. They're constantly questioning whether I can support myself, whether I'm thinking clearly enough about the future. And for the first time since I started Low-Kee Designs, I couldn't focus entirely on work."

She dropped her gaze from his and took in a long, slow breath before gradually releasing it through pursed lips.

"No, that's a lie," she continued as she lifted her gaze to his, revealing keen clarity. "It wasn't that I couldn't focus on work. It was that I didn't want to. I wanted to focus on what was happening between us. But before I realized it, I was allowing you to become more important than my career, making you my priority instead of my meetings, or the time I needed to increase my productivity."

Jacob could see the anguish slipping into the creased lines of Keely's brow. He extended his hand, running a gentle finger along her forehead, trying to smooth away those lines. He wanted to comfort her, but there was part of him that wanted to shake her too.

"I never asked to be more important than your work, Keely. As much as I want to fix things between us, I can't accept that blame. We had a deal. We wouldn't allow our connection to impact work."

She nodded, but even in her outward acceptance of his recounting of the preceding events, there was still something heavy and sad lingering in her eyes.

"We did make that agreement, and you're right, you didn't ask anything of me. But I think that's part of why I was so preoccupied. I wanted you to ask that of me. And when I realized you hadn't, I started trying my level best to backtrack, to dive into work, but it didn't help. You were making billion-dollar horse deals and I could barely do a simple catch stitch."

"Well, now." His voice was tinged with a bit of amusement. "It wasn't exactly a billion." Her eyes turned into narrowed slits, further adding to his amusement and making him chuckle aloud. She was too damn cute, even when she was working through this quasi-existential crisis.

"I'm sorry," he continued. "I get what you mean. But the truth is, I was just as distracted. It was one of the reasons I wanted you at the dinner with Ezra. I knew I couldn't afford to be distracted by thoughts of you, so

I figured if you were there, it would be less likely I'd drift off thinking about you when I was supposed to be entertaining Ezra."

She huffed, throwing her head back, and he could see some of the heaviness she was carrying press down harder on her.

He ached to make it better for her and for him. They both deserved it.

"Keely, it wasn't for lack of wanting that I didn't ask for more. Believe me when I say I wanted more. I was just afraid I'd push too hard and you'd run off. I made a promise that I wouldn't get in the way of your work. I didn't want to make you feel bad about doing a job you loved like women in my past did me."

A soft smile bloomed on her lips, instantly brightening the room while pushing away the dark cloud of worry that had marred her beautiful features.

"You want more with me?" She tightened her grip on his hand as she waited for an answer.

"Hell yeah, I do."

"But what about the distance between us? At best, it will take us four hours by plane to see each other. Are you really up for that?"

She wasn't wrong. Long-distance relationships weren't easy. Fortunately, Jacob wasn't known for doing things the easy way.

"I am."

Her eyes scanned his face, up and down, looking for any sign he wasn't being forthright. She wouldn't find any. He'd meant everything he'd said.

"Why?" She paused, looking into his eyes, her gaze cutting through flesh and bone until she was staring at the very core of him. "Why go through all this trouble for a woman you met three weeks ago who pretty much barged in and took over your house?"

He moved in closer, cupping her cheek and positioning his mouth so close to hers, all either of them had to do to connect was shift the slightest inch farther.

She licked her plump lips and he damn near gave in to the fire beginning to burn. But this was too important. He couldn't give in to the inferno that blazed so brightly between them, not when there was so much hanging on his next words.

"Because I love her…you, because I love you."

She was still. No, more like frozen. The soft intake of breath was the only sign that she'd heard him. His heart rate ticked up as he wondered if he'd gone too far too fast. But as the sound of his words trickled down around him, he realized he could never regret them. No matter how Keely reacted or whether or not she chose to have him, he needed her to know that he loved her, and probably always would.

"If you don't—"

The chance to complete his sentence never arrived because Keely had launched herself at him, taking them both down so that they lay across the cushions of the sofa. He had enough time to take in a quick breath before her lips were touching his, pressing urgently, marking her ownership of him.

And she owned him, of that he had no doubt. This glorious woman with her blunt words, her relentless determination and her amazing flair had swooped into his life, blowing away all the excuses he'd used to keep his heart protected. And he couldn't be happier about that.

"I love you too, Jacob." She shook her head, her shoulders shaking with brief laughter. "I've spent so much of my life designing every single detail of my work plan, that I hadn't considered I needed one for my life. You were an unexpected event, Jacob. One I will forever be grateful for."

"Good, because I feel the same."

He tightened his hold on her, loving the feel of her body on his. It was arousing as all hell, as was evidenced by his halfway-hard cock. But it was so much more than that.

Plain and simple, it was also comfort, making Jacob realize his mistake in his view of love prior to one Keely Tucker showing up uninvited into his life. He'd seen love as a hindrance, something that would detract from his dreams. There was no way he could've known that loving Keely would be the culmination of all his dreams coming true.

* * * * *

AFTER THE LIGHTS GO DOWN

DONNA HILL

Mom, I miss you every day.

One

"This is Paul Waverly for WNCC's *News at Ten*. Stay safe out there. Good night." He flashed his signature smile and the network went to commercial.

Layne sighed deeply from her cushy spot on the plush living room couch, pointed the remote at the television and turned it off. She lifted the glass of white wine to her lips and took a short sip. Pitch-perfect as always. But she would expect nothing less than perfection from Paul. He was the consummate professional. Audiences loved him. His rich brown handsomeness graced the covers of magazines across the country. His face lit up the screen every night at ten. He could go anywhere he chose in the television business. Rumor had it that he'd been courted by both ABC and NBC networks in New York, as well as cable news stations, and had turned them all down, touting that his roots were in North Carolina, not to mention that WNCC countered every offer. So, he stayed. As a result, WNCC bent over backward to give Paul Waverly whatever he wanted, including his penthouse in downtown Charlotte, an expense account and a six-figure salary.

She rose from the couch and headed to the bathroom for a hot shower. She had an early call in the morning and it was already near midnight.

After soothing her skin with her favorite body oil, she slipped into a pale peach satin gown that shimmered and reflected the light when she moved. She went back to the living room to refill her wineglass and returned to bed, just as the key clicked in the door.

Her pulse skipped the way it always did. Part of the excitement was the secrecy, and the rest was the sheer thrill.

"Hey, baby."

She set down her glass of wine on the nightstand, got up and crossed to the threshold of their bedroom. She reached up and stroked the hard line of his jaw that exhibited the slightest bit of stubble.

"You were fabulous as usual," she cooed and lifted up to kiss his lips. She clasped the lapels of his navy suit jacket, the one he'd had custom-made on a trip to Italy. His striped tie was loose, the top button of his snow-white shirt undone.

He slid his arm around her waist and pulled her close against him. "I bet you say that to all the boys," he said against her mouth before filling himself with her lips.

Paul thrilled her in places and ways that no man had ever been able to do. She moaned softly as his hands glided across the smooth satin of her gown and slid down the tiny straps, while she worked the buttons of his shirt, unfastened his belt and loosened his zipper.

Falling in love with Paul had kept her in North Carolina longer than she'd ever intended. She'd had a plan when she graduated at the top of her class from Columbia University's School of Journalism with a minor in political science. She would spend a year at a small station, build her portfolio, gain experience and then head to Washington, DC, and *The DC Morning Show*. It had been her goal since she was a teen and had watched in starstruck awe as Cynthia Medley, the first Black female anchor, stared into the camera and delivered the breaking political news of the day, interviewed some of the most prominent faces in government, and did it all with an ease and style that flowed from her with every breath she took. Her face had graced billboards and the sides of buses for more than a decade. There had been no other woman to compare with her then or since.

Layne believed from the bottom of her soul that *she* would be that new face of broadcasting.

Then she'd met Paul, the charismatic, ridiculously sexy anchor for WNCC News, crowned Charlotte's most eligible bachelor.

It had been July, her second week at the station. She'd been in the control room, gathering up all the notes from the day, and readying the room for the next shift, when Paul walked in. They'd eyed each other in the corridors, exchanged basic pleasantries and cordial smiles, but they'd never been alone in a semi-darkened room until then.

"I've been meaning to properly introduce myself," he'd said. The brandy-smooth voice that enthralled millions now filled the space between them. Her skin had tingled as she felt the thump of her pulse in her throat. Heat flushed the shell of her ears.

He'd stepped closer and slid his hands into the pockets of his slacks, and she would have sworn that had he not, he would have stroked her bare arm.

"Paul Waverly," he'd said instead of touching her.

She was mildly disappointed that he didn't touch her and even more appalled at herself for entertaining the idea.

She'd smiled. "Layne Davis."

He'd nodded as his to-kill-for lashes slightly lowered over dark brown eyes. "I know."

She'd blinked rapidly, tilted her head to the side. "You know?"

"I try to make it my business to know who's on the team."

"Oh." She cleared her throat. "Well, it's an honor to meet you—officially."

"I've actually asked around."

She frowned in question. "Asked around?"

"To find out who you were. What you were about."

"And?"

"Let's just say I like what I've heard. But… I've never been one to take someone else's word. I like to find out things on my own—professionally and personally."

Her throat had gone dry. She was so hot she was sure she would pass out.

"I was hoping that maybe I could take you to lunch and you could tell me all about big bad New York City." He smiled that smile, and he could have asked her to walk out into traffic with her eyes closed.

Their attraction was explosive, and before she knew it, her two-year plan had turned into a four-year stint in Charlotte, North Carolina, as she worked her way through the production department until she was offered to pinch-hit minor stand-up spots covering soft local news whenever the need arose. Her hunger for an anchor spot had lessened, but it was still willing to feast if the opportunity presented itself. When it did, she would be ready.

"All I could think about was coming home to you," he was saying now, his voice raw and hungry. He lifted her in his arms as if she was a newlywed virgin, and carried her to the bed they'd shared for the past year.

Sometimes she thought that maybe he'd sprinkled some juju in her glass of wine during their first lunch together. What else could explain the mind-altering lovemaking that left her crying out for the holy trinity, shuddering and whimpering in total submission to the power he had over her body? Like now.

Like the way he wound his hips—in homage to his Caribbean roots—when he was deep inside her, and hit and teased *the* spot, pushing her to the edge only to bring her back over and again. Shots of electricity zipped through her. She trembled. Wept. Held on.

Paul slid his hands beneath her ample rear. With a firm hold he took control of her movements as he rotated her hips against the increasing pace of his deep thrusts.

"Ohhh." She pressed her fingers into his back.

"Open for me," he whispered.

A shudder raced up her spine. She knew what was coming. Lust whipped through her.

Paul raised her thighs onto his shoulders and extended them into a wide, perfect V. He drew up on his knees. She was completely at his mercy and he at hers.

"Look at me," she urged.

Paul dipped his head to look into her eyes.

"Say it," she demanded and squeezed the muscles of her slick insides.

Paul groaned, thrust deep and hard. That was his first answer. Always.

"Yessss," Layne cried out. "Now say it," she urged and gripped him inside her again, then once more and again.

"Ahhhh!" His voice was ragged. The veins in his neck were like ropes.

She cupped her breasts that overflowed her palms and lifted them to him. "Here. Taste."

Her pink-painted toes were now reaching back toward the leather headboard as Paul continued to stroke, leaned forward and suckled and laved and suckled her offering until he was crazy drunk with her.

Tears of rapture slid from the corners of her eyes and down her cheeks. The flutters began on the soles of her feet that pointed toward the sky, down the backs of her thighs, shook her rear, coursed along her spine, shot out to her limbs and pooled in a blast of white lightning in the pit of her stomach. Whatever control she thought she had was gone. Her body became one electric charge. Her insides gasped, shuddered, gripped and released and gripped Paul's erection like a velvety wet vise.

"Say it," she cried out as pleasure roared through her.

"Ahhhhh! I love you. Oh, God. Ohhh." His back arched. Her fingers cupped him and gently squeezed. "Yesss!" He exploded, shot and exploded into her as her body conquered and captured the essence of him.

"I l-love you, too," she stammered between heaving breaths.

Spent, he collapsed on top of her. She slowly lowered her legs, locked her ankles across his thighs to keep him nestled inside her a while longer. She stroked the soft waves of his dark hair that had curled into tiny damp spirals. "I love you, too," she softly repeated.

By degrees Paul slipped out of her and rolled onto his side. He draped a protective arm across her stomach. He kissed the corner of her damp neck right above her collarbone. Just the way she loved it.

Her lids fluttered. She drew in a long, deep breath.

She had a good life. Maybe not the exact one that she'd dreamed, but she was…almost fulfilled…most of the time. She had a solid job that she enjoyed. She had friends and a man that loved her and wanted the best for her. What more could she ask for? And when the time was right, they would let everyone know that they were a couple.

She closed her eyes and began to drift off to the steady rhythm of Paul's heartbeat against her. What more could she want was the last thought that floated through her head before a satiated sleep overtook her.

Their opposite work schedules were a definite plus in keeping any rumors or suspicions about their relationship under wraps. While she spent most nights in Paul's penthouse apartment, she still maintained her one-bedroom condo for appearances. Besides, since she had to be in the studio by ten in the morning and Paul didn't need to arrive until at least three in the afternoon to prep for his ten o'clock spot, no one had connected any dots that led to them, as far as the couple knew.

"See you tonight, babe," Paul whispered, planting a soft kiss on the back of her neck.

A shimmer ran up her spine. Her lids fluttered. "Try to stay out of trouble until I see you later."

"You wound me," he teased and turned her around to face him. He gazed down into her eyes. "We won't keep us a secret much longer," he said softly. He ran a finger along her cheek. "Promise."

Layne drew in a breath and offered a tight-lipped smile. "When the time is right, the time will be right," she replied even as she wished things were different—now.

She grabbed her tote with her laptop and shoulder bag from the kitchen island counter. She gave him a quick kiss. "Later."

Layne smoothly eased her steel gray Audi—a present to herself on her thirtieth birthday—into the flow of downtown traffic. Paul wanted to buy it for her, but she'd insisted it was something she wanted to do for herself. Not to be deterred, he'd bought her a diamond bracelet and taken her away for a romantic weekend in Vail, where they were waited on hand and foot and she'd even learned to ski—a little. As much as she loved Paul, there was still something missing—not in their relationship but in her life. She was satisfied, but what she wanted was to be fulfilled, and the longer she stayed in Charlotte, the farther away her dream became.

She pulled into the underground parking lot on North Tryon in the building that the station was housed in, next to the Bank of America tower. Gathering her things, she steeled herself for another hectic, nonstop day.

If there was one thing she had to admit, it was that no day at WNCC was ever the same. There was always a constant flow of energy, and of course with the entire globe in some form of chaos from one day to the next, news was never lacking.

She rode the elevator to the tenth floor and exited onto the long, beige carpeted corridor, the walls lined with the publicity photos of the "stars" of WNCC, and the numerous renowned guests that had been in the studio over the years. Her step slowed for a moment as she came upon Paul's photo. Inwardly, she smiled. One day her face would stare out from the walls. But it wouldn't be here. That much she was pretty certain of. Her destiny was in front of her. All she had to do was figure out how to get there.

"Good morning. Good morning," she greeted as she passed the array of staff that darted up and down the corridors. She waved at her colleagues that sat in their glass offices, stopped to snatch up a bagel and a cup of freshly brewed coffee from the commissary table and continued to her office at the near end of the long hallway.

She slid her ID card along the slot and her door popped open. Within moments she'd powered up her computer, was settled behind her small and cluttered desk, stacked with folders and her to-do list on a yellow legal pad, and was sipping her cup of coffee.

Part of her responsibility, along with her intermittent reporting duties, was to schedule and confirm all guests, which often entailed cooing at and coddling handlers, whose main goal in life seemed to be to make hers just a bit more difficult. Their requests for their bosses ranged from things as benign as spring water with lemon to fully stocked limos. It was one good thing about working at a smaller station—you were able to get your feet wet in multiple areas if you showed the potential.

She dragged in a breath and reached for her desk phone just as her cell phone chirped and stopped her midway.

Layne smiled when the familiar name lit the screen.

"Hey, girl," she greeted.

"I hope you're sitting down," Tina Gerard began. Tina had opted to head straight to DC to work for the

Washington Post after they'd both graduated from Columbia's School of Journalism. With the exorbitant cost of New York living, they'd become roommates and the best of friends. Tina had tried unsuccessfully to convince Layne to come with her to the capital, but Layne had a plan, and not even Tina's pleading and faux threats of disowning her as her bestie could change Layne's mind.

"I have about ten minutes before someone will want something," she half joked.

"You need to pack your bags, your audition tapes, your bio and get your ass on a plane, train or automobile to DC."

Layne sat straight up in her leather chair. "Say what?"

"You remember my Uncle Ernest?"

"Yes, yes, of course. Talk faster, girl," she urged, excitement flooding her voice.

"Okay, okay. Anyway, he's a board member emeritus at WWDC. You know, the freaking *Morning Show*, girl! Anyway, he still has friends there."

Layne's pulse pounded in her temples. "Tina, I swear if you don't—"

"I got you an interview! Well, my uncle arranged it, since I'm his favorite niece in the world."

The air hung for a moment in Layne's lungs, then suddenly released in a gush. "Oh. My. God. Are you serious?"

"I wouldn't play with you like that." Tina paused dramatically. "And there's more."

Layne's thoughts raced. "More?"

"The interview is only a formality. If you want the job of assistant producer…it's pretty much yours."

Layne blinked so hard and fast she could have set off the butterfly effect. "Tina...no freaking way."

"Yes, girl," Tina squealed.

Layne's eyes fluttered closed. "Oh my god. I... This is what I've been waiting for."

"Exactly. Now all you need to do is pull your stuff together, tell them folks at WNCC adios and you're at your dream station. From there it will only be a matter of time before you get that anchor spot. I just know it, girl."

"Dreams do come true," she murmured.

"You need to get here by next week. The executive producer, Deanna Mitchell, wants to meet you, give her stamp of approval before anything is finalized."

Layne's heart thumped. "Do you know her?"

"No. I hear she can be a hard-ass, but she knows her stuff. *The DC Morning Show* is number two in ratings because of her. You'd be working directly under her. That's why you need to charm her out of her Red Bottoms."

Layne's brows rose. "Hmm, fancy."

"Very. I also hear she's a clothes horse. All the latest designer everything, and doesn't take kindly to her team looking like they just got off the bus."

Her mind raced through her wardrobe. Inwardly, she cringed. "Okay. I'll make it work."

"You betta. And of course you'll stay with me. It'll be like old times!"

Layne giggled. They'd definitely put their mark on the streets of New York, club-hopping and attending film premieres, art shows, plays and restaurants galore.

"So make your arrangements and let me know what day you'll be here. I'm going to text you Deanna Mitchell's email so that you can connect."

"Oh, Tina. I can't thank you enough."

"I got you. Always. But we will definitely have to do something über-nice for Uncle Ernest."

"For sure!"

A light knock on her door halted the conversation.

"Yes," Layne called out.

Marlo, one of the other assistants, stuck her head in. "Needed up front," she said, almost apologetically.

"Thanks. Be right there."

She returned to her call. "Listen, I have to go. I'll call you tonight. And… Tina…love you, girl."

"Right back atcha. And congrats."

Layne disconnected the call, closed her eyes, sat back for a moment and bathed in a moment of pure, unadulterated joy. Then her moment of euphoria burst. Her eyes flew open.

What about her and Paul?

Paul slid behind the wheel of his white Tesla. At the press of a button, the electronic dash housed on an iPad-like panel lit up. The engineless machine glided soundlessly into traffic, catching the admiring gazes of passersby.

For the most part, he didn't go for flash. Too much of his life was already on blast every night across the state. The Tesla was all part of the persona that the network wanted him to maintain. And of course giving a nod to Elon Musk didn't hurt. However, what he projected on the screen was a far cry from the man he really was, or at least believed himself to be. Of course he had ambition and he enjoyed the fame and the perks of the job, but if he had his way, he'd spend his days writing the political thriller that had been running around in his head for the past couple of years. He'd travel more, maybe get a house on the beach, and he'd marry Layne. His lips flickered with a smile.

Growing up the way he had, witnessing the love between his parents and the love they showered on him and his brother he hoped to have the same one day. But the demands of his career had put hearth and home on the back burner. He had time only for the briefest of relationships. Most women that interested him couldn't handle the demands of his job and his often ridiculous hours, and as a result they lasted a month or maybe two, which had only earned him the monikers of "Charlotte's most eligible bachelor" and "ladies' man."

What he wanted was what his parents had, and he'd never thought it was in the cards for him until he met Layne. It was that kind of crazy-at-first-sight thing. Not love, but definitely I-want-to-get-to-know-you-like-right-now vibe. The downside to that instant attraction was staying under the radar at the station. It took more work to keep it a secret than to maintain it.

He made a right turn onto Aberdeen Avenue, pushed out a breath of anticipation. All that was about to change.

He'd taken his cue from Joe Scarborough and Mika Brzezinski of MSNBC, the hosts of *Morning Joe*. They were an on-screen team for years, had finally tied the knot and remained as tight as ever. They made it work. He and Layne would as well.

Everything was set. He pulled into the parking lot of his local gym, grabbed his gym bag and got out. While he walked across the lot to the entrance, he tapped in Layne's number. She picked up on the third ring, sounded rushed and harried as she usually did while at work.

"Hey, baby," he said. "I know you're busy. I made

dinner plans for us tonight. It's been a minute since we've had a night out." The truth was they couldn't risk being seen in a candlelit restaurant or any other intimate setting as long as things remained as they were between them at work. When they did go out together it was generally on trips out of town, out of the limelight. Tonight would be different.

"Really?" she said, her voice rising in delighted surprise, mixed with apprehension.

"Yes, really. Great food, wine, maybe some dancing."

She giggled. "What brought all this on? We usually have to plan our getaways like secret agents," she half joked.

"It's Saturday, I'm off and I want to spend the night out with my woman," he crooned.

She pushed out a breath. "Fine by me. I get off at six. And… I have some news to share…over a bottle of wine."

"Can't wait. I'll see you at home. Reservations are for eight."

"I love you, Paul," she whispered.

"Love you right back." He disconnected the call and pulled open the heavy glass doors to the gym. A good workout would definitely unravel the ropes of nerves that wrapped around his insides.

Layne pressed her phone to her chest and tugged on her bottom lip with her teeth. Timing was everything, she mused as she walked toward the control room. Being out together in a great restaurant would provide the perfect atmosphere to spring her news on Paul.

Since she'd spoken with Tina, her head had been swimming, first in pure ecstasy and then in flashes of dread. As promised, Tina had sent over Deanna's contact information and Layne was scheduled to meet with the executive producer next Wednesday. *The DC Morning Show* was arranging her flight and accommodations. Everything was moving at lightning speed, after having stalled for years. What would it mean for her and Paul? How could they make it work? Long-distance relationships were difficult under the best of circumstances, but couple that with demanding jobs and unreasonable hours…and she didn't want to think about that now. She pulled open the door to the control room. The blue-green lights from consoles and computer screens always gave the control room an ethereal feeling.

She crossed the industrial-gray carpeted floor, inching behind the thick leather seats occupied by the directors and producers of *Live with Tess*, the third-best afternoon cooking show on network television. Tess Hampton was no Rachael Ray, but she had a strong following and her audience share was growing.

"Mike." She leaned down and whispered in the assistant director's ear. "Feed these to Tess during commercial." She placed three large index cards next to his keyboard.

Mike glanced up and gave a short nod. "We'll get them on the teleprompter. Another Harold Morgan request, I presume," he snarked with a half grin.

Harold Morgan was the station president, and he frequently inserted himself into the show with last-minute one-liners praising some celebrity or politician that he'd discovered liked a particular dish or fine wine. He'd brought on Tess two years earlier, and rumor had it that he was more than her mentor, which didn't make life easy for Tess. No matter how hard she worked, or how good she actually was, there was always the presumption that Harold had a hand in it. All the more reason why she and Paul had religiously kept their relationship under wraps.

"I'm only the messenger," she said, giving his meaty shoulder a light squeeze.

She walked back toward her office, but was stopped in the corridor by Linda Kreps, the producer for *Midday Charlotte*.

"Just who I was looking for. I was heading to your office," Linda said. Linda Kreps was like the dictionary picture of the harried, intense television producer. She was barely five foot five, with choppy blond hair that always looked like she'd been in a fight, and sky blue eyes that were magnified behind her glasses. She never wore makeup, and it was rumored that her closet only had one outfit: khaki slacks and safari shirts. On the opposite end, her partner could easily be a runway model. Guess there was someone for everyone.

"What's up?" Layne asked as they continued side by side down the hallway.

"The Carolina Arts Foundation Gala is happening tomorrow night, and I want you to cover it."

Did she look as shocked as she felt? "Really?"

"Yes, really. I think it will be the perfect opportunity for you to rub elbows with the right people and put you front and center with the honchos here at the station."

"Wow. Um. Thank you." She swallowed. Why now? Just when her shot in Washington was at her fingertips, a new door at WNCC was opening. Those events were peppered with philanthropists, artists, entertainment celebrities and politicians. Landing interviews with just the right person…

"Problem?"

Layne blinked. "No. Not at all. Just trying to figure out what to wear." She smiled brightly.

Linda gave Layne's arm a light squeeze. "Good. Stop by my office before you leave and my assistant will give you all the information and your press pass. Ron is slated as the cameraman." They stopped in front of Layne's office door. "Oh, and you get a plus-one. I'm sure you have someone tucked away." She winked and hurried away in the opposite direction.

For several moments Layne stood stock-still in front of her closed office door. She drew in a breath and slowly released it. This day had been full of surprises. What next?

Two

While they dressed they fussed over their outfits, and argued about who took the longest in the shower. Layne applied the finishing touch to her makeup, cheerily followed Paul down to the underground parking and slid into the comfort of his midnight blue Lexus, which he'd decided was less conspicuous than the Tesla if they wanted to keep a relative low profile.

As they'd prepared for their first evening out in much too long, they'd promised each other that they would hold on to their good news until dessert.

Layne had to admit she was more nervous than excited at this point. During the ride to the restaurant she stole furtive glances at Paul's handsome profile. Even seated, his six-foot-two frame cut an imposing figure: The charcoal gray of his suit jacket spread firmly across broad shoulders, the platinum watch sparkled at his left wrist, and the dove gray silk shirt open at the collar projected the picture of a man who understood classy and cool. She loved him. There was no doubt about that, but as she considered the reality of what her future held, uncertainty about the stability of their relationship pooled in her soul.

Paul always touted that his roots, his career, his tight-knit family, friends and Layne were in Charlotte and he had no intention of changing that. So much so that she'd ceased talking about her dream to sit in the anchor's chair in DC. For Paul, travel for work and extended vacations were one thing, but relocating was not in his deck of cards, at least not any time in the foreseeable future.

Layne laced her fingers tightly together. Could they make long-distance work?

Paul was chewing on his bottom lip as he held the steering wheel in a death grip. Sure signs that he had something heavy on his mind. Layne couldn't begin to imagine what it was, but Paul had given no indication that what he wanted to talk with her about was something awful. If anything, he seemed super excited, at least until they'd gotten in the car. When the car doors shut behind them the tension grew in waves. He was uncharacteristically nervous. A feeling she'd never connect to Paul Waverly.

"Everything okay?" she asked. She placed a hand on his thigh.

He gave her a brief look and a tight smile. "Absolutely. Why?"

"It looks like you want to cut the oxygen off the steering wheel," she said with a hint of laughter in her voice.

Paul chuckled. "No, I'm good. Just looking forward to us being out tonight—as a couple." He glanced at her again, took her hand from his thigh, brought it to his lips and placed a soft kiss on her knuckles.

Layne settled back against the plush leather of her seat. She pulled in a slow, meditative breath. *Everything will be fine*, she silently chanted. *Everything will be fine.*

When they stopped in front of the elegant, smoked-glass doors, Layne's step faltered as she actually noticed the restaurant's name etched in gold letters on the one-way windows. Guests could see out, but those on the street could not see inside. Pierre's, one of the city's exclusive French restaurants. There were times when reservations for dinner had to be made a month ahead. Clearly, Paul had planned this well in advance. Her heart thumped. *Could it be?*

The doorman dressed in all black with gold buttons on his jacket opened the door. "Welcome to Pierre's. Enjoy your evening."

"Thank you," Paul said with a short nod. He stood to the side to let Layne enter first.

The cool, dimly lit confines of Pierre's screamed elegance, from the circular tables covered in fine white linen, centerpieces of candles and lilies set in glass bowls, the gleam of silver, the hush of footsteps atop a thick red carpet, to the grand chandeliers that gave off just the right amount of illumination. Layne fought to keep her mouth from dropping open and gawking like a tourist.

Paul kept his hand at the small of her back, guiding her to the hostess's podium.

"Good evening. Welcome to Pierre's. Your table is ready, Mr. Waverly," the hostess said in an accent that was a practiced mixture of something foreign and right-around-the-corner native. Layne inwardly smiled. Mastering a universal vocal effect was part of the skill set in on-air journalism. The notion that in order to fit in one must look, behave, sound and dress the part could be exhausting. She'd love to be a fly on the wall when the young hostess was simply hanging out with her girlfriends.

The young hostess lifted her slim hand and a waiter appeared. "Table 11, Arnold." She handed him two menus and the wine and liqueur list, before he led them away.

As they were being ushered to what turned out to be a private banquette, Layne was mildly relieved that they did not cross paths with anyone they knew. But the hostess had addressed Paul by name without him saying a word, which was indication enough that they could be easily recognized. However, she was moderately soothed by the belief that anyone able to get a seat at Pierre's would be above spreading gossip. But then again…

The banquette was positioned so that the six-foot-high horseshoe-shaped leather partition faced the interior of the restaurant, with the seating tucked behind it overlooking the street. The setup gave the couple a high degree of privacy from other guests, while offering them the entertainment of life passing by on the streets of Charlotte from their coveted spot behind the one-way glass window.

Arnold placed the menus on the linen-topped table, then tucked his hands behind his back as the couple settled in their seats.

"My name is Arnold Stevens. I will be your personal waiter for the evening."

A young woman appeared by Arnold's side. "This is Michelle. She will take your drink and appetizer orders.

I will return shortly to go over the entrées." He gave a single-lined smile and whirled away.

Layne kind of wanted to laugh. This was all so shi shi foo foo. She felt as if she'd been transported to an episode of *The Gilded Age* for the twenty-first century. But it was still so cool.

"Whatever you want," Paul said as he scanned the drink menu.

She smiled at Michelle. "Let's start with a bottle of Terlato."

Paul's right brow lifted in agreement. "A pinot grigio. One of the best. I've been waiting to try it."

Michelle nodded. "I can get your wine now while you decide on an appetizer, if you wish."

"That would be fine. Thank you," Paul said.

Once Michelle was gone, Paul took a deep breath, leaned forward and covered Layne's hands with his. "So, what do you think?" he asked with a glimmer of mischief in his eyes.

Layne tilted her head to the side. "I think that if you wanted to impress me, you have," she said with a delighted smile.

Paul ran his tongue along his bottom lip. "Did I tell you how absolutely stunning you look tonight?" he whispered, sounding almost awed.

Layne flushed from head to toe. When Paul looked at her like that, with a combination of love and raw hunger, her insides lit up like fireworks. She'd wanted to look extra special tonight and had taken meticulous care in choosing just the right dress and accessories. Her sleeveless, deep royal blue satin cocktail dress with its double-layered, elegantly flared skirting flowed like a halo above her knees. The boatneck with its V cut added an extra bit of dramatic detail. Her right wrist sparkled with the diamond bracelet Paul had given her, which she'd paired with tiny diamond studs in her ears.

Layne shielded her eyes with a lowering of her lashes. "No," she said softly, "but do feel free." She glanced up, locked eyes with him and smiled with invitation.

Michelle returned with the bottle of wine, opened it and poured the delectable liquid into each glass. She glanced from one to the other. "Hors d'oeuvre?"

Paul looked to Layne.

"I'd love to try the Gougeres," Layne said.

"And, um, a plate of salmon rillettes. That comes with the miniature toast, yes?" Paul asked.

Michelle smiled. "Yes, it does. I'll put your orders in. Arnold will be around to take your dinner order." She whisked away.

Paul held up his glass. Layne raised hers. "To us. To our night. To our future."

Layne swallowed. She tapped her glass against his. "To us," she whispered before taking a sip of her wine. If Paul's plan was what she was beginning to believe it was, she wasn't sure how the evening would turn out.

She played a variety of scenarios in her mind as they went through the appetizers and mouthwatering entrée, and now the dessert had arrived.

Layne's heart had slowly begun to beat harder and faster as the evening progressed. She laughed at all of Paul's corny jokes, listened intently to his analysis of the current war overseas and the politics surrounding it, and his longing to make time to write his book.

"One of these days," he said on a sigh. He cleared his throat. "I, uh, know we promised to wait to share our news until after dessert." His gaze jumped from Layne's face to the table and back again. "I know I'm not the most romantic guy you could be dealing with and I know all this secrecy has been hard on you. But I want you to know—" his smooth baritone hitched "—that I love you. I want to spend the rest of my life with you."

Layne could barely breathe. Her pulse pounded and she swore her vision clouded over. When she looked down at the table, Paul had a tiny red velvet box sitting open on his palm, displaying a ring with a stunning sapphire surrounded by sparkling diamonds on a platinum band.

The air stuck in her chest. She covered her gasp with her palm.

"Marry me, Layne. Let's do this thing…together." He reached for her hand without waiting for an answer and slid the ring onto her finger.

Tears filled her eyes. "Paul." Her voice cracked.

"I hope those are happy tears, babe."

She sniffed, studied the brilliant stones on her finger that picked up the chandelier light and set off tiny rainbows around her hand. She blinked and blinked to stem the water building in her eyes. "Yes," she finally managed. Her head swam.

"I think we can probably make an announcement at least to HR this week."

Layne cleared her throat. "That makes sense." She nodded as she spoke. "Then we can take it from there with the staff."

Paul took both her hands and brought them to his lips. "I love you," he whispered. "We're going to be the happiest couple on the planet and I can't wait to start our life together." He kissed her hands, stared into her eyes. "Now, what is your big news?"

She swallowed the knot that was building in her

throat. Her stomach fluttered. "Well," she said on a breath, "I have two things to tell you."

"Hold that thought." He signaled for Arnold, who arrived with the speed of a ninja.

"Yes, Mr. Waverly."

"My...*fiancée* and I are celebrating." He threw Layne a smoldering look. "Can we get a bottle of your best champagne?"

"Right away."

"Happy?" Paul whispered, leaning toward Layne and brushing his thumb across the stones on her left hand.

"Very," she said, her voice slightly tremulous. "A little overwhelmed, but happy."

"You've dealt with the constraints of our relationship from the beginning, without complaint."

"Well...sometimes," she said with a smile.

"True." He chuckled, then his expression and tone grew serious. "All of that is going to change. You can finally give up your condo and move in with me." His dark brown eyes moved across her face.

Her right brow hitched. "Give up my condo?" Even though she spent most nights at Paul's penthouse, the condo was hers, bought with her own money, decorated and furnished by her. When she walked through its doors there was a sense and level of satisfaction that she didn't feel at Paul's place.

"Of course. We'll live at the penthouse until we get a house of our own. Why would you keep the condo?"

"Because it's *mine*," she said with a bit more bite than she intended.

The waiter returned with the bottle of champagne, uncorked it with a flourish and filled two new flutes. He shoved the opened bottle into a bucket of ice. "Enjoy." He hurried away.

Paul gave a nod, then reached for his glass. "Tonight is a night for surprises and celebrations. And I want to hear your news," he said, seeming to have dismissed what she'd said.

She blinked slowly before lifting her glass as well. "Yes, it is." She tapped her glass with his and took a sip. The faint bubbles tickled her nose. She pushed aside the tense moment. *Not tonight.* "Actually, I have two pieces of news."

Paul beamed. "Let's hear it." He took a sip of champagne.

"Well," she began on a breath, "Linda Kreps came to me today and said they want me to cover the Carolina Arts Foundation Gala tomorrow night!" She almost squealed out the words but remembered where she was.

Paul's eyes widened. "What? Baby, that is major. The elbows that you will rub." His grin lit up the space around them. "Proud of you. Well deserved."

"Thank you. *And*… I get a plus-one," she said with a wink.

He tipped his head to the side, left brow arched. "Hmm, and who are you planning on taking to this shindig?"

"Well," she said on a whisper and leaned in. "There is this incredibly handsome, intelligent, funny, wildly sexy guy who makes my toes curl when he makes love to me…" She ran the tip of her tongue across her bottom lip. "I was thinking of asking him to come," she said seductively. She watched his throat bob.

"This wildly sexy, handsome, intelligent guy got a name?"

She leaned in further and beckoned him closer with a crook of her finger. She whispered deep into his ear before easing back into her seat.

Paul's jaw flexed. His hot gaze never left Layne's face as he lifted his arm to signal for the waiter and the check.

"To hell with dessert," he murmured.

Her other news could wait until morning, she decided, as she curled her body next to his while they waited for his car to be brought around. She glanced down at the twinkling ring on her finger. Her heart thumped. She hugged Paul tighter. It was what she'd wanted, what Paul had promised. She could bring up DC later. For reasons that she couldn't quite name, the thought of telling Paul about it had her nerves on edge.

On Sunday mornings they'd fallen into the cozy habit of sleeping late, reading the papers in bed and ordering a lavish breakfast from their favorite Spanish restaurant, followed by slow, easy lovemaking and an old movie.

Layne rested her head on Paul's chest. The steady beat of his heart always soothed her. Its rhythm synced with her own and there was a unique harmony that they created.

She studied the ring on her finger, still a bit dazzled by the idea that this was real. She was engaged to the man she loved. He'd done everything he'd promised. He wanted to build a life for the two of them. Maybe giving up her condo wasn't so bad. Her pulse quickened. If she got the job, which Tina assured her was in the bag, she'd have to give it up anyway. She tugged on her bottom lip with her teeth. Her stomach knotted.

"You okay?" He angled his head to try to look down at her.

"Sure. Why?"

"Hmm." He turned the paper to the next page. "Your body just got all tense or something for a minute."

"No, I'm fine," she said. She shut her eyes. It was true—at times she and Paul could read each other's bodies like maps, sense mood changes with no more than a subtle look. It was one of the many things she loved about being a couple with him. It was as if there actually was a soul connection, which was why she knew she couldn't hold on to her news about DC much longer. He'd soon feel it on her skin and in every move that she made.

She flipped the sheet off, sat up and swung her feet to the floor. "I'm going to get some more juice. Want some?"

He peered above the top of the paper, then slowly lowered it to reveal a brimming smile as his gaze settled on her naked body.

"Only if you promise to bring it back dressed just like that."

"One-track mind." She tossed her bra at him that was hanging by a strap on the end of the bed. He caught it in one hand, barely moving.

"Can't help it when it comes to you." He winked.

She snatched up his discarded shirt from the night before and slipped it on, or rather swam in it, and padded out to the kitchen. She braced her palms on the granite countertop and looked around without focusing on any of the gleaming appliances. *Can't put if off forever*. She had to be in DC for her meeting next week.

She turned to pull open the left side of the double-door stainless steel refrigerator and reached for the container of orange juice. She filled two glasses, returned the carton to the shelf and walked back to the bedroom. She placed Paul's glass on his nightstand.

"Thanks, babe," he murmured.

Sitting down on the side of the bed, she ran the tip of her finger across his hairline. "Need to talk with you about something. Actually, it's the other half of the news I wanted to tell you last night." She put on a smile.

He placed the paper on his lap. "Yes!" He sat up, pulled her close. "Let me hear all about it, wife-to-be." He lifted her left hand and kissed it.

She swallowed. "Well, you'll never guess who called me yesterday."

His brow creased for an instant. "Not a clue," he said with amusement.

"Tina. You know my friend Tina from DC."

"Yeah, sure."

Layne shifted. "You know I've always talked about wanting to be on *The DC Morning Show*." She felt the shift in the room. Paul's smile dimmed. "Well, her uncle is on the board and there's an opening and she got me in to see the executive producer. There's a position open that would be perfect for me." She said it all in a rush even as she intentionally withheld the tiny fact that the job was hers and all she had to do was say yes.

Paul's eyes cinched a bit at the corners as if the morning light was suddenly too much. "Okaaaay," he said slowly. "And you're going?" he asked as if the only answer could be "no."

"Yes. I am."

He pursed his lips a moment. He shifted his body and released her hand. "Why?"

That wasn't the question she expected. "Why?"

"Yes. Why are you going through the motions?"

She blinked in amazement. "Paul. This is something I've been working my entire career to achieve. The least

I can do is hear what they have to say. I *want* to hear what they have to say," she added.

"To what end, Layne? If they offer you the job, are you seriously considering leaving?" His voice elevated in disbelief.

"What if they did?"

"That's only half of the equation. What would your answer be is the real question."

Her heart thumped. She straightened her shoulders and stood. She looked down into his pointed stare. "I'd take it."

All the air whooshed out of the room.

Paul flopped back against the down-filled pillows and looked at her in incredulity. "You're serious."

"Yes, I am."

"And what about us? I just proposed to you…last night. *That's* what you said you wanted."

"Why can't I have both?"

He tossed his head back and laughed without humor. "Both! How in the hell is that supposed to work, Layne, with me here and you in DC? For two years we had to keep our relationship under wraps. That was strain enough—on both of us, by the way. And just when we can officially get our life in order you want to add long-distance marriage to the mix? Is that what you're telling me?"

"We can make it work, Paul."

He stood so abruptly she had to take a step back to avoid being mowed over. He stalked across the room, snatched up his boxers and pulled them on, grabbed his sweatpants and T-shirt from a side chair. He turned to her, his expression a confluence of disbelief, hurt and anger. He dragged in a long breath. "Take the meeting. See what they have to say. We can talk about it when you get back." He turned to the en suite bathroom. "I'm going to get dressed and go for a run."

Even though the door barely closed, the sound of it shutting reverberated in her chest. She closed her eyes and began to mindlessly pick up their discarded clothes that had been tossed to every corner of the room the night before. They'd literally tumbled off the private elevator that opened into his expansive living room, and been so heated in their eagerness for each other that the enormous bedroom resembled the whirlwind of passion that whipped between them from one end of the room to the other and finally onto the king-size bed.

Layne picked up Paul's suit jacket and slacks and placed them in the bin for the dry cleaner. She shrugged out of his shirt and added it to the pile.

Paul emerged from the bathroom fully dressed in his running clothes. He gave her nude body a brief, hot longing look before heading to the door. "Be back in an hour or so…maybe longer."

Layne watched him go. She fingered the jewel of promise on her left hand and the sensation of uncertainty was back in the pit of her stomach.

It had been nearly two weeks since she'd set foot in her apartment. The stuffiness overwhelmed her. She dropped her carry-all on the floor of the short foyer and went from room to room opening windows. She plopped down in an overstuffed paisley side chair that faced the high windows. Late-afternoon sun streamed across the hardwood floors. She watched the tiny particles of dust dance in the beams of light. The sheer, off-white drapes fluttered ever so softly. Leaning her head back against the embrace of the cushion, she closed her eyes.

She'd straightened up Paul's bedroom, tossed the

containers of breakfast food in the trash, packed up her basic belongings while Paul was on his run, took a look around and left. A little space was what was needed. If not, she felt certain things would be said that couldn't be taken back.

If Paul was this unsettled by a simple announcement about her taking a meeting for a job, how would he react when she told him she would accept the job? He'd already voiced his doubts that long-distance could ever be a thing for them.

She released a breath, opened her eyes and pushed up from her seat. Cleaning always cleared her head, and her space could use it.

Two hours later, showered, nestled in her comfy, oversize nightshirt and curled on the couch with a glass of wine at her side in her sparkling condo, Layne took a moment to reflect on her next steps.

She sipped her wine once, then again. The bottom line was, she was going to the meeting. If what Tina said was true and the job was hers for the taking, she sure as hell was going to take it. This had been her dream for years. Paul knew this. He'd known it when they met. If he wasn't willing to compromise…well… She looked at the sparkler on her finger. Just well…

Her stomach grumbled and she realized she hadn't shopped for groceries in weeks. She placed her wineglass on the end table and leaned toward the coffee table for her laptop. Since she had a feeling she was going to be spending some time in her own abode, she was going to need some supplies.

After logging onto her favorite supermarket, she put in her order to restock her fridge, freezer and pantry. Estimated delivery was two hours. She checked the time. It was nearing four. She hadn't heard a word from Paul.

She knew good and well he was back from his run. He had to realize that she hadn't just gone for a walk. She checked her cell phone. No missed call. No text. She sighed and tossed the phone to the far end of her couch.

Fine. Just like she needed some time and some space, he probably did, too. She'd let him have it. If nothing else Paul was reasonable. His training as a journalist afforded him the skills of being organized in thought and remaining objective to issues presented, which allowed him to make rational, impassive decisions. He would think this through, weigh the pros and cons and come to realize that it was doable. She had to believe that.

"Saturday was the big night, bro. You finally pop the question?" Eric asked before taking a swallow from his bottle of beer. "That ring was boring a hole in your pocket for weeks." He stretched out his long legs and looked at his younger brother. "But by the look on your face I'd think she said no. What's up?"

Paul settled back against the lounge chair and looked out onto the waning evening from their spot on the deck of Eric's suburban home.

"Yeah, I asked. She said yes."

"That's good news, right? So why the long face?" He reached over and squeezed his brother's forearm. "What gives?" He took another swallow. "Too early for cold feet." Eric chuckled, but stilled when he saw his brother's brooding expression.

Paul exhaled, then launched into the conversation he and Layne had had earlier, his voice rising and falling.

"Hmm. So...what's gonna happen if she gets the job in DC? You plan on relocating?"

"My life is here. My family. My *career*. One that I've spent the last fifteen years building...and it's set to take another major leap," he murmured too low for his brother to hear.

Eric pursed his lips and lowered his head in thought. "You might not want to hear this, bro, but Layne has career goals, too. You knew that going in."

"She has a career. Here! One that she's damned good at and she has the opportunity to grab even more of it after the foundation event."

"So basically she should be satisfied even if she's always wanted more?"

Paul shot his brother a look. "When I made up my mind to ask Layne to marry me, I saw us like Mom and Dad. Like you and Tricia. Partners. Together. For the long haul. Not some long-distance arrangement. When would we see each other? Once a month, if that. What about a family? How the hell would that work?"

"It would work if you decided to make it work," Eric said quietly. "Listen, I get it. For all the fancy life that you live in front of the camera, at the heart of you, you're just an old-fashioned kinda guy. And that's cool. Don't get me wrong, but sometimes we have to make adjustments and they're not always comfortable."

Paul slowly shook his head. "I…can't see it."

"Is it really because you can't or you're too stubborn and you won't?"

Paul brought the mouth of the beer bottle to his lips, tipped his head back and took a long, thoughtful swallow. That was a damned good question, and if there was any way for him and Layne to figure this out, he'd have to come up with an answer.

"There's something else," Paul finally said.

Eric angled his head. "More? I'm listening."

"It's all been hush-hush. The ink on the contract isn't even dry yet."

Eric's brow rose in question. "Bruh, skip the intrigue and get to the finale."

"Earlier this afternoon, I signed a letter of agreement to host my own news show."

"Say what?" Eric sat up straight.

"Yep." He nodded and tried unsuccessfully to act cool.

"Bruh! You was supposed to lead with this. Damn, congratulations! This is major."

Paul bobbed his head and chuckled. "Yeah, man, it really is."

"Layne know?"

He shook his head.

"Why not?"

"This may sound silly but I actually didn't believe it would really happen. I mean, that's part of the reason." He placed the beer bottle on the circular wrought iron table between them. He leaned forward, rested his arms on his thighs and linked his fingers together. "It's been in the works for months but all lips were sealed. If it had gotten out, the sponsors would've bailed."

"Couldn't even tell Layne?" Eric asked, still incredulous.

"You know that for a news man who deals in facts and data, I'm a little superstitious. Truly did not want to jinx it by saying anything to anyone. Not even Layne. Once I was assured by the station president that it was definitely a done deal I knew I could ask her to marry me. I knew that even if anyone raised an eyebrow at us, they wouldn't rock the boat because of all the firepower behind the new program." He sighed heavily. "Mine was the last signature needed to seal it up tight. I'd planned to take Layne to Miami for the weekend and tell her before the station makes a formal announcement in two weeks. Sweeps."

"Wow," Eric said on a breath. "That does complicate things. For real. I mean, how *could* you leave now?"

"That's just it. I can't."

"Hey, once you tell Layne, there's no way she'd ask you to pick up and move to DC. She'll stay here. You two will get married and live happily ever after."

Paul didn't respond. He wished he could be that sure. When he'd come back from his run Sunday morning and found her gone, he knew this was not going to be a walk in the park. What would he do if she took that job in DC? They both needed some space. A few days apart were probably for the best. She'd go to the gala, make the trip to Washington, and when she got back, he'd share his news and they'd pick up where they'd left off.

"So, this new gig have a name yet? And what about your ten o'clock slot?"

Paul exhaled. "My ten will stay the same. My new gig is going to start once per month to build ratings then move to weekly. *News Hour with Paul Waverly.*"

"I am actually impressed." Eric chuckled. "You. Are. The. Man!"

They fist-bumped.

Their two-ships-passing-in-the-night schedules had their benefits, but Layne wished they would run into each other in the hall, the control room, at a meeting or the commissary. At the very least they'd have to acknowledge the other's existence, which would open the conversation door. They were both stubborn in their own way, and it would take a minute before either of them made the first move.

Usually, if they had a disagreement, they would go

to their "respective corners" until something random happened: Their favorite show would come on television, or one of them would forget that they weren't on speaking terms and rush into the apartment excited about a play or a jazz event coming to town, or they'd both be reading the same news article and start talking over each other in excitement.

This was different, though. She'd actually packed a bag with the intention of...of what? Never coming back? That was ridiculous, of course. She fingered her engagement ring.

She leaned toward the mirror and coated her lashes with several swipes of mascara, reached for her lipstick and evenly covered her lips in a hot red that lit up the undertones of her skin. She'd intricately twisted her thick, naturally curly hair into an elaborate bun on top of her head. She patted the sides and tucked one of the twisted strands back in place.

Turning from the mirror, she crossed the floor to the bed, where her dress for the evening was stretched out and waiting. She shrugged out of her robe and stepped into the sequined, one-shoulder-neckline, knee-length silver dress with a center split and draped sleeve. The dress hugged her body from breasts to knees and shimmered ever so subtly when she moved.

Layne stepped into her toe-out heels and picked up her clutch. The intercom buzzed.

She pressed the talk button. "Yes, Victor."

"There's a Mr. Ron Harrison in the lobby."

"Yes. Thank you. Tell him I'll be right down."

In case it got chilly, she decided to take her shawl, so featherlight it was almost translucent. She draped it over her arm and checked her clutch for keys, phone, lipstick and compact. One good thing about the tech age was that as a reporter you didn't have to carry around a lot of equipment. All you needed was a smartphone. She took one last admiring look in the mirror. Paul didn't know what he was missing.

Layne wasn't certain what she'd expected when she walked into the ballroom. To say that she was stunned was an understatement. Photos of these events, even the live broadcasts, did the assemblage and all the accoutrements no justice whatsoever.

"Wow," she uttered under her breath, and wished that Paul was here to share this moment with her.

Ron was at her side. He'd ditched his usual body-hugging T-shirt, jeans and the latest Nikes for a pretty slick-looking midnight blue suit, open-collar sky blue shirt and spit shine shoes. He'd even combed his shaggy blond hair so that it didn't sweep across his blue eyes. If one squinted he might be able to pass for a Brad Pitt stand-in.

"So this is that whole above-our-pay-grade kinda shindig," he said with just a hint of a soft Southern note, just enough to let you know he was from here, but he'd been around, too. He adjusted the cylindrical black bag on his shoulder that held the tripod, mics and electric cords.

Layne giggled. "It certainly is." But she believed in her heart that it would not always be this way; the little girl with her face pressed up against the window of the finest toy store wouldn't be kept out of the store forever. She'd get the shiny thing in the window. Tonight she'd been given a key—it was still stiff in the lock, but she planned to turn it, and next—DC would offer her any toy she wanted.

"Let's get settled. Linda gave me a list of who she

wants interviewed and who to get sound bites from. We'll do a few stand-ups, cover as many as we can without becoming pains in the asses."

They walked side by side, weaving between the glitz and glamour, the murmur of cultured voices at the perfect decibel, the drip-drip of diamonds, the scent of perfumes and colognes that cost more than it took to feed a family.

Three enormous crystal chandeliers glistened and captured the array of colors from below and cast them about like rainbows. The take-your-breath-away windows spanned an entire wall and rose from floor to ceiling, offering an enchanted view of the skyline and the blanket of stars that sprinkled the heavens.

"Doubt it," Ron said. "Folks like this love to 'have something to say' and see their face on the screen. You've been in the editing room. Half of what we get we can't use, 'cause folks talk too much about themselves and not the question at hand."

"Hmm, that's true to a point. I mean as news people we have an agenda as well."

Ron shrugged. "I'm going to set up over there on the left. Good vantage point and lighting for your stand-ups."

"Great. I'm going to find our table."

She wound her way around the room and nearly tripped over her own feet when she spotted the entourage at the company table. WNCC had bought a table of course, but what made her heart race was who sat at the table. Holding court was Harold Morgan, the president of the network, surrounded by the executives and their spouses and none other than Tess Hampton seated to his right and his wife at his left.

Well, just damn. She brightened her smile and moved to the group.

"Good evening, everyone." She cast her gaze around the assemblage.

"Ah, Layne. Welcome," Harold greeted. "I'm sure you know everyone."

"Yes."

Stanley Martin, the senior VP and only Black male in an upper management position, stood and helped her into her seat.

"Thank you," she said, glancing up at him over her shoulder. She placed her purse on the table.

The waiters came around and refilled wine and water glasses and served an array of appetizers—lobster bisque, mixed green salad, pâté on tiny crackers, and crabmeat on beds of lettuce.

Stanley leaned over and whispered. "If these are the appetizers I guess we won't be eating the usual dried chicken."

Layne giggled. "Clearly, the foundation is using its money well," she replied.

"I've seen some of your work," he continued. He reached for his wineglass and took a sip.

"Oh." She raised an inquiring brow. "Is that a good thing or not?" She held her wineglass to her lips and sipped.

"I think you have enormous potential." He smiled. "That's why I suggested to Harold that it should be you to cover this event."

Good home training kept her from sputtering all over his Tom Ford tuxedo. She blinked, swallowed and cleared her throat. She placed her glass on the table.

"*You* suggested?"

"Yes. Why does that surprise you?"

Did he just move closer? "I was not aware that you could pick me out of a lineup of two," she said, trying to regain her wits. He was staring at her, staring at her in a way that wasn't simply conversational and his stare held her rooted in place. She wanted more wine but she was sure that her hands were shaking.

Stanley tilted his head to the side and smiled a bit, then he rattled off her résumé as smoothly as if it was his own. Then he tossed in trivia about some of the stories she'd covered and even what some of her coworkers thought of her.

As she listened, she wasn't sure if she should be flattered or terrified. If he knew all of that, did he know about her and Paul as well? She'd opted against wearing her sparkler. There was no need to stir the pot before she and Paul worked out what they needed to work out. Equally important, why was Stanley doing all of this intel on her?

"The bottom line is," he said, lowering his voice to a whisper, "there are barely a handful of us in this business. If there is any way that I can add to that number or push someone forward, then that's what I'm going to do." He paused and seemed to move closer. "I can be a very strong ally."

"I see." She licked her lips.

"Tonight is your night to prove that my recommendation wasn't wrong." He eased back, lifted his glass in salute and finished off the contents of the flute. "You should stop by my office maybe one day next week." His attention was taken away from her by a tap on his shoulder from the woman on his right.

Layne was thankful for the reprieve. Her pulse raced. There were so many rabbit holes she could dive into with what had just happened. On the one hand Stanley came across as the laser-focused executive who had done his homework on someone he believed was worth grooming. On the other hand, it wasn't so much what he said. It was the tone, the insinuations, the look in his eyes, the closeness of his body next to hers.

As she numbly made her way through the entrée, she was happy that Paul wasn't her plus-one. Who knows what would have transpired. She offered nods and small talk when appropriate, until she was finally able to get back across the room to Ron.

"Hey," she greeted. "Did you get any food?"

"Oh, yeah. Bunch of camera folks got set up in one of the smaller rooms down the corridor. Pretty damned good, too." He smiled and then it slowly faded. "You okay?"

She glanced at him quickly. "Yes. I'm fine. Guess I'm just a bit anxious is all."

"You got this." He gave her an encouraging smile. "Ready whenever you are."

After she banished the shakiness from her voice, the rest of the evening, the interviews, the on-the-fly commentaries and the stand-ups went off without a hitch. She did her live shot for the eleven o'clock news with the chairperson of the foundation as well as a collage of sound bites from numerous guests and honorees.

"If I don't get out of these heels I'm going to scream," Layne said as she plopped down into one of the padded chairs while Ron packed up. "I just might scream anyway," she said laughing.

"Helluva night. You were great."

"Teamwork. Couldn't have done it without you. Your cues, your ability to spot the next great shot…" She pushed out a breath. "I see why you were chosen for this one."

He gave her a crooked smile. "Thanks. Means a lot."

She slowly pushed to her feet. "I hope we get to work together again."

"Yeah, me, too."

Part of her meant what she'd told Ron. The other part knew that if the vibe she was getting from Stanley Martin was any indication of what was ahead for her at WNCC and at what cost, her days at the network were numbered and she'd soon have a 202 area code—as long as things went well on her interview.

The flight from Charlotte, North Carolina, to Washington, DC, was quick and uneventful. As excited as she was about what lay ahead, part of her spirit was back in Charlotte. She and Paul had yet to really talk since she'd returned to her own apartment. Their brief phone conversations were all superficial as if no one dared to bring up the elephant in the room. He'd called her before she boarded the plane and wished her good luck, but she was sure his heart wasn't in it. She'd wanted to tell him about Stanley Martin and the vibe she'd gotten, but knew that it would only add fuel to the fire. She ended the call by reminding him that she loved him and they'd talk when she returned. He shared the same sentiment before the line went hollow.

As promised, Tina met her at the airport baggage claim area.

"Girl, girl! It is so good to see you," she bubbled, wrapping Layne in a tight hug.

"You, too, sis. It's been way too long."

"You have bags?"

"Nope, just my carry-on," she said, indicating the roller bag at her feet.

"Cool, then let's blow this joint. I'm starved. We'll drop off your stuff at my place, then get some lunch. I'll give you all the details and you will spill the beans on the foundation gala! Girl, we saw clips here. You were amazing."

Layne's cheeks heated. "Thanks. It was something."

"Um…*something*? What am I hearing?" They pushed through the revolving doors. "I parked in the lot. This way," she said hooking her arm through Layne's.

"Let's just say I need to unpack it over food and drink."

"Say no more."

They hurried toward the parking lot. During the half-hour drive to Tina's apartment, the two friends talked over, between and through each other, recasting characters and stories from their recollections from college and the many parties they'd attended, both swearing that their versions of people, places and events were accurate.

"For two highly trained and educated journalists we sure have a helluva time getting our own facts straight!" Tina said over their laughter as they pulled into the underground parking garage at Essex House.

Layne pulled her bag from the trunk and followed Tina down a short corridor and through heavy double doors to the main lobby.

"I usually just take the elevator up to my floor but I wanted to give you the fifty-cent tour first."

They stepped out into a lobby that resembled the lay-out of many of the high-priced hotels, with its marble floors, gleaming glass tables, mood lighting and lush seating. To the left was the on-site restaurant, and on the right, a state-of-the-art gym complete with trainers.

"So wait, you live in a hotel?" Layne asked in confusion as she took in the spaces.

Tina laughed. "No, silly. Everything on the ground floor—restaurant, gym, day care, business center—is for all of the residents. The apartments are from the second to eighth floor. There's also a roof deck that is open in the summer for private parties."

"Wow."

They walked toward the elevator.

"I had no idea. When you said you moved last year I didn't picture this."

Tina laughed. "Neither did I when I heard a couple of years ago that there were plans to rebuild this part of DC. Montgomery Grant—"

"The real estate developer!" Layne cut in.

"Yep. He pulled this all together. Him and his now wife, Lexington. She handled the design. The community center just opened across the street about six weeks ago. Plans are in the works for a major supermarket also."

"Totally impressive." From the moment they'd arrived and walked into the lobby, she felt something special and saw something even more special. Everywhere that she turned, she saw faces that looked like hers—from the staff to the guests, to residents.

"Grant is trying to single-handedly revitalize this area of DC. He uses only minority labor and vendors and the housing is actually affordable. For decades the buildings and the community in general were just left to disintegrate. It was dangerous, between the drugs and the muggings." She shook her head. "Now there is new life flowing through these streets. And wait until you check out the menu at the restaurant. His brother Alonzo Grant is the one that cooks for all the celebrities. He oversees the menu here."

"Get out! I've seen him on television."

Tina laughed. The elevator doors slid open. "Welcome to DC."

"So you think this Martin guy was trying to come on to you?" Tina asked before taking a bite of her salmon salad.

"I don't know. That's what it felt like. It wasn't even so much what he said, but the vibe he gave off. You know." She reached for her glass of iced tea. "I mean, I'm probably reading more into it than necessary with my own personal stuff being all messy. It could all be nothing, but it left me feeling kinda shaky."

"I hear ya," Tina said thoughtfully. "Well, my advice is to steer clear. And if you do go to his office, the door stays open or someone else is in there with you. No late-night meetings—"

Layne held up her hand. "I know the drill." She slowly shook her head. "It's a damn shame that these are the circumstances that we work under—still in this day and age."

"Girl, some things never change, just the outfits."

Layne snorted a laugh. "You got that right."

"There's an Olympic-sized, heated pool if you want to swim later on," she added matter-of-factly.

Layne grinned. "The beat just keeps going on."

The two friends high-fived.

WWDC television studios and headquarters were located in a fifteen-story eco-friendly structure located in Georgetown.

When the elevator doors swooshed open to the administrative offices on the tenth floor, a young woman in an arresting lavender blouse rose from behind a glossy glass-and-chrome horseshoe-shaped desk.

"Welcome to WWDC."

Layne approached. "I have an appointment with Ms. Deanna Mitchell."

"Yes, you are Ms. Davis. She's expecting you."

She reached for the phone, touched a button. "Ms. Davis is here," she said softly into the receiver. "Yes." She glanced up. "I'll walk you back."

They stopped in front of a frosted glass door. The young woman tapped lightly.

"Yes, yes, come in," came a sharp voice from the other side of the door.

Layne suddenly took on an extra level of nervousness.

The young woman pushed the door open and stepped aside to let her pass.

"Ms. Mitchell," Layne was saying with an outstretched hand as she crossed from the door to the desk.

Deanna rose to her feet in what felt like a film in slow motion. Every breath, movement, flicker of the eye was deliberate. She reminded Layne of a young Jane Fonda.

Deanna swept her wide, red-framed cat-eye glasses from the bridge of her flawless nose and placed them on the desk. "Ms. Davis." She shook Layne's hand. "Please have a seat. We're so happy that you were able to come in." The voice was in perfect modulation.

Layne shrugged out of her lightweight three-quarter coat and draped it across the arm of the chair and then sat. She placed her tote on her lap.

"How was your trip?" Deanna linked her long fingers together, the red of her nails matching the color of her lips.

"It was fine. Thank you."

"So," Deanna breathed. "I've already heard wonderful things about you. I've seen you on-screen once or twice, but why don't you tell me about yourself and why you think you would be a good fit here at WWDC." She leveled her mint green eyes on Layne.

Layne drew in a settling breath and clasped her fingers together. "I grew up…"

Deanna leaned back and tilted her head slightly to the side as Layne took her on a brief tour of the highlights of her life, education and the trajectory of her career.

Deanna offered a shadow of a smile when Layne finished. "You clearly have the education and experience." She paused. "So many rising journalists begin their careers in smaller markets." She pressed the tip of her finger to her lip. "Some never make it out. And that's perfectly fine, of course. But at a major network—" she paused "—it's different. The level of work and expectations are much higher. Our news programs are syndicated. As you know, the news position that we have open on *The DC Morning Show* requires extreme flexibility. The person in the spot must be prepared at the drop of a hat to cover a scene, prepare their own notes, pull a team together. And there may be, on the very rare occasion, the need to fill in for one of the anchors. Everyone has to be on their A game. Not some days. Every day."

"Of course." Why did she feel as if she'd somehow already fallen down on the job?

Deanna dragged in a breath and pushed to her feet. "I hope you've planned to stay through the day. I'd like for you to meet some of the staff and take a tour of the studio, and of course I'd like to review your tapes."

Layne's heart thumped. "Yes, I'd planned to stay through tomorrow. I'll be heading back on Saturday morning."

Deanna nodded. "Good." She came from around the desk. "You can leave your things here if you like. I'll take you around."

"Sure." Layne got up. She left her coat but hooked the strap of her tote on her shoulder and followed Deanna out.

Layne was beyond thrilled to walk the corridors and through the studio where the dream of her future bloomed. She smiled and nodded and tried to remember names and faces but the excited pulse beating in her temples made everything fuzzy around the edges.

When the tour concluded Deanna took Layne to lunch but for the life of her she couldn't remember what she ordered or what she ate. The only thing on her mind was that at some point, either today or tomorrow, Monday at the latest, she was going to be offered the job of a lifetime.

"I know we offered to put you in a hotel," Deanna was saying as they returned to her office.

"Yes, that was really thoughtful, but I'm staying with a college friend. It's giving us a chance to catch up."

Deanna nodded. "Yes, Tina."

Layne's stomach lurched. Deanna's lips barely moved when she said Tina's name, almost as if it pained her.

"I generally do the scouting for new talent on my team," she said, turning her body halfway from Layne. She angled her head in Layne direction. "When recommendations come from elsewhere…" Without finishing her sentence, she moved to sit behind her desk.

Layne's smile wobbled a bit around the edges.

"In any event, it was absolutely wonderful to meet you in person. I am going to review your tapes, talk it over with a few people and we'll get back to you."

Layne licked her lips. "Of course." She lifted her jacket from the arm of the chair and adjusted the strap of her tote onto her shoulder. She extended her hand, which Deanna shook.

"We'll be in touch," the executive producer said.

"I look forward to hearing from you and thank you for meeting with me, and the tour." Layne beamed a genuine smile.

Deanna inclined her head like Queen Elizabeth from the throne and Layne knew she was being dismissed.

"So, tell me everything?" Tina said as she and Layne sipped margaritas at Tina's favorite Mexican restaurant.

Layne ran her tongue along the rim of the salted glass, then took a sip of her strawberry margarita. "Well, Deanna... Hard to put my finger on it. One minute she's warm and encouraging and in a blink cold and distant. I got the feeling by the end that she was actually ticked off that she had to meet with me, that I wasn't *her* pick."

"Hmm," Tina mused. "Even so, you have everything that they're looking for. Period. Whether she found you on Craigslist or if someone over her head recommended you, it doesn't matter."

Layne snorted a laugh. "Craigslist? Really?"

Tina shrugged. "You know what I mean."

Layne lifted a nacho chip and scooped it full with guacamole. She took a big, satisfying bite and chewed softly, running over the events of the day in her mind.

"I know I can do great work. I feel it. This is where I belong," she insisted.

"I know that and you know that." She waited a beat. "What are you going to do about you and Paul?"

"Not much I can do until I get the official offer."

"Don't get cute. You know exactly what I mean, Layne."

Layne blew out a breath from between pursed lips. "We are going to work it out. I have to believe that. Paul loves me and I know that as difficult as it might be to be apart, he wants the best for me. He wants me to be happy."

"Okaaaay." She swirled a nacho chip around in the salsa and plopped it in her mouth. "Have you two spoken…like at all?"

Layne fingered the ring that she'd put back on. "Not really," she murmured. "But we will. When I get back."

Tina had gone into work. She said she'd be home about seven and promised they would have one more girls' night before Layne returned to Charlotte in the morning.

It was nearly 10 a.m. on Friday when Layne's cell phone rang. It was the Human Resources rep at WWDC calling with an offer. Layne squeezed her eyes shut, pressed her lips into a tight line to keep from screaming and listened to the HR rep go on about forms and signatures, all of which would be sent via email for her review and signature.

"As this is Friday, we would need your response in two business days, meaning we'd need to have your response by Tuesday."

"Of course," Layne managed between spinning in

circles and doing the happy dance. "Tuesday is certainly doable."

"Let me just verify your email."

Layne confirmed her email. "Thank you. I'll keep an eye out for the email. Have a good day."

She let out a whoop and squeezed the phone to her chest. "I did it! Damn it, I did it." She plopped down with a thump on Tina's couch and kicked her legs in the air. Suddenly, her throat clenched and burned, and tears sprung to her eyes, a combination of utter happiness laced with terror on where her life was going—and if Paul was going with her.

Three

Three years later
Washington, DC

Layne unhooked her clip-on microphone from between the two pearl buttons on her pale peach blouse and handed it off to her technical assistant, Cherie Farmer. Cherie had been more of her right hand than a tech assistant. She was a wizard with sound and lighting, and under Cherie's expert control, Layne always looked and sounded great—even in the middle of whirlwinds of Mother Nature or at the site of screaming fire engines and whirring helicopters. To add to her repertoire of talent she handled the camera as well. Layne and Cherie together were the envy of WWDC.

"Thanks, Cherie," Layne said as she stepped into the studio van that was parked outside the Great Mall. It was the weekend of the National Book Festival and any author and publisher worth their words in print was in attendance. Some of the biggest names in the industry, National Book Award winners, Pulitzer Prize winners, the *New York Times*, *Washington Post* and *USA TODAY* bestselling authors and, of course, throngs of readers spanned across the mall for as far as the eye could see.

Layne had landed exclusive sit-downs with Mia Hunter, recently minted *New York Times* number one bestselling author, and Antoinette London, the most recent recipient of the National Book Award. The fact that both of them were women and that three of the five names on the Pulitzer short list were also women was the angle that Layne was going for in her segment.

"It's going to be a fantastic segment," Cherie was saying as she wrapped up wires and returned microphones into padded boxes.

Layne grinned and lowered herself onto the bench against the far wall. "I think we got some pretty good reactions from the crowd as well." She kicked off her shoes and flexed her toes. "We are the dream team," Layne exclaimed.

The two women fist-bumped.

Cherie sat next to Layne. "I really want to thank you for always asking for me for your projects. It has made a major difference in my career and how I'm viewed at the station."

"You deserve all the flowers, sis. You have crazy skills. From day one, when we worked together on that grand opening of the shopping center that Montgomery Grant spearheaded, I knew I wanted to work with you. I can do what I do because I know you have my back."

"Always." Cherie pushed out a breath. "Do you want to sit in on the edits when we get back to the studio?"

"Sure. The live shots that streamed earlier will need to be clipped for the news cycles."

"I'm sure a spot will air on Monday on *The DC Morning Show.*"

"Yep."

"You've produced so much content for that program," Cherie said. "They really need to give you more time behind the desk."

"It's coming." Layne smiled. "Rumor has it that Brett Conway is in some trouble. If it's true he would need to be replaced as anchor."

Cherie's eyes widened. "I'd been hearing things for a while, but Brett always seems to slither out from under everything." She gave a little shiver. "So...you think you'd be in the running?"

Layne slowly nodded. "We've been doing great work. Our segment on the homeless crisis got an Emmy nomination. That's major." She blew out a breath and linked her fingers together. "It's what I've been working toward for a long time." She gripped Cherie's hand. "And when I get there, I'm taking you with me. That's a promise."

Layne sat curled on her couch, finishing off a fettuccine Alfredo and a mixed green salad while the news played in the background. Her piece on the book festival was the opening tease and had aired for a full five minutes after the commercial. Viewers were encouraged to visit the website for the full interviews and all the highlights of the event.

Layne lifted her glass of iced tea in salute. It was a great segment. She exhaled a sigh. In the background of all her shots at the festival was the outline of the Capitol Building, the White House in the distance and the Washington Monument. She remembered all too well traveling to DC to stand out on that lawn on the coldest damn day she'd ever experienced in her life to watch the inauguration of President Obama. If she ever had any doubts about getting to DC, they'd blown away with the frigid air of that January morning. That was where she belonged. With the midterm elections approaching, she was going to pitch hard to Deanna to put her out there. She'd proven she could do hard and soft news and get the interviewee to say what she needed them to say. From there, she knew an anchor seat was only a sweeps season away.

She pointed the remote at the smart TV and scrolled to the YouTube news clips from WNCC. Her heart thumped when Paul's handsome face filled the screen and the smile that had melted her heart entered the homes of millions. She listened to the smooth cadence of his baritone and remembered how that voice would whisper in her ear.

Three years seemed like a lifetime ago since they'd said their final goodbyes. Paul had said he understood that moving to DC was something she had to do for herself. He understood, he'd insisted, and he wanted her to be happy. *But…* There was always a *but*. *But* he also knew what he wanted for himself, and the career he'd built for well over a decade was rooted in Charlotte. She knew that, he'd pointed out. Knew it when they first started dating, knew it when their relationship progressed from sometimes to all the time, from like to love, from behind closed doors to an engagement ring for all the world to see. *But*…even though she'd said more times than he could count that she wanted their life together, when what she wanted was finally hers, she'd decided to throw it all away.

Layne squeezed her eyes shut and leaned back against the headrest of the couch. As much as she understood Paul's disappointment and unfounded feelings of betrayal, it still hurt. A hurt that trailed her during the day and moved through her dreams at night.

She and Paul were two focused, determined, career-driven people. That was part of the passion that had drawn them together, and the very thing that had ultimately torn them apart. While they might have been traveling on parallel paths, they'd finally come to a fork in the road.

They'd tried the long-distance thing for about four months following Layne's departure from Charlotte. But between Paul's schedule and Layne getting settled into her unpredictable on-call assignments, getting together had become impossible. The "I'm sorry, not this weekend," had turned to a mantra until it became clear that they were in a no-win situation. But she saw the look in his eyes, the way he barely touched her on the rare times they saw each other, the left-handed remarks about her "coming up in the world." He resented that she'd walked away from their life together, no matter how much he claimed to understand, but he had too much pride to say otherwise. Ultimately, over an hour on FaceTime, they'd agreed that it was over.

But that didn't keep Layne for longing for him, missing him, wanting him and wondering if he still felt the same way, even a little bit. She'd substituted nonstop work and going after her goals to fill all the spaces left empty by Paul, and when she finally claimed her seat at the anchor desk, all of the sacrifices would be worthwhile.

She might not have a life with Paul, but she had a good life. That would be enough. For now.

When Layne arrived at the studio on Monday morning, there was a decided buzz that seemed to electrify the air. Staff huddled in small groups murmuring and gesticulating, their words mostly too low-key to make out. She caught only a few as she hurried down the corridor to her office. *Deanna. Scandal. Anchor. Messy. About time.*

She spotted Cherie coming out of the restroom.

"Hey. What's going on?" Layne urged in a tight whisper.

"Girl. The mess done hit the proverbial fan," she said, almost giddy.

Layne's eyes widened. She hooked her arm through Cherie's. "You're killing me. What's up?" She unlocked her office door and they walked in. Cherie closed the door behind them.

"Word on the street is Deanna is replacing Brett Conway, girl. Security walked him out about an hour ago."

"Say what?"

"Yep." She nodded. "Apparently, charges were brought against him and the board couldn't shield him anymore."

Layne plopped down in her leather chair. She dropped her tote on top of the desk. "He's out," she murmured, her mind racing.

"There's an emergency staff meeting in an hour. The notice should be in your email."

Layne powered up her desktop, waited, tapped in her password and went straight to her email account. Her eyes raced over Deanna Mitchell's missive.

She sat back and let out a woof of air. Then a

slow smile moved across her polished lips. Her heart thumped. Thumped. "This is my shot, C. I'm the most likely replacement. No one on the *Morning Show* has my background or experience. I've been in front of and behind the camera. This is it," she whispered.

Cherie came over and perched on the edge of Layne's desk. "You got this," she said with a beaming smile.

"*We* got this."

Once *The DC Morning Show* wrapped for the morning and segued to *News at Noon*, the staff and crew of the *Morning Show* assembled in the main conference room. Everyone was whispering behind their hands. Layne and Cherie took seats in the back of the room, the better place to get the lay of the land, and Layne wanted to relish the moment she'd be called to the front of the room when Deanna announced her as Brett's replacement.

"Thank you all for coming," Deanna began. She was flanked on either side by the head of HR and an assistant. "As you all saw or heard, Brett Conway, who has been with this network for nearly ten years, was dismissed today." She lifted her cleft chin. "He'd become the face of *The DC Morning Show*. It was as a result of his work at the network that the show was propelled to number two in its market time slot." She cleared her throat. "But his success, his years of service to this network cannot override the serious allegations that have been leveled against him. We take them seriously. And after months of an internal investigation, we have determined the allegations were true. I won't get into details as there will of course be litigation and the parties involved will not be named."

"Parties," Cherie whispered to Layne.

Layne made a moue.

"As a result, there will be some major changes to the show." The tight, stricken look on her face softened and her mouth curved ever so slightly. "I am happy, thrilled actually, to announce Brett's replacement."

Layne shifted nervously in her seat. Cherie squeezed her hand.

The HR assistant went to the door and opened it.

"Please welcome our new anchor for *The DC Morning Show*, Mr. Paul Waverly."

Layne froze. Her ears started to ring. Heat rushed through her veins, clouding her vision. Her mouth opened but no words came out.

"What the hell," Cherie hissed. She flashed Layne a look of disbelief and gripped her arm. "Layne, I'm so sorry."

She couldn't speak.

Paul was talking but Layne couldn't hear anything he was saying. The room seemed to move in and out and she thought she was going to be sick.

"I...gotta go," she said, her voice choked. She slipped out the back door and darted down the hall to the restroom.

Standing in front of the mirror, she stared at her reflection. She braced her hands on the edge of the sink and drew in long shaky breaths. How could this be happening? Paul? Here? He'd said he would *never* leave Charlotte, not even for her. But here he was, taking away what he knew she wanted more than anything. What could they have possibly offered him?

Tears pooled in her eyes and dripped down on her knuckles.

Layne moved through the rest of her day in a daze, completing her tasks by rote and skipping the Paul Waverly meet and greet that had been set up at the end of the workday.

Cherie tried to convince her to go out for drinks and vent, but she declined. As close as she and Cherie had become since her arrival at WWDC, she'd never told her about Paul. That was a part of Layne's life that she tucked into a corner of her heart and soul.

She shut the door to her apartment, kicked off her shoes, dropped her tote on the floor next to her discarded shoes and dragged herself to the living room. Her cell phone chirped. She dug in the back pocket of her jeans and pulled out the phone. Tina's smiling face lit up the screen.

Layne's voice cracked when she tried to say hello.

"Layne? What's wrong?"

She heaved in a sob.

"Layne! What is it?"

"You won't freaking believe it," she managed, choking over the words.

"Believe what?"

"Paul. He's here in DC. *He* got the anchor job."

For a moment silence hung in the air until Tina sputtered a string of expletives. "I'm on my way." She didn't give Layne a chance to respond.

"So, Deanna somehow convinced Paul Waverly of all the men on the planet to come to DC to anchor the show that literally broke the two of you apart. Sh—" Tina spewed.

Layne sniffed back tears that had turned from hurt and shock to anger. She finished off her second glass of wine, reached for one of the two bottles that Tina had brought with her and refilled her glass.

"I... I just don't even know what to think, to do."

"When is the last time you spoke to him?"

Layne sighed. "Been over two years," she said, the words like pinpricks to her heart.

"I take it Deanna has no clue about the two of you."

"I can't imagine how. If she does, she didn't hear it from me. No one knows, and since we never got a chance to announce our very brief engagement, no one back in Charlotte knew, either. I mean, thinking back to my meeting with her, I got the impression that she was bringing me on board but not entirely willingly." She shook her head. "That's about it. I don't even know." She sighed.

"Deanna has been known to be totally driven and has no problem stepping on and over folks to get what she wants. And the board loves her because of it. That's why it was so major that she agreed to bring you here." Tina sipped from her glass of wine. "Well, at some point you're going to have to talk to him. He knows you're here."

"Exactly! He knows I'm here. He knows how much I wanted this and yet—" She blew out a long breath of frustration. "You're right. We will have to talk at some point. We'll be working together." She nearly choked on the word *together*. "I'm going to have to get my head... and my heart together for the inevitable." She refilled her wineglass. "We need to order some food," she said and took a long sip, "before we move from just feeling good to not being able to feel!"

"Ha! You got that right. Pizza? Or something more substantial?"

"Two pies," Layne said, her gaze drifting off along

with her thoughts. How could Paul have done this to her? Was it to punish her for leaving? Was that the man he'd become over the last three years—vindictive? She sighed. Sipped. Sighed.

Four

Paul walked into his rented apartment on Fifty-Ninth Street NW. He tugged his tie loose and unbuttoned his collar before crossing the high-glossed wood floors to the wet bar. WWDC didn't spare any expense or amenity. He poured a short tumbler of Hennessy, walked to the couch, reached for the remote and turned on the wall-mounted television. He scrolled through the channels and settled on a National Geographic special on Central Park in New York. He took a thoughtful sip as he watched the camera pan the milieu of Upper Westsiders. Most New Yorkers and ultimately much of the country could make a connection to the park because of the Central Park Five. Their notorious prosecution for a crime they didn't commit against a female jogger and their ultimate release and exoneration had dominated headlines. What many didn't know was that Central Park was once Seneca Village, owned and inhabited by a successful, thriving African American community in the mid-1800s, until the government deployed its power of eminent domain and took nearly 800 acres to build Central Park, the narrator explained.

He took another sip. Where did the people go? Seneca Village, Greenwood, Philadelphia? Those were the headline stories. But communities of color had been plagued and uprooted by either eminent domain or the other old-fashioned way—gentrification—for generations.

He changed the channel. Some things never changed, just the methods. A story for another day. He unbuttoned his white shirt and strolled into his bedroom. His living arrangements and location might have changed, but his feelings for Layne had not. He'd thought they had. He'd prayed for them to go away. For a while, burying himself in work and empty relationships had seemed to help. And then the offer had come from Deanna Mitchell.

A year earlier, he'd attended the annual convention of the National Association of Black Journalists in Chicago. He was one of the guest speakers touting the importance and relevance of local television and its ability to inform communities with the information and resources that could be used to make enlightened decisions.

After his talk, he was encircled by colleagues offering congratulations. Over the heads and shoulders, he'd spotted Deanna Mitchell, standing a bit off to the side, watching him over the rim of her wine flute. She smiled. But it wasn't a smile of acknowledgment or congratulations, it was something else.

One by one the congratulators had peeled off and Paul was face-to-face with Deanna. She was quite stunning, with her light olive complexion and startling, mint green eyes. She had the kind of features that made her origins hard to place, giving her an exotic quality. She moved catlike toward him.

"Mr. Waverly, wonderful presentation."

"Thank you." He gave a slight nod.

She extended her hand. "Deanna Mitchell, executive producer of *The DC Morning Show*."

Paul's jaw flexed. *DC Morning Show. Layne.*

"I was really impressed," Deanna was saying. "I've had an eye on your career for a while and I can tell you, going national will take you places you never imagined. You've outgrown local coverage."

Paul scoffed. "I'm almost complimented."

"You have to excuse my bluntness. I'm not always the best at being tactful."

His expression softened. "Whatever works."

Deanna laughed. "But I'm serious about what I said. You deserve more than a local spot. You have star power, Mr. Waverly. I know it when I see it." She reached in her clutch, pulled out an embossed business card and handed it to him. "In case you are ever in DC, please give me a call." She smiled and strutted away.

He briefly glanced at the card before tucking it into his inside jacket pocket. Layne was at WWDC and as much as he longed for her, it was not an offer he was prepared to accept. Besides, he had everything he could want exactly where he was. Everything except for Layne.

He put his meeting with Deanna Mitchell behind him, and dove body and soul into his work. It consumed him, keeping his longings at bay, except for the nights when the emptiness would overwhelm him and voluptuous, eager bodies didn't satisfy him.

Did she ever think of him, what they had? Did she ever regret leaving Charlotte? Had she found someone? Was she happy? When he was not immersed in work or buried in a willing body, those questions plagued him. Just when he'd finally reached a point where he could breathe without inhaling Layne's scent, Deanna Mitchell called, with an offer that literally stunned him. She truly made him an offer he would have been a fool to refuse.

Paul ran his hand across his face and close-cropped hair. Seeing Layne earlier had rocked him. A wave of emotions raced through him: shock, joy, anxiety and anger. It was the anger that seemed to linger. Seeing her again in the flesh and not in his dreams had reawakened the hurt and feeling of betrayal. And to see her get up and walk out—he huffed in annoyance. The move was a symbolic slap of dismissal.

He pushed out a breath and strode to the sauna-like bathroom to take a shower. Well, he was here now. He turned on the rain-head jet. Funny, the very spot that she so coveted was now his. The irony.

"Hey, girl, you good?" Cherie asked, meeting Layne in the hallway.

"It is what it is," she said and tried to smile.

They walked together down the corridor.

"Maybe he'll crash and burn," Cherie offered.

Layne snorted a laugh. Obviously, Cherie didn't know Paul Waverly. Crashing and burning was not in his MO. "Maybe," she said, knowing she didn't believe that for a moment. "I can't worry about Paul Waverly. I have my own job to focus on." She checked the time on her phone. "I have to prep for some interviews. They're breaking ground for another new shopping center that Montgomery Grant is backing."

"That brother is going to reshape inner city DC."

"Looks that way."

"Gotta run. I'll see you later." She picked up her pace and headed down the hall and into her office. She shut the door, pressed her back against it and closed her eyes.

Her heart was racing a mile a minute. She was sure that at any second Paul would walk around a corner or step out of a doorway and right into her path. What would she do then? What would they say to each other after all this time? Did they pretend they didn't know each other? That would be difficult, since Deanna knew they both hailed from WNCC.

She pushed away from the door and rounded her desk. She reached for the remote and pointed it at the television set mounted on the wall. *The DC Morning* show theme song and logo filled the screen and then there he was, making a brief cameo before his premiere.

The air hung in her chest. She tugged on her bottom lip with her teeth, watching Paul's marquee face fill the screen. His rugged voice filled her soul as he sat in conversation with Carl Bellows, who was filling in for Brett until Paul took over.

Transfixed, she saw Paul work the magic of his personality on any and everyone with the sound of his voice. There was no doubt that Paul Waverly was the consummate professional and would move into his new role as if it was made for him.

She sighed. Maybe it was. Maybe that anchor seat had never been hers to have. She blinked back the sting in her eyes and realized her hands were trembling. She balled her fingers into a fist. She'd given up so much to chase after a dream, only to find herself right back where she'd started.

How in the world was she going to be able to work every day? Following the show, there would be the team meeting that would go over the recording of the show to look for any hiccups to avoid next time, and set up the planning for the next show. She'd dodged a bullet for this show as it had been planned before Brett Conway was unceremoniously dismissed. But she couldn't avoid the debriefing session today, and prep for tomorrow's show, especially since she was responsible for doing two of the lead-in interviews for tomorrow's guests.

The DC Morning Show had another two hours before midday news came on. Layne had two hours to get her head on straight, look Paul Waverly in the eye, smile brilliantly and welcome him to the WWDC family. She groaned and buried her face in her hands.

The vibrating buzz of her cell phone forced her to open her eyes. Tina. She pressed the green icon.

"Hey, girl."

"Just checking on you. Want to make sure that you didn't slit your wrists or Paul's neck," she said with a snicker.

"Very funny. I'm good. I guess. I haven't seen him up close, only on screen, but that will change soon."

"How's that?"

Layne explained about the debriefing and prep.

"Oh, damn. Well, girl, you got this. He's just a man."

"Yeah."

"Um, I had another reason for calling. You know that as assistant editor here at the *Post*, I…uh…assign reporters to certain stories."

Layne's heart began to thud like a drumbeat that she could hear in her ears, like the dark music that plays when the unsuspecting victim senses something wrong in the dimly lit house. The audience knows. But she doesn't. Until it's too late.

"Whatever the hell it is, just say it!"

"We are assigning a reporter to cover Paul's first week at the station and do a close-up interview."

"You. Are. Freaking. Kidding Me!" Now her head was pounding.

Tina paused. "There's more."

"What the hell more could there be?" Her voice rose to the ceiling in a pitch high enough to shatter glass.

"I'm…the reporter."

Layne was pretty sure she'd just cussed out her best friend from here to the next millennium. She knew she'd stopped listening while Tina was trying to explain something about budget cuts and some other bs. She pressed her thumbs into her temples and slowly rotated them in the hopes of relieving the throbbing.

Truly, the world was conspiring against her. Must be that retrograde thing happening. Layne dragged in a breath and pushed to her feet. She tucked her laptop under her arm, stuck her cell phone in her jacket pocket and walked out of her office and down the hall toward the meeting room, reminding herself with every footstep—*you're a professional, you're a professional*.

Layne pushed open the heavy door, kept her expression blank and her eyes at half-mast as she inched her way around chairs and feet to find a seat as far in the back as possible.

Craig, the technical director, was up front making some adjustments to the recording equipment. He pointed the remote at the screen and *The DC Morning Show* logo appeared. He pressed pause and took a seat.

Cherie came rushing in, looked around, found Layne

and headed in her direction, dragging an empty chair with her.

"Guess I didn't miss anything," she said in a conspiring whisper.

Layne crossed her ankles and propped her laptop on her thighs. "Not a thing."

Cherie dipped her head and leaned toward Layne. She cupped her hand around her mouth for added security. "I heard Deanna plans on showing up today and there's buzz going around that she's going to make a big announcement."

Layne's stomach rolled. She and big announcements were not doing so well together these days. "What more could she possibly tell us?" she said, each word dripping with sarcasm.

"Your guess is as good as mine."

Cherie settled back in her chair just as the door opened and Paul, accompanied by Deanna, walked in. They took seats up front. Craig stood. As technical director, he generally led these meetings with input from his team and the producer of the program.

While many might think this format was punitive, it was actually extremely helpful. Praise was always meted out and critiquing was done with care. Basically, it made everyone better at their jobs. It was very easy in this business to get tunnel vision and forget about all the other players on the game board. These briefings kept everyone grounded.

Once the program ended, Craig began by telling everyone that he believed it went extremely well, then pointed out some issues with lighting and the angle of one of the boom mics. He welcomed his new cameraperson, who happened to be a woman, much to everyone's delight.

Once Craig was done and questions and comments were addressed, Deanna moved to the front and faced the room.

"Here it comes," Cherie whispered from behind her hand.

Layne tapped her foot at a blinding rhythm.

"As usual, great job everyone. You all are the reason that *The DC Morning Show* has remained number two in our time slot." She extended her arm dramatically toward Paul. "And now that we have Paul Waverly anchoring, I have no doubt that we should be number one soon."

The room resounded with applause.

Deanna held her hand up. "I'll be monitoring our numbers, and with marketing and communications launching a full press on Paul's arrival, I have no doubt that the top spot will be ours and remain ours to stay." She beamed at the gathering, then turned her smile on Paul. She beckoned him to join her.

Paul walked to the front of the assembly, looking as handsome as always, in control yet humble all at the same time. It was a magical mix. There was something unique about Paul Waverly. He had what those in the business called the "it" factor. It was something that couldn't be explained in words, but only experienced. Paul had a way of combining a tilt of his head with a gentle lift of his mouth, and the slight lowering of his lids when he looked at you to make you think you were the most important person in the world. And his shine was not dimmed from behind a television screen. If anything, it was magnified. Every one of those attributes was on full display.

Paul smiled, slid his hands into his pockets. He swung a quick look at Deanna. "Thank you, Deanna.

And thank all of you for an amazingly warm welcome. I'd promised myself early in my career that I'd never leave Charlotte. It was my home in more ways than one." He paused a beat. "But Deanna can be very persuasive," he said with a sardonic lift of his brow. The room tittered with laughter. "She's given me a heavy mantle to carry, but I'm sure that with the talent that's in this room, the weight will be light and the success will be ours because of all of you."

Layne rolled her eyes.

"And I have one more announcement to make," Deanna said. The team settled down. "Now that we are making some major adjustments to the face of the program, I think it's only fitting that Paul have one of our best to produce his show." She paused for effect. "Layne Davis."

"Oh sh—" Layne hissed from between her teeth.

Cherie clasped Layne's forearm. "Congrats, girl. That's major. A least he's not a stranger. Both of you from WNCC. And the fact that he is fine is a plus!"

Layne licked her lips and swallowed. Everyone turned toward her and clapped. She forced a smile. "Thank you, Deanna, everyone," she managed. "Very excited to be working with Mr. Waverly." She nearly choked on the faux sentiment. Her gaze jerked toward Paul and his was fixed on her. Her pulse thumped.

"Well." Deanna clapped her hands once. "That's it for today. Great job everyone. Layne," she called out over the rise of heads and shoulders. "Could you hang back for a minute?"

"Let's do lunch," Cherie said quietly. "I wanna know if he smells as good as I think he does," she giggled. "One o'clock at Mulberry's." She gathered her belongings and hurried to catch up with one of the technical assistants, better known as a TA.

Layne dragged out the process of slipping her laptop back in its case, arranging her chair back against the wall, checking the space for anything left behind, before straightening, dragging in a breath of resolve and moving through quicksand to the front of the room. Her heart began beating so hard and fast that it was hard to breathe. Her stomach did a slow roll.

"Layne Davis, Paul Waverly," Deanna said. "Paul, Layne is one of our best. As a matter of fact, she's done quite a bit of work in front of the camera as well." She smiled benevolently at Layne. "But of course you know that already. That's why I picked Layne."

"Good to see you again," Layne said. "Looking forward to working with you."

Paul's dark brown eyes flickered in a moment of uncertainty. He extended his hand and settled his gaze on her. "Nice to see you again, too. I've heard great things—from Deanna."

Layne swallowed. Her hand slipped into his. His fingers wrapped around hers and she may have gasped.

She cleared her throat. "Well, welcome to WWDC."

"I was hoping that we could sit down and talk about some ideas you may have and compare them with mine."

That raw silk voice was as mesmerizing as ever. If she didn't leave soon she would either faint or scream. "Sounds fine. Later today?"

"Say when?"

His smile made her sway on her feet.

"I think that's a great idea," Deanna suddenly cut in, angling her body so that she stood partially between Layne and Paul. "I'd like to sit in on that meeting. I have a few ideas of my own that I'd like to share with you, Paul. And we can discuss your upcoming interview with the *Post*." She turned to Layne. "I believe the reporter is an acquaintance of yours, Tina Gerard," she said, her expression and tone making clear that she knew Tina had a hand in getting Layne her interview and ultimately her job.

Layne cleared her throat and lifted her chin. "Yes. She is."

"I'm open any time after three," Paul said, cutting in.

"Let's do four, in my office," Deanna said. She flashed a tight smile at Layne.

Layne drew in a breath. "Perfect," she said, lifting her brows and widening her eyes in fake delight. "I'll see you both then." She flashed a smile. "I'm sorry. I've got to run. The show must go on." She spun away and out the door on shaky legs and a thudding heart.

Paul walked out with Deanna until they parted ways in front of his office.

"See you at four," Deanna said before whisking away.

Paul opened the door and stepped into his corner office. He shut the door behind him, tugged his tie loose and shrugged out of his jacket. He hung the jacket on the coatrack and crossed the tan carpeted floor to the well-stocked bar. It was barely past one but he needed a drink.

He poured a short shot of Hennessy and tossed it back in one gulp. He was rattled. There was no other word for it. Seeing Layne again. That close. Inhaling her. Remembering. But she'd looked at him with the same emptiness in her eyes that she'd left in his heart when she'd moved from Charlotte.

So it was a game they would play. The game of not knowing each other beyond a casual acquaintance. The game of indifference. The game of keeping it professional.

He strode to the window. The circular outline of the US Capitol Building sprawled below him. He slung his hands into his pockets and drew in a long, slow breath. His jaw clenched reflexively. He shot his cuffs and checked the platinum Rolex—ironically a gift from Layne on his thirty-fifth birthday. Three hours. Three hours and they would be face-to-face. Nowhere to run. Nowhere to hide. Let the games begin.

"Wow. This whole thing just gets weirder by the minute," Tina was saying into the phone. "You have been assigned to be his producer? I'll be damned. Hey, maybe it's a sign."

As annoyed as she'd been with her bestie earlier, she knew Tina wouldn't do anything to intentionally hurt her. She was doing her job and she was damned good at it. Besides, who was she going to rant and rave and freak out to about Paul if not Tina?

"A sign of what? The apocalypse?"

Tina sputtered a laugh. "Damn, girl, it's not that bad. Really. I mean, think about it. It's been three years. Both of you have had time to come to terms with your life. You both made some hard choices."

Layne sighed. "That's all rational and whatnot. But it doesn't account for—" her voice hitched "—how I feel."

"How do you feel?" Tina asked softly.

Layne pressed the cell phone to her cheek. "I feel… everything. Sad. Confused. Angry. Gut-punched."

"But do you still love him, Layne?"

"I don't want to," she said on a breath.

As much as Layne thought she wasn't up for Cherie's chatter, lunch with her coworker actually loosened the knots in her stomach. Cherie had a no-filter personality, and combined with their favorite comfort food—burgers and fries—and the conversations ebbing and flowing around them, Layne felt much steadier on her feet when she walked through the doors of Deanna Mitchell's office. At least until Paul turned from his seat and unmoored her with a single look when she entered.

For an instant, she faltered, but she quickly recovered.

"Layne, please join us," Deanna said magnanimously. She waved her over to the small conference table. "Would you like anything? Coffee, water?" She extended her hand to the setup on the center of the table.

"No, thank you. I'm fine." She sat and put her laptop on the smooth wood surface of the table. She flipped the lid open and pressed the power button. Paul was barely two feet away. She could feel the heat of his body. It wafted with that familiar—more natural than high-end, store-bought—scent that seeped into her pores, the way it always had. Her insides quaked.

"So," Deanna began, "I hope you are as excited as I am about this pairing," she said to Layne.

"Absolutely. This is a fantastic opportunity."

"I think so, too," Paul added. "Deanna has been singing your praises and you had a solid reputation back at WNCC—from what I can recall."

Layne swallowed. Her gaze flicked in his direction and then away. "You said you had some ideas, Deanna?"

"Yes." She tilted her head toward Paul. "A great deal is riding on you. I had to pull too many strings to name in order to get you here. But I know it will be worth it, and to ensure that it is, at least for the first month, I want to review and approve everything that goes on the air."

Layne's brow lifted. As executive producer, of course Deanna had that option, but she rarely chose it. She oversaw the producers, staff and budget, and she also was ED for *Nightwatch*, the after-eleven-o'-clock news show—enough to keep her hands full. For her to get into the weeds of *The DC Morning Show* meant that there really was a lot on the line and it was more than ratings.

Paul folded his arms across his chest but didn't comment.

"You've been an assistant producer, but stepping up to producer is going to take even more work. Every element of the program is up to you. Of course, you will work hand in hand with Paul and get his approval along the way."

"Of course." Layne licked her lips. "I want to put together my own team."

Deanna nodded in agreement. "You'll run the names by me."

Layne blinked. On one hand Deanna claimed to bestow her with so much power, and with the other hand kept a grip on it.

"Sure."

"Prepare a list of names for your team. Get them to me by tomorrow morning. I'd like them all approved and assembled in the Writers' Room by lunch." She turned to Paul. "Any show ideas that you have, contacts for interview guests, topics you want to go after, get them to Layne and she will make it happen. In the meantime, we'll finish out Brett's schedule."

The corner of Paul's lush mouth lifted into a half grin. "Not a problem." He slid a look in Layne's direction.

"That's all I have," Deanna said, signaling the end of the meeting. "Keep me in the loop." She placed her palms flat on the table. "Oh, and you might want to keep tabs on the progress with the interview—with your friend."

Layne didn't miss the dig. She rose. "I'd better get working on that list." She gave Paul a short nod and walked out.

Her pulse roared in her ears. She had to keep blinking to keep the space in front of her in focus. What in the entire hell had happened back there? She stabbed the elevator button and paced until the doors slid open. She stepped forward and, when she turned, caught a glimpse of Paul coming toward her. She stepped fully inside and frantically pressed the button for the main floor. An instant before the doors slid shut, Paul's face appeared and then it was gone. The elevator began its descent.

Layne spent the rest of her afternoon putting together her list of who she wanted on her team. Although she'd put programs together in the past, it had always been in a secondary role. This time it was all on her. If the show flopped, it would be on her, and if she had any intention of moving to that anchor chair, screwing up was not an option. Not to mention that there was only one anchor seat. Her other obstacle was that Paul was sitting in it.

Five

Paul snorted a laugh as the elevator door slid shut. He should take it as a metaphor for his relationship with Layne—closed. He boarded the next elevator to the main floor of the studio. He walked down the hallway, passed partially open office doors and bustling technicians and staff. He nodded, smiled and murmured thanks to well-wishers as he strode toward his corner office. His step slowed when he got in front of Layne's door. It was closed, but he could hear murmurs of a one-sided conversation. He hesitated, raised his hand to knock but changed his mind. He continued on to his office.

Paul discarded his jacket on the couch and loosened his tie. One full day under his belt. It was easier than he'd imagined. He'd spent his career in front of a camera, reading notes and teleprompters and convincing the viewing audience that what he said could be trusted. What was hard was seeing Layne again. Seeing her up close, hearing her voice, inhaling her familiar scent had been more difficult than he'd imagined.

He kicked off his shoes and took them to the bedroom, sliding them onto the shoe rack. He sat down on the edge of the bed, then flopped back, tucked his hands behind his head and stared up at the ceiling. The hardest part wasn't seeing Layne, it was experiencing her impervious reaction to him. He was sure part of it was akin to how they had to be around each other in North Carolina. They'd grown used to pretending to be no more than colleagues. But it was more than that. There was now an icy wall that she'd erected.

He'd taken this job against all of his vows to himself because it would put him back in Layne's path, and give them both a chance to start over or at least pick up where they'd left off. Compounded with the fact that the deal for him to host his own talk show remained in limbo and added to the last push he needed to leave WNCC.

His cell phone vibrated in his pocket. He dug the phone out and smiled at the name illuminated on the face.

"Hey, man," Paul sat up and greeted his brother, Eric.

"Hey. Congrats. Me and Tricia just watched your debut on the DVR. Not bad."

Paul chuckled. "Gee, thanks, bro."

"So, how was the first day? Did you see Layne?"

"First day was better than I expected. The people are really cool, made me feel like part of the team."

"And Layne…?" Eric hedged.

Paul exhaled. "I saw her."

"And?"

"Hard. Awkward."

After some more prodding, Paul explained everything that happened.

"So you didn't actually talk to each other."

"No. I started to stop by her office but changed my mind."

"Hmm, well, she could simply be going along with the same program y'all set up back in NC. Keeping a low profile."

"Yeah. I figure the same thing."

"At some point you're gonna have to have a conversation, especially if she is producing your shows."

"Hmm, there's that." He got to his feet and walked to the windows that looked out over the nation's capital and wondered if leaving everything behind in North Carolina and coming to DC had been a monumental mistake.

Layne parked her car in the underground garage of Essex House, using Tina's guest parking spot. She grabbed her laptop bag and small overnight tote and walked to the elevator, taking it to the eighth floor.

She exited the elevator and wound her way around the circular layout to Suite 8C. She pressed the buzzer and, moments later, Tina flung open the door and exuberantly greeted her friend.

"Let the shenanigans begin," she said kissing Layne's cheek. She draped an arm around Layne's shoulder and ushered her inside.

Tina's two-bedroom was airy and spacious and furnished with an Afrocentric flair, from the bold colored accessories on the deep navy blue seating of the six-foot sectional, chaise and club chair, to the artwork and wooden figurines that made the entire space a showroom—but cozy at the same time.

"Make yourself comfortable, sis. I thought we could have dinner downstairs. Rumor has it that Chef Alonzo Grant is visiting and will be overseeing the menu," she said with a gleam in her eyes.

"Sounds great." Layne stepped out of her shoes and shrugged out of her light jacket before following Tina into the living area.

"Wine?"

"Sure."

Tina poured them each a flute and joined Layne on the couch. "Really glad you came. Things kinda went left between us and I wanted to make sure we were good, ya know."

Layne nodded. "I know. I was totally overreacting. This whole Paul thing has me off-center."

"I get it. So we'll do dinner, talk and plan," Tina said with a wink.

Layne lifted her glass. "To plans."

"How do you see this working relationship turning out?" Tina asked as she cut into her striped bass.

"I'm a professional and he's a professional." Layne took a spoonful of risotto. "Hmm, this is delicious," she murmured.

"Told ya." Tina wagged her fork. "I'm going to be honest with you." She put down her fork and wiped her mouth with the cloth napkin. "You made a decision three years ago to follow your dream. Your dream resulted in a breakup with the man you were in love with. But three years later you still haven't snatched that star that you ran after. Not quite. And here comes the man that you put everything on the line for and he takes that seat you wanted for yourself. Totally f'd up. But that is your reality. And I'm not sure what you're most upset about—that for all you gave up, it's still out of reach or that Paul got what you wanted."

Layne sighed heavily and slowly shook her head. "Both. Everything and then some," she said, her voice arching. "When I left Charlotte for this job I believed in my bones that it would only be a matter of time until I got the seat. All I had to do was prove myself by producing quality content. Chasing the right stories to air, knowing the ropes." She blinked rapidly. "But none of that mattered because they didn't *see* me—really see me." She tugged on her bottom lip with her teeth for a moment. "But they will. I'm gonna be the best damned producer *The DC Morning Show* has ever had. I'm going to produce an Emmy-winning show with me at the anchor desk. And Paul Waverly is going to wish he'd stayed in Charlotte, North Carolina." She raised her glass and brought it to her lips. "That's the plan," she said and took a sip.

Tina lifted her glass. "Cheers to that."

Spending the evening with her best friend was as regenerating as their times together usually were. They talked, they laughed, debated and talked some more. They picked through the landmine of Tina doing an interview with Paul, with her promising to remain totally objective and that she would not allow their friendship to shape the story.

"I wouldn't expect anything less. You have your journalistic integrity to uphold. Paul knows that you and I are friends. Deanna knows that we're friends."

"All very incestuous," Tina teased.

"Ha! But seriously, we're all here to do our best." She covered Tina's hand with her own, as they wrapped up their evening with a nightcap on Tina's couch.

So, when Layne walked into the station the following morning, there was a new confidence in her step, a lift to her chin. She'd sent her recommendations for her team, via email, to Deanna, before she'd gone to bed, and found Deanna's approval in her morning email.

Buoyed with confidence, she booked one of the small conference rooms to host a debriefing and introduce the team members to each other. Today was the last day of Brett's program schedule. Beginning Monday, the show would be handed off to her and her new team.

While the technical staff and camera crew all knew each other, many had not worked together as a unit before. The balance of the day would include confirming responsibilities, partnerships and a pitch session with the writers. And, of course, sitting across the table from Paul.

"Good morning, folks," Layne greeted as she walked into the control room. The morning news had just ended and the station was in commercial break before handing the programming over to their affiliate stations.

"As you all know, I've gotten the dream assignment to produce *The DC Morning Show with Paul Waverly*." There was a smattering of applause, mixed with faux grunts and groans of protest. Layne grinned. "Anyway, we have to hit the ground running. You all will be happy to know that I have requested each of you to be on my team." This time the approval was real. "I've reserved the second-floor conference room—and lunch," she added with a grin. "I'll be expecting everyone at one sharp. Bring your energy, ideas and appetite. Cool?" She flashed a smile, walked out and headed to her office. As she turned the corner she ran, literally, into Paul.

"Oh." She clutched her iPad to her chest. "Paul."

He stretched out a steadying hand. His fingers lightly clasped her upper arm. "Layne."

Her breath hitched. "Sorry. Wasn't paying attention." She started to move around him.

"It *is* good to see you," he said quietly.

Her stomach quivered. She swallowed and forced a tight smile. "I'll see you at the m-meeting…one o'clock," she stammered before hurrying off.

Once behind her closed office door, she allowed her emotions to escape in a slow but steady stream of tears that felt endless, as if by expelling this dam of pain she could make it dry up until nothing but a dust bowl remained.

She made her way to the small two-seat sofa and curled into the corner of it, drawing her knees to her chest. She rested her head on the arm and let the tears flow until, after what seemed like forever, they finally slowed to a drizzle, then a sprinkle, and then a drip, like the last hurrah of a sudden thunderstorm in summer.

She blinked. Her eyes felt heavy and she knew she must look a hot mess. She unfurled her body and her joints ached. Slowly, she got to her feet and rotated her neck and shoulders, then went to her desk, opened the bottom drawer and took out her purse. She rummaged around for a mirror and gasped at the sight of her puffy face. She looked like she'd spent the night out drinking. The key now was getting to the ladies' room and avoiding curious looks, so she could repair the damage done by the floodgates.

She grabbed her bag and feeling like a spy crossing enemy lines, she hurried—head lowered and eyes fixed on her iPad—down the hall to the ladies' room. She tapped the code in the door lock panel and pushed the door open. There was a flush in the distance.

Layne went to the sink and turned on the cold water, quickly splashing water on her face, just as one of the interns exited the stall. She gave Layne a brief glance, washed her hands and walked out.

Layne snatched some paper towels from the dispenser and dried her face. She peered closer at her reflection. Fortunately, she didn't wear much makeup, if any at all except for special occasions. So the repairs were minimal. Her mascara had left dark smudges under her eyes. *So much for non-streaking mascara.* She cleaned up her eyes with the baby wipes she always kept in her bag and reapplied her mascara. She checked for any remnants of salty streaks on her face, then dabbed some clear lip gloss on her mouth and a light moisturizer to her face. One more close look, then she took a step back.

The slight wrinkles of her bright white blouse were hidden beneath a navy jacket over fitted dark jeans. She looked every bit the producer that she was, ready to meet her team—and face Paul.

The second-floor conference room was one of the smaller of the four in the building and could still easily accommodate twenty to twenty-five. The ten-foot table allowed for plenty of work space and the table was equipped with embedded outlets for computers, tables and smartphones. The front of the room had a massive screen that took up one wall, and a small podium for speakers to make presentations.

By the time Layne arrived, the vendor delivering lunch had just finished setting out the trays of sandwiches, salads and refreshments on a long table against the wall. Urns of coffee, tea and lemonade sat at one end.

"Thank you so much," Layne said to the delivery team. "Looks great."

"There are extra plates and utensils under the skirt of the table, in case," the young woman offered.

"Great. Thank you."

The team began filing in and by ten minutes after one everyone was seated with a plate of food in front of them.

"Will Mr. Waverly be joining us?" one of the techs asked.

Layne cleared her throat. "He—"

"Yes, I am," Paul cut in as he walked into the room. "I apologize for being late. Was in another meeting." He gave a short nod to Layne and smiled around the room.

"Um, grab a plate. Your seat is right there," she said, pointing to an empty space near the front. "We were just about to get started, so you haven't missed anything," Layne said, the most words she'd uttered to him since his arrival.

Layne flipped on the big screen that projected the information from her iPad and launched into her presentation, beginning with assignments, partnerships and scheduling. She gave everyone a chance to weigh in and got agreements all around before moving to the on-air assignments that went to Kevin Parker, who had a knack for targeted coverage of major events. He would handle breaking news. She and Kevin had worked together before and she was happy to give him a solo shot in the limelight. Della Bryant was an up-and-coming journalist who was as smart as she was camera-ready. Her specialty was political science with a twist of economics. There was plenty for her to cover in this town. Layne partnered her with Carmen Fuentes, who had the experience and the graciousness to bring a newcomer along. International Affairs went to Simon Fields. No one at WWDC was as good as Simon at what he brought to the table. Layne gave him his choice of a partner to back him up and he surprised everyone by selecting Adrienne Allen, who'd been with the company for a bit more than a year. Adrienne had shown talent by bringing hard-to-reach stories to the surface, but had yet to really spread her wings.

The meeting moved smoothly with barely a hiccup. Layne was ecstatic with how things were working out. Her newly minted team seemed genuinely pleased with their assignments and most of all with the opportunity to be heard.

Once that part of the heavy lifting was completed, the on-air members were set up with their roving crew. The crew members, once assigned, bade their goodbyes.

Now the next phase began, the pitch session and planning out Paul's programming for the upcoming week. Layne was relieved that she didn't have to deal with Paul directly but rather through the team, who pitched and tossed ideas until they had a go-ahead from Paul, cosigned by Layne. "If that's what the anchor wants, that's what the anchor gets," she said more than a half dozen times.

More than four hours later, exhausted but satisfied, she was ready to wrap up, with every piece of *The DC Morning Show with Paul Waverly* in place.

The marketing department had already changed the set. Now he had his own theme music and a tagline. *The DC Morning Show* was the only network program in that time slot that did not have a co-anchor. It made it unique but it also put a great burden on the host to carry the program from start to finish for nearly two hours.

"Well, I think that covers everything," Layne said,

the fatigue beginning to overtake the earlier rush of adrenaline. "I am very pleased with how things shaped up. I'll need each of you to have some drafts ready and any footage or cues that will be needed in the control room."

There were nods all around.

"We'll have our daily meetings directly after the show ends so we stay on track."

"Agreed."

"I'll be handling all the booking of guests, and approving or disapproving of costs. You need to have me as a friend," Cherie added with a wink.

"Unless there are any other concerns or questions…" Layne glanced around the table. "Great. Thanks, everyone." She gathered up her belongings as bodies began filing out.

When she looked up, Paul was still seated. Her heart thumped. She started for the door. Paul rose in a blur.

"Wait."

She glanced back at him from over her shoulder. "I'm really busy."

"Layne, please. We need to talk."

She turned fully around. "Do we, Paul? Really? About what? About how you wouldn't support me in my dream to come here to get *that* spot!" Her voice rose. "The spot that you swept in and took! Of all the jobs on the damned planet." She began to pace, her voice and thoughts racing. "Your personal mantra was that you'd never leave Charlotte. Never. Not even for me, Paul." Her eyes burned. She blinked back tears. "Yet— Here. You. Are," she spewed. "When it all became about you," she said, her tone dripping with disgust. "So, no, there's nothing to talk about, Paul, unless it's about the show." Her smile was a slash of her mouth. "I'll do my job and you do yours." She brushed by him and out, her heart pounding so hard and she felt slightly dizzy.

By the time she reached her office and was able to sit down, her entire body was shaking, and she had her second crying jag of the day.

Paul walked to his office, collected his things and headed to the parking garage. Layne's vehemence shook him. The look in her eyes, the deep hurt and fury, cut to his core. His decision to come to DC and take this job had been two-fold, but was it primarily selfish and self-serving as Layne accused? Had he really allowed the bright lights of national fame to blind him to what his coming here would do to her—even though his real reason was that he wanted to be near her, wanted her back and maybe even to prove to himself that he could make it on the national stage?

The sound of his shoes cracking across the concrete floor of the garage echoed in the emptiness of his soul. What had he done?

"Hey, there."

Paul stopped, turned. Deanna was walking toward him. "Hi." He adjusted the strap of his leather satchel on his shoulder.

"So, how did the meeting go today? Get everything you need?"

She stood inches in front of him. The green of her eyes sparkled in this light, he noticed. "Went well. Layne has put together an impressive team."

She angled her head to the side, studied him. "Glad to hear that." Her brow tightened. "Everything okay?"

"Yes. Absolutely."

"If you don't have immediate plans, how about a wind-down drink? Great place right around the corner."

"Wow. Thanks for the invite. I'm kinda beat, have a lot of notes to go over. Rain check?"

"Of course." She drew in a breath and released her reply. "Well, get some rest. We need you bright and ready on Monday."

"Sure thing. Good night." He offered a tight smile, turned and walked down the next aisle to his reserved parking spot. Layne had made herself perfectly clear: They had nothing to discuss—at least nothing that she wanted to hear from him. He put the car in gear and eased around the lanes toward the exit. If that was how she wanted things to be between them, then maybe now was the time to do what she wanted.

Layne was literally biting her manicured nails as the music rose and the logo for *The DC Morning Show with Paul Waverly* splashed across the screen. Her heart thumped as she listened to the technical director cue camera one. And there he was. She held her breath, not because she was concerned that Paul would fumble the touchdown, but that something else would go wrong and she would be the only one responsible. This was, after all, her show. Paul Waverly's name might be the marquee attraction, but it was her ass on the line if anything went left.

Cherie came to stand behind her. She squeezed Layne's shoulder. "Damn, he's good," she said, kind of in awe, as Paul smoothly moved from one headline to the next, knowing just when to turn his gaze, lower his voice, raise a brow or stare directly into the camera.

"Yeah. He is," she said on a breath.

The segment broke for a weather update.

Layne turned away from the multiple screens in the control room deck and went to the desk that contained the playbook. She flipped the cover open and ran over the storyboard: international news, economics, two location reports, then back to Paul for updates from Capitol Hill. The news would be fed to him in his earpiece and projected on the teleprompter. Then, another weather break and back to Paul for his interview with Senator Hamilton and his run for reelection.

The first hour was in the can and the second hour almost done. Layne paced, watched the monitors and paced some more, studying every move, every signal, every segue. And then it was over. Paul gave his trademark goodbye, held the audience in his gaze for that one extra moment, and then the screen went to commercial. A whoop of happiness and a bevy of praise was showered on Layne for her first time up producing a major program. Her spirits lifted, but she took the accolades in stride. One great show did not an Emmy-winning program make.

Stagehands darted on set to remove microphones, notes and electrical cords in preparation for *News at Noon*, followed by Tess Hampton's cooking show.

The studio door swung open and Paul walked in. The team erupted in applause and rounds of congratulations.

Paul held up his hand. "I came in here—" his gaze swept the room "—to thank all of you for doing an incredible job. You made my work a breeze."

He flashed that million-dollar smile and Layne's stomach tumbled. His eyes found her in the semidarkness. He gave her a short nod.

"Thank you, everyone. Back at it tomorrow." He gave a thumbs-up and walked out.

Layne finally breathed once the door closed behind

Paul. "Thanks, everyone. Debriefing at one," she reminded them and headed out. Cherie was on her heels.

"Big congratulations, Layne," Cherie was saying
as they walked down the corridor. "Everything moved
like clockwork."

"Definitely a team effort," Layne said.

"Good leadership. Hey," she said, when they stopped
in front of Layne's office, "I know you were hoping
for the anchor spot, but maybe this is a blessing in dis-
guise." Layne frowned in confusion. "You pull off a
solid season with this show, take it to number one and
you can write your own ticket—executive producer,
maybe even pitch your own show." Her brows lifted
for emphasis.

"Hmm." She'd been so focused on being furious with
Paul and just getting the first show successfully off the
ground that she hadn't really thought that far ahead or
the possibilities. "One day at a time," she finally said
while opening her door.

"Put it out in the atmosphere," Cherie said. "Speak
it into existence." She patted Layne's arm. "See you at
the debrief." She continued down the hallway.

Layne walked into her office and shut the door behind her. She dropped her iPad on her desk and felt the
tight cords that were holding her body together slowly
begin to unwind. She drew in a long breath and let her
eyes close in a moment of pure relief. Maybe there was
some validity to what Cherie said. Maybe it was finally
time to reimagine her future in broadcasting. However,
the pill of Paul Waverly being here at WWDC was still
hard to swallow.

The first weeks of *The DC Morning Show* went
smooth as butter. The team worked seamlessly together

and Paul was being the charismatic star that he was reputed to be. Everyone *loved* him. Inwardly, Layne groaned as she listened to the accolades tossed around with Paul's name attached. But she had to admit that things were going better than she'd anticipated. During the briefing sessions, Paul was agreeable to the line-ups and the topics and Layne's vision for each show. She was slowly beginning to accept his presence and secretly looked forward to seeing him, hearing his voice—remembering. To add to her sense of content-ment, Tina had found another reporter to interview Paul and assured her it wouldn't take more than two days the following week to finish it. The interview was over and the article slated to run at the end of the month.

And then, three weeks in, all that glittered turned to something on the bottom of a shoe. Paul began to ques-tion Layne's decisions and then challenging her choices for guests, as well as what she was assigning the team to cover. At first she shrugged it off as Paul finally get-ting comfortable in his role and wanting to get his feet wet with more input. But his displeasure only seemed to grow as he found something to critique about pretty much everything Layne suggested. It got bad enough that halfway through Paul's first month, Deanna called Layne to her office.

"Layne, come in and have a seat."

Layne crossed the threshold and her stomach rolled when she spotted Paul sitting at the end of the small conference table intent on his smartphone. He barely looked up when she entered.

Deanna got up from behind her desk and walked over to the table with a folder in hand. "I won't waste time with small talk. Paul is unhappy with how you have been handling things with the program."

Layne slowly sat down. She flashed Paul a look but he acted as if she wasn't there.

Deanna's green eyes were dark, her normally olive complexion was flushed, and her red-polished lips drawn into a tight line. She flipped open the folder. "Over the past week, Mr. Waverly has brought to my attention his…concern with some of the choices you have made with the program. For example, moving the segments around just as he was getting accustomed to the order, and setting up interviews with guests who aren't newsworthy. Besides, the debriefing sessions are not as productive as they need to be or at least as they had been when he first arrived."

Layne swallowed. "When I was given the assignment to produce this program I was also given the responsibility to run it successfully—and I have. Ratings are up and growing. We were number one in our time slot last week, the second week in a row." Her head swiveled toward Paul, her temper boiling. "Mr. Waverly may not be accustomed to the way I do things, but my job is to run a successful show and team—not hand-hold a—"

"I'd watch myself if I were you, Ms. Davis," Deanna cut in. "It might be your show to run, but without the star, you would be back on the street chasing stories and in the office booking guests. Whether you want to or not, you will get Mr. Waverly's approval *and* mine going forward, until this miscommunication is back on track. Does that work for you, Paul?"

He tilted his head slightly to the side, a half smile curving his mouth. "Works fine. Thanks, Deanna."

Layne was so hurt and humiliated she couldn't speak.

She gripped the edge of the table and rose to her feet. "Anything else?" Her knees felt wobbly.

"Nothing else for now. Thank you for coming in, Layne. I'm sure that working together, we can get over this minor bump in the road."

Layne blinked to push back the clouds that obscured her vision, turned and walked out.

Paul didn't need to make any more complaints. He'd successfully shaken her confidence to a point where she questioned her own decisions and constantly second-guessed herself. And it was becoming obvious to her team as well.

"Layne," Cherie said, sidling up to her friend after the weekly planning meeting. "What the heck is going on with you?" she asked in a harsh whisper.

Layne just lowered her head and slowly shook it. "Tired."

"Don't play with me. Tired never bothered you before. It's Paul. He has you off your game. What is going on? Did you rub him the wrong way or something?"

"Just has the 'I am the star' syndrome," Layne murmured.

"Well, whatever it is, it's taking the shine off *your* star. And I don't like it. I don't like what it's doing to you."

"I'll be fine." She offered a tight smile. "I'm going to take the weekend off and just relax for a change. Programming is mapped out for the next two weeks barring something unforeseen. So I'm going to put this place behind me for this long weekend."

"Good. You deserve it. Any special plans?"

"Not really. Playing it by ear."

"My sister is having her annual cookout. Nothing can

compare to a backyard full of family, tipsy on beer and ribs, with access to fireworks. What could possibly go wrong?" Cherie said laughing.

Layne chuckled. "Let's hope your family doesn't make the eleven o'clock news."

"Girl, you and me both. Take care. Enjoy. See you next week. You have my number if you want to come and hang out."

"Thanks."

They parted ways and Layne went to her office to check last-minute emails and pack up. There was an email from Deanna, wanting to meet on Tuesday, after the holiday, to get an update on the programming.

Layne stared at the words and the anger that she'd struggled for weeks to suppress rose from the soles of her feet, heating her blood until her temples throbbed and her breath hitched in short spurts. Tears of fury stung her eyes, but she was tired of crying, tired of being undermined. She wanted her job but not like this. It wasn't worth it. *He* wasn't worth it. Enough!

She snatched up her bag and stormed toward the door, tugged it open and came face-to-face with Paul, with his fist frozen inches before knocking.

Layne's mouth opened in surprise.

"Please, I need to talk to you," Paul whispered.

Six

Layne was stunned speechless. She'd been on her way to have it out with Paul and maybe lose her job in the process, and here he was—wanting to talk!

"Please," he asked again.

"You've done everything short of asking Deanna to fire me. You question every decision I make, undermine me at every turn in front of my team." Her chest heaved.

She was so furious she didn't even realize that Paul had stepped in and shut the door behind him.

Her eyes blazed.

"Why, damn it? Tell me why! You came all this way to ruin everything I've done for myself. Why?" Her voice cracked.

He slowly shook his head. "It… It's not like that. I want to explain. I'll explain everything over dinner."

"Are you out of your mind?"

"No. Listen." He tried to reach for her and she jerked

back. He held up his hands in surrender. "You have every right and reason to feel the way you do about me...about everything. I was wrong. I was angry and I was selfish."

Layne heaved a breath and folded her arms tightly across her chest. She rested her weight on her right hip and glowered at him.

"I want to make it up to you. All of it, and I will if you let me."

"It's too late, Paul."

He took a step toward her. "I don't think it is." His gaze trailed over her face. "I know it isn't. If you'll just hear me out. Please..."

She felt the rod in her back soften.

"After you hear what I have to say, then whatever you say or do—" he released a breath "—I'll never bother you again. And I'll do everything I can to make your job easier. Starting with not being a pain in the ass."

Layne snickered against her will.

"Just an hour. We don't even have to do dinner if you don't want. Drinks? Talk?"

Damn it, when he looked at her like that. Layne tipped her head to the side and licked her lips. "You said dinner." She rolled her eyes. "Well... Let's go. Julian's is great and it's walking distance," she said, brushing by him.

Paul stood in dutiful silence next to Layne on the way down on the elevator. He was moderately thankful that they were the only riders. The two-block walk to the restaurant was a different story. It might be July but the temperature between the two of them was below freezing. She barely acknowledged his existence as they wound their way around the after-fivers looking for a place to unwind at the end of the workday and the en-trée to a long weekend.

They stopped in front of Julian's. Paul opened the door. Layne rolled her eyes again and walked inside.

They walked in silence to the hostess's podium.

"Seating or bar?" the hostess asked with a practiced smile.

"Seating for dinner," Layne said.

"There is about a half-hour wait. I can take your name if you want to sit at the bar. You'll be called when your table is ready."

"That sounds fine," Layne said. "Davis."

The hostess made a note. "You'll be called."

"Thank you." Layne walked off to the bar, leaving Paul in her wake.

She found the last empty seat and slid onto the stool. Paul stood next to her.

"Still drinking margaritas?" he asked.

She angled her head toward him in slow motion. She wouldn't give him the satisfaction of being right. "No. Frozen apple martini."

Paul flicked a brow, then signaled for the bartender. "Frozen apple martini and Hennessy on the rocks, please."

Layne stared ahead, not daring to look at him and risk giving in. Being this close to him, with his body nearly pressing against her, it took all her willpower not to lean into him, the way she once had.

The bartender put their drinks in front of them.

Layne lifted her glass toward her lips. "So…you got me here. I'm listening. What do you have to say?"

"I still love you, Layne," he murmured.

She sputtered the sweet liquid and flashed him a look of disbelief. "Wh-what?"

"I never stopped loving you." He moved closer so that there was nothing between them but air. "I was a fool and too full of my ego to see it." He lowered his head a moment, then looked into her astonished face. "I never intended to take the job but then I realized that coming here, I could be with you again, try to make it work. If you were willing to step out on faith, why couldn't I?"

"It's been three years," Layne said. "Not a word from you."

He drew in a breath. "I know. I was stubborn and hurt. But being without you ate away at me every day. When Deanna approached me with the offer, I turned her down. Then she told me about six months ago that there were 'problems' with Brett and that if he was let go, she wanted me for the spot."

Layne slowly shook her head. "She also knew that I'd been working toward it."

"That I didn't know. I thought that if she offered it, you weren't interested anymore. And from everything I've seen since I've been here, you are one helluva producer."

She scoffed. "You'd never know it by your behavior."

"Stupid. For some reason that makes no sense I thought if I ticked you off enough it would force you to talk to me. Even if it meant lashing out." He took a chance and reached out to stroke her cheek with the tip of his finger. Her lids fluttered. "I love you. I want the chance to make everything up to you. Everything, whatever it takes. But what ultimately made me take the offer was that not having you in my life made me realize I was only living halfway, going through the motions."

"Davis!" a waitress called out.

Paul glanced over his shoulder. "Table is ready." He

helped her to her feet, thankful that she didn't smack his hand away.

They reviewed the menu in silence. Layne wasn't sure if she could eat a thing when her salmon salad arrived. Her mind was spinning, trying to make sense of what Paul confessed. He still loved her.

When she'd left Charlotte three years ago, her heart was broken in ways she could never put into words. She'd buried herself in her work to block out the loneliness and wondered every day if she'd made the right decision. She'd been on her way up back in Charlotte, but she was so fixed on this damned show that she'd given it up. And for what? She still didn't have what she thought she'd wanted, when what she'd really only wanted was being with Paul—doing this thing they loved—together.

"So…how did they take it at the station when you told them you were leaving?" Layne quietly asked.

Paul smothered a laugh and wiped his mouth with the napkin. "Let's just say it was an uproar." He went on to tell her about the emergency meetings, the promises, the added perks, the apologies for his talk show not materializing. They'd even gone so far as to say that they'd hold his spot for six months no questions asked, if he decided to come back.

"What?" Layne squeaked, wide-eyed.

"Yep."

"So does Deanna know about this six-month deal?"

He nodded.

"Wow, you really are a rock star."

He leaned across the table and took her hand. "I figured if I couldn't win you back in six months…"

"I don't know what to say," she said slowly.

"Say you'll think about it. That's all I ask."

She reached for her drink and took a sip and then another. "I'll…think about it."

His smile lit up the room and warmed that space in her center the way it always did.

Paul brought her hand to his lips and placed a featherlight kiss on her knuckle. "I'm going to make you love me again, baby."

Heat rose up her arm and tingled behind her neck. She might have sighed, she wasn't certain. Flashes of the two of them together, him touching her in places, kissing her in places… She blinked the images away but not the fire that raced through her veins and the longing that echoed in her soul.

They stood in front of Layne's car in the underground parking garage.

"Thank you for dinner."

"No, thank *you*—for listening." He cupped her cheek.

Her breath hitched.

"I want to kiss you," he whispered, drawing closer.

Heat flashed through her body. Her heart raced. She should turn away, push him away, but it was too late.

The familiar warmth of his lips touched down on her mouth and air stuck in her chest. He pressed, slowly, tenderly, parting her lips, testing the tip of his tongue along her mouth, in it, dancing until the glacier that she'd erected around her heart began to melt and her body grew soft and pliable.

Paul groaned. He snaked an arm around her waist; the other hand threaded through the twisted cotton of her hair.

Layne whimpered. Gave back and gave in. The time, the loneliness, the hurt peeled away layer by layer until she was exposed and yearning and vulnerable. She pulled away, stepped back, brought her hand to her thoroughly kissed month. She spun toward her car door, fumbled with the key fob. *Beep.*

"Layne, please. Wait," he gently urged. He lightly touched her shoulder, turned her to face him. "Don't leave like this. I didn't mean to push you. I…wanted to kiss you, to feel you again, but I can take it slow. I can. I will. I'll do whatever you want, however you want to do it."

She'd seen all of Paul's personas over the years: the consummate professional, the thoughtful conversationalist, the loyal friend, the life of the party, the counselor, the artistic lover, but never this. She'd never seen him truly exposed and raw. It was in the pleading in his eyes, the urgency in his voice.

She pulled in a breath and slowly exhaled. "What you did to me by not thinking enough of me to help me get to where I wanted, hurt me in ways that I can't even explain. For all the time that we were together it was always the way *you* wanted things, the way *you* saw things. And when I finally did something for me, *you* couldn't handle it so *we* couldn't be. Then you come here—" she threw her hands up "—after all this time, and take that one thing that I wanted for myself. You say you love me. Maybe. You say you were an egotistical asshole. True. You say you want to make it right." Slowly, she shook her head and looked him in the eye. "I don't know if you can."

His head lowered.

"You have a lot of work to do, Paul." He looked up. "And unlike the millions that watch you everyday and gobble up your every word, I won't. If you want me, if you love me like you say you do, you're going to have

to prove it. Kisses and sweet talk will not be enough."
She pulled open the car door and slid behind the wheel.
"Up to you," she added before shutting the door and
turning on the engine.

She slowly pulled off. From her rearview mirror she
watched him standing there, fine as all get-out and totally put in his place. Layne smiled. *Now, let's see what
you got.* She exited the lot and drove out into the warm
summer night.

"Get. Outta. Town," Tina chirped as she and Layne
strolled along M Street, stopping from time to time to
check out a shop window. They each grabbed a cup of
gelato, then continued on toward Wisconsin Avenue to
check out the arts festival.

"Yes. I still can't believe it."

"But do you want to believe it is the question?"

Layne scooped a spoonful of gelato into her mouth,
savored the sweetness. "I'm definitely not going to make
it easy for him."

"I should hope not. Doesn't deserve it. Make him
beg," she said wickedly.

Layne giggled.

"So." Tina lowered her voice and hooked her arm
through Layne's. "Was the kiss as good as you remembered?"

Layne threw her head back and laughed. "Girl, I almost lost my natural mind. Another minute and no telling what I might have agreed to."

"What next?"

Layne gave a slight shrug. "Up to him. We'll see."

After having roamed through the street vendors displaying their art, Layne bought a brilliant abstract of a

man and woman entwined on a meadow and Tina purchased a muted painting of four jazz musicians on stage.

Layne and Tina parted ways around three, with Tina saying she needed to get ready for a very hot date with this guy she'd met during a local journalists' conference. They were going dancing and she "needed a nap" before stepping out.

Layne returned to her apartment with the intention of taking a hot shower, ordering some takeout and reading Tiphanie Yanique's latest novel that she'd had on her to-be-read pile for months.

Just as she stepped out of the shower, her cell phone chirped. *It better not be some problem at work.* She grumbled as she padded across the bedroom floor. She picked up the phone and frowned.

"Hello?"

"Layne, it's Paul."

She dropped down on the side of her bed. "Paul—how did you get my number?"

"Your cell is on the call sheet, remember?"

She squeezed her eyes shut. *Of course.* She cleared her throat and crossed her bare legs. "Okay. And you're calling because…?"

"I don't want to waste one more minute for us. I'm sure you might have plans for the holiday weekend, but if you don't, I was wondering, hoping, that you'd want to take a drive out to Baltimore Harbor for the crab fest. I know how much you love the water and seafood. I thought it would be fun. Give us a chance to talk, spend time together. See the fireworks from the harbor."

She was silent.

"I'll do all the driving, going and coming. And I'll pay the tolls *and* gas."

She burst out laughing. "Fine. Okay."

Paul chuckled, too. "Great. I'll pick you up at about eight. The traffic will be crazy."

"We, uh, could leave tonight. Get a head start. Find someplace to stay." She swallowed. Her heart hammered. What the hell was she thinking? Too late now: The words were out, the gauntlet had been thrown.

"I'm…good with that," he stammered.

Layne wondered if she'd thrown him off by being so quick to accept his offer.

"I'll throw some things in a bag. Pick you up."

"I can check the hotels in the area…" She tugged on her bottom lip.

"Okay."

What was she doing? "Um, seven sound good?"

"Great. I'll see you at seven…if you give me your address."

She laughed and gave him her address.

"See you at seven," he said.

"I'll be out front." She hung up the phone before she really said something additionally crazy. She tossed the phone on the bed as if it was a hot poker and leaped to her feet, then spun around in a frenzied circle. What in the world had she just done?

You know what you've done. She went to her dresser and pulled open her lingerie drawer. *You know exactly what you've done.* She picked out three of her favorites: black, hot pink and virgin white. Would it be as good as she remembered? *It better be.* She shoved the drawer shut, then went to check on vacancies in Baltimore.

Layne had just stepped out the front door of her condo when Paul pulled up. She inwardly smiled with approval at his choice of vehicle. Mercedes GLS SUV in black. Hmm. Nice.

Paul hopped out, came around and took her bag. "All set?"

"Yep."

He opened the passenger door for her, then took her bag, opened the back hatch and put the bag inside next to his.

"You look great," he said, clearly nervous.

Layne angled her head in his direction. She bit back a grin and the impulse to say something snarky. Instead, she said a simple thank-you, knowing full well that an H&M T-shirt and biker shorts were not up there with Versace, but she'd take it. He was trying.

"I figure it will take about an hour and a half to get to Inner Harbor, straight up I-95." He tossed her a quick look as he slid into traffic heading to the highway. "So…did you find a place for us to stay?"

"All the hotels in the area were booked. But I found an Airbnb—a townhouse. We lucked out. The owner said there was a last-minute cancellation. We'd have the entire place to ourselves, and it's close to everything."

Paul smiled in admiration. "You always knew how to put a plan together," he said. "Remember when the station manager wanted to host a retreat for the staff and we arrived only to find out that the reservation had never been finalized?"

"Oh my goodness! Yes." She started laughing. "What a hot mess."

"You got on the phone, made some calls, twisted some arms and got us into the W hotel, *at* a discount." He chuckled. "Man." He glanced at her. "Same way you run your team with efficiency. No energy wasted." He pulled in a breath, switched the topic. "Some music?"

"Sure."

"Still love classic R&B?"

She grinned. "Is there any other kind? You still have your go-to playlist?"

"Is there any other kind?" he teased, holding her with a smile while he pressed the lighted panel on the console.

Martha Reeves and the Vandellas, classic "Heat Wave," pumped through the speakers and they immediately joined in, singing off-key and loving it, followed by "One Nation Under A Groove" by Parliament-Funkadelic, "Tracks of My Tears" by Smokey Robinson and the Miracles, and "Shining Star" by Earth, Wind & Fire.

For every song that came on they tried to out sing the other, their voices cracking over their unbridled laughter. Singing the R&B chart toppers was one of their Friday night activities, their very own at-home karaoke. They'd discovered early in their relationship that they loved the same music. What was crazy was that most of the music they loved had been popular before they were even old enough to talk. But it was their thing. They laughed and sang and reminisced for the entire drive.

After a few wrong turns they pulled up in front of the townhouse and hopped out.

Paul glanced up at the two-story redbrick structure tucked between similar buildings on either side, took in the quiet tree-lined street beneath a dusting of stars in a cloudless sky. He nodded in approval. "So far so good," he said with a wink, then opened the hatch and took out their bags while Layne tapped in the code that the owner had given her to unlock the front door.

They stepped inside, welcomed by the soft scent of lavender.

Layne flicked on the light. The squared-off foyer

opened to a cozy living room with a redbrick accent wall and a fireplace. Simple but tasteful furnishings sat on gleaming wood floors. To the right was the kitchen that led out to a tidy backyard. On the opposite side of the living room was a small study.

"There are two bedrooms," Layne offered, "and an authentic claw-foot tub," she quickly added. "Upstairs."

"Cool." He bobbed his head. "I'll take the bags up. Guess you can choose which room you want your things in." He picked up the bags and headed upstairs, chortling James Brown's "Papa's Got a Brand New Bag," much to Layne's amusement. She followed him upstairs.

The spacious bedrooms with queen-size beds were situated on either side of the bathroom along a long hallway.

"I'll take this one," Layne said, stepping into the room closest to the staircase. Paul brought her bag in and set it down next to the club chair by the arched windows.

"You've outdone yourself, Layne. This place is sweet."

She turned to face him and images of them in his bedroom back in Charlotte floated in front of her. How many nights did she listen for his key in the door—the highlight of her day.

"Thanks. I think we'll be very comfortable."

"Speaking of comfort, we should figure out what to do about dinner." He patted his taut stomach.

Layne laughed. "Definitely. I'm going to freshen up a bit and I guess we can take a walk around, see what's available."

"Sounds like a plan." He turned away and walked to his room.

Layne sighed heavily, planted her hands on her hips

and looked around. They would be there for the next four days. How long would they stay in separate rooms?

Arm in arm, they strolled along cobblestoned streets, paused and peered into shop windows, and made up outlandish stories about the people they passed on the street. They found a cozy, family-run soul-food restaurant and had the best chicken and waffles this side of Atlanta. On the way back to the townhouse, they stopped in an all-night mini-mart and loaded up on snacks, breakfast fixings, coffee and two bottles of wine.

Happy and a little tired, they tumbled into the living room and plopped down on the sectional couch.

"Nightcap?" Paul suggested.

"Sure."

He took a bottle of wine from the bag of groceries and went in search of two glasses.

Layne toed off her sneakers and tucked her feet beneath her. Paul returned with two glasses and a bowl.

"For the popcorn," he said in answer to her raised brow. He opened the bottle of Prosecco, poured two glasses and filled the bowl with popcorn. He sat a gentlemanly distance away on the couch.

Layne leisurely sipped her wine. "This was a good idea, I think," she said. She glanced at him, offering a half smile.

He studied her for a moment. "I think so, too." He glanced around. "I don't see a sound system. Want to watch a movie?"

"I'm fine. I'd just like to sit here for a few. Unwind."

He finished off his glass of wine and took a handful of popcorn. "You just relax. I'm going up to take a shower, get the day off of me." He smiled and rose to his feet. He placed the bowl of popcorn in front of her. "Good night," he said softly.

"Good night," she whispered back.

Once Paul was gone, Layne put down her glass, closed her eyes and leaned her head back against the couch cushion. If she had planned a perfect day, it would have been one like this. The drive was fun and easy. The townhouse absolutely perfect, dinner, the conversation, the walk through town…everything. Paul. She pulled in a breath and sighed. Too perfect? Too easy? Was it real or did she simply want it to be?

In his presence, she felt better. The space inside her felt warm. But she was still struggling to wrap her mind around his reasoning for doing what he did. That was what gave her pause. That was what made her put on the brakes when it was so easy to go full steam ahead.

But the truth was, she understood Paul. He was driven. He had a big ego and his ego was what propelled him to achieve all that he'd done. He was rooted to his own principles, sometimes intractably so. But as much as those traits were a strength, they were also a weakness as they blinded him very often to how his actions and his vision conflicted with others, and they would not allow him to back down. In all the years that she'd known and loved him, she'd never seen him give in. He believed it was a weakness. *You have to stand by your convictions. If you give in on one thing you'll give in on something else*, he'd told her when they'd first met. *And before you know it, what will you have? What is a man without his word, his beliefs?*

So, based on what she knew about Paul, his confession to her about what he'd done and why he'd done it went against every fiber that made Paul Waverly the man he was. For him to break his own mantra, to leave his home and job, come to DC and ultimately undress his soul was a big deal, and the fact that he was willing to do whatever it took to win her back meant this was a brand-new Paul Waverly. A Paul Waverly she wanted to get to know in a new way.

She heard the doors overhead open and close. She sighed deeply and rose to her feet. It was almost midnight and she and Paul had talked about getting an early start to get over to Inner Harbor for a full day. She really wanted to visit the National Aquarium while they were in Baltimore. She'd heard about it since she'd relocated to DC, but had yet to visit.

She went upstairs. Paul's bedroom door was shut, but she heard the faintest strains of music. She guessed he was listening on his phone. She gathered her toiletries and headed into the bath. For a moment she debated about a shower or a soak in the magnificent claw-foot tub. Ultimately, she opted for the shower. She'd save the deep soak for tomorrow. She was sure that with all the walking and touring and shopping they'd planned she would need it.

Finished, refreshed and actually revitalized, she stepped out of the bathroom and right into Paul's path.

"Sorry. Was going downstairs. Thought I'd top off the night with one more glass of wine," he said, staring at her. "Couldn't sleep."

Layne inhaled the fresh-washed scent of him—remembered it. Her heart raced.

"You're beautiful, you know," he said, his voice low, almost awed. His eyes moved over her face, down to the opening in her robe and back.

Her breath hitched. He reached out and tenderly moved a wet tendril of hair away from her face before cupping her cheek. Her eyelids fluttered close.

"Layne," he whispered. "I need you…"

She glanced up at him to the familiar love and longing in his eyes and knew that the last vestiges of her resistance were falling away. Her robe parted when she lifted her arms to drape around his neck and melted into him when he swept her flush against the hard contours of his body.

His groan vibrated in the center of her chest when his mouth covered hers in a searing kiss. Her tongue mated with his in a slow, sensual dance that sparked flames of desire.

He brushed her robe from her shoulders, kissed her collarbone, trailed his lips up her neck and across the shell of her ear. Her body shuddered with hunger.

Her robe pooled at her feet. She clutched the end of his T-shirt and tugged it over his head, tossing it to the floor. His head dipped to the swell of her breasts and he buried his face between the firm pillows. Her neck arched. She gasped as his mouth encircled a taut nipple.

Paul lifted her into his arms and pushed open the door to his bedroom. Layne was dizzy with need, the images of his room fuzzy around the edges.

In long strides he crossed the room and laid her down on his bed. For several moments he stood above her. Her gaze hungrily drank him in.

"Is this what you want?" he asked, his voice almost hoarse.

"Yes," she whispered. "Yes."

Paul pulled off his khaki shorts and kicked them to the side.

Layne sucked in a breath, taking in the beauty of him, and the memories of the feel of him inside her flooded her senses. She sucked on her bottom lip with her teeth as Paul lowered himself down beside her.

They turned on their sides to face each other.

"I love you, Layne. I never stopped loving you."

Paul captured her mouth, kissed her long and deep as his hands smoothed across her waist, her hips. He hooked his arm beneath her thigh and draped it over his waist. His throbbing erection pressed against her belly.

Her fingers threaded through the tight coils of his hair, trailed down his neck and kneaded the ropes of muscle in his back.

They took their time exploring, remembering, reconnecting, yet it was all new and thrilling.

Paul eased her onto her back and braced his weight on his forearms. He placed featherlight kisses on her lips, then her cheeks, her throat, and down between the valley of her breasts. He cupped her breasts in his palms and brushed his lips back and forth across the warm skin, nipping and suckling, teasing as she moaned and writhed beneath him.

He moved in maddeningly slow degrees down her body until he reached the heat between her thighs. Layne sucked in air from between her teeth. Paul placed a hand on each thigh and gently spread them wider. Layne gripped the sheets in her fist.

His tongue flicked back and forth across the tip of her clitoris. Layne cried out. Her hips arched. Paul cupped her rear in his palms and brought her to his mouth.

"Ohhhh!" Her inner thighs trembled. Flashes of electricity shot up her limbs.

Paul was expert and thorough, bringing her to the brink of release time and again until she begged for him.

"Tell me what you want," he urged. "Tell me."

"You," she moaned.

He moved above her. She wrapped her legs around

his waist and felt the pressure of his erection press against the welcoming wet heat. The air stuck in her chest as he pushed across the threshold. Paul groaned, and she cried his name. That instant when they became one was surreal.

What was thought to be lost became familiar again as they found their special rhythm, moving in undulating waves that ebbed and flowed through them, carried by their moans and sighs of pleasure. Hands and mouths explored, teased and urged. The sounds of desire only intensified along with the thrust and arch of bodies.

The tips of Layne's fingers pressed into Paul's back, her thighs tightened. Paul's thrust quickened, deepened, and his breathing grew ragged. Layne's moans rose until she was crying out as wave after wave of pleasure poured through her, shook her. She arched her hips. Paul pushed harder, faster. He held her hips in a steely grip. His head fell back and a guttural groan rose from his gut as the months and months of longing for the woman he loved exploded in mind-shattering satisfaction.

Their heaving breaths mixed and mingled and bubbled into joyous, giddy laughter.

Paul tumbled over onto his back. Layne looped her leg across him and curled against his side.

"You're off to a good start proving yourself, Mr. Waverly."

Paul angled his head, looked into her eyes and grinned. "And I have all the proving you need." He leaned over and sealed his promise with a kiss.

The rest of the days and hours spent together during their long holiday weekend getaway was pure magic. They laughed and talked and debated, sang, ate and toured the city, watched the fireworks, made love as often as humanly possible and tumbled head over heels back in love with each other.

It was their last night before driving back to DC, and Layne finally decided to make use of the claw-foot tub. Paul was puttering around in the kitchen with promises that he was going to prepare a great snack for the movie they'd rented and planned to watch.

Layne slowly slipped into the steamy, scented water and let out a satisfied *ahhh* when the water reached just below her chin. She leaned her head back against the pillow attached to the lip of the tub and closed her eyes. Her skin prickled from the heat.

The past few days were directly out of a perfect romance novel. *"Handsome, sexy, intelligent man sweeps reluctant, stubborn, independent and sexy woman off her feet in a whirlwind weekend escape. Will the dashing hero be able to capture the heroine's questioning heart?"* She smiled as she took a mental inventory of her body, running her hands along the wet dips and curves, noting all the tingles, tenderness and electric energy that coursed through her. If capturing the heroine had any connection to conquering her body, then all was lost for the feisty heroine. She giggled. But even so, as with all romance novels, our heroine could not let the hero think he'd won just yet.

The bathroom door eased open. She opened her eyes and turned to see Paul with nothing on but a thick towel wrapped around his waist and carrying a tray in an awful parody of a waiter.

Layne sputtered a laugh. "What in the world are you doing?"

"Your snacks, madame." He made a perfunctory bow.

"You are nuts." She giggled.

Paul crossed to the tub, pulled a small stool next to it and placed the tray of assorted cheese and crackers and red and green grapes on the stool along with a bottle of wine and two paper cups. He set the bottle of wine on the black-and-white tiled floor.

"I am here to serve, madame," he said with another mock bow. He unknotted the towel and let it drop to the floor.

Layne sucked in a sharp breath. No matter how many times he'd done it before, seeing him naked in full display always took her breath away.

"I think madame might be in need of a massage and I believe I can help." He smiled wickedly and eased into the hot water behind her. "Hmm, this is nice," he murmured into her damp hair. He reached for a grape and brought it to her mouth. With his other hand he roamed the rise of her breasts beneath the water, sliding smoothly across skin made slick and supple from the hot, scented water.

A cracker this time while he moved lower, across her belly that fluttered beneath his fingertips. He kissed the back of her neck, nibbled her earlobe, tweaked her nipples. Another grape while his hand moved between her bent knees and stroked the wet folds until she began to moan softly and slowly undulate her pelvis against his fingers. He brushed her mouth with the tip of his thumb and she sucked it in between her lips.

His erection pulsed against her. A finger slid inside her. She gasped. Arched. His palm cupped her breast, squeezed gently. Moans. Breath heightened. Her hand covered his, pressing, urging him deeper.

"I want you," he whispered hotly in her ear. "Now."

He stifled his groan in the hollow of her neck, suckling her there. She cried out. Her hips rose. Two fingers.

Heat. So hot. Her toes curled. In and out. Faster. Nip on her neck. The quickening deep inside.

"Paul! Paul!"

"Come for me," he groaned in her ear, flicked his thumb across the pulse of her swollen clitoris, and her limbs stiffened as a bolt of electricity shot through her, then shook her as her wet inside sucked on the source of her pleasure.

"Ohhhh, ahhhh!"

"Yesss," he whispered. "Come for me."

When the last wave of her release subsided, she sank against his chest, weak but utterly satisfied. That had been so damned good she wanted to cry.

Paul kissed the back of her neck and tenderly caressed her belly. Her insides fluttered, came to attention. It couldn't be possible that she could want more, but she did and after all she owed it to Paul, who obviously still had needs to be met.

She maneuvered her body so that she was astride him. He hummed deep in his throat, brushed her hair away from her face. "You're beautiful, you know that?" He kissed her, full and deep.

Layne slid her hand down between them and stroked him. His breath hitched.

"Look at me," she demanded.

Paul opened his dark eyes that had grown darker with lust. Long, steady strokes from hilt to tip. His nostrils flared. His head lolled back. He sucked air between his teeth.

Without missing a beat, Layne rose up on her knees, positioned his very hard shaft between her legs and slowly descended until they were sealed together.

Paul's fingers dug into Layne's hips, preventing her

from moving until he'd gathered himself enough not to explode on his first stroke.

She lifted up her breasts in her palms. Paul leaned in, took one tip between his lips, sucked and teased and then the other. Layne's neck arched back. She tried to rock her hips against him. Finally, he released her and rose up high and hard inside her. Not to be outdone, she rode him with abandon. Water splashed them, spilled onto the floor, stirring up a whirlpool that spun them, captured them then tossed them into the throes of release.

Later, winded but utterly satisfied, Paul murmured, "Who's gonna clean up the mess?"

Layne took a sleepy-eyed peek over the edge of the tub. "Oh my goodness."

They broke into laughter.

The drive back to DC was much different from the trip going. Now they held hands along the way, shared smiles and secret glances. They laughed more, and the initial awkwardness of being together after being apart for so long was gone. There was a renewed intimacy between them and an afterglow from their loving that hung around them like an aura.

But the closer they drew to DC and home, the more the reality of their new situation began to settle and become the third passenger in the car.

"So, um, how are we going to do this?" Layne finally ventured.

Paul inhaled deeply. "I've been thinking about it." He gave her a quick look before steering onto the entrance of I-95. "I don't want it to be like last time. Secrets and sneaking around."

"So, what are you saying?" She licked her lips. Her heart thumped.

"I'm saying that I don't want us to hide. That doesn't mean making out in the hallways or having blow-your-mind sex on top of your desk or the supply closet." He gave her a wink. She smacked his arm. "But not being afraid of being seen together. Know what I mean?"

She was thoughtful for a moment. "I get it. And I'd like nothing more than to be out in the open." She paused. "But I don't want anyone thinking that I some-how got the producer spot because of you. And—" she twisted her body to look at him "—I still want to sit behind that desk, Paul. I worked for it, I earned it. That hasn't changed. I'm a damned good producer but I know I will be a phenomenal anchor."

His brows flicked. "Where does that leave me, us?"

She sighed and looked away, then back at him. "Your contract is for six months. I'll produce the best damned news show you've ever been a part of—my way. At the end of six months we'll talk about next steps as a couple and as professionals."

"Damn, woman, you drive a hard bargain." He chuckled, snatched a look in her direction. "Deal."

"Besides, that will give you plenty of time to perfect your 'proving it to me' routine."

"I think I was off to a pretty good start this week-end, if I have to say so myself," he said with humor in his voice.

"I'll have to do some…comparisons in the coming days, weeks and months," she teased.

"Ready, willing and able."

Seven

"So, I'll see you tomorrow at work," Paul said. He'd parked in front of her building.

"Yes. Tomorrow." Should she invite him up? No. They needed a bit of distance to clear their heads. She opened her door.

Paul hopped out and grabbed her bag from the back and helped her out. They faced each other.

"I'm going to miss waking up next to you. It got easy real fast," he said, looking into her eyes. He placed a kiss on her forehead. "Tomorrow."

She swallowed. "Tomorrow." She turned and tapped in the security code and the front door buzzed open. She dare not look back because her resolve would be nonexistent and the next thing she knew she'd be making breakfast for him in the morning. She pressed the button for the elevator. This weekend was only a test. They were definitely sexually compatible. The real test would come in the days ahead when sex wasn't the answer, and the blush of the weekend had begun to fade.

She turned the key in the lock to her apartment door in harmony with the buzzing of her cell phone. She pushed the door shut with her foot, tossed her keys in the bowl that sat on the table by the door and fished her phone out of the back pocket of her jeans.

She looked at the name on the screen and snickered.

"Damn, Tina, are you stalking me or what? You see me come in the door?" She dropped her bag next to the living room couch and kicked off her sneakers, then plopped down.

"Look, I gave you the weekend. I didn't bug you for details. I 'let you live,' as the kids would say. But my sistah, time is up and I am itching for details. And if you are *just* getting back then you have some stories to tell."

Layne dropped her head back against the cushion of the couch and shut her eyes a moment. Flashes of Paul above her, beneath her, around her popped in her head. She shook it to clear the images and to calm the tingle that was blooming—again. *Damn!* She crossed her legs.

"Listen, I am literally just getting in the door. For real. Give me an hour and come on by. We'll order Chinese."

"No. Had Chinese last night. Mexican. And make it a half hour. See ya."

She hung up before Layne could protest. Layne shook her head and laughed, then pushed up from the couch and went to empty her carry-all.

"Say what now—in the tub?" Tina squealed. "Damn, I always wanted to do that." She bit down on a piece of quesadilla and chewed thoughtfully. "Hmm, have to be a good-sized tub, though."

Layne snickered. "We did more than have great sex," she qualified with a lifted brow.

"Could be, but that's the fun part." She took a long swallow of iced tea. "But on a serious note, how are you feeling, and what are you thinking with regard to you and Paul?"

Layne released a slow breath. "Being with him this weekend reawakened what I thought was dead and buried. I was reminded why I fell in love with him, but also reminded why I left. The crazy thing is," she continued, "before, back in Charlotte, it was Paul calling all the shots—the how and when. Now it's me. I'm going to do what's right for me. I'm hoping that it all works out, that Paul and I will walk through this together. But I know I'm not going to take a back seat to anyone else's vision for me. Whether I'm in love with him or not."

The work vibe on the team was decidedly different in the ensuing weeks. The undercurrent of tension between Paul and Layne had dissipated and the positive results were evident with the crew. They felt more free to speak up during briefings, and most noticeable was that rather than debate or shoot down Layne's story ideas, Paul seemed to champion them. Deanna noticed as well and made it a point to check in with Paul on a regular basis to see how things were going.

Paul returned to his office after signing off. It had been more than two months since the getaway. In between they were spending time with each other on the weekend, in and out of their respective apartments, dinners, museums and the theater, but Paul wanted more. Layne said she wasn't ready.

He shrugged out of his jacket and hung it on the

back of his chair. The desk phone rang. He snatched up the receiver.

"Waverly."

"Paul, it's Deanna. I was hoping you could join me for dinner."

"Dinner?"

"Yes. Is that a problem? I thought we could talk about the future. Your future."

He cleared his throat.

"I thought I'd order in and have it brought to my office. I have a bunch of meetings today. Does seven work for you?"

How could he say no? In the time that he'd been there, Deanna had been promoted from executive producer to program director in charge of daytime and nighttime news programing. She held the keys.

"Seven sounds fine."

"See you then."

Paul returned the receiver to the cradle and leaned back in his chair. He ran his hand across his face and heaved a sigh. In the past couple of months, Deanna had inserted herself more and more into the day-to-day activities of the *Morning Show*. Where before he'd been the one that made life difficult for Layne, for which he'd made amends, it was now Deanna that seemed to go out of her way to pinprick Layne, nixing her story ideas, questioning her decisions.

He and Layne talked about it, curled together beneath the sheets. Layne was growing concerned and had begun to question Deanna's motives. It was almost as if she wanted her to fail, Layne had confessed, to get rid of her for reasons that she couldn't put her finger on, not to mention that she felt that Deanna had a thing for him. He tried to reassure Layne that Deanna was simply trying to assert herself in her new position and was eager to prove to the higher ups that they hadn't made a mistake. But as much as he tried to allay Layne's misgivings, he was beginning to feel uncomfortable with the direction things were going with Deanna: the phone calls, after-work texts, invitations to meet for late lunch after the briefings. Hopefully, tonight some things could get straightened out, but with Layne already feeling a bit off-center about Deanna's "designs" on him, the last thing she needed to know was that he was having dinner with Layne.

His cell phone chirped with Layne's text.

I'm heading home. Will I see you later tonight?

He stared at the phone, then typed his reply.

Not tonight, babe. I'm gonna turn in early. Tomorrow?

Sure. Tomorrow. Get some rest.

Will do.

Love you. He mouthed the words but didn't text. A wave of guilt rolled through him. He'd make this dinner thing with Deanna quick and efficient, voice his concerns and get the hell out of there.

"Thanks for coming," Deanna greeted. "Come on in." She held the door open. "I've sent everyone home so that we can talk in private," she said, lowering her voice conspiratorially and placing a hand on his shoulder.

Paul forced a tight-lipped smile. He glanced at the circular conference table that had been set up for dinner complete with white tablecloth, a bottle of wine and several silver-covered platters.

"You didn't have to go to all this trouble. I'm not really hungry."

"Don't be silly." She guided him to the table. "A man has got to eat."

He pulled in a breath and walked to the table and sat in the nearest seat.

"Wine?" She held up a bottle of something very expensive.

"No, thanks. Water is fine." He poured a glass of sparkling water into his glass. "You said you wanted to talk about the future," he began, cutting to the chase.

"My, my, can't we at least have the salad first before we talk business?" She lifted one of the silver covers, revealing a beautiful mixed green salad with all the trimmings. "Help yourself."

Paul filled a glass salad bowl and slid it toward him. Deanna did the same and took a seat to his right.

"When we met at that conference…one, two years ago—" she wagged a slender finger at him "—I knew you were the one. Something special. And I would do whatever I could to get you here." She lifted her glass of wine and took a short sip. "I pulled a lot of strings and called in a lot of favors to make that possible. But you know that," she said with a dismissive wave of her hand. "And you have not been a disappointment. So far."

"I have a good team and a great producer."

Her cheeks darkened. She licked her lips. "But lately," she continued, "you haven't been the sparkling star that you were when you arrived."

Paul frowned. "What do you mean?"

"You've gotten soft around the edges. The past couple of months. You haven't been the same. The fierce anchor is coming across too touchy-feely."

"I don't think so. I deliver the news and interview my guests the same way I always have."

"I'm thinking it's time to shake things up a little. Sweeps are coming up in November. We have two months to make sure that we shine."

"What do you mean, shake things up?"

"Well, I want to reassign your producer."

His jaw clenched. "Why?"

"Layne Davis has talent, behind and in front of the camera. I want to give her some time to do for nightly news what she's done for *The DC Morning Show*, and give her some more air time. It's what she's always wanted. Isn't it?"

"You would know better than I do," he said. His mind raced.

"Did the two of you work closely back in Charlotte?"

"No. We didn't."

"Hmm. So what do you think?"

Now he wished he did have a drink. "I think you're making a mistake."

She got up from her seat and sidled next to him. She sat on the edge of the table. "I don't make mistakes. That's why I'm in the position that I'm in. And I intend to keep that track record in place. I have senior VP of the network on my bucket list." She rested her hand on his shoulder and leaned closer. Her voice dropped an octave. "We'd make a formidable team, you and I."

"I thought we already did."

She smiled. "This is nothing compared to what we could do together, *really* together. I could take your career to the next level. You could be a real shot caller—with my help."

He stared up at her. The green of her eyes sparked like emeralds.

"Your dinner's getting cold," he said, then pushed back from the table and stood. "And I really have to go."

She got to her feet and pressed a hand against his chest, halting him. She stepped closer, gripped the lapels of his suit jacket. "Think about my offer, Paul," she purred, leaned in and kissed him full on the mouth. No friendly peck but one filled with longing and power.

He stepped back. Her cheeks were flushed, her eyes simmering.

"Good night, Deanna." He brushed by her and half expected the door to be locked, like in one of those bad B movies. He flung the door open and stalked out.

He went through every variation of expletive known to man on his way down on the elevator. His temples pounded. He knew seeing Deanna after hours had been a bad idea, but like an idiot he'd done it anyway. And what was worse was that he'd lied to Layne about where he'd be.

He went to his office and actually locked the door behind him, then went to his private bathroom to throw some water on his face. He looked in the mirror and his mouth was streaked with her red lipstick.

"F—" What if someone had seen him? He scrubbed the lipstick away then checked the collar of his shirt and his jacket.

This could go left a million different ways. Deanna was a very influential, power-hungry woman and there was no telling what she might do if crossed. He sure as heck couldn't report her. Who would believe him? Best to keep this to himself and play it by ear.

He took one last look in the mirror, pulled out his cell phone and pressed the speed dial button.

"Hey, baby. You know what, I really want to see you. The heck with going to bed early." He forced a laugh. "About an hour."

He made love to Layne that night as if it was the first and the last time all rolled into one. With every stroke, he promised, with her every cry of his name he promised, and in the silence when they held each other in the dark he promised to be everything that she needed.

"So, what are you going to do, man?" Paul's brother Eric asked.

Paul paced the floor of his living room, then went to stare out the window. "I don't know exactly." It had been about two weeks since that dinner rendezvous. So far Deanna hadn't done anything about moving Layne, but he knew it was coming.

"Sounds like this Deanna can make major trouble. You have some protections because you're her star player, but if she's trying to get with you and thinks Layne is in the way, Layne is the one that will come out on the short end of the stick."

"Hmm, yeah, I know." He paused a beat. "My option is still open at WNCC," he said quietly.

"Meaning?"

"I could cut my losses, protect Layne, go back to Charlotte…"

"And you'd be right back where you started—hundreds of miles away. Didn't work before. Piece of advice…"

"I'm listening."

"Tell Layne the truth. Don't let her get blindsided. You won't be able to recover from that."

"You're probably right."

"I know I'm right. Take it from a married man.

Women know stuff. They just do. I don't know how, but it's like a freaking superpower."

Paul chuckled. "I'll tell her." He held his phone away from his ear and looked at the time. "I'm going to pick her up for dinner in about an hour. We haven't been out together in a while. I'll tell her everything tonight."

"Public places are always best," Eric said tongue in cheek. "Less chance for a scene."

"Gee, thanks."

"Good luck, bruh. Let me know how it goes."

"Thanks and I will. Tell Tricia hello for me."

"Will do. Later."

Paul disconnected the call and went to take a quick shower.

The weather was exceptionally warm for late September. The streets of Georgetown were still lined with people in the outdoor seating of the numerous cafés; couples and families strolled leisurely along the cobbled walkways, and the Galleria Mall was teeming with shoppers and tourists. Strains of music could be heard floating out of the doorways of the jazz clubs and bars. All very typical for a Saturday night in DC.

Parking was pretty much nonexistent on the weekend, so Paul opted for an Uber. The car dropped them off in front of Blues Alley Jazz on Wisconsin Avenue NW. Blues Alley was famous for its live shows with some of the greats as well as aspiring performers.

"Thought we'd do something a little different tonight," Paul said as he helped Layne out of the cab. "I have reservations for the nine o'clock performance. Thought we could sit outside a while, see the passersby, have a drink before dinner and the show."

"I'm all in." She smiled and leaned in to kiss him.

He slid an arm around her waist and pulled her close. "I was hoping you'd say that," he said.

She leaned her head on his shoulder while they waited for a table to be cleaned and set up for them.

A cab eased to a stop, waiting for the red light to change. Paul did a double take when he thought he spotted Deanna. She briefly turned in his direction but before he could be certain the cab pulled off across the intersection. He thought to mention it to Layne but shrugged it off. He was probably wrong.

Paul held Layne's chair while she sat down. They ordered a plate of calamari to share and two glasses of wine.

"To us," Paul said, raising his glass.

Layne tilted her head to the side. "To us." She tapped her glass against his and took a quick look around. "Funny, I've been living down here for three years and this is the first time I've been to Blues Alley. I was always promising Tina I'd go with her, but I'd wind up being the third wheel so I always turned her down." She sipped her wine.

"You didn't date, have anyone special?" he tentatively asked. He never wanted to imagine her with anyone else, but he would be a fool to think that she'd been totally alone.

Her gaze rose to his for an instant, then away. "Not really. No one special. I went out from time to time—" she gave a slight shrug "—but I was and am focused on my career." She forked a piece of calamari and dipped it in the sauce before popping it into her mouth. She chewed thoughtfully. "I never asked about your love life after…us."

He pursed his lips a moment. "Not much to tell. I was in and out of relationships, no one long-term."

Layne looked down at her plate. "So no one special?"

"No. No one." He reached across the table and covered her hand with his. "The truth is I didn't want anyone but you, but I was too stubborn to admit it. And the more time that passed, the harder it became. The offer to come here was the ticket I'd been needing. So I took it."

Layne sighed softly.

The waitress came to take their dinner order. They both ordered blackened catfish with red beans and rice.

"As much as I love us being together again, I have to be honest with you."

"Go on."

She hesitated. "You being here basically ruins whatever chance I might have had to anchor the show." There, she'd said it. The feeling that had been hovering in the back of her mind since he arrived was fully out in the open.

She might as well have slapped him. Although she cared for him, might even love him again, there was a part of her that resented him, no matter the reason for his actions.

"But," she pushed out a breath, "I'm dealing with it. I'm actually enjoying being a producer, more than I thought I would. And I'm damned good at it. I get the best of both worlds, working on the show and seeing you every day." She smiled.

"I only want you to be happy. And if me being here is taking away any part of your happiness—"

She cut him off. "It's not. It's not," she repeated.

The waitress arrived with their meals.

"Wow, this looks delish," Layne said.

"Babe, I need to talk to you, tell you some things."

Her fork of catfish stopped midway between her plate and her mouth. "Okay. Sounds serious." She teased the fish off the fork with her teeth, chewed slowly. "I'm listening."

"Remember that night a few weeks back when you asked me to come over and I said I was going to turn in early?"

She frowned. "Yes. But then you came over anyway."

"Yeah, there was a little more to it than what I told you."

She put down her fork. Her eyes flashed. "Whatever it is, just say it." Her tone was a mixture of demand and apprehension.

"I was invited to dinner with Deanna, in her office, alone."

"Say what?"

He held up his hand. "Please just hear me out."

Layne listened in silent hurt and fury, until Paul's confession and Deanna's plans were laid out on the table between them.

The only thing she said when he was done was "You lied to me."

"It was stupid. I didn't want you worried or upset. I—"

"You lied to me. Then you slept in my bed and made love to me as if nothing happened." Her breathing escalated. "If you could do that…" She tossed her napkin on top of her plate. She fished in her bag for her phone.

"Wait, what are you doing?"

"Calling an Uber. Maybe her little plan is all for the best. We do need to be away from each other." She pressed the app and scheduled her ride. "If she moves me to nighttime I'll gladly take it to be away from you. Because if you lied about something like that, what else would you lie to me about?"

"Layne, you have this all wrong."

"You know what, I don't care."

"It was never my intent to lie to you. I should have told you."

"Yeah, you should have told me. Then."

"I didn't and I'm sorry. You have to believe that. Layne, I love you. I didn't mean to hurt you. I was trying to protect you."

She pushed to her feet, checked her phone and then the street. Her car was pulling up. She blinked back the sting of tears. "Like I said, I don't care." She spun away and quickly walked to the waiting car. She took one look back, got in and slammed the door shut.

Layne and Tina sat side by side on a bench in Rock Creek Park that Sunday afternoon. Fall was definitely on the horizon but the last vestiges of Indian summer were holding on tight.

Layne pulled her sweater around her. "I just don't know what to think anymore."

"I have to admit, Paul can be a real screwup when it comes to doing the right thing in the relationship department, but do you really believe that he intended to do something *with* Deanna?"

"I don't know. No. Maybe." She blew out a frustrated breath.

"Do you have any space in that big brain of yours to believe that what he said was true, that he was only trying to protect you and figured he could handle things on his own?"

Layne stared off at a pair of kids chasing each other around a tree. "What he did was messed up. Without a doubt. I could probably get beyond that, but what bothers me deep in my soul is that he lied. Not so much after the fact—by omission—but before. He knew he was going to see Deanna when he talked to me and he intentionally lied. It wasn't as if it was some spur-of-the-moment thing." Her frown deepened. "That's the part I can't wrap my head around," she said with resignation.

"I get it. Believe me. Men are not always the brightest."

They both snickered.

"Well," Tina said on a breath, "I can't tell you want to do. You know what you want and you know what's in your heart. At some point Deanna is going to move you to late night with the intent of eventually getting you in front of the camera—where you wanted to be. If you can find your way clear to see past Paul's latest screwup then maybe things can work out. Or not." She flashed a crooked smile.

"You are so not helpful." She patted Tina's thigh and got to her feet. "Let's see what's on the brunch menu at Mom and Pop."

"I thought you'd never ask."

For the next two weeks Layne focused on producing her program and keeping thoughts of Paul as far at bay as possible. Unfortunately, it was extremely difficult to ignore the secret glances he tossed her way when he thought no one was looking or the apology texts that she ignored.

Maybe she should have followed his urging in the beginning and come out front with them being a couple. Maybe none of this would be happening if she'd done that. When she thought about it, it was like what Yogi Berra said: "It's like déjà vu all over again."

She was just finalizing the storyboard for the week when Cherie burst into her office without knocking.

"Did you hear?" Her voice was frantic.

"What?"

"Security just escorted Paul out of the building."

She dropped her iPad. "What? What are you talking about?"

"I was coming back from lunch and I saw it with my own eyes. Everybody is buzzing about it, but no one has any facts."

Her brain was on scramble. She pressed a hand to her forehead. "What the—"

Her desk phone rang. She flashed Cherie a glance and answered. "Yes. Okay. I'll be right up." She hung up the phone and looked at Cherie. "Deanna wants to see me."

Cherie cussed.

Layne slid her cell phone into the back pocket of her jeans and picked up her iPad.

"What do you think happened?"

"Haven't got a clue, but I'll tell you all I know as soon as I find out," Layne said, opening the door to her office. Her thoughts raced. "And don't feed into any rumors," Layne warned before walking out.

The elevator doors opened onto the executive level. Layne walked up to the reception desk.

"Ms. Mitchell asked to see me."

"Ms. Davis. Yes. You can go right in. She's waiting for you."

"Thank you." She turned and walked down the carpeted corridor to Deanna's new office now that she was program director. She knocked lightly.

"Come in."

Layne walked in. Deanna was seated behind her desk, impeccable as always. She glanced up from the pages in front of her, smiled tightly and extended a hand toward the chair in front of her desk. Layne sat down and had the unsettling feeling that she was facing a firing squad.

Deanna slapped the cover of the folder shut and linked her long fingers together. "I'm sure you've heard about Paul."

"Not exactly. What happened?"

Deanna lifted her chin. "He's been suspended pending an investigation."

"Investigation? For what?"

"I'm not at liberty to say. It confidential."

"For how long? And what about the program? This is crazy." She shook her head in disbelief, her thoughts flying in a million directions.

"The length of suspension will be as long as it takes for the investigation to conclude. And as for the program, I am promoting Cherie to producer, and you will sit in Paul's seat beginning tomorrow."

She blinked in confusion. "What?"

"It's what you've always wanted. I'm sorry this is the way you got it. But, this is a trial run. We'll see how you do. Get us through the sweeps. I think having a woman behind the desk is going to take us to the next level. Don't you?"

Layne gripped the arms of the chair. She felt as if she'd been tossed into some alternative universe. What was happening?

"I'll want to meet with you and Cherie to discuss the handoff. In the meantime, go down to Wardrobe. They'll get you all set up."

This was all surreal. Deanna was going on as if upending an entire program, ousting the lead and rearranging a stellar production team was something that happened every day.

"Of course, if you have any concerns, I'm always here." She smiled brightly. "But I don't expect that there will be." She flipped the folder back open.

Mindlessly, Layne rose from her seat.

"I know you will do great. It's what you've been working so hard for. Now it's all paying off."

Even as the words sounded like a compliment there was a viciousness to them that floated just beneath the surface.

"You can leave the door open," Deanna said, her attention already diverted.

Layne retraced her steps down the hallway and back to the elevator. The doors swished open and Cherie stood there.

"What happened?" she asked in a harsh whisper.

"We'll talk. Come to my office when you're done." She stepped into the elevator just before the doors closed.

As soon as she returned to her office, Layne called Paul. It went straight to voice mail. She sent a text. No response. He was probably in a state of shock, she thought, her heart aching for him.

What could possibly have happened? Deanna was a piece of work but this was crazy. One minute she was your strongest ally, the next she would cut you off at the knees. This was the second anchor in less than a year who'd been dismissed. Was she next on the chopping block? She rested her forehead in her palms.

The rest of the day was a frenzy of activity, between speculation, staff upheavals and general uncertainty. Layne met with Wardrobe to plan out her outfits for the rest of the week, and she'd called an emergency staff meeting of her team for the end of the day.

All she wanted was for the day to end so that she could go over to Paul's place and find out firsthand what had happened.

Her team was gathered in the small conference room next to the control room. The buzz of speculation was palpable.

"I'll get right to it," Layne began. "Management has made some major changes. As you all know, Paul Waverly has been suspended." She held up her hand to forestall any questions. "That's all I know. I don't have any other details." She tugged in a breath. "Per the program director's plan, I will take over the anchor spot and Cherie will step in as producer."

There was a hum of voices. "This is going to be a big transition for all of us and I expect that you will give your all to Cherie the same as you did for me."

"Of course."

"For sure."

"Cherie has already been briefed on what to do, and she will bring you all up to speed. Thank you, everyone, for all of your hard work and support. We'll get over this hump together. Remember we have sweeps coming up and we can't afford not to be on the top of our game." She smiled. "But going forward, I'll leave the pep talks to Cherie. Thanks everyone."

Layne walked out sad, scared and excited all at once.

She left the building, got in her car and went straight to Paul's building. She went to the concierge's desk and asked him to ring Paul's apartment.

"Sorry, Mr. Waverly left a couple of hours ago."

"Oh, um, he didn't happen to say when he'd be back? It's about work. I've been trying to reach him."

"I'm sorry miss, I have no idea. He didn't say. He did have a suitcase with him."

Layne frowned. "Oh. Okay. Thank you." She turned away. Where would he have gone? She tried his cell again. Voice mail.

"Wow, Layne, that is some kind of crazy. You still haven't been able to reach Paul?" Tina asked.

"No. I've left at least a dozen voice messages, not to mention texts. No response."

Tina tucked her leg beneath her on the couch. "I hate to say this, sis, but my mama always told me to be careful what you wish for."

"What's that supposed to mean?" she snapped.

"It's like making a deal with the devil. Sometimes the thing you think you want comes at a cost."

Layne rolled her eyes. "That just makes me feel so… much better." As much as she hated to admit it, there was a glimmer of truth in what Tina said. She'd been fixated on the damned anchor seat at the expense of everything. Now she had it, but it was only because it was taken away from Paul, the man who'd given up what he cherished for her.

Where could he be?

If he didn't stop along the way it was a solid six-hour drive to Charlotte. He could make it by ten, eleven at the latest. When he'd called his brother, Eric, to tell him he was driving down, Eric had insisted that he stay with him and Tricia, at least for tonight.

He wasn't sure what to make of what had happened this morning. He'd come in early as usual and there was a message on his answering service that he was to go to HR immediately following the end of his show. A call like that from HR was never a good sign. But maybe it was no more than firming up the last few months of his contract. The last thing he'd thought was that he would be unceremoniously escorted from the building, his credentials taken and advised that allegations had been made against him and until a thorough investigation was complete, he was suspended.

Hours later, he was still dazed by the whirlwind of events, trying to make sense out of them. *Allegations*. God, that only meant one thing in this climate. His phone buzzed in the cradle. It was Layne. Again. He dismissed the call. He didn't need to talk to her, not now. He believed that somehow Deanna was behind this, but he just didn't know to what degree.

By the time he arrived at his brother's house, his head was pounding and every bone in his body ached.

"Tricia roasted a chicken for dinner. Kept a plate warm for you in the oven," Eric was saying as he walked with his brother into the house. "Figured you'd be hungry."

He snorted a laugh. "I actually am. Haven't eaten since this morning."

"I'll get us set up. Figured I'd wait 'til you got here and I'd eat with you. You know where everything is. You'll be in the guest room."

"Thanks, bruh."

"Hennessy?"

"You know me too well."

"Coming right up."

"Hey, Paul." Tricia came downstairs. "I thought I heard you."

"Didn't mean to wake you."

"Not at all. I was waiting for Jimmy Fallon to come on." She grinned. "Kept dinner for you." She came up to him and kissed his cheek.

"Thanks."

"Okay. Good night, fellas." She gave her husband a leisurely kiss and a squeeze of his arm. "See you in the morning." She turned around and went back upstairs.

Paul walked down the short hallway to the guest bedroom on the right. He flicked on the light, looked around and for a moment wondered how he'd gotten there. Gotten to this place in his life. Deanna Mitchell. She had the power to ruin everything he'd built for himself, and for what? She might have wanted him, but not because she actually cared, but because she could and somehow believed it was her right to have what she wanted.

He set his bag down near the foot of the bed and went to the bathroom to wash up so that he could join his brother for dinner and a drink and maybe make sense of it all.

Layne had dozed off on the couch. Something woke her. The sound of sirens in the distance. She sat up and craned her stiff neck, then immediately checked her phone, hoping for some word from Paul. Nothing.

She unfolded her body and slowly stood. She considered trying Paul again, but thought better of it. Wherever he was, it was clear that he didn't want to talk to her and she had a big day coming up. Her heart ached.

Layne had stepped down from her duties as producer and worked with Cherie to get up and ready. Whispers still ran rampant about Paul Waverly. *Oh, how the mighty have fallen*, some said. Others joked that the anchor chair had become a hot seat and who knows how long Layne would last before she was kicked to the curb.

Cherie stepped into her new role and responsibilities with ease, having learned all she needed to know by being Layne's right hand. Now Layne had to call on her experiences in front of the camera and deliver. *Be careful what you wish for.* The old mantra echoed in her head as she took her seat behind the anchor desk and watched the signals for her cue.

"*The DC Morning Show* with Layne Davis."

Her red light went off.

"Good morning. I'm Layne Davis here in our studios in downtown DC. At the top of the news today from Capitol Hill…"

The two-hour segment went off without a hitch. Layne quickly found her footing and Cherie's setups were perfect. The entire team rose to the occasion and gave themselves a well-deserved round of applause when the technical director announced, "And we're out."

After one of the assistants came to un-mic Layne, she crossed the studio floor, stepping over the snaking cables until she got to the control room.

"Great job, everyone. Thank you for making my job easy."

The remaining team gave her a thumbs-up as they geared up for the next program following the local weather. Layne went in search of Cherie, but was stopped in the hall by Deanna.

"Layne, just who I want to see."

"Everything okay?"

"I watched your debut today. Impressive. I should have given you the shot long before now and we wouldn't be in yet another mess," she said, lowering

her voice. She looked her over. "You might want to do
something with your hair. Maybe you can smooth it out
some. For a more polished look." She tossed off a tight
smile and walked away.

Layne absently patted her twisted locs that she'd styled
into a topknot and muttered a curse, then spun away.

Eight

The aroma of fresh-brewed coffee wafted into his room and stirred him awake. He blinked against the light streaming in from the window. For a moment, he was disoriented. Then his reality sunk in and the events of the day before came crashing back.

He groaned and pushed up to a sitting position, tossed the blanket and sheet aside and got out of bed. After taking care of morning rituals, he padded into the kitchen.

The house was quiet. It was almost nine. It was the first time he'd slept this late on a week day in longer than he could remember. He must have been more tired than he'd realized. There was a note on the table in his brother's familiar scratch.

"Fresh coffee. Full fridge. Help yourself. Had an early day. We can talk tonight. E."

Paul smiled, crumbled the note and tossed it in the

trash. He filled a mug of coffee and went into the living room. He turned on the television and scrolled through the news cable stations until he found WWDC. He drew in a breath.

The News at Sunrise was concluding, followed by three commercials and a weather update. And then the logos for *The DC Morning Show* filled the screen.

"Good morning. I'm Layne Davis…"

Paul sat up. His pulse ticked. He stared at her, in his seat, the one she'd always wanted. She was good. Damned good. He smiled, but by degrees his smile faded.

What was really happening? Layne gets her dream job on the back of his suspension. Was Layne behind this alleged complaint? Did she lobby for the job? Deanna would have been more than happy to stick it to him since he wouldn't play ball.

The more his mind twisted around the unthinkable scenarios, the more enraged and confused he became. He turned the television off, returned to his bedroom, got dressed and went out for a walk to clear his head.

He walked about three blocks, picked up a newspaper along the way and stopped in a neighborhood diner. The waitress said he could sit anywhere, so he took a seat at a small square table in the back. The laminated menu boasted a French toast special, complete with two eggs any style and sausage links or patties.

The waitress arrived with a carafe of coffee. She turned the coffee cup over and filled it without asking. "Morning. Know what you want?"

"I guess I'll go with the special. Scrambled eggs and links."

"Coming right up."

He nodded his thanks and opened the paper, started

from the back at the sports section and worked his way forward. He'd just bypassed the arts and entertainment section and was settling on international news when the waitress returned with his breakfast.

"Here ya go, sir. Can I get you anything else?"

"No, thanks. I'm fine."

"Well, you just let me know." She paused, studied him for a moment. "Didn't you use to be that news guy? Paul. Paul Waverly!" She snapped her fingers. "Used to come on in the mornings. It is you!" She beamed as if she'd just found something she'd lost. "Can I have your autograph?"

"I…sure."

She shoved her order book at him. "Sylvia. You can make it out to Sylvia."

He scribbled his name and thanks to Sylvia and handed it back.

She held it to her chest. "So what happened to you? I don't see you on the television anymore?"

Paul swallowed. "Thanks for breakfast, Sylvia."

She flushed. "Oh, I'm sorry. Didn't mean to pry. It's just that…well, you enjoy your breakfast. Let me know if you need anything."

He turned his attention back to his meal, reached for the syrup and lathered his French toast. Between bites of food he absorbed the headlines and latest details on the war, the shakeup at NATO, and the growing threats of domestic terrorism. He ate up the news as thoroughly as he ate his breakfast. This was what gave him a rush, purpose. The idea that he might not be able do what he loved shook him. Sure, he could go back to WNCC— maybe. He still had time on his option to return. But if word got back as to why he'd been suspended from

WWDC—whether true or false—those doors would close as well.

He sat back and glanced around. *"Didn't you use to be...?"* The waitress's words played back in his head. Would that be his legacy?

He folded the paper, pushed his plate aside and put a twenty-dollar bill beneath the coffee cup. It should be plenty to cover breakfast and maybe the waitress would have a story to tell about how that *guy who used to be* left her a nice tip.

He stepped out into the slightly overcast morning. Soft gray clouds moved across the horizon. He stood for a moment, undecided what to do next, feeling suddenly adrift as if the anchor of what stabilized him had been lifted. He began walking. What he did every day mattered. It mattered not only to his audience but to him as well. It was who he was. And now it seemed he didn't have Layne, either. Without Layne, without being able to do what he loved—who was he? He was just that guy who used to be.

Light drops of rain began to fall. He picked up his pace and headed back.

"So this suspension just came out of the blue?" Eric asked as he and Paul sat on the enclosed back porch sipping beer.

"Totally did not see it coming, especially after all Deanna did to get me to come to DC, in the first place." He paused a minute, debating whether to share his dark thoughts with his brother. But if not with Eric, then who? "You know, this morning I watched the news. Layne has my spot."

"Oh." Eric frowned.

"When I saw her at first I was excited. She was great.

But then I went down this dark hole. Like did she engineer all this? She never hid the fact that she was laser-focused on getting that seat."

Eric's head jerked back in incredulity. "You're kidding, right?"

"Now I am. But not this morning. I guess I was still in shock to be sitting on the couch and not behind the desk, and then to see Layne…knowing that's what she wanted all along…" He exhaled. "I lost it for a moment."

"I sure as hell hope you found it. You know that is all the way in left field, bruh. Layne may be as ambitious as you but she wouldn't slip behind you and stab you in the back."

"Yeah. I know. Momentary lapse."

"She know you're here?"

"No. She's been calling but… I'm not really ready to talk about it. Need some time to decompress. Get my head on straight."

The brothers were silent for a moment.

"What happened to the last guy that had the spot?" Eric asked.

"He was let go after an investigation."

"Any idea what it was about?"

"Not really. There was some talk about misuse of corporate credit cards or something. Some say there were *allegations*." He took a long swallow of his beer and pulled the hood of his sweatshirt over his head. "I never met him, so I have no opinion and didn't want to start my tenure off by getting involved in office gossip."

"I'm only asking, as an attorney, to see if there are any patterns going on here."

"Patterns?"

"Yeah, dismissals that follow a similar track."

"I wouldn't really know."

"It's something that I would want to look into, if it comes to that. What exactly is the accusation against you?"

"Inappropriate behavior against a colleague."

"Could they be more vague?" Eric scoffed. "Well, I'm going to want to see the actual complaint."

"I don't need you getting involved," he said, waving off his brother's offer.

"I *am* involved. I'm your brother and I'm not going to see you get railroaded."

Paul leaned his head back and closed his eyes. In a meandering way, that was totally not how he ever presented information, he tried to tell his brother about his apprehension about his future. "Layne. My work. They make me who I am. You know I was a mess when she left."

"Yeah, and were too stubborn to admit it. You could have made it work if you didn't let your big head and ego get in your way."

"I thought you were on my side," he groused.

"I'm on the side of right. Look, one thing that I've come to terms with is that we can't be defined by just one thing—our career, where we live, how much money we make, who we love. Sure, we're a sum total of all those parts and over time some of those parts shift and change, disappear or are replaced. But that doesn't make us any less than who we are—inside. Because the key piece of who we are is what we are inside, the kind of human beings we are, how we treat other people. That's what really matters, bruh."

Paul lowered his head and smiled. "When did you get all wise and whatnot?" He glanced askance at his brother.

"Man, I been wise and whatnot. Mom always said I had a smart mouth." He winked.

Paul sputtered a laugh. "Yeah, okay."

The brothers sat back, staring up at the clear October sky, dusted with stars and a quarter moon.

"You should call her," Eric said quietly.

"I will as soon as I figure out what my next moves are going to be. This time when I come to Layne, it needs to be with a clear plan, a clean slate, no strings and total commitment. I don't feel like myself right now and I want to be in a good space and clearheaded before we talk. There's been enough confusion, secrecy and uncertainty between us for too long—overshadowing everything else. This time I want to do things right."

Eric lifted his bottle of beer. "I got your back."

"Thanks, bruh."

Lying in bed, he held his cell phone up to his face. He was hoping that there was a message from Layne, but there wasn't. She hadn't called or texted all day. He started to call her, then stopped. He wasn't ready. The one thing that he didn't share with his brother was the real reason holding him back from calling Layne: He was ashamed, embarrassed. He'd always been "the big man on campus," the star, the one everybody looked up to. He'd bought into his own hype, and now with the rug pulled out from under him, he realized just how shallow he'd become. That was not the man he wanted to present to Layne. And he wouldn't make any moves in her direction until he was sure of his footing.

Layne was in her office when Cherie knocked.

"Come in."

"Hey, you did great today," Cherie enthused and plopped down in the armchair.

"Thanks. And you stepped into those producer shoes like a champ." Layne grinned.

"We need to go have a drink and celebrate."

"I'd love to, but my first day took a lot more out of me than I thought. I'm going to head home, review my notes for tomorrow and turn in early."

"Sure. I get it. I guess I'm still running on adrenaline." Cherie pushed to her feet. "Did you hear anything official about Paul? How long is the suspension? Is he coming back?"

Layne stomach knotted. "I don't know. I haven't heard anything."

"Hmm. Okay." She stood. "See you in the a.m., and Layne?"

"Hmm?"

"I never got to tell you how much I appreciate you mentoring me and giving me this major break. No matter how things go, I'll still be able to put producer on my résumé. I have you to thank for that."

"You deserve it, C. I wouldn't want anyone else."

"Well, just know that I appreciate it." She went to the door. "See you in the morning."

The moment Cherie was gone, Layne checked her phone to see if she'd missed a call or text from Paul. Nothing. She sighed. It had only been two days. He probably just needed his space. But if she did not hear from him by the end of the week, it was gloves off.

Layne and Tina met up at their favorite after-five spot. Tina wanted to hear every detail about her debut and the latest on Paul.

When they were seated after a short wait, they put in their drink orders. Two frozen margaritas.

"So, how was it? How do you feel?" Tina urged.

"It was…amazing. The thrill was beyond what I imagined. It flowed, I didn't screw up my lines, hit all my cues. Cherie did an amazing job. Handled it like the pro she is. Made my job easier for sure."

Tina leaned in. "I am so happy for you, sis. For real. As long as I've known you this has been your dream."

The waitress arrived with their drinks.

"Thanks," Tina said. She turned her attention back to Layne. "Was it worth it?"

"Meaning?"

"Don't get me wrong. You have talent from here and back and all roads in between, but your victory was a result of someone else's loss. Someone that you love."

"What are you saying? That I don't really have what it takes? That I'm there by default?"

"Not at all. But what I am saying is that no good comes from benefitting from the fall of someone else." She held up her hand to halt Layne's protest. "What I want you to think about is how sketchy this all is. First Deanna is your bestie at work, a big cheerleader. But she hires Paul for a job she knew you wanted. Then she begins to undercut you. Then out of the blue 'allegations' are lodged against Paul and, poof, he's gone and you're in. You said yourself that you thought she had a thing for Paul and he admitted what she did in her office."

"I didn't want to believe that Deanna orchestrated everything. But she wanted Paul from when she first met him. She saw an opportunity to bring him to DC, but when he wasn't as 'grateful' as she wanted, he's out, and puts me in his spot to rub it in his face."

Tina arched a brow in agreement.

Layne sipped her drink. "Have to find a way to prove it."

"That's why you have me as a best friend," Tina said with a smile.

Layne finished out her second week and still no word from Paul. Deanna stopped by after every show to compliment Layne and offer unsolicited advice.

"What is the status with Paul?" Layne asked after the final show for the end of the week.

"I'm sure he won't be back."

"Has the investigation or whatever was going on finished?" she asked.

Deanna's eyes narrowed. She waved away the question. "I would concern myself with my own job if I were you." She gave Layne one last look. "Enjoy your weekend." She turned and walked away.

Layne sighed. What was her objective? Was she so obsessed with her own power that she simply got rid of anyone that got in her way or didn't give her what she wanted? Paul had told her what happened that night in Deanna's office. She'd been hurt and angry, so much so that she didn't allow herself to see beyond her own feelings to what was really going on. Deanna caused the toxic environment and anyone in her way paid the price.

In the meantime, Tina had assigned one of her investigative journalists to do a follow-up with WWDC and a full exposé on the history of the station. It would take weeks, Tina cautioned, but she was certain they would get to the truth.

Layne couldn't wait for the journalist to finish their work. She needed to talk to Paul, face-to-face. There was one thing she knew about Paul and that was he was a creature of habit. She was going to take a chance and drive to Charlotte.

Layne went straight home, packed a bag and was on the road within the hour. She didn't have a plan other than finding Paul. She'd figure it out when she got there.

She crossed into Charlotte a little after nine. Now that she was there, she wasn't sure where to look first. It was too late to start knocking on the doors of old friends. She'd have to find a place to stay for the night and start fresh in the morning. She drove into the center of town, better known as Uptown, and remembered the Grand Bohemian Hotel, a boutique hotel that had great rooms, wonderful service and sweet memories.

"Welcome to the Grand Bohemian. Do you have a reservation?"

"No. I don't. I just got into town and I was hoping that there was something available."

"How long will you be staying?" the reservationist asked as she keyed information into the computer.

"Um, just for the weekend."

"I have a room available on the second floor. Queen."

"I'm sure it's fine. Is room service still available?"

"Until eleven."

"Thanks." She handed over her credit card.

The reservationist returned her credit card and a room key. "The elevator is around this corner on your right."

"Thank you."

"Enjoy your stay."

Layne took the elevator and proceeded down the quiet hallway to her room. As she'd expected, it was just as she remembered.

In the early days of their relationship, she and Paul had spent a getaway weekend here. At the end of a workday, he'd found her in the break room, and checking to be sure no one could hear him, had whispered that he had a little surprise for her and that she should go home, pack a bag and he'd pick her up at six.

The Grand Bohemian Hotel was where he'd brought her. They'd had dinner in the hotel restaurant, lounged on the rooftop patio, swum in the pool and spent the rest of the weekend making love and ordering room service. When they finally emerged on Sunday afternoon, their commitment to each other was cemented.

Layne stripped out of her clothes and took a long shower, then ordered room service. While she wolfed down her burger and fries, she scrolled through her contacts on her phone. She was pretty sure she had Paul's brother's contact information.

There it was! Hopefully, his number had not changed.

She would reach out to him first thing in the morning. If anyone knew where Paul might be, it would be Eric. Before she settled down for the night, she called Tina to let her know she'd arrived safely and her plan to reach out to Eric. Much to her satisfaction, Tina informed her that her journalist was making some alarming discoveries and that she would keep her posted.

Layne barely slept and was up with the sun. She fixed a pot of coffee and waited a reasonable time to text Eric. At 8 a.m., unable to wait any longer, she typed her message.

Hi, Eric. This is Layne Davis. I was hoping you could tell me where I could find Paul. He hasn't answered any of my calls or texts. I'm here in Charlotte. Please get back to me. Thank you.

She stared at her phone, waiting for the tiny bubbles to appear to indicate that he'd received her message and was answering. More than an hour went by without a response.

If she didn't hear from him, her next move would be to visit the station. Hopefully, some of her and Paul's old colleagues had seen or spoken with him. Then again, he might not be in Charlotte at all. She should have thought this through before being so impulsive and driving all this way.

Then her phone chirped. She snatched it up from the bed and saw to her relief that it was Eric.

I'm glad you reached out. Paul is actually staying with me and Tricia. I'm not home at the moment. I had to come into my office, but call back around six and I'll pass the phone to Paul. I told him he needs to talk to you, but you know how my brother can be.

Thank you so much! I will call at six.

She exhaled a long breath of relief. He was here. She would speak to him tonight and they were going to work things out one way or another. Six o'clock couldn't come fast enough.

She went down to the hotel restaurant and had breakfast before taking a walk to think and take in the sights of the place she'd once called home.

The funny thing about the Queen City was that while other places referred to their central business district and hub of activity as Downtown, it wasn't so in Charlotte. Its main area of commerce, entertainment and culture was called Uptown.

It had been almost four years now since she'd been back. Much of what she remembered was the same. There were a few more coffee shops and a vegan café that she didn't recall, but for the most part Charlotte remained unchanged.

She strolled along N. College Street and stopped for a moment to take in the sculpture of Queen Charlotte, the city's namesake, before continuing to the Four Corners Statues at the intersection of Trade and Tryon Streets and was happy to discover that the Bechtler Museum of Modern Art was just opening for the day. On their last night at the Grand Bohemian years earlier, Paul had taken her to the museum for a jazz night that took place in its massive lobby. Even though by that time they'd discovered they both loved classic R&B, jazz tied for first place.

They were taking a chance that they might be seen by someone who recognized him from television or the both of them from work, but that night they didn't care, even though Layne wore a hat and Paul kept the hood of his sweatshirt on all night—just in case.

She smiled at the memory. It was such a magical weekend. The direction of their relationship had shifted from teasing and tentative to purposeful. Even though they had to navigate the landmines of company politics and the power dynamic of Paul's position, they'd found ways to make it work until it didn't. Was it all worth it?

On her way back to the hotel, Tina called.

"Were you able to reach Paul?"

"I got in touch with his brother, Eric. Paul is staying with him. Eric said to call tonight at six and he'd put Paul on the phone."

"Well, I have some news that you can share with Paul, but it can't go any further until we confirm some more information."

Layne pushed through the lobby doors and found a

cozy corner out of others' earshot and sat down. "What is it?"

"It seems that Deanna Mitchell has a shady history with the men at the station."

"Meaning?"

"Meaning that these so-called allegations were all smoke and mirrors to get rid of anyone that she'd set her sights on but they didn't reciprocate. If you get my drift."

"What?"

"Yes."

"In other words, Paul is not the first."

Layne's thoughts swirled. "How has she been able to get away with this?"

"Nondisclosure agreements upon hiring. We've uncovered at least five. And it seems that the board turned a blind eye because she kept churning out great programming."

"Wow," Layne said on a long breath. "So, now what?"

"Now we keep digging until all the pieces are in place and any unanswered questions are resolved."

"Man, this is like freaking Watergate."

Tina snickered. "Lights, Action, Scandal. Talk to you later. Let me know how it goes with Paul."

"Thanks, T. Really."

"I got you."

Tina's revelations spun around her head. How long had this been going on? Was Deanna that narcissistic that she would ruin someone's career just to satisfy some misplaced sense of power? Six o'clock couldn't come fast enough.

She hadn't brought anything special to wear. The best she could come up with was a white cotton pull-over sweater and black slacks. She'd always had a penchant for sexy underwear, so that wasn't an issue—*if* things got that far. So she spent some extra time in the shower and arranging her hair.

With nothing left to do but wait, she curled up in the chair by the window and kept checking her phone for the time.

When 6 p.m. popped up on the screen, she hesitated. She didn't want to seem too anxious and call on the dot. She waited a painful ten minutes, then dialed Eric's number. He picked up on the second ring.

"Hi, Eric. It's Layne. Is he there?"

"I'll go get him."

"Did you tell him I was going to call?"

"Nope. Didn't feel like hearing him tell me how I'm in his business," he said with a chuckle. "As if that would matter. Hang on."

Layne heard muffled voices. Her heart was pounding so hard and fast it was difficult to breathe.

"Layne…"

His voice was like water after a drought. It flowed through her, nourished her. She felt as if the dry leaves of her heart were beginning to bloom again.

"Hi," she breathed. "How are you?"

"Hard to say," he admitted. "One minute I'm good, the next… How are you? I miss you," he added before she could respond.

Her heart thumped. "I miss you, too. We have so much to talk about. Did Eric tell you that I'm here, in Charlotte?"

"What? No. You're here?"

She giggled. "Yes. And you'll never guess where I'm staying?"

"Where?"

"At the Grand Bohemian."

"Our first getaway," he murmured.

"Yes," she said softly. "A lot of good memories. I thought maybe you could come by here and we could talk over dinner."

"I'd like that. I can be there in about an hour. That good?"

"I'll meet you in the lobby."

"See you then."

"Okay."

"And Layne—"

"Yes?"

"I'm glad you're here. See you soon." He disconnected the call.

She held the phone to her chest, closed her eyes and smiled.

Layne felt like a nervous teen on a first date as she waited for Paul in the hotel lobby. Her goal was to look cool and collected when he came through the door but that didn't stop her pulse from jumping every time someone pushed through the revolving doors.

She was about to check the time again on her phone when she felt him before she saw him. Her head snapped up and something warm and satisfying filled her, brought her to her feet. He came straight for her and as if they were the only ones in the world, Paul took her in his arms and kissed her as thoroughly and as hungrily as a man starved.

Their lusty embrace drew smiles and murmured comments from the comers and goers.

"I think we might be causing a scene," Layne whispered breathlessly against Paul's lips.

"I don't care."

She tossed her head back and laughed, a pure, joyous sound.

"I'm sorry, baby." He cupped her cheek. "Sorry."

"So am I."

He kissed her again, then slid his arm around her waist. She curled into his side, looked up at him. "Good to see you."

He kissed her forehead. "If I remember correctly, I think the restaurant is down the hall to the left."

"Yep."

They walked hugged up together to the restaurant and were seated at a table near the rear, and placed their drink orders.

Paul immediately reached across the circular table and took Layne's hands the instant the waitress walked away. "How have you been?"

"Okay. Stressed. Worried about you."

He lowered his gaze. "It wasn't fair of me to lock you out." He shook his head. "It was a major blow about the job. I didn't see it coming, and what happened between us about Deanna…me not being up-front." He blew out a breath. "I needed to take a step back." He paused. "And when I turned on the television and saw you in my spot, my first reaction was how great you are and how proud I was of you. But—"

"But then you started to think *how convenient*. It was what she always wanted and maybe—" she pursed her lips a moment "—maybe she might have had a hand in the fiasco." She looked him right in the eye and released a slow breath. "To be honest, I probably would have thought the same thing. But then reality would kick in." She smiled. "And we'd know better."

"Yeah," he said softly. "We'd know better." He lifted her hand to his lip and kissed it.

The waitress returned with their drinks and took their dinner orders.

"None of it was out of the blue," Layne said, lowering her voice. "Tina assigned a reporter to do a deep dive on Deanna Mitchell and the dismissal record at WWDC."

"And?"

The waitress brought their dinner.

"Thank you," Paul said.

Layne took her time to explain as much as she could based on what Tina had told her.

Paul's brows rose. "I knew Deanna was over the top at times, but this?" He stared at Layne.

"I know. Tina said there's still some loose ends to tie together but they should have a full picture soon."

"Hmm." He nodded and cut into his steak. "What about us?"

Layne angled her head to the side. She ran her tongue along her bottom lip and leaned forward. "I thought that maybe if you had some time, since I'm in town, maybe we could rekindle some memories."

A slow smile moved across his face. "Hmm, I'd love to help you remember. And start some new ones."

Layne dramatically raised her hand. "Check, please."

"Nice digs," Paul teased when they entered Layne's room.

She turned the door lock and engaged the security latch. "There's some wine in the mini-fridge." She took off her shoes.

Paul poured two glasses of white wine. He stood in front of her, handed her a glass. "To making new memories."

"New memories," she whispered.

They sipped their wine.

Paul nipped the glass from Layne's hand and placed it on the nightstand. He held her face in his hands. "Thank you for not giving up on me, for being the fierce, unstoppable woman that I've always known you to be."

"I love you," she whispered. "I fought against loving you as hard as I fought for all the other things I thought I wanted. But what I discovered is that at the end of the day, when I come home alone, none of it meant anything, because you weren't a part of it. I want us in this thing together, really together."

"So do I." He leaned down and kissed her tenderly at first, and by degrees with more urgency.

Layne leaned into him, looping her arms around his neck, savoring the feel of his mouth, his tongue slow-dancing with hers.

His fingers threaded through the intricate twists of her hair until they came undone and tumbled to her shoulders. He broke the kiss and took the hem of her sweater in hand, pulled it over her head and tossed it to the floor. She laughed and returned the favor, expertly unbuttoning the tiny blue buttons of his Oxford shirt and tugging it off. He unzipped her slacks. She shimmied them off her hips and undid his. The corner of his mouth curved upward. His lids lowered when Layne reached in between the folds of his shorts and wrapped her hand around his stiffening member. He drew in a sharp breath and throbbed beneath her touch. Layne pressed her lips against his chest and covered it with hot kisses as she continued to stroke him. He groaned deep in his throat as Layne's kisses trailed lower. He gripped her shoulders and pulled her upright. His gaze scoured her face before his mouth captured hers, backing her toward the bed.

They tumbled onto the bed, sinking into the thick down comforter.

Paul peeled out of his slacks and shorts, unhooked Layne's teal-colored lace bra and matching panties in a series of seamless moves until they were both naked and heated with longing. His lips, his tongue, his fingers teased and paid homage to every inch of her body, making Layne writhe with desire.

Her soft moans rose in pitch as he kissed the inside of her thighs, stroked the tender skin with his tongue until the muscles fluttered. He pressed his mouth against her wet center and laved the sweet folds with his tongue until she begged him to stop, but he wouldn't, not until the orgasm that she tried to keep at bay rocketed through her, the force so strong that Paul had to grip her hips to slow her thrashing and allow him to bring her to total release.

Layne's soft whimpers and trembling slowly subsided. Her fingers that had been pressed into his shoulders loosened as Paul seductively moved up her body until he hovered above her.

"I want you," he groaned, his gaze boring into hers.

"Show me how much," she said, wrapping her legs around his back.

He leaned across her and grabbed his pants, took a condom from his wallet and put it on without wasting a beat.

When Paul eased inside her, filling her, sealing her body and soul to his, nothing else mattered except the two of them loving and giving of themselves to each other.

Layne lifted and rolled her pelvis to meet and invite Paul's every thrust: slow, fast, building in intensity.

Their hard, quick breathing, moans and slap of bare wet skin filled the moist air.

"Paul! Oh, yesss. Yesss." Her body shook.

Paul scooped her body tight against his and exploded, deep inside her.

And much like during their first rendezvous at The Grand Bohemian, they spent the rest of the weekend ordering room service and making love.

Nine

"I'll keep you posted on anything I hear from Tina," Layne said, as she and Paul stood next to her car. "You could come back with me," she said with an inviting smile.

He leaned down and lightly kissed her lips. "That would be so easy, but let's stick to the plan." He braced her shoulders, looked her straight in the eyes. "This is important what we're doing, not just for me but for everyone at the station."

Layne nodded in agreement. "True." A slow smile bloomed on her face. "I was getting used to waking up next to you again."

"So was I."

She dragged in a breath. "I better get on the road. I have an early day tomorrow."

He opened her car door and she slid behind the wheel. He leaned in and kissed her. "Drive safe. Call me when you get in."

"I will."

"Love you," he whispered.

"Love you right back."

Paul pushed the car door shut and watched her car drive away until he could no longer see it.

"Well, the prodigal son returns," Eric teased when Paul walked through the door.

"Very funny." He dropped his backpack by the door and joined his brother in the living room. He flopped down on the couch and stretched out his long legs. "Where's Tricia?"

"Book club meeting." Eric shrugged. "So, how did things go? I mean, they must have gone well since you've been gone for two days." He chuckled. "But did you two get any dialogue in?"

"You're just full of jokes today. And yes, we talked. Thank you very much."

"And?"

Paul leaned forward and rested his arms on his thighs. He looked at his brother. "Man, some real shady stuff has been going on at that station and Deanna Mitchell appears to be orchestrating it. According to what Layne's friend that works for the *Washington Post* has uncovered…"

As Paul laid out what he knew so far, Eric began to pace, running his hand across his head and grunting under his breath with each revelation.

Eric blew out a breath. He looked at his brother. "We usually hear about this kind of stuff coming from men wielding their will and power on women and subordinates. This is a new twist."

Paul nodded slowly. Eric continued, "If everything you told me pans out, the station is going to have a lot of explaining to do. I'm pretty sure they will do whatever they need to keep it as hushed as possible." He paused a beat. "In the meantime, if you haven't done it already, you need to put as much of what you experienced—dates and times—on paper. You might need it."

"You're right. I'll corroborate events with my calendar."

"Good. Now—" he slapped his thighs "—I was going to put a couple of steaks on the grill. It's a nice night out, and when Tricia has her book club, all the sisters bring food, so a brother is on his own for dinner."

Paul chuckled. "Steaks sound like a plan. Let me get cleaned up and I'll help."

The brothers rose.

"It's really good having you here," Eric said sincerely, "and even better that you worked things out with Layne. She's good for you. She makes you better."

"I know. She really does."

Layne was exhausted from the six-hour drive but exhilarated at the same time. The past few days spent with Paul had cast all doubt aside about the viability of them being a couple. They talked, really talked about their fears, their hopes and the role that both of them played in their relationship splitting at the seams. But they committed above all else, no matter how hard it was, to be honest and transparent with each other. And to accept the fact that both of them might want different things at different times and that it was okay. They would find a way to work through it instead of walking away.

Back home, she stripped out of her road-weary clothes, took a quick shower and checked the fridge for something quick and easy to fix, and was sorely disappointed. Everything worth eating was frozen. As she debated whether to find something easy to defrost and cook or order in, the choice was, thankfully, taken out of her hands.

The front doorbell rang. She pressed the intercom. "Yes."

"I was hoping you'd be home by now."

"Girl! You have spies or what?"

"Buzz me in. We need to talk. And I brought Chinese."

Over shrimp fried rice, dumplings and egg rolls lathered in hot mustard, Tina explained what her reporter had determined. The sources were verified and they planned to publish the story in a matter of days.

"Deanna Mitchell has used sexism and intimidation against any man that either challenged her or didn't give in to her advances. There are six verifiable victims."

Layne felt sick to her stomach with the revelations. She knew what she had to do.

"This is how it's going to go down," Layne said and began laying out her plan.

She returned to work as usual on Monday, completed her program without a hitch or a hint of what was to come in the ensuing days. Paul was also making plans on his end and Tina said that the article would be ready to go the following morning.

"We need to talk," Layne said to Cherie once the show wrapped.

"Sure. Everything okay?"

"It will be."

"Okay. Give me ten minutes. Your office?"

"Perfect." Layne walked off toward her office. She

caught a glimpse of Deanna getting on the elevator and rolled her eyes in disgust.

As promised, Cherie knocked on Layne's door ten minutes later.

"You have that determined look in your eyes," Cherie said when she came in. She took a seat. "What's going on?"

"Tomorrow we will have the programming the way you set it up. However, I will interrupt for breaking news."

Cherie frowned. "Breaking news that you already know about?"

"Yes. I don't want to say too much now. But I wanted you to know not to freak out when I go off script."

Cherie's brows rose.

"There will be fireworks and major fallout. I don't want you caught in the crossfire. The less you know the better. At least for now. I promise, I'll explain everything as soon as I can."

Cherie grinned. "This is so cloak-and-dagger! I love it and I trust you. Always have. I'll follow your lead."

"Thanks, Cherie."

"For you, anything. Hey, hear any updates on Paul?"

"Um, no."

Cherie looked at her for a moment. "Okay," she said on a breath. "See you tomorrow." She gave her a thumbs-up.

Layne offered a tight-lipped smile. "Tomorrow," she whispered in concert with the closing door.

Alone now, Layne momentarily wondered if what she planned on doing was the right thing. It would undoubtedly tank her career at the station and perhaps elsewhere. She might be perceived more as someone willing to stir up trouble rather than a dedicated jour-

nalist and professional. Tina had confirmed that the
story would run digitally in the morning and the full
details would be in print the next day and a full spread
on Sunday.

Her pulse quickened. Of course, once the cat was
out of the bag, every news outlet worth their credentials would be on it. She had to be ready to answer questions about her own hiring at the station as well. The
one saving grace was that Deanna hadn't advocated for
her in the first place and had never gone out of her way
to champion her rise at the station until Paul. If anything, it seemed that Deanna had kept a lid on Layne's
progress up the ranks, especially with regard to her
desire to work in front of the camera—which was why
she'd come to WWDC in the first place. It was ultra
important, Tina said, that this did not appear as some
kind of vendetta by a disgruntled employee. And it was
also good that Tina had assigned the story to one of her
reporters and had no hand in what had been uncovered. In hindsight, Layne realized it had been a smart
move to not make her relationship with Paul public.
That would only be fodder for more speculation in the
wrong direction.

Most important, the article was not a hatchet job.
It was transparent and did not shy away from naming
names where necessary.

Layne drew in a slow breath. She was as ready as
she could be.

Her goal was to get a good night's sleep so that she
would look fresh and alert in the morning. However,
she spent most of the night staring into the dark and
listening to her heart pounding. When she pulled her-

self out of bed, her eyes felt gritty and her body ached as if she'd overexercised.

After a long, hot, pulsing shower and two cups of coffee, she felt more human. The stylist and makeup artist would fix everything else.

When she arrived at the studio, she stopped at the security desk to leave specific instructions that she was to be notified when her guests arrived and that they should be escorted to the studio immediately.

She went in her office to check any last-minute emails and verified that she didn't miss anything on her phone. Then she went to hair and makeup. Much to Deanna's great annoyance, Layne had opted not to tame her natural hair but to glorify it. Each day she showcased her natural twists in intricate patterns, and that had become just as much her signature as her direct delivery of the news at hand. Viewer feedback had been mixed at first, but then the tides seemed to change and the viewers applauded her embrace of her Black womanhood and the positive symbol that she represented. She would miss all that, she mused as Stacy the hair stylist coiled her hair into an elaborate top bun, leaving a handful of strands draped along the right side of her face. She'd wanted to be like her idol Cynthia Medley and carve out a path for other Black female journalists to follow. But she was pretty sure that after today, her chance for that would be at an end. Funny, but she was kind of okay with that. Because today was the kind of day that she'd worked toward for her entire career, breaking that major story that would reverberate and cause change. So if today was going to be her last day, she would go out with a bang.

Today she wore a simple sleeveless navy dress with a

scoop collar and a chunky wooden necklace in a muted orange.

She had her notes in a folder, but before walking onto the set, she went to the control room and handed Cherie a tape and a revised run of the show.

"This is all part of what I talked to you about yesterday. Load this up. When I give you the signal, put it on air and follow the storyboard on that sheet. Okay?"

Cherie held the tape and page in her hand, looking at Layne. "Okay. You got it."

"Thanks." She walked out and onto the set to be mic'd and have her earpiece adjusted. Settled behind the news desk, she braced for her countdown cue and for the red light of the camera to disappear. She had a moment of panic and thought this was crazy, but then she caught a glimpse of Deanna Mitchell standing in the back of the studio behind the camerapersons, and her determination was renewed.

She drew in a breath, straightened in her seat. Watched for her signal. The theme music played, the logo shot across the screen. Three. Two. One.

"Good morning. I'm Layne Davis and this is *The DC Morning Show*. We begin today with news out of Capitol Hill regarding the most recent push for a comprehensive women's rights bill. Our political reporter Della Bryant has the latest. Della…"

While the report was being broadcast, Layne checked her notes again. Barring karma, everything should go according to plan.

"Thank you for that, Della. This is the second time during this congressional session the bill has been brought to the floor. Advocates are hoping this time there will be some success. We turn now to the international front where the war continues to rage nearly a year since its start. Aid from around the world continues to pour in, but without direct intervention from the West, we may continue to talk about this assault for many more months to come. Simon Fields is on location with the latest. Simon…"

She got the signal in her ear that her guest had arrived and was coming up. Her heart thundered. She reached for the glass of water and took a long swallow.

"Thank you, Simon. We'll be right back after this short commercial break. Don't go anywhere."

Layne's pulse raced. She gave instruction to the production crew to bring out two chairs to the round table where she interviewed on-set guests. The techs got her settled at the circular table, checked her mic and gave the thumbs-up. Stacy darted on set to powder her nose and forehead seconds before Layne got her cue.

"Welcome back. As you all know, during this portion of the program, I have the privilege of bringing to the table a wide array of guests from politicians to reverends, CEOs to grassroots organizers and everyone in between. And while I have not been in this seat very long, I do hope that what I've brought to you is both entertaining and informative. Today is one of those days. I want to begin with this breaking news from the *Washington Post*." She gave a slight nod and the tape that she'd given Cherie bloomed big and bold on the screen: ALLEGATIONS OF CORPORATE MISCONDUCT AND WRONGFUL TERMINATIONS UNCOVERED AT WWDC NETWORK.

Because of the camera and studio lights on her, she could not see beyond the camera in front of her and the teleprompter, but she could clearly imagine the chaos and confusion in the control room. "It is not often or at all that you get to report on a place where you are employed. Sadly, that is what is happening here today. Based on the thorough investigative work of Brenda Walker and Lisbeth Grover at the *Post*, rumors and allegations that have been part of the culture here at WWDC have been brought to light. Pulitzer Prize–winning journalist Brenda Walker is my first guest this morning."

She knew that Cherie had her back and would cue the camerapersons as needed. Layne's last line on the storyboard sheet was: *Do not let Deanna stop you*.

The camera went to a two-shot to include Brenda Walker, who had joined Layne at the desk.

"Thank you so much for being here. As an investigative journalist myself, I know the hours of work and research involved and the level of verification required before releasing a story like this. Please tell us how it began and what you found out."

"Thank you for having me. If you recall, several months ago, we did a piece on Paul Waverly and his superstar arrival at WWDC. Less than a year into his arrival, he's gone. I found that to be curious. When we reached out to him we got no response and the station wouldn't return our calls. That only increased my desire to find out what had actually happened."

"And what did you find out?"

"The station has a pattern of dismissing male employees, who have in some way, at some point, worked for Deanna Mitchell. And they all signed NDAs."

She could almost hear the gasp in the control room. "NDAs?"

"Nondisclosure agreements. In other words, they are not supposed to talk about the details of their employment, termination or any compensations they may have received."

"What did you discover were the reasons for termination?"

"My research goes back five years, starting from when Deanna Mitchell took over as executive producer on daytime and evening news."

Layne swallowed. "How did you get around the NDAs?"

"To date, there are six terminations that I investigated. When I reached out to them and advised them they were not the only ones and that there was strength in numbers, they agreed to talk to me."

"And we have two of them with us today." Layne signaled and the screen filled with Brett Conway. "Thank you for being here with us today, Mr. Conway. As you all may remember, Brett Conway was the anchor prior to Paul Waverly. Mr. Conway, if you would tell us about your situation."

Brett explained how about a year into his hiring, Deanna Mitchell made innuendos alluding that a relationship with her could benefit him and his career. He was flattered at first, he said, and took her up on dinners and drinks after work. But there came a time when she became more aggressive and demanding. When he got uncomfortable and told Deanna as much, he started getting calls from Finance saying there were inconsistencies in his receipts, and there were anonymous complaints from tenants in the building where his apartment was leased by the network. Finally, he was suspended, then let go.

"I know this was not easy and that there are only so many details that you can share with us. I appreciate you being here, Mr. Conway."

"Of course."

The screen darkened and Layne turned to face the

camera. "Now we have an in-studio guest that will join us."

The camera swung around to follow Paul Waverly as he walked toward the round table.

Her heart thundered. This was the nail in Deanna's coffin.

Paul walked onto the set, nodded to both women and sat down.

"Welcome...back, Mr. Waverly," Layne greeted. "I'm sure our audience is all too familiar with your presence on the screen, as you've greeted them every night in Charlotte and then every morning here in DC." She turned to the camera. "For anyone joining for the very first time, this is Paul Waverly, the anchor that replaced Brett Conway and who was then replaced by me. Thank you for being here, Mr. Waverly."

"I'm glad to be here."

"You agreed to work with Ms. Walker as part of her investigation into the allegations lodged against you. I understand that you did not sign an NDA but you have been suspended with the outcome more than likely to be your termination, like your predecessors."

"That's correct."

"Tell us as much as you feel comfortable about your experience here at WWDC."

Paul began with the day when he was approached by Deanna two years earlier, up to and including the emails, text messages, dinner alone in her office as well as her innuendos and his belief that much of her ire against him was Deanna's belief that he was involved with Layne.

"In the spirit of transparency," Layne cut in, "Paul and I have been seeing each other. For now that's a story for another day. Please continue."

"After I turned down her 'offer,' things changed."

"How?" Layne asked.

"She became overly critical. Countermanded everything I said. Essentially insinuated that I was off my game. And she continued to remind me that she'd gone to bat for me to come to WWDC. Then, I was suspended based on 'allegations' of improper behavior. I was out and you—" he looked to Layne "—were in."

Her expression tensed for a moment. "Thank you for being here today and sharing this disturbing account." She turned to face the camera. "Society has become accustomed to hearing that abusive behavior and retaliation only happens to women. But as you have heard today, that is no longer true." She closed the folder in front of her and faced the camera. "Next up, Kevin Parker is at the site of the grand opening of the community center spearheaded by real estate mogul Montgomery Grant, right after this commercial break."

The instant the cameras were off Deanna came flying across the studio floor and up in the face of Layne. Her face was red with fury. "What do you think you're doing? You think you can smear me like this and get away with it? I'll have your job and you'll never work in broadcasting again."

Layne leaned back and smiled with satisfaction. "I rest my case," she said softly.

Within moments Security was on the floor, ushering a ranting Deanna away.

The fallout from the interview was swift. There was an emergency meeting of the board to launch an internal investigation and the PR team was in damage control mode.

Layne was called into the office of the network president, Gabe Fitzpatrick.

She entered his corner office on the top floor. She'd been at the station for three-going-on-four years and this was the first time she'd actually been in the same room with Gabriel Fitzpatrick. He was imposing, to say the least, with his expensive suit, thick shock of snow-white hair and piercing blue eyes, his well-over-six-foot frame and the physique of an athlete.

"Please come in and have a seat, Ms. Davis," he instructed in a melodious baritone.

Layne lifted her chin and crossed the threshold.

"Drink?" he asked, walking over to a built-in bar on the far wall. He poured a short shot of bourbon in a beveled glass.

"No. Thank you."

"Have a seat."

He walked back to his chair and she took a seat opposite his massive desk.

"What you did today…has caused a great deal of problems for this network, of which I am president." He took a swallow of his drink. His cheeks reddened. "But it is a problem we will deal with. If these accusations against Deanna are true—" he rocked his square jaw "—she will be dealt with as well. And I can assure you that there will be no reprisals against you. That's not the kind of organization I want to run or represent." He finished off his drink and set down his glass. "The board will be meeting later today and we'll issue a statement."

She licked her dry lips and nodded.

"It took a lot of guts to do what you did on live television." He almost smiled. "A real journalist."

"I'll take that as a compliment."

"It is." He stood and so did Layne.

"Thank you for seeing me and for your support. But I'll be handing in my resignation."

Gabriel didn't respond.

Layne turned and walked out and realized that she was shaking all over.

For the next week, every newspaper, news outlet and cable station led off with the scandal at WWDC and reshaped the conversation around the power dynamics in the workplace.

"Looks like we might have started something," Paul said as they lay next to each other on Layne's bed, reading the Sunday paper.

"I've stopped taking calls for interviews," Layne replied. "I'll let the powers that be duke it out."

"Same here." He turned on his side to face her. "Know what I really want to do?"

"What?"

"Get away. A real vacation. Away from all the noise."

She smiled slowly. "Oh, really? Like go on the lam."

Paul chuckled. "We're not fugitives. But seriously, away from the calls, the demands—just relax, regroup, make love." He stroked her hip. "And plan for our wedding."

She blinked. "Our wedding?"

"Yeah. I love you, woman, and I know damned well that you love me. We've put our lives on hold for too long, and that diamond I got you four years ago has burned several holes in my pocket."

She covered her mouth with her hand. "What? You still have the ring? You didn't sell it?"

He rose up on his elbow so that he could look in

her eyes. "I couldn't. Might sound crazy but as hurt and pissed off as I was, there was this part of me that wanted to believe that we'd find our way back to each other."

Layne sniffed back tears. She cupped his cheek. "I love you," she whispered. "Let's do this, for real and for always." She leaned in and kissed him tenderly, the way her heart felt toward this stubborn, smart, handsome, sexy, loving man. And he was all hers.

Layne and Paul ducked out of the spotlight for six glorious weeks. They rented a bungalow in Hawaii for two weeks, learned how to surf, then jetted off to Belize where they toured, ate, danced, drank late into the evening and made love until the sun came up.

She had never been so happy, so full, than she had these past six weeks. It was like a pre-honeymoon, and she asked Paul what he planned for an encore.

"That," he said, "is a surprise. Keep that passport ready."

"Can't I get a hint?" she asked, kissing his bare chest before straddling his naked body.

"That would take the fun out of the surprise." He lifted his head and teased her nipple with his tongue.

She trembled ever so slightly, pressed her palms against his chest and rose up to position herself above his rising erection before easing all the way down. She felt him lengthen and stiffen inside her. She moaned. Her lids drifted closed and she held her bottom lip between her teeth as she began to move up and down along his length, sending shockwaves through them both.

As the maid of honor, Tina made all the arrangements with the management of Essex House to host the wedding, and of course she arranged to have the *Post*'s Style and Entertainment writer cover the nuptials. Layne would have been fine with a small ceremony, but her bestie wouldn't hear of it. "You'll only walk down that aisle once—hopefully—" she'd said, "so we are going to make it a walk to remember."

Actually, Layne was totally grateful that Tina had taken control of all the details for her big day. All she had to concentrate on was what her new life would be with Paul, and decorating the house they'd purchased in Georgetown upon their return from their getaway. They intended to move into it after their honeymoon— destination still unknown to Layne.

In between fittings for her dress and furniture shopping, she got news that her segment that outed the underbelly of WWDC had been nominated for a Daytime Emmy, and both she and Paul were in the running for excellence in journalism.

The past year had been fraught with obstacles for her and Paul, ones they'd created between themselves and those created outside of them. But what peeled that all away was above all else their love for each other. They recognized their faults and weaknesses and loved each other anyway, because together they made each other stronger and better.

As the doors to the grand ballroom of Essex House opened and the strains of the wedding march played, by a trio of violinists, rose sweetly to the rafters, Layne's heart soared at the magic that greeted her.

The 100-plus guests rose to their feet as Layne walked the rose-petaled aisle toward her future. The look of love and adoration in Paul's eyes guided her steps and when she took his hand and accepted his band of love, they vowed they would spend every day of their life together better than the day before.

The reception was one for the ages. A full band kept the guests on their feet, and the incredible menu, overseen by Alonzo Grant himself, was photographed as much as the bride and groom.

Whether they wanted to be or not, Layne and Paul Waverly were celebrities and reporters wanted to capture every moment.

The party went on to near midnight. Layne and Paul were exhausted but overwhelmed with happiness. As the party began to wind down and the music slowed, Paul danced with his bride.

"You are absolutely beautiful," he whispered in her ear. "And I love you more than I can ever express. We're going to have the best life possible. I promise you that."

"I'm ready to start my honeymoon," she whispered, looking up into his eyes, "and our new life together."

"My brother's advice is happy wife, happy life. Your wish is my command, my love." He grinned and kissed the tip of her nose.

"And I do believe that no one will miss us if we sneak off to our honeymoon suite upstairs. Tina will take care of everything."

"I like the sound of that." He took a quick look around. "Let's go." He took her hand and they snuck out of the ballroom and headed in the direction of the private elevator, when they were stopped halfway by a short, stocky man in a dark suit.

"I don't want to impose on your special day." He pulled a card out of the breast pocket of his jacket and held it out. "My name is Evan Miles. I'm—"

Layne and Paul cut him off at the same time. "I know who you are," they said in unison.

"Head of MSCBS," Paul offered.

Evan chuckled. "I'll make this brief. Please call me at your earliest. I have an offer that I think you'll like." He smiled from one to the other. Paul took the card. "Congratulations." The man gave a short nod of his head, turned and walked away.

Paul and Layne looked at each other. He tucked the card in his pocket. Layne pressed the button for the elevator.

"Wonder what he wants?" Layne said as they stepped on the elevator and the door slid closed.

Paul turned her toward him and pressed her against the wall of the elevator. "Frankly, my dear, I don't give a damn," he said in a really bad imitation of Clark Gable.

Layne sputtered a laugh. "Neither do I," she said, linking her arms around his neck for a kiss that lasted all the way to the penthouse floor.

Six months later

"Welcome to *Roundtable in the Morning* with Layne Davis."

"And her other half, Paul Waverly," Paul said. "We're here at the studio in Washington, DC, and we have a dynamic lineup for you this morning."

"Congressman Abrams, head of the Congressional Black Caucus, is here to talk about the efforts being made to push through the Voting Rights Act," Layne said.

"I'm looking forward to talking to him and really hearing why are there so many in Congress that continue to fight against it. And later in the hour we'll be talking with *New York Times* bestselling author Celeste Graham, who'll be discussing her book *Unraveled*, a behind-the-scenes look at what happens to a country when everyone is under surveillance."

"Scary stuff and a little too close to what is becoming a reality."

Paul nodded in agreement. "Stay where you are. Right after this break, we'll be talking with Congressman Abrams."

When they'd returned from their honeymoon in Maui and settled into their new home, Paul had come across the card from Evan Miles.

"Hey, babe," he'd said, walking into the kitchen where Layne was flipping bacon strips in the frying pan.

"Hmm," she'd said and begun placing the bacon on a plate with a paper towel.

"We never called Evan Miles."

She placed the tray of bacon and toast on the table and spooned scrambled eggs onto the tray. She sat down. "True. Do you want to?" she'd asked.

He'd shrugged. "We should at least see what he has to say."

She studied him for a moment and smiled. "Getting that itch again?"

He snorted a laugh. "Like you aren't. I see how you devour every bit of news and offer your analysis of every newscaster on television."

"Humph." She feigned offense. "And?"

"Can't hurt to see what he has to say."

She brought a slice of bacon to her mouth and crunched it between her teeth. She chewed slowly. An easy smile lifted her lush mouth. "Can't hurt," she agreed.

So they'd called. Two months after their honeymoon,

they'd met with Evan Miles, who offered them the deal of a lifetime. In the infamous words of *The Godfather*, it was an offer they couldn't refuse. They would have their own show, control over content and approval of all guests, covering everything from politics to entertainment. They would be the network's competition to *Morning Joe* featuring Joe and Mika—who, like Paul and Layne, had met through work and married.

Layne and Paul were magical together and quickly became the newest broadcasting darlings. When they sat in the corporate offices of MSCBS to sign their contract, they knew that they were embarking on their next journey together and vowed to be partners for life on-screen and off.

* * * * *

MILLS & BOON

THE HEART OF ROMANCE

A ROMANCE FOR EVERY READER

MODERN — Prepare to be swept off your feet by sophisticated, sexy and seductive heroes, in some of the world's most glamourous and romantic locations, where power and passion collide.

HISTORICAL — Escape with historical heroes from time gone by. Whether your passion is for wicked Regency Rakes, muscled Vikings or rugged Highlanders, awaken the romance of the past.

MEDICAL — Set your pulse racing with dedicated, delectable doctors in the high-pressure world of medicine, where emotions run high and passion, comfort and love are the best medicine.

True Love — Celebrate true love with tender stories of heartfelt romance, from the rush of falling in love to the joy a new baby can bring, and a focus on the emotional heart of a relationship.

Desire — Indulge in secrets and scandal, intense drama and plenty of sizzling hot action with powerful and passionate heroes who have it all: wealth, status, good looks…everything but the right woman.

HEROES — Experience all the excitement of a gripping thriller, with an intense romance at its heart. Resourceful, true-to-life women and strong, fearless men face danger and desire - a killer combination!

To see which titles are coming soon, please visit

millsandboon.co.uk/nextmonth

JOIN US ON SOCIAL MEDIA!

Stay up to date with our latest releases, author news and gossip, special offers and discounts, and all the behind-the-scenes action from Mills & Boon...

 @millsandboon

 @millsandboonuk

 facebook.com/millsandboon

 @millsandboonuk

It might just be true love...